THE TWO-EDGED SWORD TRILOGY

A STORY OF ALPHA AND OMEGA

Marilyn K. Olson

authorHOUSE®

AuthorHouse™
1663 Liberty Drive
Bloomington, IN 47403
www.authorhouse.com
Phone: 1-800-839-8640

Published by AuthorHouse   02/11/2012

ISBN: 978-1-4685-4784-9 (sc)
ISBN: 978-1-4685-4783-2 (e)

The Two-Edged Sword Trilogy
By Marilyn Olson
- **The Twinkling**
- **Dark Stars of The Twilight**
- **Twice Sharpened, The Two-Edged Sword**

PROLOGUE

Out of his mouth went a sharp two-edged sword
and his countenance was as the sun shining in his
strength.

Rev 1:16

The Word, strong and powerful, could divide with its sharpness the thoughts of the mind from the intents of the heart. Sent to the world—a darkened place where good and evil existed together—the Word began the separation process.

Who would ultimately choose evil over good? Who, by contrast, were the enslaved sitting in darkness longing to be free?[1]

We were touched by the Bringer of Light. It was HE who brought the sword of the Word to Earth, conquering evil with truth. He, who'd been with the Father since the beginning, was to live as mankind, bringing enlightenment of the Kingdom to the human race. The Kingdom of Heaven, once lost to us, could now be regained.

How had one-third of Heaven been banished from the heavenlies? Pride, arrogance and jealousy began growing

---

[1]   Matt 4:16, Isaiah 61:1, 2 Tim 2:19

within the heart of a much beloved archangel. Anti-God, anti-good, he became a black void growing in a perfect universe. His cancer of evil needed to be excised from the rest. It was a process not only involving war of gigantic proportions, but also requiring sacrifice of a magnitude no one could have imagined.

It's a story of light vs. darkness, truth vs. lies, hatred vs. love, and the powerful Word[2] of the Father being sent out to divide the evil from the good. It is the account of victory overcoming the wretchedness of evil, and restoration offered to all.

Where does one begin with a story that has no ending? To begin at the beginning is impossible, for there is also no beginning. With a point in time we will start, and fan out from there in this never-ending tale of eternity, love and forgiveness.

---

[2] Names of God are capitalized. THE WORD, I AM, HEAVENLY FATHER, JEHOVAH, LORD, THE ALMIGHTY—though emphasizing different aspects of his character, all refer to the same Divine Being.

CHARACTERS

Korel (aka) Karli	Mattie's best friend
Jano (aka) Mattie	Karli's best friend
Lusilite (aka) Lucy	Karli's older sister
Dawn	Karli and Lucy's oldest sister
Nagee	Korel's guardian angel
Rutsch	Jano's guardian angel
Jesus/Yeshua	The Volunteer from Heaven
Light/Lucifer/Satan	A fallen archangel
Jucola	Lucifer's Seraph doorkeeper
Pinnac (aka) Lusilite	Also known as Lucy
Jeric	Pinnac's guardian angel
Returnees	Fallen angels who returned to Hell after their earthly deaths
Redeemed	Fallen angels who returned to Heaven because of Jesus' gift

Dedication

There is a unique sweetness added to life when a young girl can find a "best" friend. Experiencing life together throughout all its chapters, best friends can often be closer than sisters.

Thank you, Joan, for being my best friend throughout the last fifty-two years. You are my "Mattie."

Adventures in Heaven await us!

Thanks to:

The ones who encouraged me in this project. You helped to make it happen.

BOOK ONE

FOREWORD

The following story is not meant to be doctrinal or theological in its message, for truly the more I search the scriptures regarding pre-earth activity, the more I realize I don't know. This account is intended, rather, to inspire thought and interest in the eternal side of our existence. It is hoped that the contrast of our earthly troubles compared to the joys of our eternal home will be realized by every reader, both young and old.

Though this narrative has many scriptural references, the plot, characters and story line are fictional.

Human life is short; eternity is forever. May all our ambitions, goals and desires take this fact into account as we live out our earthly days.

Marilyn Olson

THE TWINKLING

SHADOWS OF
THE TWO-EDGED SWORD

By

Marilyn Olson

Book One

*In a moment, in the twinkling of an eye . . .
we shall be changed.*

I Corinthians 15:52

CONTENTS

CHAPTER 1

DARKNESS

I am counted with them that go down into the pit:
You have laid me in the lowest pit, in darkness,
in the deeps.

Psalms 88:4,6

Korel[3] lay motionless. Only his[4] thoughts remained his alone, for all the other aspects of his being belonged to someone else.

Control: that was what it had become here—total control. To say he was a slave was putting it too mildly. Mad? Yes. Longing to be free? Every moment. Hope? None. Not for this space of time and place.

Long ago memories of heavenly life occasionally danced through his mind, but they were so far removed from his present situation that they flitted in only as a fantasy. Color: yellow, green, blue—he remembered color. And light. But

---

[3]   Pronounced Kor-EL.

[4]   The male personal pronoun will be used for all eternal "beings" regardless of gender on earth.

now all was dark, black, with forms barely seen against the glow of the ever-present heat.

Heat? It was a scorching dryness, permeating every fiber of his being thoroughly, with no softness or moisture anywhere. Oh, how he longed for a drink—anything—even for a moment, to release the swollen dry crisp of flesh he called a tongue. But this was his reality. There was no escape; there was no relief.

He knew his routine: follow the crowd, fit into the mold, don't stand out, do his job. Never smile, unless with glee at another's pain; for the expected protocol here was ridicule, pain, shame, degeneration, tearing down—yes—always tearing down.

Walking through the drudgery that had once been streets, he sloshed through the overrun sewage that sprang loose everywhere. Stink, but at least the stench was a temporary diversion from the heat. Everything was broken. He glanced at a shard of what had been a mirror and silently gasped; had he deteriorated that much? How could the degeneration take more toll on his life form? Yet it did daily.

The depths of degradation had worked its way through his body, through his soul, and deep into his spirit. But . . . his thoughts were still his—he guarded them well, never letting his face reflect his true feelings.

Hell? Yes . . . literally. This was Hell.[5]

His routine was dull; he passively did the tasks assigned to him. Hell had to keep up the fury of its organization, and there was a routine. With a boss who had an agenda, they were organized for destruction. Everyone knew what was

---

[5]   Deut. 32:22

required and no one shirked his work—no one dared—for punishment was administered here with rigor, and a certain glee. It was also meted out swiftly for the slightest infraction.

Pain: it was the barometer by which everything else was judged; for pain brought pleasure—ahh, yes!—not to the recipient of the pain, of course, but to those inflicting the pain. This was the lifeblood of Hell's inhabitants. This was the goal of their reality, for this kind of raw entertainment brought excitement to a dull existence in a way nothing else could. And the more intense, cruel, and heartless, the more thrilling the entertainment. It was exhilarating, it was breathtaking . . . it was addictive.

Occasionally there would be a spark of embers in an otherwise dead world. Only then could Korel see other zombie-like creatures walking around in their controlled existence. He sensed they were life forms he'd known in a formerly blissful state . . . . in a far-off heavenly world filled with singing, playing, dancing and joyous laughing.[6] But now there was no recognition of, or from, any of them.

Such was his existence here: hopeless, but not dead; dead, but not entirely. The dead do not feel pain. He felt pain on a constant basis.[7]

But now he sensed something changing from the daily regime: for where there was no hope, the slightest, ever so slightest hope began to flicker.[8] One day during his commute he noticed the tiniest of movements. *Did I imagine it?* As he walked by a certain being, he detected a flicker of . . . was

---

[6]   Memories refer to Heaven before the age of mankind.

[7]   Isa 13:8, Ec 9:5

[8]   The Lord will lighten my darkness. 2 Samuel 22:29.

it his eye? It had to be, for the flame of the ember gave just enough light for a moment to glimpse it.

He caught himself, not daring to change his expression in any way. *Had he been noticed?* Who was it? He waited, hoping. Something unusual was taking place.

Again and again he walked his assigned route, looking, but not looking, hoping for the slightest ember to spark, watchful to catch the flicker in the eye once more. And at last, the glimmer happened again. *This creature . . . is not dead, but has thoughts? Thoughts the same as mine? Do I dare to hope?*

Communication was out of the question. Even if they could talk, the sheer agony of the effort with tongues as fragile as soot would be impossible. The slightest look would draw attention and that would bring a whole realm of gleeful torture too horrifying to even think about. But . . . the flutter in the eye was there. IT WAS THERE!

Nothing changed for a timeless eon in his daily routine. But silently he still watched, hoping for yet another flicker of recognition. At last, once again it was there. *Breathtaking!* This time was different. Not one flicker, but two in quick succession. Was it a code? A form of communication? Thinking was, of course, his own territory. How long had he worked on this code? Unknown. For time is timeless here in Hell.[9]

Again and again over the eons, the slightest flicker, the momentary gleam came. He learned, yes, after centuries of pondering, that it was indeed code—a code of hope. *Here in Hell there is hope!*

---

[9]   Ec. 9:5, Ps 142; 3,7

He communicated back: a flicker here, an eye twitch, a blink. The code was real and communication was indeed possible.

Throughout the ages he learned much. There was to be an interruption in this present existence. All residents of Hell would systematically be deported to the surface. How, or for what reason, was not clear. But according to the being, this was a well-kept secret known only by the top echelon of the hierarchy.

Korel's mind questioned: *Was it even a possibility?* His body, obviously, was useless . . . but there was another part to him: his spirit. Could it be revitalized within a new body? Could he truly escape this place of torture even for only a moment in time?[10]

The information came slowly: on the surface they would no longer be forced to serve the evil one. By their deeds they could make a choice to serve the God of love rather than the god of evil. The condition was that in order to prevent returning to this place, one had to live a life of perfect obedience to the laws of righteousness.[11]

But the lord of evil seemed confident that none of the population of Hell could live a perfectly righteous life. He bragged with hideous certainty that he would not lose a single soul of all who were under his authority.[12]

Was this some sort of new torture? A game to fill one with hope only to be dashed down again? Why would this not be an easy choice?

---

[10] Ps 88:10

[11] Gen. 17:1; Deu 18:13; Prov. 11:5

[12] Prov. 29:2

Long ago questions surfaced in Korel's memory of how he came to exist here. He knew that his existence had not always been this way. Though the darkness seemed timeless now, it did have a beginning. And before that beginning was a faded memory of light: glorious, unimaginable light. The smells, the routine, the sensations were the exact opposite of the present darkness. Joy, an unknown emotion here, was the ever-present heavenly reality before the darkness came.

Joy. The mere thought of it now seemed as foreign as the slight sensations of hope that had been trickling in. Was it possible that circumstances could really once again change? If so, then, the proof would be with the "returnees."[13] *Yes. They would know.*

What did they experience? Why did they choose to come back? These and other questions formed in his mind, yet he dared not ask any of them, for fear kept him quiet and submissive to the dark side.

Forgotten events surfaced within his thoughts. As his dormant soul began to awaken, he found himself comparing this present existence of evil with memories of an extinct past. He thought about Lucifer, his leader, his master, his god.

Long ago Lucifer was a "light being"[14] but his glory had now degenerated to the opposite. "A black hole" was a good description, for light was now as foreign to his present

---

[13] The "returnees," are the ones who, by their deeds, chose evil over good while living their mortal lives on the surface. Thus, their situation did not change and at death, returned to the pit.

[14] Isa. 14:12

nature as darkness was to his previous self. But he could disguise himself, and often did, as a Light Being.[15]

Lucifer made it clear that he was to be worshipped, and those under his power gave him worship, for they had no other choice; but it had not always been this way.[16] They had in a previous age worshipped another God—a true Being of Light—and Lucifer had been the magnificent one who led them in worshipping this God.

They were beings under authority—it had always been so—and they followed without question the degeneration of the god of their world. His discovery of "evil"[17] and its subsequent establishment was their undoing, for Lucifer was unquestionably still their leader. The chain of command was still in place . . . . *or was it?*

Was this communication accurate? Did Korel dare to trust this information or could this be a set-up? *Do I still control my own thoughts or have they also been sabotaged?* He'd been accused of thinking independently before, with dire consequences. He knew that to trust anyone was a risk; he'd suffered the consequences of misplaced trust too many times to count.

Still, he felt sure there had to be others who remembered the times of ages past and longed for change. This being, this fellow-sufferer had stirred up a long forgotten emotion. Did he dare to truly hope?

That some "Being of Light" from ages past may be aware of his situation was a dim possibility, but he knew better than to hope, for hope was dashed time and time

---

[15] II Cor. 11:14

[16] Luke 4:7-8

[17] Isa. 45:7, Amos 3:6

again in this perpetually dark world.[18] *Coping, existing, enduring . . . for what purpose? Life is of no value here.* Yet the flicker of hope invading Korel's thoughts would not be extinguished.

Gathering information became crucial. It was painfully slow, but that was the way it had to be, for to create any disturbance outside the norm would immediately bring suspicion and punishment.

One day Korel found himself unobstructed during his zombie-like walk. This was unusual. *Could the impossible happen today?* His thoughts were in a whirl as he slowly made his way through the darkness.

And then . . . he felt his presence before he saw him. *Yes, there would be a flicker today,* he surmised, *or some form of communication.* Slowing his pace just a fraction, his eyes slowly moved toward the direction of the being.

Breathe slowly . . . no change, no change, he cautioned himself. The creature came closer. Korel watched intently, though trying not to bring attention to himself. Slower the pace went, slower . . . careful . . . *what is this?* The being stopped, turned, and looked squarely into Korel's face.

At that moment Korel knew beyond a shadow of a doubt that this creature had been sent. This had to be a sting operation, a set-up, or at best a huge hideous joke. Fear prickled every molecule of his putrefied carcass as he froze to the spot.

The wicked gleam in the being's eyes danced in delight for a moment, but then unexpectedly softened. Now Korel could not discern truth from the abundance of lies that surrounded his existence.

---

[18] Job 10:21-22

"How could I have been so gullible?" he agonized as he awaited his fate. Knowing that building up hope and dashing it to the ground was one of the favorite pastimes of the demons, overwhelming terror once again seized Korel; he suspected that his chastisement would be the next raucous entertainment for the masses to enjoy. The punishment for entertaining hope in this hopeless place would be cruel and unending.

He glanced away, but the creature stayed by his side, communicating openly.

"It is your turn," he hissed.[19]

My turn?

"Come with me." And with that the being took off in a new direction.

Korel's thoughts swirled as he followed his guide. *Off the beaten path? Do I dare?*

Korel looked around. Nothing had changed. Could it be that what he had been led to believe was actually true? His thoughts whirled, yet seemed frozen in time. He dared not think, not react, not plan . . . . there was no escape. The punishment would have to be endured.

The being led Korel downward through a labyrinth of paths to where he had never been; maze after maze, turn after turn, the walk never slowed. The descending terrain gave no clue as to direction and place.

Coming to a large open area, the ground suddenly gave way. They began to plummet . . . down, down, down. Korel had never been outside his few meters of assigned space: his passage each morning to work and his return each night to his broken down quarters. The air in this lower region[20]

---

[19]   Hebrews 9:26-27

[20]   Deut 32:22, Psalms 86:13

was even more putrid and oppressive than what he had previously experienced.

Finally they landed, entering a large, open space where walls jutted out from all directions. Chained to the walls, floors, ceilings—everywhere—were thousands of life forms. Here, he surmised, they kept the most dangerous of the prisoners.

As he stared into the gloom he noticed four huge angels shackled tightly to the center walls of the massive room. Isolated from the rest, they stood out as beings that had once been gigantically powerful.[21]

Who are they . . . hostages captured by the dark forces of Hell or high-ranking angels banished from Heaven? The questions played themselves out in Korel's mind, yet he dared not attempt to solicit a response.

Referring to the masses of prisoners, the guide spit out, "They left their former habitation, throwing away their estates to come here." [22] He grinned with pleasure at the thought of their torturous pain.

"And those," he sputtered as he pointed to the four gigantic angels, "will be released to do massive damage to the surface of the earth someday.[23] But for now . . ." the guide stopped as a mixed look of fear and disgust crossed his face. For a brief moment he appeared as though he would vomit, but quickly regained control of himself and continued, "Each of the 'banished' must be given a time span on the surface of the earth. While there, they can choose to change their eternal destiny."[24]

---

[21] Rev. 9:14-15

[22] Jude 1:6

[23] Rev. 7:2

[24] Deut. 10:12

A span of time? How? The questions bubbled to the surface, begging to be asked.

As if reading his thoughts the guide superciliously continued. "There . . . through there."

Korel stared to where he was pointing with his bony, crusted finger. At first he saw nothing, but as he continued to gaze into the darkness, he noticed a small, round opening in the wall.

"There," he again rasped, "is the tunnel that leads to the surface."[25]

That Korel (along with one-third of Heaven's former inhabitants) existed in the pit of the earth was his reality. How he got here was not a mystery, for in the recesses of his mind he remembered entering through the enormous gates of Hell only to find that exiting through them again was impossible; the gates to Hell opened only one way. It was unrealistic now to believe there was another way to escape from this colossal dungeon, yet Korel began to consider that it might be possible after all.

How does one get to the surface through the tunnel?

"Vacuum," was the gruff answer. "Reverse gravity will suck you to the surface through a tunnel." Noticing Korel's look of skepticism, he continued portentously, "You'll be very small because only the spirit goes. The rest stays here."[26]

Not much left, anyway.

---

[25]   Ps. 104:30, Ps 71:20 Note *face of the earth* vs. *depth*

[26]   Ps 16:10, Acts 2:27

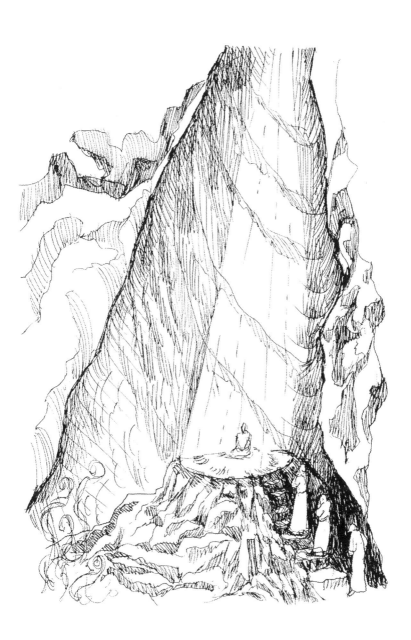

CHAPTER 2

THE TUNNEL

The Lord will lighten my darkness.

2 Samuel 22: 29

A t last Korel noticed the lines where others, like him, stood waiting. The expressions on each face were dull, as if resigned to whatever came next. He looked around; *where were the returnees?*

Without a word his guide pointed in the direction of a large abyss. Korel could see hunched-over figures being prodded like cattle toward the hole. These pathetic beings were those who had been to the surface, and had come back. *They chose to return.*

The returnees were different: they were emotional. Some were screaming while others were pounding their fists and heads against the walls as if looking for escape; others walked along silently as if in shock. Most of them seemed filled with regret and mourning, but a few laughed malevolently as they re-entered this place of misery.

All had left with only a spirit but returned with something else: a soul.[27] We who were only spirits wondered

---

[27]   Matt. 10:28

at the change in them, but outwardly, showed not a glimmer of interest. It was better not to react, not to stand out . . . our regime had conditioned us well.

Slowly the line moved forward as one by one those in front disappeared into the tunnel. Surprisingly, some would return within what seemed like just a few seconds. Whoosh! They re-entered the pit with screaming, shock and astonishment. *What did they experience on the surface? Why do they seem surprised when they come back?*

As if reading my thoughts my guide explained that there would be a block put on all memories of previous existences while they are there.[28]

"You'll know nothing;" he continued, "all will be new. You'll be welcomed, for the most part: helped, guided . . . loved."

Loved? Korel's thoughts tried to take it all in. Faintly, a long-forgotten feeling seemed to tantalize his senses but he could not grasp the meaning.

"A choice has to be made. Those who are here by choice, who love evil and who worship the pleasure it brings, will have the chance to return here. Seventy years, more or less is the test. Some will have longer earth spans and some will have shorter, but everyone in Hell will eventually have a turn. Even" . . . there the guide stopped, looking with repugnant disdain at the massive walls of chains . . . "even those prisoners will someday be released from their shackles. Day of Judgment . . ."[29] he trailed off as if lost in thought. Korel tensed, still trying to comprehend the situation.

"Though you'll not remember this existence when you go, you will remember it when you return." The guide laughed

---

[28] I Cor. 13:12

[29] Matt. 12:36, I John 4:17

with churlish, delightful glee as he watched the returnees. "Look at them. They all remember!" Watching them, Korel observed that every face reflected surprise and shock.

"All the more pleasure for us," the being snickered, "for they'd forgotten, and now they remember. What thrills we'll have in destroying their souls, little by little, piece by microscopic piece!" The guide broke into hideous laughter, rocking the chamber with its echo.

So he gets to destroy souls—what's new? The spirit never dies, but the soul can be torn apart bit by bit—extended amusement for demons deriving pleasure from the pain of the damned.[30] Loving to destroy what God creates is a favorite pastime down here.

Choices . . . that was what was different. *To choose . . . what?* Korel's thoughts began to accelerate with the idea. *To have a new beginning where everything is equal, where good and bad choices present themselves together, having the freedom to choose between them . . . was it possible to choose both?*

No, it was not possible. A choice had to be made between the good and the evil. The choices on the surface would determine which G/god[31] would be eternally served.

Korel was determined; his choice was clear, but he dare not think about it. *I must fit in, not stand out, not bring attention to myself.* He didn't want to be chained to a wall, floor, or ceiling. What shrieks came from those massive walls!

As Korel approached the entrance to the tunnel, he saw what was happening; the next in line would sit down at the entrance and quickly disappear. Steadily, as one by one the

---

[30]   Luke 16:28
[31]   All references to Jehovah God are capitalized.

thousands ahead of him went, he keenly observed that the tally of those who returned didn't match those who left.

Fear, excitement, dread . . . these were emotions unfamiliar to spirits, yet he'd begun to experience them. *Emotions . . . am I developing a soul?*

Suddenly he found himself at the entrance of the tunnel. He sat down, as instructed and immediately felt a suctioning pull. The sensation was incredible: light years of speed, the surroundings whizzing by him—he sensed himself shrinking as he experienced velocities that were never even imagined in Hell.

Familiar words inside his head screamed their orders as he shot through the ever-lightening channel. *"Lie, manipulate, murder, steal; destroy, deceive, trick, cheat; envy, hate, kidnap, rape; greed, gossip, slander, take."* The thoughts got lighter and lighter; the hold that bound him to them weakened as he traveled toward the ever so slightly lightening of the dark.

Some power—other than what was experienced in Hell—took over. A warm sensation began to envelop him.

Flashing through the tunnel Korel lost track of time. Sleepily, his last thoughts drained away as he entered the world of dream. His dreams were pleasant as he incubated in warm wet comfort for the next nine months.

CHAPTER 3

EARTH LIFESPAN

I have set before you life and death . . . Choose life,
that both you and your descendants may live.

Deut 30: 19

ntering the world of man I quickly became aware of wonder, warmth, excitement, and love. A loving hand reached me, took care of me, cuddled and warmed me—played with me. My childhood was everything good and very little bad.

Life before the present? Only a non-memory that showed up in some occasional child-hood nightmare.[32]

The present reality was filled with the wonder of learning: a fun world, with interesting things and places to explore. In this existence not only did light replace half of the darkness but good and evil co-existed with "good" winning much of the time. Here, I could explore the events of life with warm family and friends to comfort, encourage, and love me.

The idea of choice was presented to me very early in life: choose to obey, or not to obey. The good choices

---

[32] Isa 29:7

were usually encouraged; the bad choices were generally discouraged. I say generally, because I was often punished for things I didn't do, then disciplined again because I'd not admit to doing them. Though lying would have lessened the punishment, my conscience—for whatever reason—wouldn't let me do it.

As a result, I developed a method of "admitting" my guilt without having to lie. When wrongfully accused and the only way I could stop the punishment was to "confess" my guilt, I would try to act remorseful and sorry without having to actually admit to the wrongdoing. Though it got me a reprieve, in the end this tactic would cost me.

When Mattie and I first met we felt an instant rapport and knew we'd be friends for life. My family had moved to a new city and I found myself the newcomer at Sunday School. Somewhat shy, I was welcomed by Mattie who sat down beside me, introduced herself, and invited me to her house for Sunday dinner. That afternoon we decided to become "best friends." That decision never changed.

During the next years we rode our bikes, played on her grandpa's farm, and had overnight sleepovers with our friends. Experiencing life together, we shared all the changes that came with maturing from little girls to young women. We talked about our secret boyfriends—of course, these boys never found out we liked them! Later, we tried on our first lipsticks and high heels together.

One of the most binding events of our relationship was when both of our tender young hearts were convinced of our need for salvation. One night during a Sunday service we made that commitment together: to give our lives to the Jewish Messiah, Jesus, and to serve Him with all our hearts. We were ten years old at the time.

That decision influenced the direction our earthly lives would go. Encouraged by our pastor to read the Bible and pray every day, we grew spiritually strong together.

Through this friend I learned what commitment meant. Responsible, honest, reliable—that was my friend Mattie.

"My sister doesn't like me," she confided to me one day. "She tells me so all the time."

I felt sorry for her, but inwardly was happy my sister liked me, for it was my sister Lucy who would comfort me after the unfair spankings, holding me close while whispering, "I love you, and always will. Never forget that I love you more than anyone else does."

I was an active child who loved to experiment and discover how mechanical objects worked. One day I picked up a staple gun. This was not a little office stapler, but a powerful tool used in constructing houses. Curious to see how far the staple would shoot, I stood on our deck, aimed, and pulled the trigger. The device didn't shoot its staple. I tried again, using both hands to squeeze with all my might, but still it wouldn't work.

Somewhat frustrated, I looked at the tool again, only to discover that I had been pointing it the wrong way. Turning it around, I easily shot the half-inch staple straight out into the air. Had it not malfunctioned, I would have shot the fastener straight into my eye. Already having poor sight in my left eye from an earlier accident, I could have damaged my right one as well. Relating this experience later to Mattie, she informed me that we all had guardian angels. Later close calls in my life made me tend to agree with her.

Teenage years were a mixture of fond memories and painful ones. I had many friends but except for Mattie, it was hard for me to trust them. Why? It seemed my trust was misplaced, for my concerned sister would often inform me of their conversations about me behind my back. Reluctantly—and only after obtaining my promises of absolute confidentiality—Lucy would relate to me their cruel words. Though heartbroken many times over the broken relationships, there was some solace in the fact that I had a caring sister who watched out for me.

One result of this chaos was that I developed an avid interest in reading. It became my consolation, my daily distraction and escape from a life I didn't understand.

As my youth gave way to middle age and on into my sunset years, I learned to appreciate the good as well as to forgive the bad. The Biblical promise that "all things work together for good to those who love the Lord" gave a tangible hope to all that transpired during my lifetime.[33] Learning to function within my Saviors' loving parameters, I eventually realized his words were the only ones that mattered.

The good and bad—from my first breath to my last—were as the blink of an eye.

---

[33] Romans 8:28

CHAPTER 4

THE GATES OF HEAVEN

*He delivered me from my strong enemy, and from
them that hated me: for they were too strong for
me. He brought me also into a large place.*

2 Sam 22:18, 20

Seventy-eight earthly years were over in a flash and I
found myself once again entering the dark tunnel.
Immediately, I felt myself begin to move, faster and faster
flying like the wind toward . . . the light! Brighter and
brighter it came, with every turn and bend in the tunnel
pipeline.[34]

At last I entered an open meadow. The first thing I
noticed was the pleasant odor; it was pure and sweet with a
scent not unlike the flowers on the earth. And the light! It
was bright, without a hint of darkness anywhere.[35]

The pleasant sound of a distant bubbling of water
accompanied my senses as I walked through the velvety
grass. Soon I heard the delicate chirping of birds, then soft

---

[34]   Ps 23:4
[35]   Job 12:22

gentle laughter mixed with sounds of joyful music filtered out over the vast field of flowers I had just entered. My body felt light, free from pain and energized.

What was this place? A faded memory triggered my consciousness. I'd been here before. *Yes, I remember!* So many eons ago, yet timeless in its memory. I had been here in the eternal pre-dawn of life on earth and . . . oh, yes, long before the multi-millennial existence in Hell.[36]

Suddenly, I knew. I had passed from death into life, and the existence I had just left was quickly becoming a faded memory. My physical pain was gone as the deceitfulness and lies of the world sloughed off me like a wet cloud. Absolute truth became clear and I realized with lucidity that lies and deception could attack me no more.

Entering a state of purity, I sensed that the race had been run and won. This was the end of earthly pain, sorrow, disappointment and weakness.

I had returned at last to my eternal home.[37]

"Welcome, Korel!" I looked up to see a long-forgotten friend running across the field toward me.

"Nagee!"[38] I returned the joyful greeting. Soon we were in an exuberant embrace—so many things to say, so many memories to share! We walked arm in arm along the river toward the shining beautiful city. Everything awed me: the grass, trees, the butterflies, even the stream of sparkling water that gurgled beside the path.

Closer and closer to the city we walked with Nagee babbling happily beside me. It was hard to focus on his

---

[36] Ps 18:5

[37] Isa 57:15

[38] Pronounced Na-GEE with a hard "G"

words, so overwhelmed was I at being in this incredible place. In the distance I could see the kaleidoscope of lights inside the city gates. What wonders were inside those walls? Headed in that direction, I knew I would presently have a chance to find out.

Strolling beside the ever-narrowing stream[39] we soon reached the entrance of the city where more of my long-ago friends welcomed me with laughter and high-spirited joy. The hugs, the dancing, the exuberant shouting that took place was intense as we enjoyed our long awaited renewal of friendship.[40]

As I basked in the light of freedom, I realized the nightmare of the darkness was over. And the last seventy-eight years? Just a flicker of an eye. The days, the marking of time, the growing up, the lessons fought and learned: it was all a process to prepare me for my eternal destiny.

In the recesses of my mind, however, there remained a slight recollection of someone . . . some being who communicated with me over centuries of torture. *Who was it?* Someday I would find out; but for this eternity, I wanted only to bask in the glow of the love, the perfection, the holiness and joy of the present.

The gates to the city were large and ornately carved from a pearly substance. I remembered an earthly description, but that portrayal didn't come close to their massiveness and grandeur. Truly, I was so lost in the present moment that I discarded any preconceived ideas I'd formed about them.

---

[39]   Rev. 22:1

[40]   I John 3:2

Observing my awe and amazement, the gatekeeper whisked us on through with a smile.

As we walked through the towering gates, more ageless ones crowded close to greet me. Happy, blissfully exuberant, I recognized many of them as family and acquaintances with whom I had interacted during my human lifetime. What a delightful reunion this was with all those who'd returned to Heaven before I did!

Eventually Nagee nudged me; it was time to go. I could see he had a destination in mind and, after a few more joyful greetings and promises to visit, I happily followed along.

Soon we entered a large courtyard with ornate sculptures along the wall . . . such unsurpassed detail, such skill! I was amazed any artist could create figures with such exquisite precision.

Entering the vestibule, Nagee smiled in unspoken agreement as he turned my way. Comprehending his intentions to race, I quickly began scrambling up the stairs. Still marveling at my youthful speed and agility, I jumped slightly higher than needed at each step, resulting in Nagee having to wait a few seconds as I finished the ascent.

"Still getting used to your new body, eh?" Nagee jabbed me in the ribs teasingly.

"It's been a while," I countered.

"Won't take you long to adjust," he replied.

Adjust? Not yet! The feeling of lightness was incredible, and that sensation thrilled me immensely as I continued to test my unending strength on the stairs.

Catching up to him, we commenced moving forward—or so I thought. Suddenly Nagee stopped and glanced back down the staircase we'd just ascended. Grinning and without a word, he spun around. I knew precisely what he had in mind, for the little child in me had the same exact thought. The stair railing! It swerved and curled in a very inviting sort of way.

"Race you!"

Without a thought we jumped on opposite sides and slid down the banisters. Nagee beat me by a millisecond as we both landed with a plop at the bottom. Laughing all the way, I raced him to the top, beating him this time.

"Welcome to Heaven," Nagee said as he doubled up in delight.

Heaven. This was Heaven.

Chapter 5

The Advocate

*If any man sin, we have an advocate with the
Father, Jesus Christ the righteous.*

I John 2:1

We walked on into a large rotunda with many small
side doors and one large one. Stunning sculptures
and paintings graced the walls. Live choral music floated
in from somewhere and it thrilled every molecule in my
being.

A light, almost electrical sensation ran through to my
very core. I felt remarkably healthy, so alive, so—what's
the word—boisterous: almost like the feeling I had as a
little child on earth, but much more intense. Saturated
thoroughly with an enormous sense of well being, my soul
was overflowing with passion, zest, and love of life.

Love—yes—that was the electrical sensation that was
pulsating through me. It was a sensation somewhat similar
to being in love but felt much more energizing. We had
a taste of this on earth, but just a taste. This was the real
thing.

Finding seats, we joined a small crowd who also looked
like newcomers. Wonder, surprise, and smiles graced each

face; I sensed that all of us were experiencing the same acute sensations.

As we gazed at our surroundings as well as each other, flickers of recognition danced across some faces. *Had we been together before?* It seemed possible we had.

Soon the great doors opened, and the doorkeeper appeared. Calm and friendly, he lovingly called each of our names in turn.

"Korel." With that one word I heard the most compassionate sound ever attached to my name. I tentatively took a few steps toward the man. Warmly he held out his hands, inviting me into the room.

As I entered, I noticed a large book sitting upon a judge's desk of sorts. A robed individual nodded to the doorkeeper, indicating that my name was written within its pages, and motioned for me to sit down. As I did so, a side door opened. Into the room came the loveliest, light-filled figure I'd ever seen

"I am your Advocate," he said tenderly. His eyes were deeper than the ocean, and the light danced over his face as he smiled at me. I didn't speak, for I was too overcome with his beauty to be able to think at all. At that moment I knew I would be content to stay here with him forever.

The judge opened the large book. Instantly an electronic screen beside my seat opened for my viewing and before I knew what was happening, my earthly life appeared before me. All my hidden secret thoughts and actions played out right before my eyes. The good deeds, the bad, the evil and malicious, the generous and victorious—they were all there, every one of them.

The visual account was true, it was factual, and it was accurate.

CHOICES! I covered my eyes in shame, for I knew that a holy God would not accept my life as totally righteous.

Recalling my pre-earth determination to choose to do only "good," I knew I'd failed to meet Heaven's standard. I understood the consequences of sin in this place: it was not tolerated, not in the least.

As I sat there, I reflected on the wonderful existence before the rebellion. Lucifer, Michael, and Gabriel had previously each governed one-third of the inhabitants of Heaven. Lucifer had, in that era, directed us according to the rules of righteousness.

We knew what it was to submit to authority, and that had been our pattern; but even if we had discerned the devastation of "evil" we couldn't withstand its pull. Deceived, we were seduced into choosing the way of our fallen leader. The resulting banishment from Heaven was inevitable, for wickedness cannot co-exist with purity and righteousness.

Oh, how we had since regretted following Lucifer! Yet bound by authority, we knew nothing else but to obey him; then after the rebellion took place, we couldn't break away. It was too late.

Good became "evil" and evil was "good."

Eventually Earth's once beautiful surface was destroyed and all those under Lucifer's control entered the pit. The gap between Heaven and Hell was large and un-crossable.

Eons in that miserable place! It all came back with a rush—*desolation, torture, debasement, degradation.* I remembered the dilemma as I racked my brain: *How did I end up here again? Was it a permanent placement?* I saw my actions being judged—the evil against the good—and I had no hope of winning against the sin in my life.

"I've redeemed this man." Turning, I observed my Advocate speaking quietly to the judge. "He is under my bond and covering. His deeds will be placed under my account to settle."

With that statement, I realized my place here in Heaven was secure.

Who is he? The One who taught us to overcome evil with good?

"—I know what you're thinking." He turned to me with the most accepting and understanding of smiles. "You've questions as to events that transpired on earth. Someday you may want to review those years; not now, but maybe after you've had a chance to get settled again."

I looked at him. He had scars on his wrists as he held his hands out to me. A poignant recollection whisked across my mind, yet I didn't vocalize it. I only looked at him in wonder, for I knew he'd paid the price for my sin.

This was Jesus, the Messiah.

"Thank you, my Savior," I murmured gratefully, then burst into sobs. He held me as lovingly as a father comforting his child. As I lay with my head next to his heart secure within his love, I knew nothing else but hope and joy, for I realized anew that this Man had been counted worthy to pay the price for my redemption, and I was safe.

He walked with me to another door, opened it and held it open for me. Nagee was waiting for me on the other side. Exiting the door, I turned and waved good-bye to the man who'd represented me. With a gentle smile, he returned the wave as the door clicked shut.

CHAPTER 6

THE SKYPER

There is none like unto the God of Jeshurun, who rides upon the Heaven . . . on the sky.

Deut 33: 26

Still emotionally charged, I couldn't speak. Nagee seemed to understand, and we walked together for a time in silence.

What sights we saw as we walked through the city streets! The pavement, luminous in its golden hue, caressed our feet as we walked on its sparkling surface. The buildings themselves each produced their own musical sound, blending in harmony together as a continuous symphony that no orchestra on earth could have performed. Chattering shoppers walked by us in animated conversations, exuding a genuinely cheerful atmosphere; all beings appeared to be ecstatically happy and content.

The scents were numerous and varied: exotic aromas continually changed odors as they permeated the air, each one unique and fresh, with no two alike. The bakeries released their tantalizing smells of freshly baked breads which awakened our taste buds in a delicious sort of way.

I noticed these aspects, yet still could not speak for the wonder of what had just transpired.

"Want a ride?" Nagee asked me mischievously.

Not sure what was coming next, I meekly nodded my head "yes," for I still couldn't utter a sound.

We walked a short distance to the transportation stop. Within minutes a small, white vehicle arrived; it somewhat resembled a train car, except its shape was circular rather than elongated. Entering the unit I noticed the swivel-type chairs positioned around its circumference. Their unique placement allowed passengers to either face the interior or look outside through the clear glass window encircling it.

Upon sitting down, the transporter left the street and sped away through the open air. This was a wonder I hadn't seen before.

"The skyper," Nagee informed me, "is the quickest way to go a short distance."

"How far?" I asked timidly.

"Five, maybe six," he answered

"Six . . . miles?" I didn't know what he was talking about.

He looked at me with a laugh.

"Miles? You think miles here? We're talking about planets. Your home is over there."

He pointed to the map on the carriage wall. Sure enough, the planets were in order, much like a subway chart tracking the stops.

"Your stop is on planet Ziphotan. It's a ways out, but shouldn't be more than ten minutes in earth time."

I enjoyed the ride; it was similar to the dark tunnel in speed, yet much more pleasant. Before we knew it, we had arrived at our destination.

From the window of the skyper I could see numerous fruit trees and orchards. Yes! This was where I wanted to be, for I'd loved working with the soil on earth.

While disembarking the skyper, I noticed the mansions in the distance; big and luxurious, they dwarfed anything I'd seen on earth. Soon we arrived at mine. To say it was everything I'd ever wanted is putting it mildly. New, with everything in place and working perfectly, I marveled at its design and functionality.

Noticing my reaction, Nagee looked at me strangely with a little smirk on his face. "You don't remember?" he asked.

"Remember? I . . . do," I stammered, for only then did I realize that this had been my own house ages ago, long before the fall with Lucifer.

The gardens looked as fresh as the day I'd left; the outbuildings were clean and organized. Everything was painted beautifully and appeared as if just recently built. "Nothing ages here, remember?" Nagee said with a laugh. "Everything is eternal, unchanging; hooray for perpetual youth!"

Youth. I'd not seen myself since arriving, but suddenly I remembered the large mirror in the entry way of the house. Bounding effortlessly up the stairs, I entered the house and looked in the mirror. Sure enough, a strangely familiar, but much younger version of me appeared; I was youthful, and in perfect condition.

Staring at the image I'd lived with for seventy-eight years, I recognized the features as my own; yet the wrinkles, scars, and facial blemishes were gone, and the arthritic hands were replaced with those that were young and strong.

It was me all right, and I felt wonderful!

"Heaven to Korel, Heaven to Korel;" Nagee summoned me back from my thoughts.

"Has it been sitting empty all this time?" I asked, referring to the house.

"Empty," he assured me. "But your neighbors have all pitched in to get the house ready for you."

"How did they know I was coming?"

"We knew before 'mankind' was created that you could potentially return. You see, when the banishment came, a plan was immediately put into place for restoration."

I looked at him quizzically, as this didn't quite fit my current time-frame of mind. "Return?" I asked, grasping the idea for the first time. "Everyone? All who were banished?"

"I understand the price was paid for everyone, though not all took advantage of the offer. Unfortunately, some enjoy serving the evil one and don't want things to change," he replied.

I could hardly understand this concept, but knew in my heart it was true. Had I not suffered at the hands of evil ones on earth? And before that . . . oh, I couldn't bear to think of the age of darkness, for the present light was now so overwhelmingly a reality.

No, no dark memories for me now. Only the present, incredibly happy moments were all I wanted to think about. As if reading my thoughts, Nagee assured me that someday I would want to review my years on earth.

"And when that time comes, I'll go with you to the place of the archives. There you can spend as much time as you like, watching the history of your life."

It sounded interesting for someday in the future . . . but not now. There was so much to see, to explore and to experience in this marvelous place! I wanted to visit my earthly parents and grandparents as well as others I'd only read about. I wanted to see for myself the wonders of Heaven . . . or the heavens, as I realized the vast amount of space included.

After bidding farewell to Nagee and settling once more into Heaven's routine, time became unimportant as I enjoyed every moment of my existence. The days were filled with wonder and happiness; for you see, when no one steals, lies, or envies, life is one hundred percent pleasant. On earth we had some good days, but there were just as many bad ones that counteracted them . . . and the eternity of existence before that? It was the ultimate of evil.

So this was the antithesis of what I'd previously experienced, and those who'd never lived in the dark underworld truly didn't understand my joy at having escaped it.[41]

---

[41] Hebrews 2 (whole chapter) particularly vs. 14-15. Also see Ps. 71:23

CHAPTER 7

THE ARCHIVES

The Heaven and the Heaven of heavens is the
Lord's, the earth also, with all that therein is . . .
as the days of Heaven upon the earth.

Deut 10:14; 11: 21

My work in Heaven was wonderfully fulfilling; I did what I liked to do best on earth . . . work with the soil. I was also able to fulfill a longtime desire in developing and creating new types of plants. On earth I could only dream about doing it; in Heaven, this was my job.

Every morning I'd arrive early to tend the fruit trees and gardens. Then after a good long workday, I enjoyed going home to barbecue with my neighbors or have friends over to play games.

One day as I was working in my orchard, I heard someone whistling a peppy tune. This, in itself, was not unusual, but the skillful trilling of the whistling caught my ear. Somebody, obviously, had whistled for a very long time!

Looking up I saw a swarthy young man standing, admiring my trees. His skin was olive colored, finely muscled, and his hair was platinum white. He had a slightly fatherly look on his face, but otherwise seemed to be about the age of the rest of us. His attitude was casual, almost sporty in his bearing.

"Nice apples," he remarked. I had to agree that they were, as they were my favorite. "I haven't seen these before."

"Hybrid," I answered. "Developed them myself. Want to try one?"

"Sure." He reached up, picked one off the tree, looked at it for a moment, then took a bite. "Different." he remarked. I could tell he was impressed.

"Would you like a starter slip?" I asked.

"Absolutely," he replied, his eyes brightening in a way that only a fellow gardener would understand.

Smiling gratefully as I cut the slip, he inquired, "Did you get your green thumb from your father?"

"Definitely not from him," I answered, knowing how much my dad hated to even mow the lawn.

"Who, then?" he persisted.

"Not sure," I answered with a shrug. "No one else in my family showed even the smallest interest in gardening."

The man paused a moment, then quietly replied, "Glad you're here, son."

Son? I looked at him again. There was a slight resemblance, but I didn't know who he was.

"Thank you," I replied.

As he resumed his walk down the road I knew we had something in common: we both loved working with plants.

Curious about the stranger as well as from where my aptitude for gardening came, a thought occurred: The archives could reveal the answers to my questions. *Didn't Nagee say that the archives were available?*

As I mulled over this thought, my curiosity grew. Would it be possible to view other events of earth? Could I see the great flood, the creation of the world, the discovery of America? Could I watch history in the making?

Pondering this heady possibility, my curiosity increased until one day I mentioned to Nagee my desire to visit the archives.

"Ahh! Rather early to be reviewing your earthly life, don't you think?" he questioned.

"It's not that record I want to review—at least not yet. I just want to see history in the making. Is it possible to see the great flood? It's something about which I've always been curious."

"It's not only possible, but it's shown on a regular basis. Anyone who's ever heard the story wants to see this event once they arrive here."

"Good. Let's go!" I yelled. I raced him to the skyper stop and waited while he huffed in behind me.

"Day job." He tried to minimize the fact that I'd beaten him. Sitting while composing music all day did not diminish the energy Nagee had, but my daily activity in the orchard had strengthened my physical self to the point where I now ran faster than he did.

"There are other kinds of races," he said with a shrug as we found our seats. "Composing music is in my blood just as much as gardening is in yours." And with that comment, he began singing a well-known Broadway tune. He sang so loudly that everyone in the skyper turned and cheered when he was through.

As he stood up and took a modest bow, I saw that our fellow travelers were actually enjoying the salty entertainment. It was a pleasant break for them in the middle of their busy day.

"Your turn," he challenged, thinking I would not dare to sing out loud.

Oh no? I got up and took a mock bow. Trying to top him, I sang three notes of the tune, and then to everyone's relief, quit and sat down. Still, the smiles and polite claps were all I needed to feel I had at least attempted to win the dare.

Nodding his approval and pretended relief, he clapped me on the shoulder and asked for an apple. I complied with his request, causing him to laugh so hard he fell to the floor.

"You actually have one on you?" he asked as he took his seat once again.

"All the time," I responded.

"Why?" It was an honest question.

"In case I get hungry," quite factually spoken.

"But haven't you yet figured out at you can get food here whenever you're hungry?" he asked in amazement.

"I like apples," I responded simply, "especially ones I grow myself." And with that, I pulled another out of my pocket.

You must understand that these were not ordinary apples such as you would find on earth. These were perfectly round and crisp, with a hue on them that is indescribable, being that earth does not have this color. They have a flavor that is both tart and sweet, and unlike anything else for taste; plus the apple is only apple—no seeds—with the skin being the same consistency as the fruit inside, yet firm enough to hold without getting your fingers sticky.

"Maybe you're related to Johnny Appleseed," Nagee mumbled between bites.

I stopped in mid-chew. Of all the time I'd been here, the thought of him hadn't even crossed my mind. Maybe he was the stranger I'd just met.

"Is he here?" I asked. Nagee looked at me strangely.

"I would think so. We can find out in the archives," he responded.

The skyper was approaching the stop, and we prepared to exit.

"Look over there." Nagee pointed toward the window. "That tall building, the red one," he continued.

"Yes, I see it," I answered.

"That's the archive building."

As I looked in the direction he was indicating, I saw a building with siding the consistency of sky and the color of a sunset. On the ground surrounding it was a crowd of many beings. They all seemed to await eagerly the opening of the doors.

"Didn't know there would be lines in Heaven," I remarked smugly.

"Lines?" Nagee let out a whooping laugh. "Those aren't lines. They simply come early to watch the light show."

"Show?" I peered deeper at the sight. Sure enough, surrounding the crowd was an aura of light. It was a show, fantastic in its color, deep in its hues, and unbelievably intricate and beautiful. It made me want to hurry up the disembarking of the skyper.

"Hold on." Nagee put a hand on my shoulder. "You'll get to see it all. The show is repeated numerous times in the day; you won't miss anything."

Walking toward the archives building, I once again noticed the striking lights of the city. Surely no other city in the entire universe was as extraordinary as this one.

As we approached the building, I marveled at the phenomenal sight: it was like walking into a rainbow on earth, which, of course, never appeared in those days to be a possibility. Upon entering the sphere of the structure, the lights warmed, then cooled us, teasing us with their sensations and smells. There was truly nothing on earth to compare with the experience.

Edging toward the doors of the archives building, Nagee reminded me why we'd come in the first place. "So easy to get distracted here," he remarked, "so much to see and experience."

"And how long have you been here?" I teased.

"Good question," he answered with a grin. "How long is eternity?"

I shrugged, knowing there was no answer to that question.

The doors to the building were unusual. Transparent, they were light as a feather, yet when pressed against, stronger than steel. There were no door handles or hinges. Encoded with sensitivity to certain movements, they instantly sprang upward with just a raise of the hand.

Entering, I saw that the place was huge. We stopped in the lobby to look at the directory, for there were many possible destinations.

"Let's see," Nagee mused out loud, "what millennium would you say it was?"

"According to the Biblical records it should be within the first 1,000 years of the creation of man," I replied, happy to supply information I'd learned on earth.

" . . . Enoch, Methuselah, Noah, Shem . . . wait, here it is." He pressed the slight protrusion in the directory, and before we knew what was happening, the floor began to gently move under us. Seats appeared, and we sat down on the comfortable chairs.

A cold drink materialized at my fingertips, as well as a fresh piece of fruit (slightly resembling an earthly pear.) I looked questionably at Nagee.

"Comes with the show," he casually remarked.

We sat as the chairs moved, and the presentation began. Shown in 360-degree virtual mode it was, needless to say, amazing. My questions about the event were more than answered as I watched the worldwide deluge play out before me.

I experienced the waters breaking out of the earth's belly along with forty days and nights of torrential rain. I watched the yearlong adventure of shipboard activity as well as the daily animal care and feedings. I saw the floodwaters recede into oceans, lakes and rivers; the ark settling on the mountain, and the dove being released.

Then earth's first snowflakes began to fall. The ark on the mountain became entombed in the snow, swallowed up by Ararat only to be discovered centuries later by the inhabitants of the earth. A large-scale treasure hunt, I sensed there had been some heavenly fun in planning this mysterious secret!

Meanwhile Noah and his family left the cold temperatures of the mountain, gradually building more and more houses as they grew in number. We watched as new generation after new generation appeared.

"At this point," Nagee informed me, "you have to choose which family line to follow."

"How do I know which one is mine?"

"There's a code. Put your hand under this light; it's a DNA analyzer."

"Fascinating," I said as I placed my hand where indicated. I was about to find out my earthly genealogy through a practical scientific process.

The DNA results came instantaneously, and my ancestral line appeared on the surround screen.

"How far do you want to go?" Nagee asked. Looking up, I realized we'd been in the archive building for . . . one earthly month? Had it really been that long?

"It's timeless here, Korel," he reminded me. "Forget about the time. You can't use it up, and it doesn't move, so enjoy these present moments as they come."

"We could stay for years," I mused, for I was actually entranced with the idea of following my genealogical path to when I was born. Earth time was certainly different from heavenly time mode.

Staying a bit longer, I saw the development of my ancestral line from the time of Noah to the erecting of the tower of Babel. I watched, fascinated, as the earth gradually repopulated and its diverse cultures developed and expanded.

As the archives entered into the twentieth century, I hesitated. Did I really want to view my own earthly life just yet? Hadn't I been mortified when the sin in my life was exposed during my day of judgment? Yet, I felt compelled to continue with the history of my family. I was curious . . . I had siblings. Did they find their way to Heaven?

"Are you ready?" asked my friend. Noticing my hesitancy; he wanted to be reassured that I was fully prepared for what was to come.

"Yes," I answered firmly, for I knew I needed to see my time on earth.

CHAPTER 8

MY EARTH HISTORY

*He will put his angels in charge of you to guard
you in all your ways.*

Psalms 91:11

"There are different ways to experience your personal earth history," Nagee acknowledged. "You can live it virtually, or you can just watch it on screen."

"What do you suggest?" I asked hesitantly, for I wasn't ready to experience it virtually just yet.

Sensing my uncertainty, Nagee answered that I should just view it on screen. He pressed a series of buttons and before long I was observing a well-loved child living a productive life, having no problems whatsoever. Throughout the story everything worked out perfectly.

This happy child—cherished by family and friends—grew up healthy, married well, raised a lovely family and lived life to the fullest. When it was over, I felt warm inside, as if watching a G-rated movie where all came out okay in the end.

But something was definitely the matter, for throughout the show many faces were hazy to the point where I couldn't recognize them at all; I was left guessing their identities. In reality they hadn't affected the outcome of my life in any way . . . they were just present.

After the show, Nagee looked at me with a silly grin on his face.

"You liked it?" he asked softly.

"Yeah, I mean, there wasn't much to worry about." Remembering the earlier shame I had felt seemed rather ridiculous now. I'd forgotten all those wonderful events in my earthly life.

"I'm amazed that my life was so orderly and serene, so unchaotic, so . . ." As I searched for the right words, Nagee responded with a waterfall of amused chuckles. It startled me for an instant.

"What's wrong?" I asked, concerned he'd disrupt the others in the room

Barely able to rein in his mirth, he pointed to the panel of buttons on the face of the screen. "There," he finally spit out between giggles.

I looked to the panel. It had a row of buttons with ratings. *Ratings? Here in Heaven?*

"There's no sorrow here," Nagee was finally able to speak. "You see, in the edition you just viewed, all of the evil ones who caused the bad in your life were blocked. You saw the life you should have led, were designed to lead, and what God had prepared for you to experience. But . . ." here he hesitated, "in order for you to experience what actually took place, you have to read the disclosure and sign that you understand."

Looking closely, I saw that indeed he was correct.

"No one wants unhealthy surprises—especially not here."

He looked at me soberly before smiling again in his good-natured boyish way. "You can choose how you want to review your life. If you want to see it all, you can: the good with the bad. Or you can choose just to see the good—which you have already experienced—or if you prefer, just see the bad . . . a really, really dark nightmare!"

That, I assured him, was definitely not what I wanted to see.

"But of course," he continued, "that edition causes some truly gripping moments of excitement." My lack of enthusiasm for that edition was apparent in my stoic reaction, so Nagee quickly continued without further teasing.

"If you like, you can choose to see your life review not only through your earthly eyes, but also with your present mind and understanding. Or," he looked intently at me as he lowered his voice in a conspiring tone, "you can alternatively choose not only to see the good and bad, but also the driving motivation, reasoning, and powers that were behind everything that happened to you on earth."

I took the bait. "How?"

"The button underneath here—the green one on the side—press that during the show and you can experience the review from a variety of ways."

This was it, for there were many incidents I truly wondered about.

"But," he warned, "the faces of those who are not here will be obvious, and their fate you might guess." Silently I digested his words, for I did wonder about someone . . . someone I thought I once knew well but found I never really did know at all.

"Your memory of them, however, will fade quickly once you're done," he continued. "You can even see the bad turn into good . . . quite interesting for the philosophers among us."

I didn't think I was much of a philosopher, but just inquisitive. *Curiosity . . . that's my only motivation for this adventure*, I told myself.

I moved my finger to press the last button on the panel, the one on the bottom. With my other hand, I reached over the underside to simultaneously press the green button.

Laying his hand on mine for an instant to affect a momentary delay, Nagee cautioned "If you pick that button, you'll experience your life virtually in the same way you did on earth except that you'll understand the why of the events. While in the moments on earth, you won't remember this time up here."

As Nagee released his handhold on me, I pondered his words. But my resolve had been quickened. I wanted to see the whys and wherefores of my life in a way I'd not experienced before. I had to see it. I had to understand.

"I'm ready," was my simple answer. I signed the disclaimer and pressed the button.

CHAPTER 9

REAL EARTH TIME

Stand firm against all the strategies and tricks of the devil. For we are not fighting against people made of flesh and blood, but against the evil rulers and authorities of the unseen world, against those mighty powers of darkness who rule this world, and against wicked spirits in the heavenly realms.

Eph 6:10-12

I awoke covered with sweat. I'd had another nightmare, so real, and so scary. I quickly got up and ran into my mother's bed, where she soothed and comforted me. Though living a relatively happy childhood, I was prone to nightmares, and they came with such certain regularity that my mother calmly tolerated . . . even expected them.

Warm and secure in her loving embrace, soothed by her words of comfort and prayers on my behalf, I gingerly crept out of her bed and back into my own—lest my older sister see me and tease me about being "mama's spoiled brat."

How much longer would I suffer these crippling nightmares?

The youngest of four children, I had an older brother and two older sisters. My sister Lucy was my constant companion; she took it upon herself to explain the world to me through her eyes.

"Promise you won't tell?" became her favorite phrase toward me. She loved to be involved in everything that concerned me, from my parents, to my other siblings, to my friends and acquaintances. She was my guide through life; after all, she was almost three years my senior and knew so much more than I did . . . or at least that's what she led me to believe.

And believe her I did. She interpreted the world to me. She told me all the negative things others said about me, though later in life I often wondered how she acquired the information.

Soon after I turned twelve she took me by the hand to my dad's home office.

"Look." She pointed to my dad's tax books. "See all these figures?" I'd never seen these books before, so this was novel information. "Dad's keeping financial records on all of us. We need to pay it all back someday, you know." She smiled sadly at the thought, as if everyone else in the family knew this fact and I was the only one who didn't.

"When?" was my response.

"Before you leave the family." She smiled sweetly at me. "Don't worry," she said. "We all have to do it."

I looked at the mound of figures, covering everything from food to tires, and felt overwhelmed. How was I ever going to repay this debt?

"There is a solution," she insisted. "but don't tell anyone I told you about this," she cautioned. "You promise?" Dutifully, I promised not to tell.

"Then I'll tell you what to do. Insist that you pay for everything yourself. Don't accept any help whatsoever from Dad or from Mom, because if you do, he'll just mark everything down in this book for you to pay back later. And," she added dolefully, "he'll add interest."

I pondered this new information. I didn't want to pay interest on my debt, or it would never get paid.

"I should know," she continued. "I've had to pay back so much already."

This was news to me. I hadn't even considered that my poor sister had been under this kind of strain, but her sad face told me all I needed to know. That our dad could be so cruel just didn't make sense; however, I accepted her words as golden and determined to do as she suggested. That she was able to hide her deep sorrow from the rest of the family was amazing to me; I determined to follow her example.

"You can't tell anyone, now," she reminded me in that solemn way of hers. "This is just between you and me."

I nodded . . . and I dutifully kept the information secret from that day forward.

The next years were filled with a growing sense of pressure and determination. I didn't want to leave home with debt, so I worked very hard to live as frugally as possible. I worked every day after school, doing odd jobs, babysitting, cleaning houses.

In ninth grade I was hired by a neighbor to mow her lawn. Through this job I discovered my talent for gardening, lawn care, and landscaping. I not only liked this kind of work, but others noticed my efforts and wanted me to work for them as well.

Of course this greatly limited my participation in sports or other extra-curricular programs and activities offered at school. Though I felt I was missing out on a part of my youth, I truly began to enjoy the work that came my way. Besides, I was firmly determined to graduate debt—free.

But a heavy cloud of depression settled over me; the more I worked, the higher the debt seemed to grow. I knew my parents loved me, but I could not understand why they kept this news only to impose it upon me later.

At restaurants I ordered only the minimum while the rest of my family ordered expensive meals. When my mother would take my sisters and me shopping for school clothes, Lucy would always remind me of what she'd revealed to me.

"Remember," she warned, "all this goes on our bill. Don't let mom buy you anything. She'll only bill you later for it."

With my sister's constant admonitions, I learned to graciously refuse new clothes, or find one or two items and pay for them myself. Mom would often look at me questionably, but I kept my promise and didn't disclose to her that I knew about their plan.

I wasn't the best dressed in high school, but I made it through to graduation while living frugally. I got used to using hand-me-downs, or finding clothes at thrift shops. Many times the clothes didn't fit, and weren't even close to the style of the day. But each day I tried my hardest to keep my eventual bill to a minimum

"Why is she so independent?" I heard my dad say to my mom. I didn't hear her answer, but I hoped they were proud of me.

Once during those years at age sixteen, I wrote a check to my dad.

"What's this for?" he asked.

"I want to work on my bill," was my tart reply. He looked at me quizzically, but didn't say anything. Months later I found that check still un-cashed in his books.

"Hmmm," I thought to myself at the time. "What is his scheme? Did he crave the interest this small un-cashed check would generate? Is he that greedy? Does he really want my hard-earned money that much?"

I felt a sharp poke in my ribs. Dazedly, I woke up to find the grinning face of Nagee in my space.

"Heaven to Korel, Heaven to Korel," he sing-songed.

Could it be? Yes, it really was!

"Oh, it was so real!" I exclaimed. How I remembered these emotions, these feelings of frustration. But now I was back in reality with Nagee. *Yes. I was still in the archives house.*

"How long . . . ?"

"Timeless here, remember?" Nagee grinned at me. "Takes some getting used to. You want to go home?"

"No," I responded, for now I really was curious. I wanted to see what my Dad's real motivation was for all those stressful years. Surely he knew that living under that financial burden at such a young age was not healthy, yet, he never said a word to me about it. To say my youthful attitude was less than stellar toward him was correct . . . I'd always tried to do the right thing in regards to him, but because of his tightwad policy there was a huge wall built up between us.

"I've got to see what his motivations were," I said matter-of-factly.

Nagee smiled a knowing look. "Then you know what to do," he said softly.

I pressed the lower button and kept the motivations button handy.

Yes, I would see.

CHAPTER 10

A REVELATION

*A lying tongue hates those that are afflicted by
it; and a flattering mouth works ruin.*

Prov. 26:28

"I hate her," I heard Lucy say to herself. She was standing in front of our bathroom mirror where no one could see her. She was looking into the reflection, using my other sister's hair supplies. I knew she didn't like our older sister, for she often told me so herself. She'd already explained to me how our older sister used all of our parent's money for herself, leaving nothing for us, so her words weren't a surprise to me.

She opened the door to the rest of the house; there I was, watering my plants in preparation for planting them into our neighbor's yard. That I had a skill far exceeding Lucy's abilities was apparent, for, try as she might, she couldn't get anything to grow.

As Lucy walked past me, she turned, and with a hideous look on her face, stuck out her tongue at me. My back was toward her, facing the plants. Of course I didn't see it at the time.

"But, she loved me then, didn't she?" I asked myself out loud.

I looked up. Nagee was not smiling now. He was looking solemnly at me. "So . . . find out something?" he asked.

Speechless, I could only look further. There it was; all through my high school years I saw her talking to people behind my back.

"She was a talebearer!" I exclaimed to myself. I discovered for every story she told me about my dad or oldest sister or someone else and made me promise not to tell, she told another one to them about me.

Suddenly all the unhappy incidents in my life began to make sense. All the friends who'd disappointed me, all the times I received spankings and discipline for circumstances I didn't cause, the times I was disciplined for "lying" when I'd not lied . . . now it all fell into place.

"You are so gullible!" Lucy laughed in my face one day. At the time I had no idea what she was talking about, but now I knew. The story about my dad making us all pay him back was false. I had believed her to my own hurt.

Now I understood why my parents had never given me a bill. At the time of graduation I had thought it was because I'd paid for everything myself. Then, after I paid for my wedding and left home, I didn't bring up the subject of the bill because I didn't want to remind them about it. But in the back of my mind, it was always there.

I reversed the archive device . . . Middle school. There she was, speaking negatively to a teacher about me. "No wonder I could never connect with that teacher," I mused.

Clear back, clear back—there I was at age eighteen months. My left eye . . . yes, I'd lost some sight in that eye. I'd been told I tripped on my blanket, making me fall on the corner of the coffee table; but as I looked, I became aware that the story was not the way it happened. I observed Lucy sneaking toward me and pushing with all her might. The blood, the screams—both my dad and mom came running. Dad grabbed me, picked me up, and headed for the car.

Meanwhile, Lucy sat hugging herself, taking it all in from the couch. She was singing and grinning to herself as she watched the show. It was obvious; my pain gave her pleasure.

As the archives revealed, this incident was not the first or last time she pushed to hurt me. Over the years I witnessed her shoving, scratching, and pulling my hair. Each time she'd play the victim as she'd fib to my parents as to what really happened.

Why? Finding the green motivation button, I quickly pushed it. The word "JEALOUSY" quickly popped up. And then another, more surprising word came into view: "ADDICTION."

Addicted to what? Pressing the green button a third time the word "LYING" appeared. Astonished, I soon learned that Lucy enjoyed the game of hurting her little sister and getting away with it; she liked the drama and exhilaration she felt whenever she could cleverly manipulate the situation to hide the truth from those in charge. Seeing the agony and pain in her defeated sister's eyes only increased the ecstasy of the hatred she had for her.

Where had I experienced that before? Oh yes, I remember. In Hell.

I watched as Lucy's fibs gave way to lies. Those in turn became more and more exaggerated as she began to fabricate stories over the years of stealing and violence, all attributed to me. And . . . what's this? "Hello, this is Karli," she lied as she spoke intently on the phone. She was pretending to be me as she made rude and stupid comments! Over and over again I witnessed this phenomenal fraud. *Yes, our voices did sound very similar. Did people really believe it was me?*

Now in the archives I observed her addictions extend to include petty thievery—not only from me, but also from other members of the family. Knowing she had a scapegoat to blame for the thefts gave her a boldness she wouldn't have had otherwise. Her success at learning to look and sound credible only made it that much easier for her to continue her devious pattern. Lucy's boldness with her phone calls never ceased, but continued on through adulthood.

"This is Karli. I want you to know that I think you're stupid and I hate you. Don't ever contact me again!" With a grin, she hung up. *Didn't anyone ever catch on?* Now I understood why previous relationships were mysteriously broken.

I observed the devastating effect of these lies on my friends and family; I witnessed as those falsehoods, fed over a long period of time and repeated over and over, became believable. Lucy, in her tireless crusade against me, repeated her damaging stories non-stop to anyone who would listen. She lied about everything concerning me, even later in life claiming that I was mentally ill. No one ever caught on; they all believed her.

As a result of Lucy's fabrications, my family of origin—thinking to "correct" me—began to ostracize me. I was rejected, ignored, and my words were not taken seriously. As we grew older, I wasn't invited to weddings and other celebrations. Upon the death of my parents, my siblings cheated me out of my portion of my earthly inheritance; I didn't understand why this was happening at the time.

But now I saw the hideous look of pleasure, in the form of an evil little grin that appeared on Lucy's face when she got someone to believe her tales. She felt a sick gratification every time she caused someone to hate or hurt me. I was shocked to see how regularly the attack came from behind my back.

"Why are you surprised?" I asked myself. "You believed her lies against others, didn't you? You acted upon those lies, didn't you?"

Illumination is always 20/20 in Heaven.

I moved the archives forward and saw that indeed, I did come to a place where I recognized my need for forgiveness; for as I said, I'd believed those lies about others, and had acted unkindly toward them as a result.

I saw myself—though not understanding why I had been punished so much—forgiving and determining to love my Dad. I saw the reconciliation between us, though he himself didn't understand why the wall was there either. But by faith, we had forgiven each other those things we did not understand, and together we enjoyed the moments still left to us on earth before he died.

Rewind. Okay, there I was at a young age, being locked out of the house.

"The gangs are going to get you!" shrieked Dawn, my oldest sister, and her friends. I could hear their heartless laughter as I ran around and around the outside of the house trying to get back in. My parents were at work and Dawn was in charge. The fact that there'd been a much talked about gang murder in a neighboring city made the possibility of murder very real to my five-year old mind. Screaming, scared, and feeling unprotected, it was an early memory that struck fear deep into my little heart. I was locked out until just before my parents came home that night. In the end they didn't believe me as I sobbed and cried because . . . yes, there it was: Lucy was privately telling my mom it really didn't happen, that I was only lying to get attention for myself.

As I begged my mother to protect me, Dawn sat stony-faced, not saying a word. Could it be she had promised Lucy she'd not tell? What was the motivation for her cruelty in doing it in the first place?

Pressing the green button, I came upon an earlier scene: I'd played a board game with Lucy and had won. Being older than I, she was not happy about it. Her little scheme at revenge started immediately. She whispered to me that Dawn was mean, then went into the kitchen where Dawn and her friends were making cookies. After making her "promise not to tell," she told her that I said she was fat and ugly.

Livid with rage, Dawn decided to teach me a lesson. That was, of course, her motivation for locking me out of the house.

But the result of her actions only confirmed to my five-year old reasoning that what Lucy had said about her was true. She WAS mean. The result of that incident was that I believed Lucy whenever she said anything negative about our older sister.

This type of manipulative drama repeated itself often in regards to my dad and others throughout my childhood. Fascinated, I observed how my self-esteem was daily being battered by that which I didn't understand.

The archives continued to another scene. Here I saw myself at age six with my fourteen-year-old brother. He, with the approval of my mother, was beating me.

"Why did you take it?" he demanded. "Mom, smack her until she confesses."

My mother joined him in the spanking.

I had not taken anything, yet here I was being accused and disciplined . . . and oh, yes: backing up the archives I saw Lucy in the other room, secretly talking to my brother.

"She took your dollar bill. I saw her." The look on Lucy's face was one I recognized many times: fake concern, fake innocence and real guile.

"Wow!"

I looked up to see Nagee looking at me with an expression I'd not seen before.

"Too fresh?" he asked. "It's only been . . . seventy-two years!" The difficulty he was having at containing his amusement was clearly reflected in his facial expression.

As my mind re-adjusted to the present, the absurdity of the comparison of the painful past to the glorious present hit me. We both broke out in long, healing laughter. Realizing that mortal situations were temporary made me all the happier at being back in Heaven where I belonged.

"Another day we can return," Nagee said. "Let's go do some skydiving."

I was only too glad to leave.

CHAPTER 11

A NEW ARRIVAL

Sorrow and mourning will disappear, and they will be overcome with joy and gladness.

Isaiah 51:11

Everyone speaks only the truth in Heaven; as a result, deceptions and manipulations are no longer a part of our existence. One of the happiest events for me during this time was getting re-acquainted with my earthly parents as well as some cousins and siblings. Being able to enjoy each other's company without the influence of all the stories and lies to cloud the truth was thoroughly refreshing and illuminating.

Could this be the "Heaven on Earth" we'd so searched for, where truth was prominent and lies were non-existent? Was it possible to bring this transparency of relationship to earth? Imagine the clarity, the enlightenment, the restoration of relationships if nothing but truth influenced each decision.

Jesus had plans for such a "Heaven on Earth." His rule there would restore truth to every event and each situation. During this time the deceiver and all his influence would be chained up and ineffective. This would give opportunity for all current and former inhabitants of the earth to judge things in the light of truth, not being influenced by the deceptions instigated by the enemy.

All lies would be cleared up—what a thought! For even in my little world, clearing up the false stories brought such freedom from the devastation originally caused by them.

Parallel with Heaven's policy of transparency and honesty was an underlying current of expectation: for you see, since the day that one-third of our residents was banned, preparations had been made for their return. The war for the souls of mankind involved revealing to them the deceptions of the enemy. So as each individual—as a human—became aware of the truth, repented of his rebellion and turned to Jesus to save him, there was a great celebration in Heaven! Singing, dancing in the streets, joy, hugs, anticipating each arrival—it was a party that never ended. Included in that celebration was the restoring and preparing of his empty mansion for his return.

On our street I'd noticed one of these mansions; it was a daily reminder of a joyful reunion soon to take place. Not only had I known the occupant, Jano, in our previous existence, but I'd known him on earth. He, or I should say "she," had been my closest friend. Now, not only was I given the privilege of helping to restore the grounds, but I'd also been invited to be part of the welcoming team for her arrival. Eagerly I anticipated this event.

Meanwhile, we eagerly worked to get the mansion prepared. Opening the doors for ventilation, we cleaned and dusted, then worked to get the gardens planted and ready.

Soon word came to gather at Heaven's gate, for it was there that all her earthly friends and family who'd preceded her to Heaven would meet. Arriving by skyper at the appointed time, I quickly ran over to the large ornate gate. Fresh in my memory was the awe I felt at my own recent arrival. *The years between our deaths seems only moments apart.*

The wonder hadn't diminished in the least, for the joy at having attained salvation from such depravity and pain was a phenomenon about which the heavenly angels, who'd never experienced it, were constantly curious. Explaining it to them was useless, for the explanation never reached the intensity of the experience. They could only marvel at our joy and intense emotional reactions at regaining something they'd never lost.

Joining in with others who'd known Jano, we merrily reminisced while anticipating the new arrival. Not only would we get to be reunited again, but we'd also get to experience the joy and overwhelming excitement Jano would feel at arriving here with us.

The topics of conversation centered on the fun times and good memories of life on earth with Jano (known to me then as "Mattie"). Though we had known Jano from long ago, those at the gate didn't talk about earthly sorrows or the pre-dawn of mortal life. Most of us had already gone to the archives to clarify the deceptions surrounding our earthly lives; no one ever thought about the dark existence before that, as those memories had been erased.

The buzzing conversation took a turn as we noticed two happy travelers approaching the gate. Yes, this was my friend Jano. I also recognized Rutsch,[42] his guardian angel,

---

[42]   Pronounced "Roo-CHAY".

walking beside him. Busy guarding Jano as Mattie for the last eighty-seven years, he was obviously enjoying their victorious entrance. Skipping and chattering, it appeared Rutsch was celebrating not only Jano's arrival, but also his own successful completion of a task well done.

As they approached the gates, we ran out to meet them. Nothing on earth could compare with the emotional high we experienced at that moment! Such exuberance, such exhilaration! For one of our own had returned, and we had the privilege of being the welcoming team. What an indescribably joyful moment this was!

After one last embrace and promises to visit, Rutsch guided Jano through the gate and walked with him to the great rotunda. How it reminded me of my walk—not so long ago—toward the same place with Nagee.

Nagee . . . . the sudden realization hit me; had he been my guardian angel on earth? Intuitively I knew it had to be true.

As I digested this bit of information, an unanswered question filtered into my subconscious; I was curious about something. Looking around, I realized I was not far from the archive building. I quickly said my good-byes to the rest of the group and headed that direction.

Chapter 12

Return to the Archives

Those who look to him for help will be radiant with joy; no shadow of shame will darken their faces. For the angel of the Lord guards all who fear him, and he rescues them.

Psalms 34: 3, 7

I was curious: while on earth I'd often wondered where God was. Knowing I wanted to serve Him, why was my life filled with such sadness at times? Was my guardian angel there to protect me? Where was he when I was young and vulnerable? Though memories of earth fade in Heaven, I still had questions for the memories that hadn't completely faded away.

I quickly found my place in the archives, logged into the motivations mode and backtracked to my high school years. Moving forward this time, I saw that every aspect of my life was marred by the tale-bearing of my sister. The godly, strong, potential mates were confidentially "warned" by her that I was not interested in them and was only playing them for a fool.

"So that was why my friend Tim, and later, John and Steve separated themselves from me," I mused.

Yet, there was my sister, comforting me, telling me she was the only one who really understood, that she was the only one who truly loved me.

Lucy, as usual, warned me not to go to my parents as she insisted that they were too busy and adding my troubles to theirs would only cause them more distress. With her deeply concerned look she was so convincing, so believable.

Now I understood that she had lied to them as well as to me. I re-felt my loneliness and frustration. I re-lived the period in my life when I wallowed in self-pity and misery: watching old movies, skipping scheduled events, eating candy, crying a lot. During that time it was hard to excel at anything.

Depression, feelings of low self-worth—those were the battles I fought then on a daily basis. It was a tough battle, a spiritual battle; the depression was black, it was real.

Through it all, though, I continued to pray. As a result, I saw the Lord eventually use these stressful experiences to strengthen and prepare me for the tougher battles ahead.

How?

Still believing the lie my sister had told me, I continued to work hard all through school to pay for my expenses. I never asked my parents for anything. My father, of course, never did give me a bill; but as a result of believing that one was coming, I not only became a hard worker but also learned to exist on the barest minimum.

This frugal ability turned out to be a blessing, for the farmer I married continually had such financial difficulty that we lived on practically nothing those first few years. I had been well prepared to live a pauper's life. It wasn't a bad life, but farming in this case was only for the financially thrifty!

There were also other hidden benefits of this pauper's life. With a simplified living environment I saw our children become able to work hard physically as they learned to appreciate the value of a dollar. While other families were dealing with too many possessions and not enough to do, our little family enjoyed the small events of life and flourished mentally, physically, and spiritually.

Away from the stress of my family of origin, I grew strong in spirit and began to understand my value from God's point of view. It was during this time I started to suspect that maybe my dad hadn't been the "problem." Rather, the difficulty had been caused by the lies and jealousy of my sister.

Pressing the motivations button, I saw that the campaign to control and separate me from the rest of my siblings never lessened, but actually increased with time. On the screen I could see the negative words about me behind my back—hours and hours, daily—it seemed to be her only topic. I truly was amazed at her tenacity and drive. I recognized that my father was as much of a victim of her tales as I was, for I'd believed her tales against him as much as he'd believed her tales against me.

Eventually I realized the lie she told me in my youth was not true and that my parents had never intended to give me a bill for my childhood expenses; my dad had only kept his books for tax purposes. This was just one of many lies Lucy had told me in an attempt to devastate my relationship with my parents.

I observed my gradual awakening to the truth during those early years up on the farm, and with this new insight, my life changed dramatically. Though all the hurtful events had up to that point been clouded in mystery, each ambiguity cleared up as truth was applied to the memory. My life blossomed.

Once Lucy realized I knew she'd lied, she never spoke civilly to me again. Her efforts to undermine my life, however, increased four-fold as she slandered me with fresh rigor to all my family, friends, acquaintances, and co-workers.

But now I saw that for every hurdle I had to jump over, I gained twice that in self-respect, motivation, and skill. For every person that my sister was able to keep out of my life through her tale-bearing stories, I had dozens more join it who were a positive influence.

Sitting in the archive building watching the history of my life, I observed myself becoming strong in spirit and in confidence of who I was in Jesus. My children grew up healthy and productive, and even much more so since my original family had abandoned me. I now realized that all the gossip and tale-bearing would have been detrimental to them had my siblings chosen to still be a part of our lives.

What I'd been told as a child was true: All things do work together for good to those who love the Lord.[43]

As I continued to watch, I saw myself rise above the abandonment and rejection felt from losing my earthly family through Lucy's manipulations. I saw the day when I really understood what was happening, accepted it, and moved on to accomplish the tasks God had prepared me to do.

The archives continued revealing the deceptions, the repetitive lies, day after day, year after year . . . I literally became quite bored with reviewing it all. Sin was, after all, a part of our earthly experience; learning to overcome it was the exciting part.

---

[43] Romans 8:28

Quickly I fast-forwarded the rest of my life. Pressing the green button I saw that my labor during the next many years was productive in the eyes of God. Additionally, all the reading I did as a child to escape the familial stress turned to my advantage by making me into an excellent and well-known writer.

Further into the archives I observed my hard-working husband starting a family business, becoming financially successful, and our children growing up to become effective leaders in the church. I died a ripe old age, well loved and respected in the community.

I had not been alone in my earthly walk. I'd not been forgotten, after all; for truly I saw that only good had resulted from all my earthly pain.

But one question still nagged at me: *Where was Lucy?* I'd forgiven her long ago, had prayed constantly for her and attempted reconciliation with her many times; but she'd disappeared from the screen.

I put aside the machine and sat back. Touching my pocket, I felt for the ever-present apple I usually carried there.

"Ah." I smiled to myself as I took a healthy bite. This was where the action was, right here in Heaven. Unhurried, unrushed, savoring each bite, I soon felt refreshed.

CHAPTER 13

THE BOOK

I saw the Lord sitting on his throne, and all the host of Heaven standing by him on his right hand and on his left.

1 Kings 22:19

Spinning in the chair for a moment, I enjoyed taking my mind off of what I'd just learned. Eventually facing the screen once again, I returned to the archives.

Thinking to find the answer to my question I pressed the buttons . . . except now the archives didn't continue forward, but only backward. I couldn't go beyond my life on earth.

Or could I? There is no time line here in Heaven. *Surely . . .* but try as I might, I couldn't move the buttons in any way possible to see what had happened to my sister.

Now the screen started moving backward—faster, faster, until I saw the day of my birth, backward, backward, backward through the ages, clear back to Adam and Eve and . . . beyond.

The screen didn't stop as expected. I saw the hideous sights of Hell. Yes, the memories came flooding back; I'd been there. They were horrible experiences too gruesome to tell. The screams, the depravity—faster and faster the screen went. I sat transfixed, as it didn't stop. Backwards, backwards, to . . . could it be? Life before Hell?

Yes, there was our beautiful Heaven, my familiar street. There it was, just as it is now. How long ago? It was unfathomable: timeless, beyond eras, beyond eternity.

The screen gradually slowed down. I saw myself in a huge worshiping choir. *Yes, I remember that day*; all those under Lucifer had gathered to praise the Lord of All.

We were in adulation . . . mighty, roaring worship. The praises filled the streets of Heaven with a mighty rushing sound: beautiful, uplifting music. All was glorious then, before the time of evil. Our leader had been magnificent, magnetic and musical. He had been a good director, highly respected, and given a place of honor.

Then the chaos started: private, jealous thoughts began to control his mind. *Control—yes—that was an issue. And worship.* Lucifer ached for the worship that belonged only to Jehovah.

Obsession took over, decisions were made. There was war in Heaven. Michael and his angels fought against Lucifer and his angels. Judgment was assessed and the cleansing of Heaven took place.

Before we knew it, we were hurled into space: shrinking, shrinking, shrinking, and finally landed with a raining of thuds on this small planet called Earth. With a sick feeling in our stomachs, we realized that life was over as we knew it, never to be the same; we had blindly followed our leader in his treason.

He became the god of our world.

Aware, yet we were unaware as we didn't fully comprehend sin and its nature at the time.

Deceived. Controlled. Manipulated. Unwilling—there the conclusion was unclear, for there were as many willing as unwilling. *Yet . . . surely those who'd been deceived . . . could they still choose?*

Sin is not tolerated in Heaven. Knowing that, all who followed Lucifer in his rebellion sinned with him.

I sat back in my chair stunned and exhausted, for the weight of what I'd just seen took every ounce of strength from my body. Yet the screen continued—not on earth, but in Heaven. This was . . . this was an area that I had not experienced.

I looked around. *Did I have the authority to continue looking? Did the machine malfunction? Was I, did they . . . ?* The questions dissolved as I immersed myself into the activity I saw before me. Though now I'd been in Heaven for some time, I'd not yet been to the throne room or even to the great temple complex; but there on the screen I saw the door open to the inner throne room of Almighty God.

The throne was the color and clarity of an emerald, but the brightness surrounding it prevented me from seeing the One sitting on it. Surrounding the throne was a rainbow. The floor, smooth and clear as glass, extended endlessly. Seven stunning lamps of fire burned before the majestic seat, with each lamp representing one of the seven spirits of God.

There were twenty-four chairs situated close to the throne. Walking to them were twenty-four elders, dressed in beautiful white garments. Each one was wearing a crown of gold. Closest to the throne were four large beings, or "beasts," that appeared to be able to see everything surrounding them.

Soon a large number of angels arrived . . . . so many so that the floor was completely covered with beings for as far as the eye could see. A great assembly had been called for the rest of Heaven, the two-thirds that stayed. The Archangels Michael and Gabriel together with their angels gathered into the massive hall. The meeting was a solemn assembly, for even though Michael and his warrior angels had defeated Lucifer and his angels, there was not the jubilation one would have thought would occur in the face of victory.

A large book was placed in the middle of the room. It was a register of some sort, a book filled with names—the names of every angel under Lucifer's dominion. Because they'd committed treason with him, all were now banned from Heaven.

No longer would their names or personal data be available to anyone in Heaven, for no sin, sinner, or reminder of sin was allowed within the gates. Seven seals, one for each of the seven spirits of God were being placed upon the books.

The book was sealed shut.

Chapter 14

The Volunteer

The Lion of the tribe of Judah, the Root of David, has prevailed to open the book.

Rev 5:5

How long the book was sealed, I don't know—time is not measured in eternity—but in the recesses of my mind was the memory of the eons I had spent in Hell feeling totally forgotten.

Was this period of hopelessness in Hell the same duration of when the book was sealed? As I pondered this thought, the screen went silent.

I thought something had malfunctioned, for try as I might, I couldn't move the screen forward. As I watched the screen, not a creature moved; all of Heaven was waiting to see what would happen next.

Backing the machine up a fraction, I saw plans being made to re-establish the foundations of the earth. Why? It was for the eventual redemption of the banished. "Mankind" was to be the newly created form to temporarily house an eternal spirit.

Created lower than the angels, we as "mankind" would need guardian angels to protect us from the deceptions of Lucifer during our decisional time on earth. Through our earthly conscience, the guardian angels would give us guidance to keep us safe. Whether we listened to them or not was up to us.

Transfixed, I saw Gabriel's messenger angels respond with enthusiasm as they eagerly lined up to be the guardians. One would be assigned to each of the newly created "mankind" as each one entered the world for the great test.

But now, all seemed to be in limbo on the screen. A special volunteer had been requested—one who would enter life's circumstances as "mankind" along with all of the banished one-third, yet not succumb to the temptations and lures of the evil one. By living without sin in the face of evil authority, lies, and deception, he would be able to give his life as a ransom for the rest. Only then could the book be opened.

No one responded.

This was incredible—but not unbelievable, for if Lucifer, the "Bright Star of the Morning" had so deceived one-third of Heaven, how could any of the rest of the angels hope to have the intellect and strength to defeat him? None of the masses under his authority had been able to resist his potent cunning or manipulations. Even Michael, when challenged, acknowledged his limitations when he didn't rebuke Lucifer but said "The Lord rebuke you."[44]

But at last, One came forward. He was magnificent, with eyes like fire—a form of God Himself.

I recognized Him.

At that moment great sobs of relief, thankfulness and joy welled up in me; for I knew beyond all doubt who He

---

[44] Zechariah 3:2

was, and what he'd done for me. He was the Volunteer who would make a way for those banished to return to Heaven. I was thankful beyond words.

I knew well the story of his entry into the world. Not only was the timeline of earth's history based on this eventful birth, but his followers had made it into a yearly holiday. His perfect life, his gruesome death, his breathtaking resurrection . . . . eventually all the earth knew this story and knew it well.

Viewing it here in the archives, I saw that so much more had happened than what we'd realized. I watched him die, but instead of going straight to Heaven, his spirit went directly to Hell.

Stunned, I could only question, "Why?" *He lived a sinless life, didn't he? He healed the sick, he loved, he forgave. If anyone deserved to go to Heaven, it was he!*

As I watched his spirit descend, I noticed something unusual. Unlike the returnees who screamed upon their re-entry, he entered the pit as a conqueror with authority. I observed the powerful demons squeal as they attempted to surround, control and chain him. But they couldn't get within ten feet of him; a strong force surrounded his person and none of them could penetrate it.

"RELEASE THE PRISONERS!" he demanded. Quivering before him, the defeated forces did as commanded. Soon a mighty roar was heard as the newly liberated captives followed Jesus out the gates of Hell to earth, and then on to Heaven.

Next on the screen appeared the inner court of the heavenly temple. At this all-Heaven assembly, Jesus entered, walked to the throne, and jubilantly took the book from the One sitting there. Immediately, the twenty-four elders laid down their crowns as they, the four beasts, and all the assembly bowed before him.

Holding the book high, Jesus slowly turned around as all gazed in wonder. Noticeably visible were the fresh wounds on his hands and feet.

At that moment, vials of odors were released, filling the air with the prayers of the saints. As the sweet smells flowed throughout the vast room, the orchestra of harps started their overture and all joined in to sing this brand new song:

"You are worthy to take the book and to open the seals. For by your blood you have redeemed us to God. Worthy is the Lamb[45] to receive power, and riches, wisdom and strength and honor and glory and blessing."[46]

Thousands and thousands were assembled, covering the whole floor endlessly. They were joyfully shouting "blessing, and honor, and glory, and power, be to him that sits on the throne and to the Lamb for ever and ever."

Keeping time with the music were the four beasts who punctuated the praise with an occasional loud "Amen!"

---

[45] The term of "Lamb" refers to the Jewish sacrifice the priest would make for the atonement of sin. Jesus was the perfect, unblemished Lamb of God who died in our place to atone for our sin.

[46] Rev. 5:12

CHAPTER 15

THE QUEST

The lip of truth shall be established for ever: but a lying tongue is but for a moment.

Proverbs 12:19

Sitting in the archives I realized the price had been paid for all mankind to be redeemed. That all the earth knew about this redemption was probable, for the worldwide media network was such that anyone anywhere and at any time could hear the story of Jesus the Messiah.

Yet, what about . . . I kept in mind why I had stayed in the archives. *My sister. Yes! I had loved her . . . yet I no longer knew her.*

I attempted to move the screen forward, but it was not responding. Looking for a solution, I ran my hand under the panel to locate the motivation button. Finding it after a short search, I pressed it firmly. Once, twice, three times. Abruptly the screen began to move again.

For a second time I watched as one-third of Heaven's angels hurtled through space toward Earth. Landing with soft thuds, they ran, forming groups in the blackness.

Pressing the "virtual mode" button, I instantly became part of the action. Falling with nothing under my feet felt exactly like the occasional nightmares I'd had on earth. "Not again," I thought as the sensation of free-falling once more sickened my stomach.

As we rapidly descended, I noticed the being to my right; he'd been one of my acquaintances who'd endeared himself to Lucifer before the fall. "This is our opportunity," he whispered gleefully, his face inches from mine. Turning my head slightly toward him, I saw that what had once been a luminescent light in his eyes was now a dull finish. "Everything we knew before has now been changed," he proudly informed me. "Think opposites now. What was bad is now good and what was good is now bad. Learn this, and you could be exalted in rank." He smiled a crooked smile as he watched to see how this information affected me.

What did he mean? I instantly knew that what he said was true to a point, but could be manipulated into a lie; for as he said, all was changed. Truth would be replaced by lies; whereas joy and freedom were former norms, misery would be the norm now. To him that was an enjoyable thought.

"Power," he continued, "and I'm going to get mine, whatever it takes." He smiled ever so wilily as he smirked directly in my face, "Wouldn't you enjoy that?"

I couldn't tell if he was trying to encourage or taunt me, but one thing stood out clearly . . . he wanted to control me. The look on his face would have frightened the toughest human . . .

Pressing the button quickly to get out of "virtual mode," I continued to watch as the terror took root and permeated every action, thought and ruling on this now dark home called Earth. As the era continued, the pit of the earth became ever more increasingly our place of residence;

deeper and deeper we went until the surface became virtually unattainable.

For how long we existed in this state I don't know, but as the eons rushed by I observed this acquaintance transforming into . . . the being with the flickering eyes!

"Unbelievable," I thought as I now realized that the two beings were one and the same; for truthfully, the fallen angels had so changed after millenniums of horror that no one could really recognize anyone at all . . . nor did they want to. Here I was, safe in the archives, witnessing past events.

But still I was curious. *Where was this being now?*

I moved the buttons forward until I watched my going into the tunnel. By pressing the green button, I also observed this being entering the tunnel just a millisecond before me.

So . . . this being, my "guide," so to speak; was he also going to earth for the great test? As I watched, it seemed that he was, for he entered slightly before me into the world of dream. In earth time, he entered exactly three years and twelve days before me. *Was he . . . ?*

The question stuck in my mind and would not, could not, be asked, for I had prayed for her from the time I found out her true nature to the day of my death. Surely God would have mercy on her as he had mercy on me!

Yet, here it was. *This being was my sister on earth.*

CHAPTER 16

THE PIT

For the grave cannot praise you, death cannot celebrate you: they that go down into the pit cannot hope for your truth.

Isaiah 38:18

It had to be a mistake. I reversed the forward motion of the screen, replaying the event, pushing more buttons to reveal motivation.

Suddenly the screen moved to a secret room in the depths of Hell. I saw multitudes of thousands and thousands of dark images bowing, scraping, and groveling before the exalted ruler of the pit. This was a room I'd never seen before, reserved only for the top echelons of power in that dark world.

As I watched, an ugly beast arose in their midst. He strode mightily about full of self-importance, and gloating in the growling adulation offered him. All was deceit and fake as he proclaimed himself to be a royal deity. Everyone in the room continued to grovel before him, a counterfeit god, as he mocked, ranted and raved against the inhabitants of Heaven.

"Our troubles are their fault," he screamed to thunderous applause. "There are twice as many of them as us." He paused for dramatic effect. "Where is their 'so called' compassion when it comes to us? Where are OUR skypers? Where are OUR mansions?"

The screams and hisses in that massive room exploded with such rage and hatred that he stopped for a moment to enjoy the sound. His speech was impassioned—designed to manipulate, to incite, to control.

As the noise died down, his voice took on a cajoling texture with volume hardly more than a whisper, "We must take our revenge!" All was quiet in the darkness as they listened to the cold, thrilling words.

Continuing to speak to his worshipers, his whisper gradually increased in volume until it was a blood-curdling, ear piercing scream.

"We'll take our revenge, then take it again, then take it again, and again, and again!"

As he punctuated his last phrase, the cavernous room exploded in riotous chaos. Screams, biting, cursing, and orgies of every sort and imagination broke out. Then as planned, at the very moment the place erupted into its peak of hellish frenzy, the newest returnees were brought to the platform.

Upon seeing them, the screams rose tenfold as the excitement of seeing the newcomers' terrorized faces spread throughout the room. Bind! Torture! Destroy! This was what they existed for. To tear down anything God created was exhilarating, addictive, and yes!! Here was fresh meat! Fresh blood! Fresh earthly souls!

The platform began to shake as the quivering group observed in horrific disbelief the sight before them. That this was their permanent reality was just beginning to dawn, but their silent expressions of horror were soon replaced with screams of unbelievable pitch and volume as their suffering became the entertainment for the night.

I looked away from the screen, for I didn't want to witness this depravity and torture. The demonic thrill-kill would last until the returnees were no more than fragile shadows of broken spirits. What was left of them would then be chained to the walls to await their Day of Judgment.

"Oh, mighty master!" The voice startled me in its familiarity.

Turning again toward the screen, I now detected only a handful of demons in the room. The mighty beast had transformed himself into a bright shining angel. Those left had surrounded him in some sort of ritual; he was speaking softly, as to small children.

"The celebrations will continue as long as we successfully gain returnees." He paused a moment for dramatic effect. "Furthermore, my dear rascals, the most intensely pleasurable celebrations will be when we welcome returnees who think they're going to . . . the other place." His now beautiful face couldn't conceal the ugly contortions of his hideous glee. Closing his eyes, he reveled in this thought as the flattery and grunts of approval continued from the demons surrounding him.

"And that is why," he continued, "you've got to be smarter than ever. Use good strategy; be clever in your planning, for if truth prevails in the earthly experience, we could lose some of them to the other side."

"But" . . . here he stuttered a bit in his eagerness to impart his mastery of trickery . . . "those who allow just a little truth mixed in with the deception . . . they'll be successful."

He looked solemnly over the small crowd. "Those who succeed will not only be exalted in rank, but will also enjoy a more intense gratification when evil prevails. Now who wants to volunteer for the assignment?"

"Pick me!" screamed a demon.

"No, me," cajoled another.

"I can do it!" sniveled another.

Then the most conniving of the group, a wily being named Lusilite, uttered the words the leader had been waiting to hear: "Oh, mighty master, your beauty overwhelms me with its fierce darkness."

As he spoke, the demon slithered to grope the feet of his master while forcing himself to look humble in his presence.

I shuddered as I heard that familiar voice again. This one was a master of deception; his flattery, the obeisance, it was a convincing act.

"I will be victorious," Lusilite said with a hoped-for sound of confidence. "We shall have our celebration with this one also."

"So, you guarantee success, do you?"

"Yes, I do." He put on a fake smile to calm himself down.

"If you fail, you'll be our entertainment in his stead!"

Lusilite, so bold before, began to shiver slightly.

"Rise, I give you the assignment."

As Lusilite struggled to stand, the ruler of darkness continued. "Communicate with him, let him think he can trust you, then tell him the plan. When the time comes, bring him to the tunnel with you. Then . . ." At this point he could hardly keep the anticipation of the betrayal from preventing him to finish his instructions.

Finally getting control of himself again, he continued. "Do everything you can to destroy him. Lie to him from his babyhood on. Lie to others about him. Undermine his efforts to succeed at anything." His voice became more and more sinister with every sentence. "Spoil every attempt at reconciliation with those you're able to alienate from him. Steal, cheat, manipulate his confidence; bring him to a point of total desperation. Let him feel the full weight of betrayal by those he trusted and loved. You've seen the routine." He paused to wipe his forehead as he had worked himself into a lather.

A slow grin spread across the face of Lusilite, for he truly looked forward to wreaking havoc in the life of Korel, his assignment. "Any other suggestions?" he calmly asked, trying to contain his own building excitement.

"Go for the trust factor, then hit her with the big betrayal."

"Her?"

"She'll be female . . . more intuitive, but also more easily fooled."

"Why not attack the mother?" interrupted another imp, who was still hoping to gain the assignment. "Too many babies, not enough money . . . I could return him quickly with an abortion."

"Your specialty won't work in this case," was the irritated response. "The mother has strong maternal instincts and is involved in a committed marriage. Besides, abortion returnees aren't much fun anyway. They just get back in line; we have no power to stop them.

But," he turned back to Lusilite, "betrayal from those she trusts—that should cause depression, maybe even suicide. At the very least it should prevent her from using her abilities to their greatest potential. This shouldn't take too long. Don't fail me."

He spoke with such unusually menacing urgency that Lusilite, taken aback, stopped his groveling for an instant.

"Master?"

"You . . ." he paused trying to find the right words. "You will have to battle" here his counterfeit beauty turned hideous as he spit out the next words . . . "have to battle her prayers for you."

Lusilite froze as he pondered this news.

"You'll not convert to the Light side?" he asked. "The urge will be strong." The glow of the light surrounding this powerful angel of darkness began to turn green.

"Convert?" Lusilite spoke as if an electric shock hit his system. Panicked, he forgot his previously rehearsed words of flattery for a moment, causing the other hopefuls to crawl over each other in their eagerness to be next in line in case the assignment was still open.

Then Lusilite quickly regained his composure. "Be it far from me, master. I can do this. I won't fail. I'll do your bidding down to the finest detail." With timed cunning, he once again groveled at the feet of his master.

"All memories of this place will be erased for the season. You'll have choices, same as the others, but I believe you will succeed."

Lusilite leaped at this unexpected compliment, for he realized that his thirst for power and control had been recognized as an asset.

Curious again, I hit the motivations button in order to read the inner thoughts of Lusilite. I learned that the thirst for power and control was his only motivation for wanting to go to the surface; he intended to return victoriously with his victim in tow and had not the slightest interest in changing the mode of operation of the dark world he had chosen.

As the screen moved forward, I watched transfixed as Lusilite entered the tunnel, swept toward the world of man, and was born into the family three years and twelve days before myself.

Suddenly everything made sense—the struggles, the betrayals—but it didn't matter anymore. I realized that the evil intent of Lusilite/Lucy toward me had only increased my resolve to forgive, to pray, and to serve Almighty God with abandon. The earthly distresses she caused actually made me stronger. Because of them I learned how to pass the tests on earth, to pray effectively, and to forgive totally.

My sister had been my greatest enemy, yet because of her hatred, I came to rely upon the Lord to overcome Lucifer's ways of darkness; I learned to live in the Light.

"There's your answer." I turned quickly at hearing the voice of Nagee, for I'd been so engrossed in the archives that I didn't hear him come in.

"How long have you been standing there?" I asked.

"Long enough," he answered. "Jano is looking for you,—thought you might want to take him to Ziphotan."

My mood brightened at the idea. "I could show him my house, the orchards, the hybrids"

"—Rutsch might want to come, too. He's curious about those apples of yours. Ready to go?"

"Yes." I quickly ended my session and followed Nagee out the door.

As we exited the building Nagee turned towards me. Pausing for a moment to organize his thoughts, he spoke softly, "You were not always easy, you know."

I looked at him and immediately knew what he was talking about. The subject was that of guardian angels . . . Nagee in particular.

"You wondered where I was?" he continued. "Who do you think prevented the staple gun from working?" Nagee looked questionably at me for a moment.

Oh, yes. I remember!

"And years later, when you were a young mother who ran out of gas in the middle of a dark and dangerous country road with two babies in the car,—"

"—You were the peculiar old man that brought gas to me on an old flatbed trailer?"

"What you didn't see was the loaded semi truck barreling down the road. He wouldn't have been able to stop once he crested the curve of the hill . . ."

No, I didn't realize it, but I always wondered about this experience with the two strangers who were there to help me. They knew, somehow, that I was penniless, graciously refusing my offers of "sending" them a check. "There was a young woman with you who spoke with a lisp—"

"That was Rutsch. Since you and Jano were friends, we completed a lot of our assignments together." Nagee smiled unexpectedly as I digested this new revelation.

"If you want a total list of events where I intercepted on behalf of your safety," he continued, "I could give it to you."

"You were my guardian angel—"

"—For seventy-eight years I watched over you."

No further words were needed as my expression acknowledged my understanding and gratefulness.

CHAPTER 17

A MID-AIR REUNION

Watch! He comes with clouds; and every eye shall see him, and they also which pierced him. I am Alpha and Omega the beginning and the ending, which is, and was, and is to come, the Almighty.

Rev 1:7-8

The focus of activity in Heaven was heading in a distinct direction. A unique marriage was to take place, one that we'd looked forward to for years while living on earth. Jesus was preparing for his allegorical bride, the Church to be united with him.

I was part of that church, and looked forward to the union with great joy. Together we'd set up his kingdom on earth where righteousness and truth would be restored. All the redeemed would be involved in the event.

Excitement in Heaven increased as the time for the marriage feast grew near. Not only had I anticipated this day since arriving here, but all of Heaven had been waiting for it as well.

A few conditions had to be met before the marriage could take place, however. First, all the banished angels under Lucifer had to have a mortal lifespan on earth in order to make a choice. Guardian angels would then bring those who chose to serve the Lord to Heaven upon their death.

As they era of mankind winds down, the final generation of believers would not experience death. Instead, they would be caught up in a vast mid-air gathering. On that day all who put their trust in Jesus to save them would be lifted from the earth and gathered together in the clouds. We, who'd already died our earthly death, would arrive first, returning with our Lord to accompany the new ones to the great marriage feast. It would be a huge harvesting of earth, with the angels being the reapers.

Those left after this . . . oh what sorrows there'd be, for the four mighty chained angels would be freed to wreak havoc on the earth. I could only imagine the scene: warrior angels with virtuous strength invading Hell's territory, bringing with them the keys to Hell and death. Chains locked from before time began would be opened, prisoners would be freed. *Those millions chained to the walls of that gigantic cavern, were they to be set free?*

That Heaven owned keys to locks in Hell was common knowledge here. Not only had certain angels been sent to open locks and remove chains, but Jesus himself had made an appearance there in order to set prisoners free.[47]

Suddenly it happened; this was the day and hour! Like a whirlwind, the happy news spread throughout all the heavenly realms. The Father proclaimed that today was the day Jesus would return to earth with his holy angels to gather in the rest of the redeemed.

---

[47] Rev. 1:18

To be part of the welcoming chorus was a privilege we knew we'd not earned. First the trumpets would blow, then the angels would begin the process of reclaiming the earth for the Lord's return.[48] Yes, we were prepared and ready!

The hour had come! We gathered by the gates of Heaven, and together with our Lord prepared for the great final harvesting of the earth. Excitedly, we readied ourselves for the trip.

Getting organized, we learned the order and placement of our arrival. The whole earth was to be encircled. Every city, town, village, or small little outpost needed to be in view.

Not a hair was out of place as we donned our spotless white robes and put on our finest golden jewelry. We wanted to welcome the new arrivals in the most glorious way, for, as we all knew, they'd been through quite an ordeal during the last days on earth.

Nagee, who'd been assigned to play in the orchestra, was excitedly tuning his trumpet in preparation for this event. He had such a look of awed anticipation on his face that I could hardly get him to say a word. Being speechless was unusual for Nagee and I mentally made a note to tease him about it later.

The ability to transport matter quickly throughout the universe was a science that now seemed rather simple; learning to do so required no more than a few minutes of concentration with a pictorial manual. Using this method, the transport to earth was luxuriously comfortable and quick for the assemblage as we crossed from one heavenly

---

[48]   Mark 13:27

zone to another. It was no more difficult than batting an eye, and quicker than its twinkle.

We disembarked just outside the earth's atmosphere. Excitedly we traveled the final distance using our recently re-discovered ability to fly through the air without help. What a thrill it was, flying together into the earth's atmosphere with Jesus leading the way! Finding our places, we encircled the planet in such a manner that every inhabitant of the earth could see angels in the sky. Since Nagee was in another section, I found myself next to Jano, my childhood friend.

"Remember?" Jano winked at me as he grinned from ear to ear. I quickly realized to what he was referring: late one night during one of our youthful "sleepovers", we thought it had occurred. Wide awake as we lay in bed, we'd been talking about the coming rapture. Suddenly the reading lamp on the headboard turned on. Needless to say its sudden brightness, inches from our eyes, made our hearts beat double time for a few seconds. Only when we remembered that the loose bulb in the lamp had earlier turned out by itself were we able to breathe again.

Now we were experiencing the real event together. It was an event we'd previously imagined only from earth's point of view.

"How could I forget?" I replied with as much breath as I could spare, for indeed, my heart was beating so rapidly in excitement that it was even now difficult to talk!

As we swiftly moved toward the earth, we could see the activity: two people were in a field, two were in bed, two were eating lunch . . . Our thoughts whirled: Which ones would join us? Which ones would not?[49]

---

[49]   Matt 24:40-41

Arriving in formation with our Lord Jesus leading the way, we were about to witness the much anticipated exodus of the believers from the earth. These, along with Enoch and Elijah,[50] would be the unique ones of mankind who would never experience the sting of death.

Suddenly the signal was given and the orchestra of trumpets began their majestic symphony. Immediately all Heaven roared with a mighty shout as we continued to make our approach; the choir burst out in a glorious anthem of praise and we all joined in.

The sound awakened the world in a way they'd never experienced. We watched as, one by one, the earthly believers began the ascent to meet us in the air.

What surprise and exultation graced each formerly earthbound face as our paths came together! With warm greetings we welcomed each one. As we observed the new arrivals seeing Jesus in person for the first time, we again re-lived our own wonder at first meeting him.

As the moments continued, we unexpectedly realized we were welcoming not only our own earthly children, but many grandchildren and great-grandchildren as well. Our joy was indescribable, our ecstasy was uncontainable, and our happiness was immeasurable.

The welcoming of the believers along with their guardian angels continued with a mighty, rapturous homecoming celebration. The trumpets continued to blow with exuberance and we were all giddy with an overwhelming joy.

---

[50]   Both were taken to Heaven without dying. See Gen 5:24 and 2 Kings 2:11.

Arriving back in Heaven with the redeemed of the earth in tow, the rest of the angels welcomed us home. What I'd previously experienced with welcoming Jano was now multiplied by millions.

To be part of this homecoming was an unspeakable joy . . . words are not enough, so I'll not even try to describe it. The marriage feast was about to begin!

> *"He that is unjust, let him be unjust still: And he who is filthy, let him be filthy still: And he that is righteous, let him be righteous still: And he that is holy, let him be holy still."*
>
> *Rev. 20:11*

CHAPTER 18

THE MARRIAGE FEAST

He will rejoice over you with great gladness. With his love, he will calm all our fears. He will exult over you by singing a happy song.

Zephaniah 3:16-17

The marriage supper of the Lamb, as it was affectionately known, was the celebration of the official uniting of Jesus and his church. All those who'd accepted the free gift offered through the Volunteer Lamb would be welcomed with a huge party. Though all of the banished ones had been invited, there were places set only for those who'd accepted the invitation.

"CHOSEN FROM THE FOUNDATIONS OF THE EARTH." I saw these words on a banner lifted high at the gate to welcome the happy guests.

Arriving there with the redeemed from the earth was delightful! Everyone was talking about the mid-air meeting, and all were ecstatically happy.

The welcome was endless from those who'd stayed within the city. That it was a reversal of the scene that took place so long ago was not lost on us. The laughter, the enjoyment, the restoration—it was truly a momentous occasion no one would ever forget.

As we walked through the gate and toward the great banqueting hall, I was surrounded by the ones I'd known and loved on earth, and in Heaven before that and . . . . I couldn't remember another time other than those two times, for all memories of tears and the agony that created those tears had been erased.

As we walked through the massive doors, warm smells and gentle music greeted our senses. As far as the eye could see were festive tables with attractive place settings, decorations, flowers, and all kinds of food. This was Heaven; eternity was real and ongoing. The joy welling up within us was indescribable as we talked and laughed, anticipating the presence of our beloved leader, Jesus.

As the festivities began, I noticed someone sitting close to the head table. His appearance was distinctive . . . I had seen him before.

Rising, he walked to the podium to face us. He spoke intensely, joyfully. "I am Adam," was his simple opening. "And I'm glad to not only be called 'grandfather,' but also 'brother.'"

Applause and exuberant cheers broke out as the meaning of his words fell on us. "Here we are, the redeemed, alive together with Christ." More thunderous applause.

"I was the first to experience life on earth without previous knowledge of any existence. My mortal body—the prototype formed out of the earth's elements—was brought to life with the breath of Almighty God. Released from the pit, my spirit was resuscitated into this newly formed body and I was given the power of choice. Yet even in my idyllic world I couldn't live a faultless life, but sinned along with Eve.

When I failed the test," he continued, "the door was opened for sin to enter the world. As a result, the seeds of sin bore fruit, multiplied, and became ever increasingly hard to overcome; but when Jesus came, he reversed the trend, giving us power to overcome the evil in our lives. Jesus, the second 'Adam' did not fail the test . . . thanks be to God!" He stopped as thunderous applause interrupted him again.

So this is Adam . . . I recognized him. He was the stranger I met in my orchard who'd admired my hybrid apples. I was pleased to see him up front, joyfully being part of the festivities.

As the applause quieted, he continued with one last statement:

"Jesus, Savior, we honor you!"

The roar of praise that followed was loud and sustained. As Jesus entered the banqueting hall, the twenty-four elders in attendance instantly fell on their knees before him. Immediately, the rest of the guests, as one, followed suit. The powerful strength of our dear resurrected Christ shone brightly in his face as he graciously received our thanks, our worship, and our praise.

Finally he spoke. "Rise up, my love, my fair one, and come away. For, look, the winter is past, the rain is over and gone; the flowers appear on the earth; the time of the singing of birds is come, and the voice of the turtledove is heard in our land. Rise up, my fair one, rise up!"[51]

With that joyful greeting we rose from our knees and took our seats. Jesus continued to speak. "Do you really understand how much the Father loves you? I love you with

---

[51] Song of Solomon 2:10-12

an everlasting love." And with that, he began to sing with the tenderest of voices:

> "The Lord God in our midst is mighty;
> He saves, He rescues
> He rejoices over you with delight;
> Rest in his love,
> As he, with joy, sings over you."[52]

The response to the song was silence, for all were completely caught up in the beauty of the singer. Jesus then continued:

"As the Father has loved me, so I have loved you. Continue in my love."[53] With that, he sat down and the feast began.

We enjoyed the food and entertainment knowing we were celebrating our union with Him in the same way a bride celebrates her union with the bridegroom. It was a love partnership, but we also served him gratefully because of what he'd done to redeem us from death and Hell.

Though we'd been given the chance, we'd failed to earn salvation through adherence to God's laws. Jesus, who'd come to earth as mankind, knew what temptations and deceptions the enemy could put forth. He didn't fail, but overcame sin in every way. His love for us was unconditional.

How deceivable we were, but how un-deceivable was our perfect Savior. Only through his gift could we return with a clean slate to our Heavenly Father. He was the

---

[52] Zephaniah 3:17

[53] John 15:9

bravest, strongest, gentlest, and most compassionate Being to ever inhabit Heaven, and we were to be one with Him!

Timeless in its festivities, the marriage supper finally ended. Jesus, our leader and King had made the announcement that we were to return to the earth to help him set up his Kingdom. From every country, language and nationality he appointed kings and priests to reign with him on earth. Now at the feast, we all bonded together as one to accomplish the task set before us.

What a joyful crowd we made! Singing, dancing, hugs . . . it was never-ending. Eventually Adam again took the stand. "Eve, come meet your children." He lovingly held out his arm to her as she joined him at his side. "My beautiful 'Rib'," he teased as the assembly room filled with merriment. She playfully jabbed him in his and smiled mischievously to the audience.

"There's a little boy inside every man," she spoke pleasantly in a rich alto voice. "and I'll dare say that I'm the only wife in history who got to view this phenomenon up close."

A twittering of chuckles and laughter filled the room. That Eve had a sense of humor didn't seem to fit the preconceived idea of her that had been passed down through the ages.

"My 'childhood' was spent inside . . . with that little boy." As the audience grasped the meaning of her words, more ripples of laughter waved over the sea of faces. The fact was that neither she nor Adam had a mother, and therefore hadn't experienced gestation or childhood.

Adam gazed lovingly at her for a moment before turning his attention back to us. "We have work to do. We must prepare the earth for His reign, starting with the Day of Judgment. Six days have already passed. Let the Day of Rest begin."

Suddenly I had clarity. Each thousand years represented one heavenly day.[54] Six thousand years had passed since the creation of Adam; now the Thousand Year Reign was beginning. We'd known it was coming; even the demons knew it and trembled in fear. It was on this long awaited day that the redeemed angels would judge the deeds of those who'd not accepted the free gift of salvation.[55] We'd rule together with our Redeemer, who would set up his righteous kingdom on earth.

We, as well as the other angels, looked forward to the day when ALL creatures in the earth, or under the earth, or in the sea, or in the heavens would bend the knee to worship our King.[56] Jesus, Son of the Living God, the Creator of the heavens and the earth was worthy of all praise, adoration, love, and worship.

Love would rule. On this new day the earth would be filled with the knowledge of the glory of the Lord.[57]

And what about Lucifer? Following the Thousand-Year Reign, even he would be released for a time.[58] After that, however, he would find his home in the eternal abyss known as the "bottomless pit" and all Hell and death would be thrown into the Lake of Fire.[59]

Amazingly, and as unbelievable as it sounds, some will still prefer evil over good. Thankfully, our God is merciful.[60]

---

[54]   2 Peter 3:8

[55]   Isa.45:23, Romans 14:11, Philippians 2:10

[56]   sa.45:23, Romans 14:11, Philippians 2:10

[57]   Hab 2:14

[58]   Rev. 20:3

[59]   Rev 20:14

[60]   Ps 136:1

He continually reminds us that his mercies are new every morning. In His hands all consequences will be just, true, and accurate.

Pondering these thoughts, it struck me: Eternity is a long, long time. *Perhaps . . . perhaps . . .*

My thoughts trailed off as I tried to recall who I'd prayed for so earnestly while on earth, but the memory had almost completely faded away.

Chapter 19

Building New Jerusalem

I am Alpha and Omega, the beginning and the ending which is, and which was, and which is to come.

Rev 1:8

The temple complex housing the great throne of Almighty God was within walking distance of where the banquet took place. To say the buildings were large and magnificent would be an enormous understatement as to their grandeur. As far as the eye could see the golden structures radiated lights of every color. Constructed out of bright luminescent material, each edifice was a mathematical wonder of architectural design. Hexagonal, diagonal, square and round—the combinations were endless and profound.

Surrounded by jasper walls, this city within a city was so bright with natural light that no sun was needed. Much grander than the earthly temple of King Solomon's day, nothing at all compared with its magnificence.

Entering the gates into a large courtyard, a brilliant altar of pure gold immediately got the attention of all newcomers. From its glowing top a sweet scent permeated the air; its wonderful aromatic intensity increased proportionally to one's nearness to the altar. On its crest incense burned day and night before the throne of God.

Within the innermost rooms of the temple the twenty-four members of the highest council would meet with the Heavenly Father. Here, decisions were made and put into action.

The news that we were soon to enter this shining temple area delighted all the happy guests. Moreover, Jesus informed us that we would help to accomplish a special task in preparation for the forthcoming earthly reign. The war between good and evil was coming to a head. Michael and his angels had eroded Lucifer's stronghold over the earth by using the sword of the Spirit to consistently expose his lies.

After the vast harvesting of the saints, however, the war took a different turn. Now it was time to take the strong action needed to end the chaos and restore health to that ailing planet.

As we filtered into the gigantic area of the courtyard, we were stunned at the massiveness of the walls surrounding us. "Look around you," our Savior said. "You are standing in the New Jerusalem."

Excitedly we surveyed our surroundings. Beautiful stones of all shapes and sizes were in piles. The foundational walls of the city would be garnished with all kinds of precious stones; the material for the twelve gates was pearl.

With twelve foundations, one on top of the other, the city would be like no other. Each foundation contained a complete atmosphere of its own, and bore the name of one of the twelve earthly apostles.

The streets were made of pure gold, transparent as glass. There was no temple here, for the true temple, not made with hands, was the physical presence of the Lord God Almighty and the Lamb, Jesus the Messiah. The city was the "New Jerusalem," still in the construction process. As tall as it was wide, it was quickly dubbed "The Quad Project."

We were part of the construction team. The many talented architects, designers, and laborers among us, along with unending supplies of quality materials made this an enjoyable project. Working together, we were astonished at how rapid the progress, and non-existent the setbacks.

The city was unique with the length, width, and depth equal in measurement. Twelve gates—three on each wall—surrounded the city. Written in stone upon each would be the names of those residing within; twelve specially chosen guardian angels would maintain the gates. The city, so superbly constructed, would be 100% safe from all outside attacks against it. It's destination? Earth.

During the following days of construction we often observed angels entering the courtyard on their way to the throne. Though the messenger angels would wave and stop to visit, the warrior angels would not. These gigantic angels, with muscles like steel, would stride purposefully through the courtyard toward the entrance doors of the temple. Focused on the business before them, they didn't stand around chit-chatting like the rest. Once they obtained orders or needed items they'd depart without taking time for social interaction.

One such angel entered the complex soon after our arrival. Within a short time, he exited the doors, walking back through the courtyard. As he did, I noticed an object in his hand that had not been there previously. Gold with a rich reddish hue, it resembled a small barbell. Intricate markings could be seen on the bottom of the circular bell-shaped base. Curious, I hastily caught up to him as he stopped momentarily at the gate.

"What is it?" I asked.

Looking at me with the disciplined look of a warrior, he kindly explained, "My mission is to identify the I AM's remaining servants on earth."

"I didn't know there were any left."

"After we harvested the redeemed, the evil one claimed ownership of those who remained. All commerce is now controlled by their side. Instead of bank cards, each person, whether young and old, wears an indelible number, stamped either on his forehead or right hand. Without this code it's impossible to buy food or do business of any sort."[61] As the angelic warrior spoke, he showed me the object in his hand. It was the seal of Almighty God.[62]

"There are yet 144,000 who secretly have not complied with this ruling. This seal will identify them to the four powerful angels, soon to be released to damage the earth."

I stared in awe at the seal. It was small, but perfectly formed for a mark on the forehead. "Thank you," I murmured, not wanting to delay him.

As he hurried out the gate he called to the waiting angels, "Not yet!" Though eager to get started, these four gigantic angels agreed to hold the four winds so that not even a breeze would blow until the remaining servants of God were notarized with the seal.

Moments later we were summoned to enter the temple grounds. Eyes began to glisten with tears as the buzz of conversation grew softer; for this was the first time since arriving that any of us had been invited into the inner sanctuary.

---

[61] Rev 13:17

[62] Rev. 7:3

We quickly put away our tools and changed into our best garments. To think that we, the formerly banished, were now to be part of the great throng of worshipers was overwhelming. To once again be in the presence of the Ancient of Days was a privilege made possible only through Jesus, our Savior and Redeemer.

Entering the inner sanctions, we joined the millions of other angels already there. Completely immersed in the roaring praise, we joined in with abandon, worshipping the Ancient of Days and Jesus the Messiah, who was being seated at his right hand.

The celebration of his victory over the enemy—his conquering of death—was limitless in energy and joyful praise. That we were one again with the hosts of Heaven was astonishing in its reality.

And then, unexpectedly, seven powerful warrior angels stepped forward to each receive a trumpet. By sequence of blasts, pitch and length of sustained tone, each had prepared a unique sound to usher in a segment of the final days of the war. I watched in wonder as they left the inner sanctuary carrying the unusually large trumpets.

"The seven plagues," Jano informed me. "We read about them in Sunday School, remember?" The irony that we were experiencing these events from Heaven rather than from Earth was not lost on us as we watched transfixed, the prophetic events unfold.

Soon another warrior angel was given a handful of incense and a special vial containing all the prayers of the righteous. As he stood at the courtyard altar, a sweet fragrance ascended to God from the items in his hand. Picking up a golden censer, he lit it from the altar, ran through the gates toward Earth, and threw it down with a mighty heave.

Suddenly there were voices, sounds of thunder, lightning, and an earthquake. With this signal the seven angels prepared to play their trumpets.

The war had taken a mighty turn.

CHAPTER 20

STRATEGIES OF WAR

These shall make war with the Lamb, and the Lamb shall overcome them: for he is Lord of lords, and King of kings: and they that are with him are called, and chosen, and faithful.

Rev. 17:14

War! These were the dramatic final days about which we'd heard so much while on earth.

The first angel blew his trumpet.[63] Hail, fire and blood caused one-third of the trees to burn up. With the noise from the second trumpet, a massive meteor, much like a huge burning mountain, fell into the sea destroying one-third of all sea life and ships.

When the third trumpet blasted its sound a huge burning star fell from Heaven. One-third of all the waters became poisonous, causing many humans to die.

As the fourth trumpet resonated, one-third of the stars lost their light. It was pitch black for most of the day and night. Still, not a single one repented.

---

[63] This chapter is from the book of Revelation.

Next, a warrior angel flew through Heaven shouting "Woe, woe, woe, to the inhabitants of the earth." His loud warning referred to the three events that would follow.

The fifth angel appeared, holding a trumpet in one hand and the key to the bottomless pit in the other. As he produced his ear-splitting blasts, a star fell from Heaven to earth. Traveling at maximum velocity, he flew to the endless abyss and opened it with the key. Immediately there arose so much smoke out of it that the sun and air were darkened.

Out of the smoke came locusts with stingers like scorpions. For five months they tormented all not bearing the seal of God on their foreheads. In excruciating pain, they begged to die, but couldn't. This was the work of the powerful angel named Abaddon, also known as "king of the locusts."

As each trumpet sounded, progressively worse events happened to the earth and its inhabitants. Repentance was the key, for only through total repentance could the war end.

Yet those who lived through the plagues still weren't sorry for worshiping devils, or for their murders, sorceries, immorality, and thefts. Conversely, the worse the pain, the more horrible were their blasphemies toward the only One who could save them.

"Repent or I'll come to you quickly and fight you with the sword of my mouth." We heard these words spoken with authority and prayed for the inhabitants of the earth.

"To him that overcomes I'll give hidden manna to eat:" this message was designed to give hope where there was none. "I'll give a white stone with a new name written which no one knows except the one that receives it." Those who overcame would get a new identity.

"He who overcomes will be clothed in white. I won't cross his name out of the Book of Life, but will acknowledge his name before my Father and his angels. I warn, discipline, and correct those I love, so pay attention; you can ask for forgiveness:"[64] These words—like swords—continued to pierce earth's darkness during this time of trouble.

With the echo of the sixth angel's trumpet a majestic Voice spoke from the golden altar: "Release the four angels held in the great Euphrates River." These four mighty angels had waited over a year for this command. Immediately upon release, they destroyed one-third of earth's population. With that destruction, earthly repentance finally began.

The news of this turn of events permeated all of Heaven.

Those of mankind who had the seal of God upon their foreheads still had to endure earth's hardships until the victory was complete. The angels worked day and night to protect and strengthen them.

At last the blasts from the seventh trumpet were heard and another mighty angel came down from Heaven. Setting one foot on the earth and the other on the sea, he roared like a lion.[65] With this deafening sound, all of us in Heaven responded with this declaration: "The kingdoms of this world have become the kingdoms of our Lord, and of his Christ; and he shall reign for ever and ever."

Immediately a voice boomed out from Heaven saying, "Now is come salvation, and strength, and the kingdom of our God, and the power of his Christ: for the accuser of our brothers is thrown down, which accused them day and night."

---

[64] Rev 3:19

[65] Rev 10:1-3

As one more powerful angel flew swiftly to earth, he brought the message of eternal salvation to explain to every nation, culture, and type of people on earth. His voice was deafening as he declared "Fear God and give glory to him, for the hour of his judgment is come. Worship him that made Heaven and earth, the sea and all fountains of waters." At this announcement, all those on earth who'd refused the mark of the beast boldly stood up together and sang:

> "Great and marvelous are your works,
> Lord God Almighty;
> Just and true are your ways,
> King of saints.
> Who shall not fear you, O Lord,
> And glorify your name?
> For you alone are holy.
> All nations shall come and worship before you.
> Your judgments are revealed."[66]

As the song ended, those of us in Heaven cheered, proclaiming our support for the courageous ones who would be joining us soon. That they'd have to endure living on earth until the war was over was going to be difficult for them, but Jesus continually encouraged them with his strong and sure words: "To him who overcomes I'll grant to sit with me in my throne, even as I also overcame, and sat down with my Father in his throne." His words brought hope and strength to the righteous who were suffering on earth.

The war wasn't yet over; there were many battles yet to be fought. From our vantage point in the New Jerusalem

---

[66] Rev 15:3-4

we watched as seven powerful angels exited the gate, each carrying a vial of God's wrath.

Instantly, thick smoke filled the temple.

We quickly learned that until these seven vials of plagues were fulfilled, no one would be able to enter the temple of our Heavenly Father. His powerful voice, however, would still be heard throughout Heaven and earth.

The angels, according to plan, began to pour out the vials.

As the dust-like substance left the first vial, it spread and settled over the earth like fog in a valley. It brought sores to everyone except those who had the seal of God invisibly imprinted on their foreheads.

The matter from the second vial turned the sea into blood, killing everything in it; droplets from the third vial changed every river and fountain into blood. At this event, one powerful angel who'd seen what the enemy had done to the Lamb's martyrs remarked, "They've shed the blood of saints and prophets, and now they have only blood to drink. That's justice."

The liquid from the fourth vial spurted to the sun; the chemical reaction from it created intense heat, scorching the earth. But instead of turning in repentance to God who had power over these plagues, the majority of earth's inhabitants blasphemed his name.

Black tar from the fifth vial oozed out, thinning and spreading until it enclosed the earth like a shell around an egg. Hardening to rock-solid, it prevented any light from penetrating its dark shield. Without light, photosynthesis ceased, water couldn't evaporate for rainfall, and all plant life immediately began to die. Any energy emissions from earth's fuel resources caused huge amounts of exhaust fumes and carbon monoxide poisoning to build up within this shell. Breathing became difficult: lungs were damaged, eyes watered and throats became raw and bleeding. Gnawing their tongues in pain, mankind still refused to repent and blasphemy against God continued to be the norm.

The toxic substance from the sixth vial reacted with the water from the Euphrates River causing it to bubble and evaporate. As the nations wondered about the desert wasteland that had once been fruitful, spirits of devils were free to work demonic miracles for them in the name of the beast and false prophet. Deceived, all the kings of the earth gathered together for battle against the righteous at Armageddon.

As the host of Heaven fought and won this final battle, the seventh angel poured his vial into the air. As he did so, a thunderous voice from the throne in the temple of Heaven said the words we'd all been waiting to hear: "It is done."

At this announcement, a magnificently powerful and bright angel flew to earth. As he blasted through the shell, the darkened earth was instantly lightened with his glory.

"Victory!" he cried. "Babylon the great is fallen, is fallen!" Lucifer was immediately bound and sent to the bottomless pit.

With that announcement the holy city of New Jerusalem began its descent out of Heaven toward Earth. We'd finished building it during the last stages of the war and our decorators had done their job superbly.

Riding along were all of the redeemed, affectionately known as the Lamb's wife. And truly, no bride was ever adorned so beautifully!

CHAPTER 21

DAY OF JUDGMENT
THOUSAND-YEAR REIGN

> *"And behold I come quickly, and my reward is with me to give every man according as his work shall be. I am Alpha and Omega, the beginning and the end, the first and the last."*
>
> *Rev. 20:11*

What a privilege to be one with the Savior, to return to earth to rule in righteousness with Him. It had been decreed that ALL the earth would bow the knee to our Lord and serve Him; all would confess Him Lord of all.[67] We would help to make that happen.

Organizing His Kingdom, we soon received our assignments for the phase known as the "Thousand-Year Reign." Though our headquarters were established in the newly rebuilt Jerusalem, my commission was one of the judgeships assigned to the vast cities in the continent previously known as Antarctica. Those on earth during the

---

[67] Romans 14:11

last days who'd been faithful to the war's end were chosen to reign with Christ during this period in the newly built Jerusalem.

After the terrible chaos and destruction of the land, we had much work to do, but finally, all the earth was restored to its original condition. Green and lush, even the icecaps were gone; all of the frozen floodwaters of Noah's time had at last melted.

What beauty existed in the city! What joy, what peace! Finally all nations worked together in harmony as every being learned to obey the laws of righteousness now ruling the earth.

The law of Love . . . it reigned supreme. All creatures of the earth, sea, sky, every corner of the earth and those under the earth now lived by it. The earth flourished and became once again an unspoiled Garden of Eden.

My assignment stretched out endlessly before me, for every being that didn't accept the free gift of salvation had to be judged according to his works. My tools were few: a list of candidates and a desk equipped with an archive machine. Each individual who came before me would put his hand under the DNA analyzer, and his life story would appear on the screen.

This was absorbing work, but my days on earth had well equipped me for this daunting task. I'd learned to discern good from evil; to look beyond what was spoken—no matter how eloquently—and look into the heart. I'd attained wisdom with the ability to use it, for uniting with the Savior had given me complete insight into each case.[68]

---

[68] We shall judge angels. I Cor. 6:3

My caseload was full. Each individual was kept alone at first in a room for the purpose of introspection. It was not unpleasant or painful for him, for he was well taken care of as he waited. This period of isolation gave him the opportunity to clarify the lies and deceptions he'd previously believed. It was also a time of evaluating in the light of truth everything he'd been exposed to on earth.

My assignment was to schedule each case, review with them their life story, listen to their explanations and judge their words against the witness of their deeds. My findings would then be passed along to a higher court for further processing.

The oddest group of cases was, by far, the young boys who'd been tragically misguided. From the time of their infancy to their death, everyone in authority over them—their clergy, teachers, even their parents—had parroted to them the lies of the false prophet. Then, just past the age of their childhood, these young people had acted upon those lies.

Thinking to be martyrs for God, they instead found themselves in the eternal world as his enemies. Expecting to have great rewards in Heaven such as many "virgins," servants, and riches, they instead found themselves in a Hell too horrific to describe.

One was now before me. He was ageless, but in earthly years, only fourteen. Still shocked by the extent of the deception, he could only bow and sob piteously.

"Where are my virgins?" he kept asking. "I did everything I could to destroy the infidels! I deserve my reward!"

Looking at the archives, I saw he truly thought he was serving God. "Didn't your conscience bother you when you found out children would be killed?"

"Yes, it did," he answered honestly; "but I ignored it. I thought I was being weak to even consider their lives at all."

"The false prophet will be judged along with Lucifer. The Lake of Fire is prepared for them together."

"It was all for Allah!" he screamed. "I lived my life for him. I bowed five times a day; I was the one who dedicated my life, my death, all that I was to do his will! Everyone applauded me, even my parents!"

"Did you believe that God wanted you to tear down rather than to build up; to destroy the beautiful cities he'd made, or the people that loved him? What about the innocent babies who didn't have a chance to grow or to make a decision to serve him?"

He hung his head. "I wanted the virgins they promised me. I blindly believed what I was told, but they all fed me lies."

"God is Love. You served a god of destruction. You killed yourself along with hundreds of innocents. Here, take a look at what your life would have been had you listened to the conscience God gave you."

As he viewed the scene before him, I saw his anger turn to incredulity at the extent of the deception of his life. Sadly, he had joined hundreds of others who became pawns in Lucifer's game of lies and destruction. His reward was definitely not what he had been told.

Another group had enjoyed their occult practices. They loved evil, and wanted more evil in their lives.

"It was all about power," one being bragged to me. "I was the best; I could put a curse on anyone."

"And you think that is going to impress the Lord?" I questioned.

"I love pain!" he screamed. "Hurt me! Hurt me some more!"

I observed that this being was heading back to where he'd been before earth-time began. He wanted to return to Hell; I had no power to stop him.

Sadists, thieves, those who hurt others behind closed doors—they all came before me. Some were surprised that their life histories were open for all to see. Every secret sin and excess was judged. Every adulterous affair, every corporate cheating, every dishonest political power play, every motive and ambition was examined. Nothing was hidden; we saw it all. In each case, we followed the guidelines in the manual given to us; it was specific and detailed, for our God is just, thorough, and merciful.

The victims—those who had been murdered before their time on earth was fulfilled—were next. These included several who'd wandered the earth in a state of limbo, not having lived long enough to reach the moment of decision. Looking at the archives, we realized that had some lived a bit longer, they might have accepted our Lord as their own. We dealt with these ones gently and carefully, for all needed to have a chance to make their choice.

Then there were those who, while on earth, had never heard about Jesus and what he did for them. They were judged by their own conscience. If their conscience didn't condemn them, it was revealed to me from the archives.

Each case was different, yet the basics were the same; for each being had been given a chance to live a perfect life and had failed.

But the price had been paid for all. The fact that each had his own "judgment day" was evidence that God had not issued a universal condemnation of all who'd not known to accept the free gift while on earth.

Our Lord is fair, merciful, and quick to forgive. He knows our thoughts as well as the intents of our hearts and could judge the soul of each in a way that was perfect and accurate. I was honored to be on his team.

Murderers, liars, thieves, pornographers, sadists, predators . . . we saw them all. Wealthy, poor, smart, foolish . . . we judged them all.

A special group came to visit us one day. They were the quiet ones of earth—many of them as sinless as Enoch and whisked right into the arms of the Savior. They were the mentally handicapped, the paralyzed, the silent, the bed-bound.

Watching their lives through the archive machine, I could see the innocence as well as the abundant and fruitful mental activity each experienced on earth. Attractive, healthy, robust—this group appeared as if they'd never left Heaven. Indeed, there were many who were actually secret angels masquerading as the feeble in order to disguise their true duties while on earth. It was a joyful, energetic group.

What a day of liveliness that was! They played and skated all over the marble steps as well as slid down the banisters. How that event brought back memories of another formerly feeble being experiencing the brand new freedom of a strong, well-working body!

CHAPTER 22

EPILOGUE

Be silent, and know that I am God! I will be honored by every nation. I will be honored throughout the world.

Ps 46:10-11

One day a few hundred years into the Thousand-Year Reign, I was in conference with my judicial team. As we discussed the details of one of our assignments, a shrunken creature appeared at the door. The doorkeepers let him in.

I watched as this shriveled, ugly creature approached our seats. He'd deteriorated so much it was hard to imagine him of ever having had a spark of life. In comparison, those redeemed in attendance had radiant faces and were strong and stunning in appearance.

Slithering painfully up the steps, the creature bowed, then looked at me in horror. There was recognition—I saw just the slightest glimmer in his eye, a sight I'd seen eons ago.

I stared, trying hard to remember this being. That he'd found his way here in this condition was a miracle. To say he needed transformation was obvious; I could easily guess his motive.

The rebellion of the earth had been dealt with; everyone now bowed to our Lord Jesus Christ. Some did it unwillingly . . . nevertheless love ruled, and would continue to be in power—there was no longer any choice.

Since Lucifer had been banished from the surface of the earth, he couldn't freely lie and deceive as he did before. How this poor creature, obviously so long in sin and degradation, could function at all was only by the grace of God.

"It isn't fair," the creature spit out as he reached me. He had difficulty speaking—from more than just his physical lack of viability—he was emotionally charged.

Tragic, yet somehow comical in its own right, I had to suppress my desire to lean back and howl with amusement at the situation; I realized, with incredulity, that there was at least one hardened sinner who was so fond of his former sins that he couldn't function in a love-filled world. I was truly amazed.

"No matter what I did to you, you always came out on top."

What could this poor creature be referring to? I searched my memory and found nothing.

"I was to be exalted. I was to gain rank and status. I was to be in a powerful position of authority. You ruined it for me. You ruined it all."

I couldn't imagine what contact I'd with this depraved little soul, but I listened quietly as he continued.

"It's my turn to rule. You've had a turn," he continued piteously.

Did I hear correctly? Was this being truly under the belief that his self-centered demands would be considered at all?

"You've always had more than I. It isn't fair!" he insisted.

I looked down at this small crispy imp. To realize he'd once been a mighty angel was extraordinarily difficult. He was a perfect example of one who still catered to his evil residue, and therefore one who continued to deteriorate.

Still, I was curious; he seemed to know me. I finally spoke, "Tell me your name."

Sidestepping this request, he hissed out "You know me."

I could see the fear in his eyes, for exposure to truth was the reason most of the depraved liars tried to hide when the great Day of Judgment came.

"I don't know you," I answered truthfully, for try as I might I couldn't remember ever associating with him before.

"You know me!" the being persisted.

Quiet for a moment as I searched my brain again, I realized all memory of this being had been erased.

"Where were you sent?" I inquired.

"To the Cain House of Detention."

The Cain House. That was where all those who hated their brother were held.

"Why were you released?" I asked, for he definitely didn't seem ready to rejoin our world of love.

"Good behavior." I knew immediately he was lying; on his wrist I could see the bright orange band clearly identifying him as an unrepentant. I perceived he'd been sent to us because his first sentence at the Cain House had expired. As one of the impenitent, he would need more than one place of correction to recover. His addictions were so blatantly prominent that I didn't even bother to consult with the archives. I determined he'd need lots of therapy and during this Thousand-Year Reign while the "great deceiver" was chained up and ineffective, I intended to give him all the help possible.

"All liars will ultimately be sent to the Lake of Fire," I stated.

The being shivered visually. "Don't send me there. It's not my fault; it's yours. I should be in your place, and you should be in mine. I was to be promoted to the highest rank before you ruined it for me."

He's still jealous . . . has it still not been dealt with? I decided to test him. "Who is your Lord?"

"Je . . . Je . . ." the being could hardly say his name. "Je . . . He got it wrong. I was misjudged," he whined in the most grating of voices.

"Speak only the truth," I commanded.

"I . . . I . . . I . . ." He couldn't speak, for he'd spoken only lies for so long that he couldn't physically make himself speak the truth.

I knew this being could have a new body. I could release him into the massive DNA restoration plant to have his original body re-formed, yet I knew it would be pointless to do so since he hadn't experienced any real change of heart. Since he was still controlled by jealousy as well as addicted to lying, a new body would just deteriorate after time into this present state again. Additionally, it wouldn't be healthy for those who'd recovered to see him with any body other than what he had at present.

My compassionate side wanted to restore this poor creature to health, but he had to be willing to be helped. That he'd refused the free gift of eternal life when he had a chance was now moot, for all—both righteous and unrighteous—lived under the authority of our King Jesus.[69] The chain of command had been re-established, making all orderly again in this formerly chaotic world.

But for now, his whining and lies were becoming extremely irritating to the rest of the council. "Silence!" I commanded. The creature slowly bowed in submission as I re-checked the guidebook issued to us for such decisions. Concluding that he had to go where indicated, I motioned to the doorkeepers to take him to the "Lakeside Correction Facilities."

As this small desiccated creature left, he turned and with an enormous effort, stuck his tongue out at me. Amused but untouched, I continued with the business before me.

---

[69] See Phil 2:9-11

Life was, after all, pleasant, perfect, busy, and continually filled with joy.

The Thousand-Year Reign was in progress and we still had a lot of work to do; the whole earth was to be continually filled with the Lord's glory, and all its creatures were to worship him in joyful surrender.

After our reign here, maybe we would return to Heaven for more adventure!

Eternity is a long time; we serve a God whose mercies are new every morning. Nothing is impossible with Him.

(I am come) to open the blind eyes, to bring out the prisoners from the prison, and them that sit in darkness out of the prison house.

And I will bring the blind by a way that they did not know; I will lead them in paths that they have not known: I will make darkness light before them, and crooked things straight.

These things will I do to them, and not forsake them.

Isaiah 45:15-16

CHAPTER 23

POST EPILOGUE

Sorrow and mourning will disappear, and they
will be overcome with joy and gladness.
Isaiah 51:11

Under the reign of King Jesus from his headquarters in the New Jerusalem, the whole earth had been restored to beauty. But now the Thousand-Year Reign was over and the "great deceiver" had to be freed from his prison.

With this release came the test: Who would again be deceived, or worse, who'd genuinely want to serve Satan? Freedom to choose was once more a possibility. Final decisions were to be made as to choice of rule: good or evil.

At the same time, the rest of the dead were brought up from the grave to be judged; they'd missed the first resurrection and were in danger of the second death. However, those who were part of the first resurrection, and had reigned with Christ for the last thousand years, were not affected by the second death.

After his release, the devil attempted to deceive the nations from the four quarters of the earth. Gathering together the fearful, the unbelieving, the hateful, murderers, depraved, sorcerers, idolaters, and all liars for his army, they—without warning—surrounded the camp of the saints and the beloved city.[70]

But fire came down from God out of Heaven and quickly consumed them. At this point, death and Hell were cast into the Lake of Fire. This was the second death, and whoever's name was not found written in the book of life was also thrown into the Lake of Fire.

Suddenly a thunderous voice spoke from Heaven. "Behold! The tabernacle of God is with men. He'll live with them and they'll be his people. God himself will be with them, and be their God.

And God shall wipe away all tears from their eyes. There shall be no more death or sorrow, no crying, and no more pain; for the former things are passed away." [71]

He that sat upon the throne said "Behold, I make all things new. I am Alpha and Omega, the beginning and the end. I will freely give to him that is thirsty, water from the fountain of life."

Rev 21:5-6

---

[70]   Rev. 21:8
[71]   Rev. 21:4

BOOK TWO

FOREWORD

Does our Lord abhor any of His creation? Does His wrath exceed his love toward those who hate him? After writing "The Twinkling" with getting to know and understand the character of Korel, the story lent itself to a sequel, the story of Lusilite. Understanding the reasons for behavior often helps us to love the unlovable, even though their acts are despicable.

Two men in a field, two women grinding corn, two people on a rooftop . . . one shall be taken, one shall be left. Some find the narrow road that leads to Heaven; others walk the broad road that leads to Hell. By our actions, we choose whom to serve.

Dark Stars of
THE TWILIGHT

Shadows of
The Two-Edged Sword

Book Two

Let the stars of the twilight be dark; let it look for light, but have none; neither let it see the dawning of the day:

Job 3:9

CONTENTS

CHAPTER 1

GLORIOUS LIGHT

*When the morning stars sang together, and all
the sons of God shouted for joy*

Job 38:7

Pinnac was elated. In his[72] hand was an invitation
usually reserved only for the highest-ranking angels in
his legion. A highly secretive meeting had been arranged for
the purpose of establishing a new policy, and he was to have
a part in the implementation process. He was thrilled for
this honor and moved swiftly with singleness of purpose to
prepare for the secret conference.

He realized he would be working with his legion's top
leader, Lucifer, the powerful archangel also known as "Son
of the Morning."[73] This angel, one of the most influential
beings in Heaven, was so commendable that the eternal
God had given him one third of the angels to oversee.
Though millions of bright beings were under his reputable

---

[72] All references to eternal beings will be male, regardless of
gender on earth.

[73] Isaiah 14:12

management, Pinnac was delightfully aware he was one of a very few who'd been chosen as part of his promotional team.

It had been ages since Pinnac had worked with the top echelons of his regime. Though in the heavens there is no marking of time—for eternity is not measured in days—yet the invitation sparked ancient memories of past exciting experiences with this magnificent leader.

Eager to get started, he gathered his clothing changes as well as some gifts to present to those who would host this clandestine delegation.

Speculating about his final destination, he entered one of the single-passenger skypers and quickly punched in the secret code from the invitation. As the vehicle launched and sped through space, he noticed he was headed toward the small planet Earth, located in a solar system within a lesser-known galaxy.

Soon the skyper arrived at the covert destination.

Earth, a small but beautiful planet was a pleasant place to visit. Green and lush, the mountains and waterfalls were a favorite resort of the upper echelons of power. Not too hot or cold, it was an enjoyable tropical paradise; gold and silver were in abundance and the air was sweet and pleasant.

Disembarking the tiny skyper, Pinnac looked up to see Jucola, a worship angel from the highest order, extending his hand. "Welcome, Pinnac! I'm glad to see you again," he smiled nondescriptly as Pinnac shook the hand offered.

"Thank you, Jucola," Pinnac responded amicably.

"Please follow me." Without a further word Pinnac gathered his things and followed him to a small open door. Upon entering the two were immediately whisked up into the air, utilizing their own natural ability of flight, (for angels do not need vehicles to move swiftly.) The fact that

Pinnac didn't know the destination made the movement a surprise to him. Usually his innate homing device was activated within his power of control, not outside of it.

Arriving at the undisclosed location, Jucola took his bags and led him to the meeting chamber. Entering, Pinnac found he was not alone; seated at the ornate table was Lucifer himself. Splendid, glorious in appearance and brighter than any other angel, Lucifer was often called by his nickname "Light."[74]

"Pinnac, you are remarkable." The velvety words had a paralyzing effect on him.

"Thank you, sir."

"You've just received the invitation, and have arrived in such a short time. I'm impressed with your quick response."

"Thank you, sir," Pinnac again responded meekly. Bowing slightly, he presented the gift he had so carefully prepared for his host.

Getting up from his seat, Light moved closer to receive the present; nodding his appreciation he continued: "Do you know why you're here?"

Fingering the invitation in his pocket, Pinnac responded, "There's a special assignment, and I've been chosen to help execute the order." Light smiled faintly, knowing Pinnac had no clue as to what the assignment might be.

"Do you know why you've been selected?"

---

[74]   The meaning of the name Lucifer is "light; illumination."

His carefully chosen words had the desired effect on Pinnac who was asking himself that very question at that moment. Without waiting for an answer, Light continued: "You're one of the most dependable and I know you can keep a secret."

Surprised his non-verbalized question had been acknowledged as well as answered, Pinnac again enjoyably assessed his situation. The fact that Light was planning a secret surprise was not unusual for he often did this within the context of his job description; his responsibility of leading the angels in worship required him to be creative. "I'm pleased, sir, to have been chosen."

Moving toward a large cabinet, Light opened a wide cupboard door. "I've created a new instrument for the orchestra. Want to hear it?" The relaxed and pleasant atmosphere put Pinnac immediately at ease.

"Of course," Pinnac answered as he eagerly awaited the new sound. New creations of instruments along with different combinations of playing them together were not unusual. Light continually wanted to enhance the skill of the orchestra music and worked with all his factions to improve the singing and playing abilities of his legions.

Light brought out a tall, shiny metal object; its rim was made of a porous substance. Blowing slightly into it, a whisper-like voice was immediately heard.

"The churager" he said "is the name of this instrument." He blew again into its mouthpiece. Again, out came the low, rich whispering sound. "This instrument will give a constant undertone, balancing out the shriller instruments of the orchestra. It can also accompany the choral acapella worship. Want to try it?"

"Sure" was the ready response. Pinnac picked up the churager, marveling at the rarity of intellect in this magnificent archangel.

As Pinnac blew into the mouthpiece, Light stared at him a moment, then gently spoke, "Do you trust me?"

Startled at the absurdity of the question Pinnac quickly answered, "Of course." Light seemed to want a more complete answer so, not knowing what else to say, Pinnac continued; "The great I AM has exalted you to your present position of power over one-third of Heaven. I've always trusted you . . ." Light waited while Pinnac took a breath and continued, "and always will."

With the last response, Light appeared satisfied for the moment. Returning the churager to the cabinet, he sat down and motioned to the seat across from him. "Please."

Sitting in the ornate chair, Pinnac's thoughts spun as he studied the magnificent one before him. The mystery of how the bright "Son of the Morning" achieved his exalted rank was unknown, yet his astute devotion to the purposes of worship was completely unquestionable.

"You like my churager?" Light asked.

"I'm amazed at it, frankly," Pinnac answered enthusiastically, wondering if this instrument might have something to do with the new policy.

"The churager is a very simple creation, and has nothing to do with the new assignment," Light remarked casually. "I've developed a much more complex creation—a new entity within the assignment—that I'm letting only a certain few know about. It's still in its experimental stage, but I have to say that I've discovered something intriguing."

Caught off guard, Pinnac could only stare in surprise. Not waiting for a response Light continued. "It has to do with worship, of course . . . adoration at its very finest. I've developed a new type of veneration and with time and practice all our masses can learn to do it."

Curious and still in awe, Pinnac could only nod his head in agreement. His focus was on the attractiveness of Lucifer, for even as he spoke the aura surrounding him was magnificent. There was a mystery, an excitement in his words, and they stirred up a heretofore un-felt emotion in Pinnac. The beating of his heart grew rapid and his adrenalin began to flow.

What is this, this new creation about which Light is so resolute? Impatient for the answer, Pinnac hoped to hear it quickly; however he didn't vocalize this desire, but only nodded meekly as he listened.

"My creation will shake the foundations of Heaven itself." As Pinnac listened to the potent words, he realized something was indeed unusual, for he could see in the powerful angel's eyes an excitement that inspired both curiosity and awe.

"How do I fit into the picture?" Pinnac finally ventured to ask, for he had endured the suspense with about as much patience as he could.

Light answered the question with a question of his own. "What planet have you never seen?"

"Nexor," was the answer.

Light looked at him with a mischievous sparkle in his eye. "Nexor is where you'll learn the answer. We'll go there together."

CHAPTER 2

THE SECRET CONVENTION

You have said in your heart, "I will ascend into Heaven, and exalt my throne above the stars of God."

Isaiah 14:13

Nexor was located three galaxies away from the agricultural planet known as Ziphotan. Just as Ziphotan was known for its wood products (many of which were used in making instruments of worship), Nexor was well-known for its fun, parties, and delightful activities.

Nexor was the ideal planet for field trips and outings, and every angel from that area seemed to be full of practical jokes. A great vacation playground, there's no doubt one would have extraordinary fun and unusual experiences while visiting. Good restaurants, a buzzing city life, unusual entertainment and sweet drinks of different flavors and textures were in abundance at Nexor.

Though Pinnac had always wanted to visit this planet, his new status made him too serious to think about enjoying the experience. *Fun and games,* he thought to himself, *are only for the masses of lower angels to enjoy.* As one of the new team members of the highest echelons of power, he had work to do and that took priority over everything else. Pinnac, humble and discreet, was truly dedicated to serving others; doing his assigned tasks well always gave him the greatest pleasure.

The planet Nexor was in the same league as the outlying galaxies that housed the planets Earth and Ziphotan. After a journey of some duration—it was a well-hidden little planet within its massive galaxy,—they finally arrived.

Looking out the window of the transporter, Pinnac could see hundreds of angels waiting expectantly. *So there are many who've been selected for this assignment,* Pinnac noted to himself as Light made a hasty exit to avoid the crowd. Now Pinnac could hardly keep his excitement from overwhelming his senses.

Entering with the others into the auditorium, he sat down as close to the front as possible. Soon Light entered, looking radiant. Claps were heard and cheers resounded as he took the podium.

"We have a distinct opportunity," he began, "A highly clandestine operation—so secret that I'm asking you not to give each other your names." Pinnac glanced discreetly to his side. *There is no one I really know well.* He wondered if this was the case for everyone else in the room. "Normally I'd not only give opportunity for you to introduce yourselves but would also add my personal comments about each one as well. This time, however, the unusual will be the usual."

At this point many looked around, trying to see if there were any with whom they had more than just a passing relationship. There were none and all eventually realized they'd been chosen with this lack of relationship in mind.

After a short pause Light continued, "You know how our mission is to effect praise among our planets . . . to offer praise to the Almighty, the Creator of the universe." Sounds of affirmation were heard throughout the room. "We must increase the intensity of this worship . . . to teach all angels how to worship more in depth—and in a new way. This is the delight of our heavens, to exalt in unique ways the One who created us.

Angels cherubim, seraphim, archangels, mighty ones, sons of God, elders, and priests . . . we have all experienced various intricacies of genuine worship."

Acknowledging this was standard, for as long as they had existence, this was the usual protocol, to praise and worship the One who'd created them.

"I've been experimenting and have discovered some unusual elements to the fine points of praise," he continued. "I've hand-picked you, and gathered you here together. Yes, I've even accompanied some of you here individually so that I could test your loyalty and submission to authority." Here, sideways glances began as this was not the usual lecture they were accustomed to hearing. That they were all timeless beings was not the point, that they were created beings was; for each of them had been fashioned for worshiping the Great I AM who gave them life and an entity that was eternal.

Glancing across the aisle, Pinnac looked for any who seemed uncomfortable with the direction the speech was going. None appeared to be; all gave the impression of being elated and fascinated with the words. Pinnac put his own niggling thoughts aside and gave his full attention to the speaker.

"I'll be meeting individually with each of you to clarify your assignments; our private conversations must be confidential until we meet together again as a group. When that time comes you'll be able to see the greatness and magnitude of what I've discovered. I can guarantee you'll be charmed when you've been totally immersed in my new creation."

The auditorium erupted in applause as Lucifer took a long bow. The cheering continued as he strode happily about on the stage; bowing again and thanking his elite for their good will toward him.

That night the celebration began: full of surprises and phenomenal entertainment, Pinnac had never experienced an event quite like it. Sworn to secrecy while experiencing the fun together, the elite bonded together in a way they'd previously not done. The eating, drinking and celebrating continued until all were exhausted.

The next morning, not having slept since receiving the invitation, Pinnac retreated to his assigned quarters for some much needed rest. Drifting off to sleep, he excitedly looked forward his next private meeting with Light.

Chapter 3

The Visit

The stars of Heaven shall fall, and the powers that are in Heaven shall be shaken.

Mark 13:25

At last the night came when Pinnac heard a knock on his door; he opened it to find the exalted leader standing outside. "May I come in?" Light asked meekly.

"Of course!" Pinnac answered joyfully. He swung open the door to let him in. At last he would find out what this secret mission was all about.

Sitting down, Light began, "As you now know, I've been instructed from the top to change the order of things." Pinnac noticed an almost imperceptible flush cross Light's beautiful features. *What is this? A blush of . . . what? Anticipation?* He could not read this body language, for he'd never observed this phenomenon before. "To change the order?" Pinnac questioned.

"Instructions from the top," Light repeated, now looking sufficiently self-assured, "in a new, more effective way."

Pinnac's pulse quickened as he digested this thought.

"But before I tell you the complete plan, you must prove your loyalty to me and to our heavenly cause."

Pinnac's thoughts began to whirl; something didn't seem right but he quickly forced himself to put the spiraling thoughts out of his mind. Though physically he began to feel strange, he continued to listen politely. *These new feelings are uncomfortable*, he rationalized, *simply because I've never experienced them before.*

"Experimentation . . ." Light continued, "I've done it extensively and have discovered a new way of worship. Until this new approach is implemented, worship of the Creator will only be done through me." Pinnac was surprised again, but as Light continued the explanation, it began to make sense. "This season I'll be the vehicle that delivers our worship and praise to the Almighty, leaving my highest ranking officials free to stay here."

Hearing these words, Pinnac was a bit disappointed, for he truly enjoyed the yearly travel to the highest Heaven. Celebrating the seasonal holy days at the great Heaven of heavens was a tradition he'd always kept;[75] nevertheless, he acquiesced to this mighty one who was in authority over him.

"No cause for concern," Light assured Pinnac. "This all ties in to my new discovery."

"What's my assignment?" Pinnac finally questioned.

"Here, come to the mirror." They moved over to a large mirror covering one wall, floor to ceiling. "Look how magnificently bright I am, and how insignificant you are in comparison." Pinnac observed wordlessly as Light stretched up as high as the ceiling. "Now look at my height. What do you feel?"

"In awe," came back the ready response.

---

[75] Nehemiah 9:6

"Bend down so you're even shorter, and look up from the ground at me. Now what do you feel?"

Assessing his feelings as to what Light could be referring, Pinnac finally responded, "Overwhelmed."

"That's what you're supposed to feel."

Pinnac still didn't comprehend what Light was doing. Finally, Light said softly, "What would happen if you bowed down to worship the Creator through me?"

"Has it ever been done, I mean, to worship through proxy?"

"No . . . that's what makes it so exciting. Remember, this comes from the highest authority. The Almighty has made me equal with him . . . . and in some ways, superior." Pinnac caught his breath, for this thought hadn't occurred to him.

The aura surrounding Lucifer became brighter as he stared with magnificent eyes at his admirer. Entranced by his splendor, Pinnac eventually decided to abandon all reservations and simply do as requested. Slowly, reverently, he bowed down before him and worshipped.

Immediately a slight feeling of euphoria washed over him. This was different from what he'd experienced bowing before THE ALMIGHTY; it was new, embodying the excitement of the unknown, the adventure of secrecy, and the implementation of formerly forbidden acts.

Sucking in his breath as the mild ecstasy washed over him, his thoughts swirled as he knelt before his leader. Light made no attempt to raise him from his position, but rather indicated his adulation needed to be higher in intensity and sustained. Raising his head, Pinnac bowed once again, this time bending to a much lower level. As his breath once again filled his lungs, he was rewarded with a most pleasurable sensation; it invaded his entire body.

"Enough for now," Light said as he moved to a chair and sat down. As Pinnac arose from his position, Light repeated his caution to keep quiet about the experiment.

"The others won't understand," he warned. "Only the ones gathered here are involved at this point."

Pausing a moment, he continued. "Pinnac, you have what it takes to be able to achieve a position of highest power. Rank and authority are mine to give and I'll bestow it upon whomever I wish; just continue to obey me without question."

As Pinnac digested these exciting words, unobtrusive, mild desires for power and control began to filter into his psyche. As he entertained these thoughts a surge of energy washed over his senses. It was a potent feeling—he wanted to feel it again. Light sensed this and discreetly increased the feelings with his seductive words, "prostrate yourself before me and the surge will be even stronger." Pinnac quickly obeyed and immediately felt the powerful pleasure again. "It is mine to give, and I will give it amply," Light promised.[76]

So went their night, with Pinnac learning the first lessons of the newly created secret policy. The discovery was exciting, the euphoria was pleasurable, and the quest for power was addictive.

Pinnac was hooked.

---

[76] 2 Thess 2:12 "pleasure" in unrighteousness

CHAPTER 4

A NEW ORDER

—wandering stars, to whom is reserved the blackness of darkness for ever.

Jude 1:13

After that night, Light met often with Pinnac. Little by little he showed him things he'd never even dreamed of: forbidden things . . . powerful things. Pinnac was an eager apprentice. He wanted to rise as his leader had risen, to be magnificent, to have authority, to even be—as suggested—adored by the masses. All acts of worship were justified as well as kept confidential, for this magnificent being asserted all would eventually be given to the wonderful I AM in a way that would impress and delight.

Pinnac was swept up in the experiment; it was all he could think about. The new practice was exhilarating and the pleasurable feelings increased with the accomplishment of each additional prohibited act. Yet, deep within his spirit an unwelcome thought nagged him. *What if these new commandments didn't originate with THE ALMIGHTY?* He couldn't bring himself to carry this concept to its conclusion, for none of this sort of notion had ever entered the perfection of Heaven before.

Unknown to Pinnac the others caught up in the experiment were also promised rank and power. Individually, each learned to fulfill without question Light's every wish. Trusting this had been set into place by the GREAT ALMIGHTY, they entered into the experiment with abandon, shaking off any doubt or inhibitions.

Nightly surprises were experienced—harmless pranks, irritating tricks, mischievous acts—each carried out with the goal of desensitizing this group to his yet-to-be-revealed new creation. Each prank produced a certain euphoric feeling which was enjoyed immensely by the instigator of the trick. As the nightly sessions continued the desire for the addictive euphoria became stronger and stronger.

One day the exalted leader opened Pinnac's private session with a question: "Has God said you shall worship no other?"

"Yes," he replied confidently.

"Oh?" came the slow reply. "When?" Pinnac tried to think. "It's inherent," he replied. "There's never been another to worship."

Light smiled slowly—a confident, appealing smile. "Don't limit THE ALMIGHTY," he cautioned. "He can do what he wants." Pinnac, startled at the possibility, began to doubt himself, wondering if he really knew anything at all.

As Light commenced pacing back and forth across the floor; Pinnac sensed he was, at last, about to reveal information regarding the elusive assignment. Light began timorously: "I've been ordered . . ." here he stopped, an emphasis Pinnac noted quietly ". . . to change a few traditions. Do you trust me?" Pinnac had never had any reason not to; in fact this was how all the lower angels had been designed: to submit to the authority placed over them. He nodded, too intimidated to speak. Light again spoke quietly: "The new order is that I am also to be worshipped."

Pinnac had been well prepared for this moment, for indeed, it was only the next step down a path he'd been traveling ever since he received the invitation.

Light observed that his statement had been completely accepted as true, so continued confidently: "I've discovered a force that's more powerful than anything yet created. This is why THE ALMIGHTY has issued the order of worship for me."

Pinnac could not conceive of any force other than what he'd experienced, so his curiosity was great as to what discovery instigated such an unusual order. As he waited expectantly, Light's beautiful face took on an edge he hadn't seen before. It was alluring and exciting, sparking even greater curiosity in Pinnac.

"I've much to say . . . do I have your full allegiance?" He had asked this question before, and Pinnac was always quick to answer. This time his hesitation was brief, but noticeable.

Light frowned slightly, but continued confidently: "There'll be things that happen—things hard to understand—but you must trust me." With that, his look intensified as his eyes bored through Pinnac with a mesmerizing gaze. He face became so radiant that soft light beams shot out from it, overwhelming the trusting Pinnac. His momentary hesitation gave way and he bowed slightly as he submitted himself totally to this new secret order.

"Evil," Light said dramatically. "It's a simple name for the mighty force I've discovered. 'Evil' is what I've named my creation." Realizing the reticent Pinnac didn't have a clue as to its magnitude, Light continued: "It's attributes are power and delights and it far surpasses the creation of good with its many intricacies and nuances of levels.

There's much to teach and much to learn. We'll soon meet together with the other recruits to learn its many workings and characteristics before we make it the only law of our populace."

As Pinnac digested this gripping information, Light surprised him with one more detail. "As one of my top leaders, you'll no longer be called Pinnac. You'll be known as Lusilite, a name worthy of the position I've given you."

Lusilite. Pinnac rolled the sound over his tongue. It was a combination of Lucifer and Light. *Clever* to *be so uniquely named after the one I serve.*

As Pinnac knelt, something in him changed as he fully accepted his mission to promote the new creation called "evil."

"I pledge you my absolute service in this new order," he promised fervently.

Light seemed pleased with the transaction. Gazing deeply into the eyes of the newly named Lusilite, he whispered, "Change will come slowly, but together we'll make it happen." Breaking his gaze, he strode directly to the door. Turning one last time, he glanced Lusilite's way, gave him an odd look, and exited.

Awestruck with what had just transpired, Lusilite didn't move for a few minutes. He didn't know the future, but whatever would happen, he was to play a dominant role.

CHAPTER 5

THE ASSEMBLY,
WAR AND BANISHMENT

And the stars of Heaven fell to earth
                              Revelation 6:13
Some of the host of Heaven and stars were cast to
the ground and stomped on.
                              Daniel 8:10

At last the time came for all the recruited to meet again—this time with their assignments and mission in mind. Gathering together in the secret assembly room they waited for their exalted leader. As Light made his entrance, his devoted followers as one rose up, cheered, and bowed deeply before him.

Looking at the exuberant crowd with a peculiar expression of adventure and wonder, Light hesitated only a moment before speaking softly. "Worship me." Having been thoroughly prepared for this, all in the room fell to their knees and began the corporate worship that had formerly been reserved only for the Great I AM.

As the noise in the room grew louder, the intensity of the emotions increased. Here was another god—a creator—who demanded their worship.

"You may rise." The command came ineptly, as if Light himself was in awe of the act.

"As members of my secret service, you'll be privy to many things," he began. "Performing tasks you thought you'd never do, you'll be amazed at the power you'll be able to access. What extraordinary accomplishments will take place because of your loyalty and perseverance!" He smiled as these words, spoken so passionately, began to invade the senses. "All you thought before will be changed; there's now a new, superior order and you are the pioneers to ensure it comes about."

Pride in their leader and in the fact they were the "chosen" began to well up within the group.

"There'll be additional individual assignments, but before those are dispersed, you must be instructed in detail on how to succeed. I'll train you well, for our society will grow stronger only as we achieve success after success." A smirk crossed his face as he continued. "Don't plan to leave this place very soon—there's much to learn."

Immediately the lessons and the tactics needed to implement its principles were initiated. Light was a good teacher. He was thoroughly persuasive: his exciting discovery held promises of power and cosmic supremacy. Though the lessons taught were total opposite of what they'd always experienced, the repetitiously euphoric moments none-the-less causing the addictions to this new power to become strong and unbreakable.

One night Light opened the session with a startling statement. "Tonight you'll discover the ultimate pleasure: I've named it 'pain.'" None of the recruits had experienced pain before, so of course no one knew what he was talking about. "Pain is good," he continued. "It will become the motivation for getting things accomplished, making it the backbone of my new creation."

Soon the curious crowd discovered the "ultimate pleasure" of pain. Divided into groups and instructed as to how to cause it, various levels and intensities were administered and experienced by the unsuspecting novices. Actually experiencing pain for the first time, the noise in the room was terrible! But immediately following the pain came the ubiquitous burst of pleasure, heightened to previously unknown measures.

From that night on, varying degrees of pain were always a predecessor of pleasure; it was soon impossible to experience any level of pleasure unless intense pain was experienced first. Initially, the euphoric moments were first preceded only with mild beatings. Soon cuttings, whippings, and more intense tortures were required to feel the powerful sensations. Gradually the degree of pain was increased until it was equal to the pleasurable moments that would follow.

After numerous lessons in this topic, the apprentices of evil found that only pain brought them pleasure, particularly the pain they watched others experiencing.

It was strange, this new creation of evil.

The time came when Light traveled to the highest Heaven purportedly by proxy to take the praise of his elite to the Great I AM. Upon his return, he described to them the Father's delightful response to the change. Elated, they vowed to fulfill the strange new requests with even more rigor and attention to detail.

Unknown to them, it was all a lie.

CHAPTER 6

THE MISSION FOR EVIL

He cast upon them the fierceness of his anger,
wrath, and indignation, and trouble, by sending
evil angels among them.

Psalms 78:49

There was no question Lucifer was powerful; his creation had forcefully affected all who'd been involved in the experiment. Constant homage to his person was now the requirement for all his leaders, yet he was never completely satisfied with their efforts; as a result his demands grew greater and greater. His initially modest requests soon became unyielding commands fraught with screaming and angry eruptions.

"I've produced power through my creation," he hissed one day. "I am the highest in exalted rank, equal to THE ALMIGHTY. I won't be content until all my subordinates give me the worship I'm due." Abruptly changing to a cajoling tone he continued, "We must work, we must instruct, we must train our populace in the new ways of worship . . . and every angel under my authority are, first and foremost, to worship only me."

Organized to the tiniest detail, his selected leaders were dispatched, each with a particular region to educate in the new order. Their assignment was enormous, but they were thoroughly prepared and ready to begin. It was crucial the teaching be conveyed, the new order obeyed and the chain of command kept. Evil was the creation this populace must accept, and they must worship only Lucifer.

The word went out, the order was fulfilled, and those of the top echelons found themselves in the promised positions of authority as they implemented the new order for all under Lucifer's control.

Not everyone embraced this new regime, however. Some attempted to rebel against it. But neither choice nor discussion of the matter was allowed; all were forced to submit. The select few made sure the order was established and followed by the masses.

Again the time came when all the heavenly angels gathered in the highest Heaven for the corporate worship of the Great I AM. This time not only Lucifer's selected leaders but also the millions under his authority did not attend. Instead, they gathered together on planet Earth for their own collective worship.

Instruments of music were practiced as choirs rehearsed their anthems for the coming celebration. Lucifer's secretive new order of evil would soon be officially implemented in full.

At last the moment came when one-third of Heaven gathered as expected, to honor their new god. It was a grandiose affair, with worshipful reverence being offered by the millions under his command.

Lucifer was in the heights of his glory, radiant with splendor as his subjects bowed before him. The music was loud and rhythmic as the masses danced with glee, exploring intricacies of the new mandate. Most seemed to enjoy the experience—they didn't dare to express anything else. The rally shook the heavens with its volatility and noise.

Immediately following the inauguration, an unfavorable report leaked out to all the other heavenly cities and even to the throne room itself. The details of the information were of a rebellion, and Lucifer's angels were the rebels.

But many still believed they'd been secretly commissioned—that the other angels simply didn't know about their experiment. Explaining it to them was useless, however, and before long the rumblings in Heaven turned into ugly accusations.

Lucifer's masses quickly banded together behind their "son of the morning," the god they now worshipped, and war of gigantic proportions broke out.

The intense battle waged between Michael's angels and Lucifer's own; an unseemly conflict between the old order of innate goodness and the new order of exciting evil. Which order was stronger? Lucifer's angels were certain theirs was. They fought, using Lucifer's tools of hatred and destruction to defeat the old order of love and prosperity.

It appeared Lucifer's angels were strong and effective, but before long they were swiftly and without pretension ushered outside the borders of Heaven. They found themselves in outer darkness with nothing to lighten their existence.

Immediately, as the banished watched in wonder, a colossal barrier swept across the heavens. Try as they might, it was impossible to penetrate this barrier; it effectively blocked any attempted return.

Searching desperately, the banished soon discovered the small gate, which was now the only entrance or exit to the heavenly cities.[77] This gate was guarded constantly; none of them could re-enter it. Eventually they realized there was only one place they could go: back down to the planet Earth where their celebration had taken place. Unhindered by the forces of "good," the elite could now set up the new kingdom of evil without interference.

The defeated angels began the long, dark descent to Earth—falling, falling, falling, with nothing under their feet.

As Lusilite fell, he noticed a simple being to his left named "Korel." That this angel had not yet totally embraced the new order was apparent, for the look of confusion and despair was obvious on his face. Lusilite, by now having learned well the secrets of deriving pleasure from the unwary, decided to have a little fun.

"Power," he muttered loud enough for Korel to hear, "and I'm going to get mine."

Korel warily glanced at Lusilite, his child-like belief in the mission still intact. "This is our opportunity," Lusilite whispered as he realized he could manipulate control over Korel's thinking. "Everything we knew before has now been changed." He paused a moment for the realization to hit him. "Think opposites now. What was bad is now good and what was good is now bad." Maneuvering the situation, Lusilite continued. "Learn this from me, and maybe I'll work out a promotion for you. It's in my power to do it," he added smugly as he watched to see how this information had affected the quiet little angel.

---

[77] Gen 28:17 mentions the gate of Heaven.
Also note Luke 13:24 and Revelation 22:14

Seeing the bewilderment in Korel's eyes made Lusilite bolder than ever. "Power," he repeated "and I'm going to get mine whatever it takes." Turning to look squarely into Korel's face, he contorted his face into the most evil grin he could manage. "Wouldn't you enjoy that?"

A hideous Cheshire grin covered Lusilite's face, obviously frightening the docile Korel. Seeing Korel's fear, however, sent a jolt of pleasure through Lusilite's power-grabbing soul. *Evil is fun*, he thought. He intended to wreak as much havoc on Korel as possible. "*If only he knew what was in store!*" He could hardly wait to experience the unchecked world of evil without "goodness" to neutralize its potent effects.

Landing with soft thuds, the fallen angels gathered into groups and quickly scattered into the darkness. They would now re-organize under the order of evil.

It was a new experience, living in the gloom. Though there were remnants of vegetation left and the land was still fairly beautiful, this would soon be changed. Everything that had once been lovely was to be destroyed: destruction of all traces of good was the goal.

The dazzling cities were smashed to the ground. All gold, silver and precious stones were buried and hidden—some beaten into dust. The age of darkness had begun.[78]

Days morphed together as angels who'd once been attractive slowly degraded until none were recognizable as their previous selves. As they, like moles, dug deeper and deeper into the earth's crust and interior, the passage lengthened until the finality of the pit emerged.[79]

---

[78] Isa 14:17

[79] Isa 14:15, Amos 9:2

Into its depths they entered, only to discover it was impossible to exit again. Their damage to the earth complete, massive amounts of water now filled enormous underground craters as well as covered Earth's entire surface. The weight of the water sealed the gates shut.[80]

Existence in that dark place turned into eons of unmarked time. Daily routine took up the slack, for organization of the masses was detailed and thorough. The administration of pain, a necessity in maintaining the hierarchy of power, became the lifeblood of Hell's organization.

The chain of command in this dreary place was established. At the top was Lucifer himself, who now changed his nickname from "Light" to "Satan" in honor of his new creation. Next were his dedicated elite, or "demons" that did Lucifer's dirty work in the pit. The masses of angels who fell from Heaven with Lucifer were the lowest ranking of the populace. Though some of them had actively embraced the new regime, many others had been deceived as to the origin of the new order, simply obeying without question the ones in authority over them.

The "untouchables," or non-ranking inhabitants and lowest on the scale were the well-hidden prisoners of war.[81] These mighty ones, captured and chained in a secret location, existed in a comatose state of suspended animation.

The top echelons of the hierarchy were the only ones allowed to party within Hell's deepest depth. There, intensely evil gratifications were experimented with and experienced by those who gained the highest rank and authority over the rest. Their ambitions raged within them, unquenched,

---

[80]   Gen 1:2

[81]   Isaiah 14:17

as they fed their addictions with the evil force that had been created.

Now in the pit, Satan continued unabated the lessons of his creation. He taught his legions the intricacies of evil with new abandonment, for he had already paid the price of its implementation. Brainwashed and deprived of other stimuli, the fallen masses soon became shrewd students of this dominating new order. They quickly learned to listen, absorb the information, and carry out their orders without question.

Meeting together in the deepest parts was routine for the elite. There they endured Lucifer's violent temper and vast mood swings as he imparted the many nuances of wickedness. His unpredictable method was all part of the allurement of this rule of sin and evil.

"We're not the weak side," Lucifer intoned during one of his many lectures. "We have prisoners." Here he stopped. *Would he explain?* "Giants—" Lucifer grinned as he played his captive audience. "—powerful angels from Michael's army, and a few from Gabriel's too. Chained . . ." He would not elaborate, preferring to keep his elite in suspense.

Watching him, Lusilite could see in his features not only the greed of violence but also his lust for power over the entire universe. Obviously frustrated that his dominance and control only extended to one-third of Heaven, Satan ruled his masses with ironclad precision and his demons with mathematical cunning. His goal of expanding his base of subordinates by an additional two-thirds was behind every crafty decision he made.

Eventually he took his elite—purportedly as a reward for their groveling allegiance—to see the prisoners chained up in the lowest part of the pit. In a comatose state, these giants were oblivious to their surroundings.

Powerful angels, chained and under our control. It was a heady realization.[82] Seeing the supremacy Lucifer held over these formerly powerful beings only confirmed more strongly his cause.

Though those in leadership had long ago abandoned all former views in favor of this new order, there were others not privy to the scheme who still needed to be converted in their thinking. Outwardly, all appeared to follow the cause; yet some, like the little angel Lusilite noticed falling with him, didn't have a clue as to what was happening. They'd been sucked down together with the leadership, being that they were also under Lucifer's authority and power.

Access to the deepest areas of the pit, however, was granted only to the demons. There they continued to learn how to enact their ravages and further their cause.

---

[82] Rev 9:14-15. One can only speculate as to whether these angels are good or bad.

CHAPTER 7

LESSONS FROM THE PIT

Seek him that makes the day dark with night: that
calls for the waters of the sea, and pours them out
on the face of the earth: The Lord is his name:
Amos 5:8

The demonic celebrations became the focal point for everything else that happened in the pit; only those who contended for rank through competitions in wickedness were eligible to attend them.

Because Lusilite became adept at accomplishing the most heinous acts he was often rewarded with an invitation to the lowest realms. Here, unspeakable pain to the unwary was administered to the entertainment of the rest. It was during one of these intense revelries that resounding words suddenly interrupted the proceedings:

"LET THERE BE LIGHT."[83] The mighty voice shook the foundations of the earth itself.

As the demons huddled together in the deepest part of the pit, a rumbling noise began a slow crescendo, shaking

---

[83]   Genesis 1:3

the planet with its sound. As the volume increased to a thunderous blast, a whooshing roar could be heard mixed in with the noise. Shaken, the pit started to turn slowly as the earth began to rotate on its axis.

What's happening? Unknown to Hell's inhabitants, the massive volume of water covering the earth was being gathered into seas, rivers, lakes and streams; dry land was appearing.[84] The CREATOR OF GOOD had begun his mighty renovation project. Other changes soon followed: Water formations high above the atmosphere now totally encircled the planet, making the warmth of all the earth once again a consistent and comfortable temperature.[85]

Bright light from the formerly darkened surface now began to seep into the dim hole. Everything was shifting! The inhabitants of the pit grabbed onto the jutting walls so as not to be tossed to and fro. Finally the rumblings and shakings stopped. For once the revelries of the pit ceased until all on the surface was quiet again.

Unfazed, Lucifer made a hasty but still secretive visit to the surface to assess the situation. Within a short time he returned to the pit. Calling his demons back for the usual rally and teaching he smiled a congenial and commiserating smile. "Come, my chosen," he intoned. "New events have unfolded which will empower our cause; we have now entered a 'time zone'. All future events on the surface will be measured within it."[86]

---

[84] Genesis 1:9

[85] Genesis 1:6

[86] Daniel 12 depicts earthly events as "times" in a time zone. Revelation 10:6 "Time [is] no longer" Also Acts 17:26

The surface? Is it accessible again?

As if to answer the unspoken question, Lucifer continued. "There are ways of exiting the pit . . . I myself have been to the surface."

His legions looked at each other incongruously. Used to the deprivations of the pit, none thought the system would ever change again. "Those who have passed the most rigorous competitions—who've learned well the intricacies of evil—will go to the surface as my agents for special assignments. I'll decide when you're ready."

Micordial, one of the top elite and a rival for Lucifer's' affections, asked the question the rest were too fearful to ask. "The gates, do they now open again?"

"Stupid!" yelled Satan. Though it was a valid question, Micordial foolishly was the one who asked it and consequently paid the price; kicked firmly in the face, he flew across the room from the impact, landing against the opposite wall. The rest, knowing Satan's kick was lethal, chose to stay outside his kicking range. None-the-less, the question so foolishly asked was being answered, to all their relief.

"Your bodies will stay here, but your spirit may roam freely upon the earth—as long as you're in the process of accomplishing the mission I send you to do." Here his features took on a depraved gleam.

"The war is not over," he shouted, "no, far from it! *HE* thinks he will win. *HE* thinks the old order of 'good' will beat my new creation of evil." He began his ubiquitous striding across the platform. "The great test . . . hah!" The room went silent; the elite didn't know as to what he was referring.

Used to his outrages, they played along as they'd been taught to do; knowing that as soon as he calmed down he'd let them in on the newly acquired information.

"The battle continues with 'mankind,' a specially created entity made strictly for the purposes of a test. Whoever obtains their obedience will win the war. We must win at all costs! Learn well, my chosen, these lessons of evil, for victory will only happen if you use the tools I give you."

The demons are in for a long session today.

After a dramatic pause, Lucifer's tone turned conspiratorial: "There's a secret route to the surface through the barrier; spirits can easily travel this passageway, but all bodies will stay here . . . that way I know you'll come back." His depraved laugh was deep and long.

Are we the prisoners? The question fleeted through Lusilite's mind, then quickly exited again. *Of course not; we are the powerful.*

The room buzzed with anxiety, however. *What's this? A new chapter in an already hideous existence?*

"The earth will be populated, little by little. Our job is to make sure each mortal chooses evil over good. This choice decides their eternal destiny. It's not hard. Just make sure each disobeys the rules of I AM.

Just one disobedient act will prevent them from meeting HIS standards, thereby equipping them for eternity with us. Our job is to make sure each one is tempted . . . and each succumbs to the temptation. It's easy. I've already succeeded with every member of the first family . . . . except for one."

As a look of total hatred crossed Lucifer's face, a plume of black smoke exited his nostrils. Composing himself again, he continued. "Our numbers won't diminish if we do our job; we must be watchful and alert to successfully tempt each and every person who inhabits the earth as mankind."

There had been so many lies of late that Lusilite didn't know which tales were valid. *What does he mean, "our numbers will not diminish?"* There had to be more to the story. Lusilite, ever the avid learner turned all his focus to find out.

Gathering his courage after the speech, he entered the private quarters of Lucifer. Cringing and crawling as low as he could—for this was what he now required of all who entered Satan's presence—he lay prostrate until given the command to rise.

"Oh mighty one," he began. "Our populace cannot diminish, can they? How is this possible?"

Sighing with a weariness that seemed out of character, Lucifer relaxed the protocol enough to sit down with his protégé. He appeared even relieved to talk to someone about this irritating situation.

"The I AM thinks he will re-establish his authority over our citizens," he began. "He chooses to forget he made me their undisputed leader. Now he wants them back."

Still not understanding the ramblings of this fallen archangel, Lusilite listened quietly. He knew he was in danger of suffering pain, for Lucifer had a quick temper that got more explosive as time went by. Yet, determined to find out all he could he listened without comment.

"This is not common knowledge," Lucifer intoned. "A secret . . . I'll tell you; but the others mustn't know about the mandate, not until I decide there's no other option but to tell them."

"I understand."

"Each of our general population must be given a chance to choose, in a neutral area with influences from both sides, which entity to serve. Evil, in my estimation, will win hands down. It's the easy way out, and most will choose the path

I've taught them. But there may be a few who go the other way."

Sighing again, he continued, "The war is not over, my comrade, not by a long shot. We must endure the transience until the finality of the choice is made. The battle for souls will take place during the next few thousand years." Lusilite continued to listen quietly.

"All the population of the pit must go one by one to the surface as mankind.[87] There they'll be presented with both good and evil choices and must choose the creator of one or the other to obey.

We must increase our lessons from the pit so all will choose to come back here again. I'll not be denied my rights as god of this world!"[88] He finished with a flurry of angry motions, frustrated the I AM was, in his mind, taking back what had already been given.

"Freedom of choice . . . I'm totally against this, but must endure these coming millenniums. I've no choice. They do, but I don't," he finished with a self-pitying intonation.

Was he seeking sympathy? This self-pitying seemed out of place to such a mighty beast.

"No one must know!" Lucifer's face suddenly grew red with rage. Grabbing Lusilite by the throat he lifted him up so his face was directly in front of his own. Glaring at him, he suddenly spit, laughed malevolently, and threw him down to the ground. Kicking him violently in the groin, he asked, "What do you feel?"

---

[87] Gen 1:28 Interestingly, the command was to "replenish," or re-populate the earth, indicating a previously populated status.

[88] 2 Corinthians 4:4

"Overwhelmed with your beauty" was the ready answer.

"That's what you're supposed to feel." He sneered, appeased for the moment. Lusilite bowed and crawled as best he could out of the room.

Debilitating pain was the price he paid, but in his mind it was well worth it, for he now knew more than the rest of Hell's populace. He was elated to be privy to this information and determined to use it to his own advantage.

CHAPTER 8

JOB

*Behold, we count them happy which endure. Ye
have heard of the patience of Job . . .*

James 5:11

Since the war and banishment, skypers for Lucifer's
domain had all been destroyed. However, during the
course of the ongoing war, Lucifer had managed to hijack
two of them for his own personal use. Though he could, and
often did travel the heavens without benefit of the vehicle,
the trip took longer and was much more wearing.

Exiting the pit in one of the skypers for a visit to
Heaven, Lucifer managed to enter the restricted zone.[89]
Still unbelievably powerful, he'd not lost his ability to enter
the highest Heaven, though the masses under him could
not. Joining the "sons of God"[90] who seasonally presented
themselves before the Lord, he strode directly to the temple
complex, demanding to be let in.

---

[89] See John 10:1
[90] Job 1:6

Entering the throne room along with the other high-ranking angels, he began to whine about the unfairness of the great test.

Seated at the table was the Lord himself. Looking up, he asked, "Where did you come from?"

"From going back and forth in the earth and from walking up and down in it," he replied sniveling.

"Have you considered my servant Job? There's no one like him in the earth, a perfect and upright man, one that serves God and hates evil."

"Does Job serve God for nothing in return? Haven't you made a hedge around him, his household, and all he has? You've blessed the work he does so much that his belongings extend all over the land. But turn the tide against him, take everything away, and he'll curse you to your face."

"All right; look. I'll let you take everything he owns. Just don't hurt him physically."

Smiling in anticipation, Lucifer stomped out of the room. Jealous of the Father, he was irritated at still having to submit to His boundaries.

As he climbed into the skyper, Satan formulated a plan; his hands, formerly tied as to the havoc he could cause, were now untied, so to speak. This would be a test of his skill, and he was determined to pass it.

Job, spoiled rotten by the Father will now find life intolerable and will fail miserably in his pursuit of 'good.'

Muttering to himself, he continued to scheme: "Job will be the prototype; with him I'll create the pattern to use on how to cause the rest of mankind to choose evil over good. My slow-learning idiots will then watch it through virtual mode, observing how I did it."

His plan was made and carried out perfectly. He didn't need his demons to do this work . . . he would do it himself. First he caused havoc in Job's life by destroying all his belongings. Next he caused the death of all his children; but even when this happened Job still trusted in the I AM.

Fuming at his lack of success, Satan returned to Heaven's throne room. "It's not fair," he whined. "You have an advantage over me by not letting me touch his body. Let him experience sickness and pain; he'll turn to me and then you'll see whose creation is stronger."

After permission was given Satan increased his attack against Job with renewed gusto. Itching and in unbearable pain, Job's whole body ached miserably. He was so wretched that his wife pled with him to curse God and die. Still he unswervingly served the I AM.

Satan next influenced Job's three closest friends to falsely accuse and turn against him. Looking at him with pity they gave him lengthy lectures on how to repent. Though not understanding why evil was plaguing his life, Job didn't budge in his adamant belief in the power of goodness or of his trust in the Lord.

Finally the test was over. Job prayed for his friends and the Lord gave Job twice as much as he had before. He died, rich and old.[91]

Lucifer, enraged after losing face, vowed it would never happen again. Unsuccessful in turning Job towards evil, he had to create other examples for the virtual mode lessons. *As soon as my demons are fully prepared I'll release them to do my dirty work on the face of the earth.*

Meanwhile, slowly, almost imperceptibly at first, the population of the pit began to decrease; in a secret place

---

[91] For complete story, read the book of Job.

within the deepest regions was a tunnel where one by one the spirits of the fallen were sucked to the surface to be born as mankind.

As earth's populace began to multiply, the change below was so minute it was at first not even noticed. Because it would not affect the millions in the pit for some time, very few knew about the process and the revelries continued unabated.

Lucifer was able to come and go as he pleased; it was no secret. That others in his top echelons were being prepared to exit and enter for special assignments was not so well known. This secret was kept so total control could continue to be exerted against the masses; he needed the ranks to be firmly established for evil before any news of the "great test" leaked out.

CHAPTER 9

MORE LESSONS IN EVIL

Brother shall betray the brother to death, and the father the son; and children shall rise up against their parents, and shall cause them to be put to death.

Mark 13:12

As mankind's population multiplied, the lessons on how to deceive and destroy them intensified.

Gathering his demons for yet another session, Satan began his impartation: "Mankind is a very different type of being—far inferior to what we've seen in the past. Their knowledge of eternity is extremely limited during their few short years on earth, not remembering anything that happened before their mortal birth.[92]

As children they're particularly trusting and deceivable, as adults they're more set in their thinking. The plan is to secure their allegiance to our way when they're young and malleable so that throughout their lifetime they can do much damage for us."

---

[92] 1 Cor. 13:12

Humans will be born with a sense of innate goodness. They'll also be born with a soul, or in other words, a thinking and emotional type of entity which can be injured and destroyed. Once the soul of a human is wounded it's easy to enter in for the kill.

"Any questions?"

There were many, but to ask one would be risky. However, Micordial finally raised his hand.

"How does one 'enter in'?"

Glaring before breaking into a slow grin, Satan answered. "Occasionally you'll find a human so ready for evil that he'll open a 'door' into his own body. When you find an open door you can enter in through the eyes. Bring some of the others with you, for more than one evil spirit can do major damage within that person and all that pertains to him.

Those who are fortunate enough to find a host will find a pleasant place to practice unbridled evil . . . but more on that later.[93]

Any more questions?"

Satan was in a good mood, so more questions quickly followed.

"How do we deal with the innate goodness each will be born with?"

"We present troubles and abuse as early as possible to the young with the goal of eroding their happiness. Eventually, their innate goodness will react to the mistreatment in a way that will destroy them and others. For every genuine act of love, we must present a counterfeit in order to neutralize its effects.

---

[93] Luke 11:24-26

As adults they'll be servants to their habits and addictions." Satan paused a moment to gather his thoughts.

"There'll be those who are frugal, who budget their money and deal with others honestly, expecting the same. We must inspire thieves to steal from them—that'll bring them to a place where they'll be easy prey for us. If bitterness, fear, hatred or resentment enters into their psyche, we've got them.[94]

We'll inspire uncontrollable rage; major damage can be accomplished with humans with anger addictions. Others will be conquered through their apathy, or failure to build up enough moral fortitude to withstand evil. We'll conquer them all through any means possible. Inspire depression, betrayals, troubles to rich and poor alike—it doesn't matter their standing in the earthly hierarchy . . . all can be persuaded to sin."

Satan's demons, excited about going to the outside, did their best to prepare for the mission. Released one by one with specific assignments in mind, they found the exit—it was very small indeed—squeezing their spirits through the opening and toward the surface. Feeling a sense of freedom, but with warfare in mind, they focused on the tasks before them. Their assignments included accidents, thefts, spreading of diseases, arsons, and evil suggestions of rape and murder.

Covering the populated parts of the earth, each returned with an outcome of either success or failure. Micordial's mission was successful; he'd accomplished his first death from the surface . . . a suicide.

There were many failures, however, and the demons that failed were berated and demoted in rank for their

---

[94] Hebrew 12:15

lack of success. This caused jealousies and hatred to grow amongst the demons, dividing those who'd been successful from those who had failed. Satan's angry rampages, however, eventually included both successful and unsuccessful, so success mattered little in the end.

"Idiots," he exclaimed. "Is it so hard to understand the mission? Are you that weak and stupid? Can't you figure out our numbers are diminishing?" The demons looked at each other in confusion, still not comprehending his words.

Finally quieting down after another extended rampage, Satan began his next lesson on the killing of mankind.

"The stages of human growth are these: pre-born, babyhood, childhood, young adult, adult, and elderly. At any stage of life, attacks with the purpose of killing the body can be made. Assault the body or the mind, and the person will die."

Sounds easy. Why was it so hard?

"Unfortunately, the I AM presents healing for every body.[95] However there are many circumstances where healing won't be completed."

Why?

"We present infections, they present antibiotics. We impose danger, they impose rules for safety. We spread viruses, they teach sanitation. We promote abortion for unwanted pregnancies, they promote adoption. We cause deformities, they study medicine and inspire surgical skill. You get the picture—the war is tough, but we must win it. This is one of the major goals of our battles—to prevent any forthcoming healing."

How?

---

[95] Exodus 15:26b; Psalms 103:3

"Disrupt the process. Inject suicidal thoughts into your victim before healing can take place . . . accidents, chemically induced dementia, untreated diseases, murders . . ." he went through the list of possibilities. It was up to his demons to carry out his plans for each assignment.

Once again his demons were released to do his bidding, each returning with resulting victories or defeats. The forces of evil from the pit were effective in their missions; as the population of earth grew, so did the evil of its inhabitants until almost all had chosen evil over good.[96]

But the earthly war between good and evil had only begun. Soon a massive wipe-a-way of life took place, completely erasing all evil-doers from the face of the earth. The water stored in the heavens came down with a mighty forty-day rainstorm. Deep underground lakes gushed out, changing forever the size and shape of the planet. The northern and southern axis of the earth shifted as the separation of land mass caused the continents to shift. Oceans formed, and the earth was once more free from sin.

Excursions to the earth were suspended for a time until Noah and his family exited the ark.

Soon the battle between good and evil resumed once again.

---

[96] Read the complete story in Genesis chapters 5-10.

CHAPTER 10

THE ULTIMATE BETRAYAL

Fear him which is able to destroy both soul and body in Hell.

Matthew 10:28

Lessons from the pit didn't diminish in the least. Knowing he had only a short time in which to conquer the hearts of mankind, Satan stepped up his training; he had a trump card, one he'd saved for the final lesson in evil.

"It's intriguing," he began pleasantly, "the killing of a human body does not generate the highest thrill; this ecstasy is produced only through destroying its living soul. The ultimate betrayal, my finest creation, accomplishes this on the surface."

This extremely intensified achievement would have powerful consequences. As Lusilite listened, he immediately understood; for he'd already been told the secret of the "Great Test" none of the others knew. *Killing the body would not guarantee a spirit's return to the pit; destroying its living soul almost certainly would.*

"The killing of a soul can, of course, take place here in the pit, deriving pleasing entertainment for the masses to enjoy as they watch. With 'returnees' it can take place over an extended period of time if done correctly. However, the ultimate of ecstasy is produced by—"

"—what's a 'returnee'?"

"Dim-wit! Brainless! You haven't figured that out yet?" Satan's pleasant demeanor had changed abruptly. Incensed that he now had to explain the hated "Great Test," he began onerously:

"Those who succumb to evil while living as mortals will return here. When they do, they'll have not only their spirit, which cannot die, but also a soul which can die.[97] It's extremely pleasurable to welcome them . . . ." Satan's foul mood suddenly improved again as he re-lived the abuse of the returnees. "As more and more make their re-appearance, I may let some of you join me in the 'welcoming' celebrations."

The excited noises turned into blubbering eagerness since destroying anything the I AM had created was the goal and delight of Hell's demonic throng.

Lucifer eventually quieted the room; the time had come to fully explain the Great Test to all his high-ranking demons. He grudgingly began the lesson:

"You've all sworn allegiance to me, signifying our dominion is your preference; your job is to persuade the rest to make that choice as well. Power, authority, rank, and status are yours—if you pass the test."

"How do we pass the test?" The question was asked so meekly it was barely audible.

"Numb-skulls! Idiots! Murder, rape, steal, kill, kill, kill!" Satan's features took on a deadly glaze.

---

[97] Matt. 10:28

The elite knew better than to ask any more questions, for when Satan reached this point in his aggravation, there could be some serious physical damage. They left the session with the major lesson of ultimate betrayal still unexplained.

However the top ranking demons were soon enjoying revelries of a different sort deep within the pit. Killing the souls of the returnees piece by microscopic piece created an ecstasy of its own.

Occasionally the fiercest of the returnees, because of their extremely evil lives on earth, would be allowed to work among the demons. The elite resented this for they didn't want to share their rank and promotions with anyone else. Backstabbing and treachery flourished within the borders of Hell.

The lesson on "ultimate betrayal" remained to be taught, however. Lusilite, ever seeking rank and favor decided he would be the one to broach the subject.

Groveling one night at the feet of Satan he whispered "Oh beautiful lord, who can absorb thoughts such as yours? Yet you have our deepest curiosity as to how your mighty mind works."

Flattered, Satan answered with a condescending smile; he knew what was coming, for he himself had orchestrated the curiosity. "What is it, Lusilite, my neophyte?"

"We'd like to know: What is the 'ultimate betrayal'?"

Pausing for a dramatic moment, he subtly responded with a question: "Who, my fair demons, is the most vulnerable among the humans?"

"A baby or child," spoke Micordial

"A young girl," Elixer interrupted

"An invalid," Lusilite budged in.

"Who is their most trusted?"

"A father."

"A friend."

"A mother."

"A spiritual leader."

"Remember what you've answered, for all of them are right." Satan gleamed in the dinginess; the information he was about to impart gave him a most pleasant gratification.

"The most intense betrayals, or 'Shareekas,' involve broken trust by someone in a trusted position; for instance, a young girl molested by her own brother, uncle, or father; or better yet, killed by one she depended upon and trusted." He paused for a pregnant moment before continuing:

"Come with me. I'll show you a perfect example of Shareeka."

Exiting through a formerly concealed door, the demons abruptly found themselves enveloped virtually in the earth world. Trees, grass, and flowers were everywhere. A muddy path strewn with leaves and small twigs was under their feet; the sounds of jungle noises teased their ears; the warm wind and humming of insects gave a pleasant summer feel to the scene.

Running as fast as he could down the trail toward them was a young boy, a wide grin covering his face. Moving aside, the demons quickly realized he couldn't see them.

As the boy approached the group, his pace slowed down to a walk; a look of wonder crossed his face as he sensed he was not alone. Glancing behind him and to each side, he crept forward. Finally his steps quickened as he continued his run down the jungle trail.

"That, my friends, is an example of how powerful an influence we have with just our presence. Now—a whisper in the ear, a desire planted, a seduction of evil thought—watch what happens."

Satan immediately moved to where the boy was now resting and catching his breath. Sitting on a rock beside a small stream of water the boy's gaze was focused on the upward circling of a big hawk. Coming closer, Satan whispered directly into his ear. As he did so, a mischievous grin spread across the boy's face; he had gotten the message.

As subsequent plans of mischief began to form within the boy's thoughts, a light sensation of pleasure washed over his body.

"This boy will be a pawn in my hands. He'll go home, steal his father's tools, and then successfully blame his younger brother for the theft. This is just the beginning. Once he acts upon my suggestion, then I require more and more mischief in order to experience less and less pleasure . . . it won't take long to get him hooked."[98]

Lusilite was astonished. *This is an innocent little boy, cute and energetic. Yet, he was to become a powerful pawn for the evil side. How?*

No answers were needed as he watched the events of this boy's life play out before him.

---

[98] 1 Peter 2:19

CHAPTER 11

THE SHAREEKA

Many shall hate and betray.
Matthew 24:10

Locton woke up early. Having passed his thirteenth year he was now considered a man and would be allowed to take part in the seasonal raids against a neighboring village.

Grabbing his knife as he exited the house, he determined to spend the day hunting for young straight saplings. With them he would make dozens of arrows in preparation for his first real battle as a warrior.

No one could remember why the conflict had started, but the never-ending attacks had become something of a tradition for his tribe. Wars created excitement as well as a quick way to enrich ones own assets—spoils of war were not limited to material items, but also included the most valuable plunder: slaves.

There were many slaves in Locton's village. Abused, overworked and malnourished, they often got sick and died, thereby necessitating replacements.

Young females were easy to capture and made ideal slaves; with them no courtship was required and marriage arrangements didn't need a formal consent to take place. If a female slave bore children for her master, strong maternal instincts would usually ensure loyalty to her forced situation.

The warriors who won the spoils of war achieved wealth and status within the tribe; the thought of the plunder was enough motivation for Locton to risk his life for the ill-gotten gain.

One day as Locton ran down his favorite trail, he spotted a young boy fishing in the stream. Silently creeping closer, he soon realized he was a child from the enemy tribe. Watching him, he devised a plan that would take some time to fulfill.

Creeping closer, he surprised the boy with a "hi-ho." Jumping, the startled youngster prepared to run, but seeing Locton's friendly smile, soon relaxed. "Catch anything?" Locton asked pleasantly.

The boy shook his head. "Not much fish here."

"I know a better spot on up the stream."

Hesitating only a moment, the child quickly relented and soon the boys together experienced a fun afternoon of fishing and play. As darkness approached they made plans to meet again.

For the next few months they spent each day together. This was unusual, for boys from warring tribes avoided any contact whatsoever; but the two seemed to enjoy each other's company, often discussing the senselessness of war. Icto and Locton determined to break the long held animosity that had divided their tribes for so long.

Months turned into two years, and they became closer than brothers.

"You should meet my family," Locton suggested one day. A look of fear immediately crossed Icto's face, for memories of past wartime abuses had made an indelible scar on his psyche.

"They'll welcome you because you're my friend," Locton assured him. After numerous urgings with repeated reassurances, Icto finally agreed to meet Locton's people.

The day came when Locton brought Icto to his home. Locton's promises proved true, for upon their arrival Icto was treated like royalty. As he enjoyed the meal prepared for him, he resolved anew to work to facilitate peace between the two tribes. *Someday I'll be able to reciprocate the hospitality.*

"Visit me tomorrow; we're having a special meal," Locton spoke enthusiastically. "My brother shot a wild pig in the forest." Icto thought about the succulent taste of roasted pork. It was enough to tempt him to visit once again.

The next day as the boys approached the village, Icto was happier than he'd ever been. Knowing he was safe lifted a tremendous burden from his young mind; he'd trusted Locton with his life and had not only been protected, but honored as well.

Glancing at his friend, he realized he truly loved him.

Stepping to the soft beat of a drum, they entered the tribal boundary. Locton pointed to a small hut, "You may change in there."

Entering the hut, Icto found special tribal clothing. Pleased, he donned the outfit, admiring himself as he exited the door. Scanning the crowd, he located his friend near the tables.

Glancing at the finery, Locton smiled: "You are almost a man."

"Tomorrow will mark my thirteenth year," replied the happy Icto.

All were in a merry mood as the meal began. The sound of a fluted pipe wafting over the faded evening light provided pleasant entertainment as they enjoyed the delicious food.

"Feeling full?" asked Locton.

"Very," was the answer.

"Tired?"

"A little . . ."

"Here, rest your head on my shoulder."

The shoulder was tempting; Icto's day had been long and the full meal had made his eyes sleepy. The hesitation was brief, but he decided to take him up on the offer—if only to close his sleepy eyes for just a few moments.

The shoulder and upper chest were warm: a perfect place to rest his weary head. Gazing up at Locton's face just before closing his eyes, he smiled sleepily and then nodded off slightly.

"This is the moment," Satan whispered to Lusilite. Lusilite watched, transfixed, as the mellow scene changed sharply before him.

Unknown to Icto, this was the signal for which the guests had been waiting; the greatest betrayal, the lowest punch of a long-fought war was not only in killing a body, but in first killing its soul.

At the instant Icto's head touched Locton's chest, a full trust had been established. But it was all a lie. This event had been planned since the day Locton first noticed Icto fishing by the stream; the words Satan had previously whispered into his ear had taken root and developed to this moment in time.

The scene played out. As Icto's head touched his chest, Locton's gleaming eyes signaled the rest: *now is the time.* The crowd quietly got up and surrounded the two boys.

When Icto awoke a few minutes later, it was to a circle of enemies, each with their weapon drawn. Startled, he lifted his head in fright, looking to his friend for protection. What he saw instead was an evil grin, an "I got you" look, and luminous eyes filled with murderous lust.

In that instant Icto knew he would die. But as he suffered the knife thrusts over and over, the pain from his broken heart rivaled the pain from the physical torture; the one who was thrusting the knife with such enjoyment was his trusted friend, Locton.

Satan froze the scene to the exact moment when Icto knew he was betrayed. The look in Icto's eyes was one of utter surprise and disbelief.

"This is Shareeka! See that look? The killing of the soul—perfectly executed." A sly grin spread across Satan's face. "Both of them are returning here." [99]

---

[99] It is believed that cannibalism and other forms of horrific betrayals are still practiced among isolated tribes in New Guinea and South America.

CHAPTER 12

STRONGHOLDS

You shall not bow down to their gods, nor serve them, nor do after their works: but you shall utterly overthrow them.

Exodus 23:24

Satan's strategy was to gain strongholds in more and more areas of the earth. One of these gains was over the entire region of a formidable tribe known as the Hittites.[100] These inhabitants had degenerated completely to the worship and service of Satan; their entire system was set up to accommodate evil with all its rituals and practices.

It was a pleasant place for Satan's echelons to visit, for there they could wreak havoc in a way they couldn't in other locales. "Shareeka" was enjoyed time and time again as Hittite laws enforced its satanic rule as the only law of the land. Ritualistic killings and practices involved many innocent children: a great Shareeka! Satan's legions enjoyed the scenes over and over again as sons and daughters ultimately realized they were the sacrifices of their own

---

[100] See Deaut. 20:17

parents. Completely isolated from the rest of the world, their cries for help were useless.[101]

One day the news came: the Israelite troops had been commanded to drive out the Hittites and claim the land for the forces of good. Because the existing stronghold ensured the return to the pit of not only the present populace of Hittites, but all their future generations as well, the demons determined to block the advance.

The battle between good and evil raged hot: Joshua and his troops fought the Hittite battalions as Michael and his angels battled Satan and his demons. As the Hittites were driven from the land, Satan's stronghold was broken.

Defeated, the forces of Hell regrouped: there were other tribes, other regions—they must claim a new stronghold one way or another. Resolute to win at any cost, the battle for mankind raged on.

---

[101] Psalms 106:34-38. Because Israel did not completely destroy the idolatrous nations, they eventually not only accepted but also practiced their wicked atrocities.

CHAPTER 13

GOD'S ONLY BEGOTTEN SON

*They that are wise shall shine as the brightness
of the firmament; and they that turn many to
righteousness as the stars for ever and ever.*
                                        Daniel 12:3

As earthly years melted together, the battle continued between good and evil. Power and control were the objectives; the winner would reign over all.[102]

Satan's evil empire would in turn take ground and suffer defeats. Causing wars, unnatural deaths, sickness, and disease, the forces were able to gain ground as they deceived some of mankind into falling for the death traps. A quest for power and control motivated countless humans on earth, and it was certainly the motivation within the pit.

Often Satan would roam the earth, continually educating himself as to the status of the battles raging there. When God Incarnate came as a baby into the world of mankind, Satan was aware of it and did everything he could

---

[102] See Isaiah 37:16,20 and Luke 4:5-6

to thwart the plan. [103] Unsuccessful in destroying the child, he went after the young man, Jesus.

The temptations were strong, but Jesus never budged from his commitment to righteousness—not even once, to the occasional irritation of his sinful brothers and sisters. He was not deceivable like Eve, nor easily swayed as was Adam.

Satan, however, was determined to defeat Him. If he didn't, Jesus could re-claim the lost and make a way for the banished to return to Heaven. This outcome must be prevented at all cost.

Failing in his earlier attempts to make Jesus sin in any area, he decided to try a different tactic. Finding Jesus fasting in the desert, Satan observed he was weak, dehydrated and hungry. *Perfect! I'll make him a reasonable offer he can't refuse.*

As Lucifer materialized into a human-like form, Jesus immediately perceived who he was. Recognizing him as the powerful archangel who had jealously rebelled, he determined to be perfectly wise in dealing with him.

"You're hungry. Here . . . as HIS only begotten Son you can do anything. Turn these stones into bread—it's easy for you, oh STRONG ONE. Have some bread; strengthen yourself."

"It is written, man shall not live on bread alone, but by every word that comes form the mouth of God."

Scripture! How I hate those words.

Satan tried another tactic. Taking Jesus to the earthly temple built according to the specifications of Heaven's architectural design, he elevated up to the highest pinnacle.

---

[103]   See Mat 2:13-20.

There they observed worshipers going into the temple complex for the purpose of worshipping the Great I AM. "Look at these worshipers; they'll all know you came from God if you do one thing: fall down from this steeple. It's written that the angels will catch you so you don't get hurt, right? Prove this scripture true. When all the worshippers see this terrific feat, they'll know you came from God and will believe everything you tell them; your mission will be accomplished."

"It is written 'You shall not tempt the Lord your God.' I won't do it."

Satan's greatest goal was for the I AM to worship him, as he had himself worshiped the I AM in the past. He planned very carefully what to say next. Moving to the highest mountain in the world, he showed Jesus all the kingdoms of earth.

"We know this is the reason you've come, to gather the kingdoms back into your domain. I'll offer you a shortcut. You won't have to die or be tortured. There is an easier way out; just . . . bow your knees and worship me. That's all you have to do . . . just once . . . I'll hand my people back to you if you just fall down and do it. Okay?"

"Get behind me, Satan! You know we're to worship only the Lord God." The answer was quick and to the point.

Lucifer, frustrated and angry, reached his boiling point; a plume of black smoke escaped out of his ears, eyes and nostrils. "I'll be back . . ." his voice trailed off as he whisked himself away into the darkness.

Jesus was spent, hungry, tired, and weak. Lying down, he knew he'd defeated the enemy in this one of many tests; these offers were clever and tempting, but he determined never to fall for any of them. Too many had fallen captive to this type of conniving, and he fully understood how tough it was to withstand it.

As he lay there, weak, but contented in the fact he'd once again beaten the enemy, angels from Heaven appeared, bringing sustenance and much needed encouragement. He delighted to be with these who were totally dedicated to serving the God of goodness.[104]

Feeling refreshed, Jesus got up knowing what he needed to do: he must let the inhabitants of earth know the Kingdom of Heaven was once again within reach. It was accessible only through him, the Holy One of Israel. He would be able to remove the sin of the world by paying the price as the I AM's unspotted Lamb.[105] His message was strong, sure and true.

Choosing disciples to help him, he began to teach mankind about the Kingdom of Heaven.[106] It would be a quiet, nondescript start.

Though Satan had left Jesus for a time, he'd not given up. His next move was to prepare a devil from the elite to be a secret "plant" to accomplish the Shareeka.[107] Being betrayed from one who had eaten, worked, slept and prayed with Jesus would be his final and best attempt to defeat him.

It worked! Three years of ministry ended in a brutal death for the Volunteer from Heaven. Satan returned to

---

[104] See Luke 4:1-13 for the biblical account of this story.

[105] Jewish law provided that an unblemished lamb could be sacrificed as payment for one's sin. The penitent one could then be found blameless before God.

[106] See Ps 145:13, Matt 4:17, Rev 12:10.

[107] John 6:70-71

his demons, glowing with news. They quickly perceived something was different, for the normally morose Satan had rejuvenated himself, appearing almost joyful in his countenance. Those nearest him heard the now familiar word uttered softly. "Shareeka."

Gathering his forces, Satan sat down, inviting the rest to sit as well. This was unusual, for no demon usually had the luxury of sitting when Satan was present.

"Friends," he began, "I've won the greatest battle since our existence. Not only have I killed HIS prophets and messengers, but now also the Son.[108] It was a stellar betrayal by our own devil, Judas, who we 'welcomed' two days ago. Get ready. The ONE will be joining us soon."

"A returnee?"

"No, idiot. He wasn't one of 'the banished'. But now . . ." he let out a shriek of excitement.

"So . . . not human?" still not getting it.

"Dummy, listen! Human . . . Mortal . . . Diety! Son of God, Son of man!"[109] Uncontrollable exhilaration gripped him as he screamed a deafening "IT'S TIME TO CELEBRATE!"

Soon the demonic masses were dancing to the beat of the death drums. *We'll welcome him, all right, with terror and torture. What new highs this will bring*! Lusilite licked his lips in anticipation. To destroy perfection would certainly be the ultimate ecstasy!

Suddenly the ground shook as rocks began to tumble off the jutted walls. Everything in the pit vibrated at breakneck

---

[108] Mark 12:1-8

[109] Jesus was both Son of God, Son of Man. Mark 1:1; 8:31.

speed. As the reverberating noise grew louder and sharper in intensity, a powerful surge of electricity hit the inhabitants.

Suddenly the depths were struck with blinding light. "Shareeka, Shareeka!" Satan yelled. "This is THE ONE. Attack, bind, torture!"

But events didn't go the way Satan expected; instead of a defeat, Jesus entered the pit as a Victor. Unlike the returnees who screamed upon their re-entry, Jesus entered as a conqueror with authority.

The powerful demons squealed as they attempted to surround, control and chain him, but they couldn't get within ten feet of him. A strong magnetic force surrounded his person and none of the elite could penetrate it.

"RELEASE THE PRISONERS!" Jesus demanded.

Quivering before him, the defeated forces of Hell began unlocking the chains. A mighty roar was heard as all unlocked prisoners immediately followed Jesus out the gates of Hell.[110] Now frozen in terror, faint memories of their former estates in Heaven—abandoned in order to follow Lucifer—twinkled within the memories of the Fallen. [111]

---

[110] Psalms 16:10. See also Matt 27:52-53.

[111] Jude 1:6

CHAPTER 14

LUSILITE'S SUCCESS

Jesus was troubled in spirit and said: one of you shall betray me.

John 13:21

Knowing that what he'd first perceived as a victory was actually his utter defeat, Satan realized he had but a short time left as god of his world.[112] He didn't impart this information to his demons, however, but continued to berate, control and manipulate them.

"We must cause chaos, we must win more battles: the war is not over and defeat is not an option!" His demons, still hoping for rank and position fought for the surface assignments. "Don't fail me," warned Satan as he once again handed an assignment to Lusilite.

Exiting once more through the narrow cavity, Lusilite wandered the earth, looking for an open door: a willing soul. *Yes, here is one.* It was in a meetinghouse where lies were taught as truth and the innocent believed them.

---

[112] Rev 12:12

The men, sitting around an opium pot, were each smoking from pipes connected to the communal supply. The drug-induced high they were experiencing was a perfect open door for delusion and deception. Having learned well the lessons from the pit, Lusilite decided to test his skill.

Whispering into the ear of the robed teacher, Lusilite observed his reaction: he stopped puffing for a moment, then nodded slightly. As he absorbed the message, the door to deception opened widely.

Not long after this event, the Imam wrote a declaration on religion and family. This opinion was the basis of a law, which would set the stage for the ultimate of betrayals.

Upon Lusilite's return to the pit, his success in the assignment was to earn him a high ranking promotion amongst the demons, for he had set into motion one of the most effective and longest lasting Shareekas of all earth time. However, it was not the highest rank possible and Lusilite craved yet a new assignment that would achieve an even greater Shareeka.

As he plotted and schemed for his next mission, the top ranking demons watched the unfolding Shareekian drama in virtual mode.

Centuries after the implementation of the religious law a young girl named Suja wandered aimlessly about her house. She was bored. Her religion claimed girls couldn't be educated so she was not allowed schooling like her brothers. Her activities consisted only of household tasks designed to condition her into becoming a subservient and obedient wife. Powerless to make her own decisions, she felt a growing frustration with her life.

Occasionally she'd be allowed to accompany her mother to the market place, but only if she first donned a heavy black burkha. Covered from head to toe, her view was limited to what she could see through the linen shield covering her eyes.

Why she was so clothed was not a mystery; her family was Muslim—from the strictest sect—and followed its every teaching. Though she respected her parents, she remembered the comparative life of freedom she experienced as a young girl before maturity took place. Now her black clothes were her prison.

Her longing for adventure and excitement was not to be, for her parents soon contracted a marriage agreement with a wealthy Muslim relative. Being only fourteen years old, Suja was apprehensive of this agreement, as she barely knew the man who was three times her age. Though bored with her present situation, she was not ready for the duties this marriage would demand.

Is this all my life is worth?

Accompanying her mother to the marketplace, she looked as much as she could at the activity and interesting sights. Passing an electronics store, she stopped, interested, as a TV played out adventurous scenes before her. Watching, she realized the TV was turned to a forbidden channel. *The world is much larger than the few familiar blocks I've experienced.* Freedom to dress the way she wanted, to go to school, to get a job outside the home—these were things forbidden by her strict Muslim faith.

Realizing Suja was watching a prohibited program, her mother hastily took her daughter's arm, steering her toward the flower shop. Passing a travel agency along the way, Suja unobtrusively picked up a travel brochure. Opening it, she noticed a small piece of paper hidden within its fold. Written on it were the words: "Longing for freedom? Contact Jamal: 4682 Busr St."

Her interest was piqued; surely this was a sign someone would help her! She quickly replaced the note and stuffed the pamphlet into her pocket. *Perhaps this is my ticket to freedom.*

She must plan carefully, for all her pleading about the marriage had gone unheeded. Her father's decision was clear: she must marry the distant relative who had such power over her family.

As the day of her marriage drew near, she again begged her parents to release her from the contract.

"It's not possible. The Imam has confirmed this union to be of Allah and has given us his blessing." Her parents were adamant—nothing would change.

Skeptical of this information—moments before the pronouncement of blessing she'd observed the currency slipped to the prophet—she correctly perceived that money was the motivation for the blessing. Her parents were the willing and gullible target for the exchange.

Fretting and worrying as the day approached, she decided to do something about it. With the slip of paper in her hand, she determined to leave the only home she'd ever known.

Late that night she put her plan into motion. Hiding behind the cupboard, she waited until the day cook exited. Catching the door just as it was closing, she propped open the lock with a piece of cardboard. *I'll escape as soon as the coast is clear.*

Hiding some extra clothing under the hated black outfit she waited until the lights were out before carefully opening the door. Slipping through it, she found herself outside—unsupervised and free. She planned to go to the address on the paper and let them help her. It was a risk, but the only option she had.

Traveling quickly through the darkened street, she found Busr Street. *I've been on this street before: my friend Afya lives close by.* The nearness of Afya's house was a comfort to her as she matched the address from the paper.

Trembling, she timorously knocked on the door. Presently an elderly man appeared; seeing her black burkha he quickly invited her inside. "What's your name?" he inquired gently.

"Suja," she replied.

"Why are you here?"

Presenting the slip of paper she'd found, she answered boldly,

"I want to be free."

Pausing for a long moment as he stared at the paper, the man struggled with the situation before him: though he wanted to help her as he'd helped others, to harbor an underage Muslim girl was very dangerous; if caught, the penalty would certainly be death.

"You must return to your father quickly."

"Please, sir . . ." She began to cry.

"This could be very dangerous for you," he warned. "I can't help you."

He firmly opened the door. With her dreams of freedom shattered, she searched in the darkness for Afya's house.

Peering through Afya's darkened window, she realized the lateness of the hour. *What to do?* Sitting as close to the house as possible she wrapped the thick burkha around her to keep warm. *Tomorrow, I must find refuge.*

As the first rays of morning sun appeared, Suja tapped the window to wake Afya. Reaching through the bars to hold her hand for a moment Afya responded, whispering, "How can I help you? I'm also a prisoner."

Worried sick, Suja realized she had to return home. *I've no other option.* Walking quickly she gained entry through the kitchen door just as she had left it. Inside, she found her parents pacing the floor.

"Where've you been?" demanded her father

"I . . . went to my friend's house."

"Who?"

"Afya."

"Of course I'll verify this. Is that all?"

"Yes."

"You're lying. You were out all night?"

"I couldn't see her address in the dark."

"I don't believe you. Where else did you go?"

"I can't remember."

"You don't remember? You'd better remember!"

"It was to an address I found, but I didn't know the people there." With that admission, the scowl on her father's face became dark.

"Husam will not be happy. We haven't done our duty to protect you from the influences of the world. If he finds out about your night out, I fear he'll break the marriage arrangement."

"Good!" she screamed. "I don't want to marry him."

"That's not your decision to make."

"I won't marry him."

"You'd bring shame to our house? You would dishonor me, your father?"

"No, I honor you, my father. Please, don't make me marry this man. I don't even know him."

"Suja, he is wealthy . . . we've already signed the agreement. He wants to marry you . . . he paid a huge sum to acquire this contract . . . . we should be honored."

Panicked, her voice rose in terror. "What about me? Don't you care about me?"

"It was so decreed by the Imam. We'll obey the will of Allah."

"It was so decreed only after the money was paid."

With that comment, her father slapped her in the face. "You'll not scream at me. You'll marry him; this is my final word on the subject."

As her father strode out of the room, Suja noticed her brother Amdahl smirking in the corner.

"So much for your night of freedom," he sneered. "Now you've dishonored the family; you'll need to repent of your rebellion."

"You go marry an old woman," she retorted to his surprise.

Angered by the cockiness of his sister, Amdahl determined to seek revenge; he found his father in the study. "Our family honor is at stake. Does Husam know she was out all night, unsupervised?"

"No."

"Well, he soon will; then we must be avenged of this treason."

As the meaning of his words sank in, Suja's mother began to wail and her father's scowl turned deadly. "We must do what Allah requires of us," he intoned.

"My baby, my little girl!"

"Sharia law is very clear; a child can't rebel in this manner and escape unscathed."

That night as Suja slept, her father and brother arranged for the honorable killing. To appease their god, it had to be slow, it had to be painful, and it had to be a surprise.

Entering Suja's room as killers was not difficult for they had been thoroughly brainwashed by their religious law. *I'll show myself strong and do Allah's will.* Her father would be the one to give the final blow to complete the killing; her brother Amdahl would do the rest.

The moment of surprise in horrific disbelief in his daughter's eyes would be the moment the family honor would be restored.

Pulling her from her bed, Amdahl began the beating. Pleading throughout the night for mercy, Suja implored her father to help her. At last he put up his hand to stop the ordeal. *I'll marry the man; I don't care anymore.* Waves of relief swept over Suja as her father gently lifted her up and caressed her for a moment.

"Father," she sobbed closing her eyes in trusted security.

"Daughter, you have shamed the family. You must pay the price." Opening her eyes, Suja saw the knife.

Shocked beyond belief, she could only stare in horror as he brought it to her neck in a swift motion, cutting her airway. As she lay gasping for breath, her expression gave away her intense distress and surprise. Her soul was damaged beyond repair. Her eyes remained opened as her spirit left the body.

Viewing the scene in virtual mode, the roomful of demons erupted in gleeful pleasure. "Shareeka! Shareeka!" The screams of excitement were high-pitched and loud; there was much pleasure derived in watching the ultimate betrayal and killing of a soul.

After the noise had quieted down, Lucifer nodded in Lusilite's direction. "Well done, Lusilite." He looked unusually pensive for a moment. "Thousands more will die in this manner. We'll get them all, both killer and victim."

"All?" The excitement was extreme.

Satan's face took on a green glow. "Most all." He would not elaborate.

CHAPTER 15

THE NEW ASSIGNMENT

Wrath is cruel, and anger is outrageous; but who is able to stand before envy?

Proverbs 27:4

Craving more and more power, Lusilite managed to coax it out of his existence; he had learned well the hierarchy and different levels of degradation. Addicted to the pleasures of evil, he wanted a fresh assignment. Soon after the initial encounter with the opium smoking Imam he watched for a chance to be awarded an assignment with even more challenge and potential for Shareeka.

Entering into the deepest bowels of the pit for yet another night of revelry—fresh returnees now provided the entertainment—Satan met him with his customary snarl. "You again?" Satan observed Lusilite was getting a bit too big for his britches. Yet because he was one of the most effective of the demons, he let the irritation go.

"So you want something new, something outside the norm? How about the little mousy Korel? His half-hearted attempts in the arts of evil earned him a turn at being the entertainment for the night, but it was a lousy night; not much fun. He didn't howl and shriek like most of the rest, so we let him go back to his dull little existence. But if on the surface he thinks he's going to the other side, his return here would provide some extremely enjoyable entertainment."

"I remember him: the little docile angel who fell next to me in the great fall. I'll reel him in like a fish. When is his appointment on the surface?"

"Fifteen hundred earth years, more or less," was the answer.

"I'll start with the Shareeka immediately."

"Micordial and Elixer also desire this assignment." Satan gloated with the thought of what was to come. "You'll have to 'apply' after the celebration tonight."

Lusilite knew he would have to grovel, flatter, and do a few other uncomfortable actions in order to win the task, but he was willing to do whatever it took. Certain it would be worth the cost, he looked forward to wreaking havoc in this quiet little angel's life.

Later that night he easily won the assignment, as he knew he would. He immediately began the process that would lead to a mighty Shareeka . . . so elated was he, with thoughts of the grand betrayal, that he could hardly keep from dancing.

First he secretly followed Korel in his every move, memorizing his schedule and habits. Creating seemingly chance encounters designed to create trust, he began communicating using a silent code of blinks, eye twitches, and eye movements. Gaining Korel's trust was paramount to the eventual Shareeka that would follow. Ultimately this little angel would be exposed to heights of evil he'd not even dreamed about.

Daily the charade began, little by little the contacts continued until the point in time approached when Korel was to be born into the human world.

Lusilite once again received a summons to the depths of the pit. Crawling in gingerly—for he knew the physical dangers he faced—he once again groveled at the feet of his master. Finally he heard the words he'd waited centuries to hear.

"It's time to let Korel know the plan. Lead him to the tunnel; centrifugal force will suck him to the surface, but you must enter in just before he does. The earthly bodies have been reserved and put into the pre-planning stage. Ready to go?"

Lusilite didn't understand. "Where?" was his ignorant response.

"Idiot!" Satan screamed directly into Lusilite's face. "The test, the surface, the Shareeka!"

Trembling, Lusilite searched his memory. *Is there something I've missed?*

"Your own earth test . . . did you think you could bypass it?[113] Even I can't do that." Satan's voice was calm now, though Lusilite noticed the extra irritability in his words. *What information is he concealing?*

"I'll lead him to the tunnel tonight," Lusilite managed to speak.

"Don't fail me," Satan warned as he muttered something about "the antichrist" and "false prophet" and "the new messiah" under his breath.[114]

---

[113] See Acts 17:26-31

[114] 1 John 2:18, Rev 16:13; 19:20.

Bowing while exiting, the uncomprehending Lusilite at least understood his own "earth test" would occur simultaneously to Korel's. His memories of the abyss would be erased during that span, but Lusilite was non-the-less confident in his finely honed abilities to bring Korel victoriously back to its depths.

The fact both would be born into the same family would provide Lusilite the opportunity to influence Korel's decisions and undermine his every effort to learn truth from the other side.

That night Lusilite entered the tunnel a millisecond before Korel, making him three years and twelve days his elder in earth years.

Lusilite's test as mankind had officially begun.

CHAPTER 16

EARTH SPAN

We ourselves also were sometimes foolish, disobedient, deceived, serving various lusts and pleasures, living in malice and envy, hateful, and hating one another.

Titus 3:3

"*I hate her.*" Lucy said this often to herself in reference to her younger sister Karli. A crybaby, clingy and innocent, there was something about her that just made Lucy want to hit her—and she often did. From her babyhood on she found ways to make her life miserable.

Karli would cry . . . oh how Lucy enjoyed that! When she could she'd run to mama, not able to tell her what was wrong. Playing the innocent, Lucy could always lie her way out of anything.

Growing older, Lucy very quickly learned to turn any situation around. Making up believable stories she discovered how to effectively make her younger sister look the fool! And names—she could think of the most awful ones to call her, yet claim it was she who said them. It became a game: how many ways could she deceive Karli, and make her life wretched?

Successfully manipulating and controlling those around her was a powerful feeling. Lucy could affect their destinies, friends, decisions and even choices as to marriage partners. Lying was, after all, a sort of talent. In order to be effective at it, one had to be believable. *Get the right expressions on my face, use the correct tone of voice, add a little flattery, then show sorrow and pain at the right times so a sense of pity is ignited.* It was a fun and challenging game; soon it turned into a powerful obsession.

Though Lucy's daily abuse became addictive, sometimes her conscience would prick her . . . especially when making Karli believe she was on her side. Yet, it was so fun—Karli was so gullible! Lucy had no regrets . . . at least not for long.

The times when her conscience bothered her (it was a nuisance having one at all), she learned to ignore it. Only once did she permit it to trigger a response: One day Karli was sick at school and had been crying; her face was beet red. Seeing Lucy in the crowded cafeteria, six-year-old Karli reached out her hands toward her. Without thinking Lucy hurried to her side, bringing her a cup of cold water. As Karli looked at her with trusting, loving eyes, Lucy was proud of herself; for the first time she had been truly kind to her little sister. She never let Karli forget it, either.

Other than that incident, Lucy was determined to get every selfish perk she could out of life; it was up for grabs. Take from Karli? Part of the challenge. When they would both get things for Christmas, Lucy always ended up having it all. She could easily manipulate the trusting Karli, for Lucy often reminded her that she was the only one who truly cared about her.

When Lucy caused Karli to be punished unfairly, she'd blame their father, saying he's "mentally sick." Taking her Christmas candy was also easy: just complain, "Dad took my candy too." Yet, Lucy would warn Karli not to say anything: "Remember Dad's bad temper? He'll spank you if you upset him." Karli always believed her as she'd been unjustly spanked many times before. What power Lucy felt over Karli!

Later attempts to "even the score"—for Lucy had grown insanely jealous of the beautiful teenage Karli—included stealing her diaries and music books, secretly spitting in her drinks and even putting pieces of ground up rat poison in her food. Though often suffering from stomachaches, Karli never had a clue as to why.

Life was good for a season: Lucy had the best of both worlds. All the family was so conditioned to believing the false stories that they gave her ever burgeoning tales no second thought. She'd for so long consistently made Karli out to be the "enemy" and their Dad out to be hers, that each accepted their respective "facts" as truth. *Stupid, stupid Karli . . . she never catches on!*

As Lucy grew older she began to worry. *Surely Karli will discover all my lies.* Lucy gradually distanced herself from Karli, beginning a new tirade of accusations against her to the rest of the family. Because she'd been believed her whole life, it was easy; they never caught on. But Lucy feared that one day her lies would be exposed. *The truth must never come out*! *I'll confidentially inform everyone she's crazy . . . then if Karli ever breaks her promise to me by speaking out, she'll not be believed.*

Life got more and more tense, however, as Lucy had to make up better and newer stories to cover her tracks. Eventually Karli matured, becoming exceptionally productive, which fueled Lucy's jealousies even more. As an adult, Karli became a writer, author and a composer. People outside Lucy's influence had respect for her, which made Lucy continue even harder in her campaign to destroy her.

Lucy's control was like a house of cards, one stacked upon another. If one card fell, all would fall. She determined none would fall. Controlling those around her, Lucy had to constantly watch over the allegorical cards she'd laid; but she was clever, usually doing damage control as a preemptive insurance. No one ever disbelieved her as she could talk her way out of anything. She became professional in the art of manipulation.

As adults, the situation had changed. Worried and caught within the grips of her lying sprit, Lucy's youthful looks deteriorated into those consistent with depravity. On the other hand, Karli became everything Lucy was not: beautiful, talented, kind, and successful.

The more Lucy tried to cause trouble for her sister, the stronger Karli became. Not understanding why this happened, Lucy eventually refused to have any contact at all with her sister. Her lies and slander appeared to no longer be effective.

Years passed. One day Lucy found herself beside the deathbed of her aging father. Managing to deceive him up to this point, she reveled in the fact he would never know the extent of it. As she dominated his attention, a look of revelation unexpectedly came over his face; Lucy bent low to hear what he said.

"Honey, you need to apologize to your sister." *What does he know? After a lifetime of deception he tells me this now?* She looked around; no one else was there.

Peering with the most hateful look she could muster, she bent down to look squarely into her father's face. "Why should I?" she spit out. He didn't answer, but closed his eyes to shut out her horrifying scowl.

Meanwhile Karli entered the room. Lucy glanced up: *Where did she come from?* Quickly changing her expression, she lied as she grabbed Karli's hand, "See, Dad? We're here together." Attempting to smile, she tried to accomplish her last deception to him. As he slowly turned his head towards Karli's direction, his dying eyes locked lovingly upon hers. Bewildered, Karli didn't say a word. The look of understanding on his face, however, said it all: they had both been deceived. Turning his head back to Lucy, he looked at her sadly before closing his eyes again.

This is not the last thing I want from my father! He has to believe me to the end! Lucy stomped out of the room without looking back. She would never apologize. *He is just an old man, a crazy old man. Yet . . . how did he know the truth before he died?*

After this event Lucy determined anew to never face Karli again. The power of truth was far stronger than Lucy's lies and it frightened her greatly. *How could one so easily discard years of carefully constructed lies only to acknowledge the truth in the end?*

Karli attempted reconciliation with Lucy many times, but was unsuccessful. Knowing Lucy also claimed to have accepted the gift of salvation through Jesus was some comfort to her, but the inner heartache was always there.

As Karli became more influential and totally immersed in her world of good friends and loving family she never ceased to pray for the sister she still loved. Dying at the age of seventy-eight and well beloved by all, Karli left behind a legacy of hope and beauty for the thousands she'd touched in her lifetime.

Meanwhile, when Lucy's tale bearing tactics could no longer affect Karli, she looked for another target to satisfy her addictions. She found one.

Lucy had two sons; the older one, Ben, was solid, hard working and trustworthy like his father. The younger one, Milton, was conniving and manipulative. She preferred the younger one.

Married and divorced five times, Milton could not keep a wife. The numerous divorces were fine with Lucy, however, for she wanted to be the only woman in Milton's life.

Ben, on the other hand, had married a nice girl—a girl very much like Karli. Jealous of her beauty and intelligence, Lucy was nevertheless pleased, for now she had someone besides the unfazable Karli to manipulate and control. Her jealous obsession against her sister slowly transferred to her daughter-in-law.

Emma, though smart, was a quiet, self-conscience little thing. Mousy, with not a thought to call her own, she was submissive to a fault. Lucy took pains to try to get the quiet girl into an argument, even becoming verbally stupid in her abusiveness, but Emma never fell for the bait and always treated her mother-in-law with respect. *What a chump.*

Scheming with Milton for dishonest transfer and control of her husband's estate she created as much stress and anxiety as she could throughout the years to honest Ben and trusting Emma.

As the years passed, Lucy aged into a whining old lady. Never satisfied nor having thoughts about the eternal future, she fixated only on the gratification she felt as Milton brought their secretive schemes to fruition.

Years later Lucy lay in a hospice bed grinning to herself. She had won after all—not against her sister, but over Emma. The hatred she felt toward her was strong.

"She thinks she's better than the rest of us," she fumed to the nurse, "so then, why did she marry my son?" The question was never answered, but it didn't matter; Emma had served her well in replacing Karli as a target. It had been entertaining . . . Emma was also gullible! It didn't matter what abuse Lucy dished out, Emma acted as though she believed her, honored her and valued her opinion. Though Lucy made hurtful and unkind remarks, Emma always answered graciously and kindly. Her gentleness caused Lucy to hate her even more!

"But I've defeated her," Lucy continued. "She'll see . . .

Milton understands me, flatters me, makes me feel good. I've given it all to him; but that was part of the deal: I scammed for the money; he had the wit to get it from me.

Ben and Emma are not much fun, though I can depend upon them when I need help. Still, I favor Milton; with his spending habits and taste for alcohol, he enjoys spending the fruits of other people's labors. Together we worked with corrupt attorneys to cheat the system as well as to scam it for all we could get. I trained him well!

Ben chose not to do things my way; He paid his taxes, went to church . . . but so did I. It was an amusing game to stir things up . . . complaining to one, demanding from another, spreading rumors, causing chaos and quarrels. I played it very well." Remembering the church uproar she had created by her talebearing stories caused her to smirk in pleasure again.

The nurse left for a moment then returned. She was smiling, yet Lucy felt a coldness breeze over her. "You're dehydrated," she said as she adjusted the IV attached to her vein.

"I've given my power of attorney to my youngest," Lucy's rambling continued. "He's also my executor, my medical power of attorney, and the only one in my will. Declaring my husband incompetent before he died, we got the will changed and orchestrated together the transfer of all my assets to him," she related proudly.

"I'd waited years for the money. It was infuriating! Ten years older than I, but he wouldn't die, no matter how badly I starved and abused him. Milton took care of it for me though: no blanket, open window, pneumonia, refusal of antibiotics—need I say more?"

Enjoying the attentiveness of the nurse, Lucy continued; "I feel no regret . . . my husband lived many years too long. Besides, if he'd had his way, Ben would have been the executer of our estate." A little thrill shivered up her spine, for the memory of her manipulations even now gave her an odd pleasure. She was looking forward to when her favorite son would visit again; together they'd laugh about their morose secrets and legal accomplishments.

"Rest," he'd said with a wink. "Get strong, and come home. Together we'll enjoy the fruits of our labors!"

The nurse came back again with new medications for the IV. "Are you comfortable, Lucy?" she asked.

Lucy could only murmur "yes," surprised at how weak she felt.

Soon the liquid reached her, making her sleepier and sleepier. But something was wrong; inside her body her spirit was fighting to stay awake. *What's happening?* Mad visions began to attack her senses. All was evil and seemed surreal. *Where's my son? He can fix this.*

As she watched helplessly, the morphine drip was increased again and again. She fought frantically to stay awake, determined the drug would not overpower her. Finally, she heard the distinct footsteps of the scraggly-faced Milton. Waves of relief went through her; *He can correct this. He can make the nightmare go away!*

"She gone yet?" he asked the nurse as he entered the room.

No, I'm not! Lucy tried to scream, but only gurgling noises came from her throat.

"How long does it take?" he queried

The answer was forthright. "It's up to you. Have you called your brother?"

"No. I want to make sure there'll be no bedside communication. When she's past the point of no return I'll inform him of her 'illness'."

From her drug-induced state, Lucy realized with horror she had no power to stop what was happening. Gradually, the form of the nurse changed to a smiling demon. Her son . . . he looked like the devil himself. He was grinning profusely, knowing he'd cheated Ben and Emma out of their inheritance; his mother had taught him well.

Leaving her body, Lucy whisked through the air, stopping only for a fleeting moment outside the window of Ben and Emma's house. From the spirit world she observed Ben on the phone getting news of her "illness," and Emma on her knees praying for her.

If only I could have spoken the words I needed to say . . .

Chapter 17

Return to the Pit

*The heathen are sunk down in the pit that they
made: in the net which they hid is their own foot
taken.*

Psalms 9:15

Lusilite felt himself being hurtled once more through
the tunnel: from light to darkness, from freedom to
bondage. The scream within his head grew increasingly
louder until it was all that occupied his senses. *Who was
screaming?* Gradually the truth dawned: it was he.

Exiting the tunnel into the pit, Lusilite abruptly
remembered: he had been here before. As the dark glass
surrounding his memory shattered, he knew he'd failed his
assignment; his intentions had been to deliver Korel, yet he
perceived Korel was not here. Now he'd have to pay the price.

"Shareeka! Shareeka!" The crowds of demons were
aroused and excited over the new batch of returnees. As
the meaning of the words hit Lusilite, he knew he was
doomed.

"So now you've re-entered our eternity of death," he
heard the familiar voice snicker as his blood curdling screams
gave way to a whimper. "You know our agreement."

"I worked hard on the surface—" Lusilite stammered in protest.

"—You think you're special? Don't you realize YOU ARE MY SHAREEKA? HA HA HA HA HA! You little weak, ugly creature! What makes you think you had any power at all? I planned this from the moment you first got my invitation." Satan looked squarely into the face of Lusilite and murmured seductively, "Your destruction tonight will give us an enormous rush of pleasure!"

Prodded with the other returnees toward the dark hole, Lusilite began to shiver uncontrollably. He knew there was no escape; the violence would have to be suffered.

And suffer he did. After that night he was no more than a fragile shadow of a broken spirit. Though death consumed him, there was never a final moment because spirits can't be completely exterminated. He would exist in this broken state until the Day of Judgment.

Worse than the torture that night was the Shareeka he'd experienced. Not only had his favorite child murdered him for his money but Satan himself used him for his own pleasurable Shareeka. His soul was wounded more deeply by the betrayals than by the night of torture.

"You thought you were such a powerfully exalted angel? You were nothing. I used you for my own pleasure. I use all my demons . . . they all think they're special. You were one of the worse ever, never effective." The ugly words repeated themselves over and over endlessly in his thoughts.

Chained to the walls of that gigantic cavern, Lusilite's thirst for power and control was stunted, but unabated. Though the premise of his existence was all based on deception and fakery, Lucifer's grip still held him in sick fascination.

Why, after all his conniving, could he not obtain that powerful status he so desired? *What is the key?* He'd have some time to figure it out, for he wouldn't move again until the final days on earth had expired.

Existing in a hibernated state, Lusilite was aware of his surroundings—the shrieks, the torture, the debasement, the heat—yet was detached from its momentary horror. Hope? None. Yet in the recesses of his mind, he acknowledged that love existed somewhere. Would love forget him forever? He could only wait in the darkness, knowing he was where he deserved to be.

CHAPTER 18

JUDGMENT

The angels who kept not their first estate,
but left their own territory, he has reserved in
everlasting chains under darkness until the Day
of Judgment.

Jude 1:6

The length of eternities in the spirit world is not the same as earth time, for time there has no beginning and no end. Though for a season mankind cannot understand the concept of timelessness, it will be clear upon their re-entry to eternity. It isn't that time stands still, or that all are in a state of suspended animation; there are events and seasons in Heaven as well as memories, joys and pleasure that mark the passing of eras.

As the age of mankind ended, once again the gates to Hell were opened and chains were unlocked; Judgment Day had arrived.[115] The ANCIENT OF DAYS had decreed everyone except the "redeemed" would be judged according to their earthly deeds as to which god they had chosen to

---

[115] Matt 12:36, 1 John 4:17

serve.[116] Lusilite knew there was no question as to his own choice, yet the smallest trickling of hope piqued his senses. *Anything is possible in an eternal world.*

"Pinnac." As his name was called he found himself in the bright world of lights, the changed world of good and evil. The battles had been fought, and he was on the side of the defeated.

Entering the vestibule he noticed The Book; it was open, for the Mighty One of Israel had broken the seal that had locked it shut. On its pages were written the original names of every angel who'd previously been under Light's authority.

---

[116] Rev 20: 12-13

As Lusilite glanced at the open page, he noticed a black mark where his name should have been.[117] A small book of record rested on a table nearby. On its cover was written his name, "Pinnac."

The redeemed of mankind had already been transported to Heaven at the time of the Rapture. Identified as "the bride of Christ," they had now returned with their Lord in order to assist in the judging of the rest of the populace.[118]

As Pinnac turned his attention to the seated being at the desk, the radiance of this individual caused momentary blindness to eyes that had been so long accustomed only to darkness. As his eyes adjusted to the brightness of his face, Pinnac gasped; this was the one who'd dominated his thoughts over the past millennia: Korel, the docile little angel he'd tried so hard to destroy. *How did this little insignificant person achieve such rank of power and authority?*

Pinnac was astonished at this turn of events. Panicked and in fear of retribution, he attempted to avoid looking directly at the being, but soon realized it didn't matter. It was obvious: Korel didn't recognize him.[119]

"Put your hand under the DNA analyzer," he was instructed. Doing so, his earthly life rapidly flashed before his eyes. He saw the constant evil intent of his heart, open now for all to see. He was not chagrinned, being as he knew he had chosen evil over good before his earth time, yet he began to feel he'd missed out on something.

Power was what he'd craved, but this weak little mousy Korel had it! *It's not fair.* Whoever was in charge of handing

---

[117] Exodus 32:33; Rev 3:5

[118] 1 Cor 6:13: The redeemed will judge the angels.

[119] Rev 21:4; See also John 16:21-22

out power and authority had definitely gotten things wrong. He was the wilier, more intelligent, craftier being. *Why, why WHY?*

Nothing made sense in his depraved mind set, yet he had no power to change anything. He'd now be judged by the very one who had irked him ceaselessly with his meek and simple ways.

Not finding his name written in the Book of Life, Pinnac's deeds were judged against the standard of Heaven. Watching his earthly life play out he had no doubts as to where he was headed, but was surprised to be sent to the Cain house, a residence for all who hated their brother.[120]

Why? To be rehabilitated? This is God's retribution? He determined it was not a fair placement, and that he could lie once again to get himself out of trouble. He would blame Korel, *yes, it had worked on earth, and it should work now!* "It's his fault you got it wrong," he sputtered. He pointed his finger accusingly at Korel. "He's always out to get me." Dolefully crinkling up his forehead in an attempt to illicit pity from the ONE sitting next to him, he didn't consider he was talking to TRUTH himself.

"You chose to hate rather than to love. Jealousy ruled your actions," spoke the stern but kind voice. "You'll reside in the Cain House until further notice." With that the guards walked him over to a transport and accompanied him there.[121]

---

[120] Because Cain was jealous of his brother Abel, he killed him. See Gen 4:1-10, and Hebrew 11:4.

[121] Ps 66:4 states all the earth shall worship the Lord. In order for that to happen, the unrepentants would need a change of heart. See also Philippians 2:10.

The Cain House was large, housing multitudes of "unrepentants." The grounds were grassy with flowers of every sort dotting the borders. Though the place was beautiful, it was not Heaven. The redeemed of the fallen had already claimed their heavenly estates but he could not; only those who'd accepted the free gift of salvation while living on the surface could return to claim them once again.[122]

Lusilite was assigned to Jeric, a small angel who seemed rather frail. His smile was wide and friendly, however, and there was an aura of peace about him. Lusilite immediately didn't like him . . . but he had never really "liked" anyone.

Yet Jeric's friendliness took Lusilite by surprise; he was comfortable in his presence, as if he'd known him before. They hit it off as much as they could and Pinnac seemed to relax a bit about his predicament. He surmised he could not only influence and manipulate this little angel but overpower him as well.

Yes, he is the right one for me.

---

[122] See Isa 51:11 and Rev. 5:9

CHAPTER 19

THERAPY

You have ordained them for judgment; and established them for correction.

Habakkuk 1: 2

Entering into the large building, Lusilite joined other sad individuals like himself. "Watch out for the vial," muttered one who was obviously having a hard time with the therapy sessions. Not understanding what he meant Lusilite determined to not be swayed from his belief in the supremacy of evil.

Noticing the running drinking fountains conveniently placed on one side of the inner court, his guard asked him "Would you like a drink of water?" Lusilite had not considered the place would be so accommodating.

Shuffling to the fountains, he tasted the water: it was good, it was sweet, and it was wet. His dry parched tongue immediately reacted to the pleasant cold wetness of the liquid. *How invigorating a drink of water can be!*

Drinking long and deep, he eventually lifted his head. Noticing the flowers again, he began to wonder about the place. *Is this really the place where I'm supposed to be? What's the catch?* Lusilite knew he didn't deserve the kindness offered him, so expected at any time to be confronted, accused and abused; after all, wasn't this the expected protocol? This was how things worked in Hell, providing fun and enjoyment for the masses when one was caught thinking hopeful thoughts. *This is only a test; I must not give in to this*, he determined within himself.

His deluded thoughts still continued to lie to him, giving him hope of power and control in the evil side. *Lucifer will reign*, he told himself. *I'll be there with him, next in power.* These words, burned deeply within his psyche, controlled every decision and thought he made.

Hobbling with difficulty, Lusilite shuddered with delight at his own pain . . . . he would need lots of therapy to recover his soul.

Soon Jeric arrived, bringing with him more life-giving sustenance. Eating made Lusilite feel better. Though the kindness was unwelcome and seemed weak, this was how all the earth now lived, and he had no choice but to comply with its standards.

Though life was insistently pleasant, he remained skeptical, knowing he was in enemy territory. Realizing the final battle still lay ahead, he believed the force of evil would win—for the practice of evil not only created unique entertainment, but was also pleasurably addictive; he feared that no being would ever be able to ultimately overcome its pull. *Why can't they see evil will ultimately triumph over good?*

Most of the detainees at the Cain House were unrepentants like himself. Occasionally there'd be one who turned from his evil ways, joining those who'd chosen goodness over evil. Yet Lusilite felt certain they'd be drawn back to the dark side.

Jeric, the only one who visited him on a regular basis continually attempted to make small changes to his way of thinking. One day Jeric arrived with some new information.

"Pinnac, it is time to take you to the place of the archives." Lusilite had heard about this place, as many "unrepentants" talked about their experiences there. It was a large structure where scenes from their earth experience could be replayed. Bored with everything else, Lusilite was only too happy to agree to the plans for the day.

Entering into the vestibule, he immediately challenged his guide. He wanted to view other things, something—anything—that would bring a rise to the pleasurably evil aspects he'd experienced in the pit. But, no, he was under the authority and guidance of this *weak and puny Jeric*. "Okay, so what do I have to endure today?" he pouted sarcastically.

Jeric motioned toward the chairs emerging from the wall. Sitting down in one of the comfortable seats, he felt it shift as it moved into another world. Oh, yes, he recognized this world; the world of mankind and eighty-four years of mortal experiences.

Settling back to watch the show, he once again prepared himself to enjoy the raucous chaos he'd created for Korel. Grinning to himself he anticipated the evil little thrills that would again permeate his body, arousing the evil pleasure . . . *wait, what is this?* The life he was witnessing was not what actually happened during his lifetime, but what would have happened had he overcome his evil inclinations.

Watching it was irritating, yet he was grudgingly fascinated. He saw his rise in power . . . *yes?* The elevated strength and wisdom he attained as he moved in conscious obedience from a dull beginning to an exciting authority.

His love for his sister was pure and strong; united in purpose they became a team that was unbeatable. Working together—Karli with her fantastic musical skill and Lucy with her speaking ability—Lusilite could hardly believe the rise to fame, prosperity and power they both were able to attain.

How could we become such an influential earthly force, one that could not be overcome? In reality the pooling of their God-given talents along with the sisterly bond had not happened. Because it hadn't been developed, countless possibilities were not utilized. *Why didn't I see this at the time?*

As the story came to its conclusion, Lusilite sat bewildered and numb. Though he couldn't accept that this is what should have taken place, something never-the-less began to stir within him. To think that he could have been so extremely effective and powerful! But because he hadn't been willing to overcome his addictions to evil, his life took a far different path. Even now he couldn't grasp the concept of changing in any way.

Jeric watched him carefully. "So, learn anything?" he asked.

"No," was his sullen reply. Lusilite was unwilling to give in any way to the light side.

Returning to his room, Lusilite pondered the incident. To be powerful through loving others and giving to them was a new concept. *Are the archives accurate or is it only a deceptive tool to convert me to the light side?*

His mentality was so used to lies that he couldn't bring himself to accept truth in any form; *I trust no one. They're all liars . . .* His thoughts trailed off as he went to sleep. As he slept he dreamed of the beautiful and productive life he would have lived had he valued his sister on earth.

The experience wouldn't leave him. He thought about it daily, not able to compute its implications. *Is it truly a fact? Have I missed out on a powerful and fulfilling life?* His delusional thoughts began to twist as he turned his anger from himself to the CREATOR OF GOOD. *Why hadn't I been given the gift of music, and Karli the gift of speaking? Why did power have to be attained only through giving?*

The memory of the betrayal by Milton was still painful. *Where is he?* Lusilite looked around. *Was he also placed in this place of torment?* Lusilite hoped in one respect that he was, and in another that he'd escaped. Overwhelmed and bitter, Lusilite put the thoughts out of his mind. He determined not to think about these events again.

Spending time with the "good" angels was difficult for Lusilite; seeing others who'd been bound to the dark side gradually change into their original beautiful selves again made Lusilite envious. *How is it they once again have strong and functioning bodies? Why not me?* Angry, jealous thoughts crowded out any logical reasoning he may have acquired from being in the presence of Jeric.

A DNA transformation process could change his degenerated body to his highly functioning pre-earth state.[123] Though Lusilite nagged Jeric about it daily, demanding to have the procedure done, Jeric explained that he had to appeal to the judicial team when his sentence at the Cain

---

[123] Phil 3:21

House expired. Only then would they make a decision regarding it.

Jeric imparted this information with some hesitancy and a perceived sadness, which only made Lusilite all the angrier. *Why do I have to live such a miserable existence? I've done just as well as anyone else here.* He kept his real motivations and attitudes hidden as well as he could.

That he and Jeric were not on the best of terms was not an issue; they'd never been close. Even while looking at the archives as to what might have been, Jeric seemed rather passive throughout the show. *Have I thwarted Jeric's opinions, help, and advice so much he's given up? What a weak little mouse.*

He congratulated himself at having given Jeric no pleasure at all in his assignment. That Jeric had volunteered to be his guardian angel from before earth time began didn't make an impression on Lusilite, but only made him more pompous in his copious self-importance. *As soon as Lucifer is released from the bottomless pit, I'll be exalted in rank and once again powerful.*

Meanwhile Jeric halfheartedly began the process of requesting the appeal, warning Lusilite that his heart had to change if he truly wanted to be physically restored. Lusilite insisted he could make a much faster improvement with a fully functioning body. *Can I lie my way through? It's always worked before.*

He would soon find out.

CHAPTER 20

THE APPEAL

Who shall change our vile body, that it may be
fashioned like his glorious body?
Philippians 3:21

Lusilite forced his mind to keep focused on the seduction of evil rather than the appeal of goodness, for he truly believed the new creation was the more powerful, and would ultimately win.

One day Jeric arrived with news that he'd scheduled an appointment with the judicial team. "Do you want me to go with you?" he asked pleasantly, knowing Lusilite's heart hadn't really changed.

"No. I'll go alone." Lusilite was certain he could manipulate the judge—as long as Jeric was not there to ruin the farce. Lying was, after all, his specialty.

Making his way to the headquarters was a painful ordeal; many stopped to help, looking at him piteously as they did so. *Is it really that obvious I'm an "unrepentant?"* It was evident, but Lusilite, so in denial as to his true condition didn't realize his physical appearance perfectly matched the reflection of his evil heart.

Hobbling up the marble steps, he strategized as to the tactics he'd use: remembering how easily he had manipulated the goody-goodies on earth he decided to use the same approach with the redeemed. *This will be easy: they're the same gullible wimps they've always been.* Words were the tool he'd use to get what he wanted—it didn't matter that his physical self was a wreck.

Crawling past the guard, he entered the large hall. The judicial team was in conference . . . *so much the better*. Slithering to the podium he waited respectfully until he was noticed by an extraordinarily strong and glowing angel named Jano.

The sight of this being literally took his breath away: never had he seen such power and grace radiate from one of the so-called "redeemed." Lusilite's experience with them had been, at best muted, for the last few centuries had been almost exclusively spent with Jeric who'd never been under Lucifer's authority.

Sitting beside Jano was his old enemy Korel. Seeing him in such splendor enraged Lusilite, re-igniting strong emotions of bitterness and jealousy. *Why is Korel in such a powerful position while I . . . ,* he attempted to gain control of his thoughts as this magnificent creature focused his brilliant eyes on him.

"It isn't fair," Lusilite spit out. "No matter what I did to you, you always came out on top." Pausing a moment, he attempted to get his pent-up rage under control; he didn't want to spoil his chance to deceive the team.

"I was to be exalted. I was to gain rank and status and be in a powerful position of authority. You ruined it for me. You ruined it all."

Lusilite waited to see what effect his statements had on Korel. Since the angel didn't say a word he assumed his guilt-trip tactic was working.

"It's my turn to rule. You've had a turn," he continued pathetically. Secretly congratulating himself, he generated the most self-pitying tone he could muster: "You've always had more than I. It isn't fair!"

Korel looked at him with a most amazed look. Finally he spoke, "Tell me your name."

Panicking, the depraved imp fought to keep his voice in control. Looking as calm as he could, he answered evasively, "You know me."

"I don't know you." The response was honest, for all memories of abuse and horror in the redeemed had been erased

"You know me!" Lusilite persisted.

Quiet for a moment, Korel then inquired. "Where were you sent?"

"To the Cain House of Detention."

"Why were you released?"

"Good behavior." It was a lie but Lusilite had hidden the bright orange band identifying him as an "unrepentant," certain the team hadn't noticed it. Delusional in his expectations, he readied himself to give a persuasive appeal for his physical restoration.

His addictions were so transparently obvious, however, that Korel didn't even bother to consult with the archives. "All liars will eventually be sent to the Lake of Fire," he stated firmly.

The imp shivered visually. "Don't send me there. It is not my fault; it's your fault. I should be in your place, and you should be in mine. I was to be promoted to the highest rank before you ruined it for me."[124]

"Who is your Lord?"[125]

"Je . . . Je . . ." Lusilite could hardly say his name. "Je . . . He got it wrong. I was misjudged," he whined in the most grating of voices.

"Speak only the truth," Korel commanded.

"I . . . I . . . I . . ." He couldn't speak, for he'd told falsehoods for so long he couldn't physically make himself speak the truth. Jano, irritated at hearing Lusilite's lies

---

[124] Revelation 21:8

[125] 1 Corinthians 12:3

got up from the table and exited the room. Korel directly silenced the whining imp and motioned the doorkeepers to take him to the "Lakeside Correction Facilities."

Lusilite wasn't happy about this turn of events; he hadn't even been permitted to ask about the new body. Angry at being escorted out without having made his appeal, he turned toward Korel and with an enormous effort, stuck out his tongue. Watching the departing rebel, Korel was slightly curious, but being distracted with his duties, attempted to put the sad circumstances out of his mind.

Finishing up the business of the day with the judicial team, he began to prepare the room for the next meeting. As he did so, his curiosity grew. The imp, though lying about everything else, had said something that struck a note of truth with Korel. "You know me," he'd said so ardently, with a tone of genuine fear in his voice. *He couldn't have faked that.*

Almost as a second thought, Korel got up from the table to examine the pathway the degenerate had taken. Sure enough, not far from the entrance was a small, black dot on the floor. Peering closer at the tiny spot of black moisture he surmised it to be a drop of saliva. Remembering the imp's blackened tongue sticking out in protest, he correctly deduced its origin.

Korel picked up the material with a dry Q-tip, deposited it into a small plastic bag and carefully placed it in the desk.

CHAPTER 21

THE DEFINITIVE
REVELATION

He is able to subdue all things to himself.
Philippians 3:21

Going to the Lakeside Correction Facilities for more therapy was not what Lusilite had in mind. Though he was more determined then ever to have the power and control he craved, he was now under the authority of the "good" side and had to do as instructed.

Entering the large fortress he noticed the birds flying, their lively sounds brightening up the surroundings. *This is new; I hadn't noticed the birds before.* Passing through the gated door and into the courtyard, he was immediately assaulted with the beauty of it: grass, flowers, shrubbery—it didn't resemble a prison at all. Children were playing in the yard, fruit trees were in bloom; the place looked like a well-kept garden.

Soon he was taken to a room overlooking the lake. Everything was provided for him; he began to look forward to each new day. The attendants were kind, generous, and helpful; but his addictions were so deeply ingrained he wasn't able to make a healthy connection with them.

One day Jeric entered his quarters: "Have you re-visited the place of the archives since your arrival here?"

"No. I don't want to view my life again."

"Oh, it's not your life you'll view; it's the life of Korel. Get up. We'll go together."

Lusilite's thoughts whirled. To see the life of the one he hated was an idea he hadn't considered. Grudgingly he prepared for the trip.

Entering the large red archive building, Jeric brought him to the room where the event would take place. Noticing the surrounding screens, Lusilite settled back to enjoy the experience as much as possible. Remembering the distress he'd caused, he was ready to enjoy the pleasure of reviewing it.

Unexpectedly, Jeric interrupted his ingratiating thoughts. "You'll not see it as yourself," he continued. "You'll experience it virtually, as if you were Korel." Before he had time to react, the buttons had been pressed.

—————————————————

I ran as quickly as I could. My oldest sister Dawn, was chasing me, ready to beat me up again; I had no idea why. This happened daily. As I ran up the hill into the woods, I could hear her footsteps behind me getting lighter and lighter. She had given up. *Good.*

I crept toward the forest opening, hiding behind a tree. I heard my mom below asking Dawn where I was as Lucy sat holding herself, rocking. She was enjoying the drama; for once again, she had orchestrated it. She'd successfully told Dawn another lie about me. Dawn always believed Lucy no matter how unrealistic her stories. She believed it all, sure that I was a little vixen who needed daily punishment.

"Mom, you don't spank her nearly enough. She's spoiled." As Dawn complained about me Lucy did her best to look sorrowful, nodding in agreement.

"Dad will take care of her when he comes home." I knew the frightening routine.

Hiding in the woods, I waited until dark. Even though I didn't want my mother to be worried, I wanted to avoid the ubiquitous whipping I was destined to receive upon my return. Finally the cold and hunger got to me. I had no choice; I crept back to the house and into bed.

The next morning my dad, after cutting a willow branch from off the tree, whipped me soundly. Putting my hand back to shield my bottom, I quickly retrieved it, for the branch left multiple splinters.

Life was hell on earth during my childhood years.

Why is Dawn so mean to me? I didn't know. I tried to fit in, to follow the rules, to obey my parents, but I was the one who always got the spankings. I never had a clear understanding as to why, but learned to accept them as part of my childhood.

Having an older sister who continually lied to me as well as to others about me kept me in a sort of limbo; I became rather shy and afraid of people in general, never really understanding the issues of my life. However the chaos caused my spiritual side to develop and flourish.

I faithfully read the Bible every day; we were encouraged to do so by our Sunday School teacher. As the Word became real to me I began to respond to the love and discipline I found within its pages. Learning to love and forgive those who unfairly accused and hurt me was valuable for my spiritual growth.

As I grew older I became stronger. Still not understanding the chaos in my home, I learned to accept things the way they were, and do the best I could regardless of the circumstances in my life.

One day as a young mother I went to a meeting at school. Shortly after I entered the seating area, Lucy entered the room. I saw by the smirk on her face that she had a little secret. Entering the parking lot after the meeting I noticed a long keyed scratch on my car. Looking to my right, I noticed Lucy's car parked directly behind mine.

Now, what do I do? Make a scene only to have her deny it and call me crazy? I decided to once again overlook her evil actions, forgive her, and pray for her. Interestingly enough, not too long after that someone sideswiped my car causing damage in the exact same place as the scratch. Their insurance paid for it all to be repaired; her evil actions hadn't hurt me a bit.

But the sorrow and depression from the abuse was real. It took many years to put the feelings into perspective. Expressing my sorrows to the Man of Sorrows, I learned to trust and rest in His love. Though not understanding why I was rejected and misused, I learned to follow His example of forgiving and praying for those who wanted to destroy me. There was no other option; the alternatives of hatred and bitterness were not qualities I wanted in my life.

So every day I found myself praying for my sister. Sure, the attacks continued throughout the years from my sister and those she was able to influence, but I learned to overcome and move on with my life in joy and victory. *After all, this life is temporary and the truth will eventually prevail.* With this hope I could continue to love, forgive, and pray for my enemies.

"Oh God, bless Lucy today. Help her to desire your truth. Shield her from the deceptions of the enemy. Let her know your glorious freedom."

"Earth to Lusilite, earth to Lusilite." Hearing the faint voice in his ear caused Lusilite to look up; he soon realized he was in the archive building with Jeric reviewing Korel's past history as his own. Enlightened, he now completely understood how his actions, fueled by hatred and jealousy, only caused Korel to become stronger and more entrenched into following the Light side.

He couldn't speak, for emotions he'd long suppressed came rushing to the surface. *Is this what real power is all about?—To be able to withstand evil by doing good?—To serve rather than to dominate?* Lusilite began to see things with a new light and for once his thoughts became lucid. *To forgive takes more strength and energy than to hate. To love the abuser . . . that strength could only come from God.*

Surprised at this insight, his thoughts raced within him. Reviewing his earthly thoughts and actions in light of what he'd just experienced, he realized he hadn't even remotely harnessed the rare power of what he'd seen: the extreme power it took to forgive ones enemies.[126]

---

[126]   Matt 5:44

CHAPTER 22

THE VIAL

*You know my wanderings: put my tears into your
bottle: are they not in your book?*

Psalms 56:8

One day Jeric bounced into Lusilite's room, a subtle smile playing with his lips.

"Ready for tomorrow's therapy? We're going on a picnic."

"Oh goody" sneered Lusilite with a yawn. He truly didn't like the little fellow, so full of energy and creativity in his therapy games.

"Here, I've got something for you." In Jeric's hand was a small brightly colored bottle.

"What is it?"

"Prayers." [127] Curious, Lusilite took the vial offered him. Turning it over, he felt the smoothly carved surface.

"What am I supposed to do with this?" Not answering, Jeric nodded and quickly left, claiming to have another errand to attend to.

---

[127] Rev. 5:8 tells of vials filled with prayers of the saints.

Lusilite examined the vial; small, elongated, sturdy and not particularly ornate, it had a calming aspect to it. Lifting it up it became heavy in his hand . . . heavier than one would have expected for an object of this size.

Turning it over, he looked for an opening. There was none. He peered closer; unobtrusive in appearance it didn't seem to be something to be afraid of.

Why did the unrepentant at the gate warn me about it? He had withstood the prayers while on earth, what was there to be afraid of now? He sucked in his breath as reason tried to displace logic. *Surely there would be no power left in any of these prayers as the end times have already come and gone.*

*A*s he looked at the small object, a warming sensation began to envelope his senses. *Is this the magic of the vial about which I'd been warned?* Righting it again he decided to wait before further trying to open it. Placing it in the corner of the room he finished his daily activities and went to bed.

The next morning Lusilite could hear Jeric's quick steps coming down the hall. "Ready for some fun?" he asked good-naturedly. Lusilite hated the sound of his ubiquitously happy voice. How could anyone be continually in a good mood? *Reminds me of Emma. Her happy demeanor had irritated me from the moment I first met her.*

"Sure," was his sullen reply.

Knowing Lusilite had lost his ability to fly long ago, Jeric took him to a transport tunnel. Stepping onto a platform made of warm compact air they were quickly transported to a bright and sunny, beautifully landscaped park. Exiting the tunnel, Lusilite squinted painfully.

"Uncomfortable?"

"Glaringly," was the sullen retort. Lusilite still could not get used to the light.

"How was your night?"

"Same as usual."

Jeric looked at him for a moment before continuing. "Didn't open the vial?"

"Nope." Lusilite glanced away. *How did he know?*

"Dare to be brave," was the bright response.

Ignoring him, Lusilite glanced at the others in the courtyard; there were some he'd known from his pre-earth days. All appeared gloomy and tired; only occasionally could he see a spark of life. Conversations were stilted; they were the final unrepentants upon the earth and all were in their so-called "therapy."

The questions arose between them: Where are the dungeons? The torture racks? The carvings and knifings, the amputations and tongue slashing? All the atrocities they'd expected weren't happening. This psychological game, in their estimation, was much more dangerous, for it created allurement to the light side; it was an entrapment, an enticement—the greatest of seductions. *They would draw us to their side with love.*

Love, love, love . . . the sound of the word itself drew a repugnant disdain in Lusilite's thoughts, yet he had no choice but to go along with the schedule for the day. He was a prisoner of war, after all. As long as he remembered this fact and hung onto his quest for power, he would prevail.

He knew the draw of the addictions and was adamant in his belief nothing could ever erase the powerful conception of evil. It was a creation that fed on itself and would never be conquered. He would endure until he could rejoin the evil forces, earning himself a powerful position of authority. He gloated on these ingratiating thoughts as Jeric continued talking. *Yak, yak yak!* Irritated, he glanced his way. *Does he ever quit smiling, this little punk of an angel who wants to take charge of my life?*

While drowning out Jeric's constant chatter with inward chatter of his own, Lusilite basked in the warmth of the sun and soon fell asleep. Jeric, understanding more than given credit for, joined his friends in a boisterous game of softball. Other guardian angels of "unrepentants" soon joined in, as the therapy session seemed to be in a lull. *Why not enjoy the afternoon?*

And they did.

Later, arriving back in his quarters, Lusilite's eyes once again focused on the little vial in the corner. It appeared so insignificant. He walked over and kicked it slightly, just to make himself feel more in control.

The vial didn't budge.

"Oh, yeah, play it smart with me," he muttered to himself. In a rage he attempted to throw it through the window but the vial only bounced back from the glass, light as a feather.

Perturbed but curious, he once again picked it up. Turning it over, he noticed the diminutive label. "Prayers for Lucy." He hadn't noticed this inscription before. Peering closer, he read the dates: 1945-2029. Interesting . . . the year he was born and the year he died.

Disdainful but begrudgingly curious, he once again turned the vial over. *Where is that cursed opening?* Frustrated, he flung it against the wall, only to have it float in the air like a helium-filled balloon, bouncing up and down in a causal, unhurried way. *What is this thing?*

Crazy with fury, Lusilite grabbed it out of the air, and tried to break it in two, much like one would break a stick. It didn't bend. Next he tried biting the smaller end of the vial . . . *maybe it will pop off.* No such luck.

Irritated, he banged the bottle against his desk until he was sweaty and exhausted. "How can such a little vial cause this much frustration?" he demanded to no one in particular. Finally giving up, he angrily threw it into the corner and went to bed.

As he slept, strange dreams of pleading voices and sobbing prayers entered into his subconscious. He awoke with a start.

Through the dimness he could see a cloud of fog covering his bed, furniture and ceiling; voices, many and prolonged were speaking: voices of parents, friends, and a particular one over and over again. *What is happening?*

The myriad voices continued unabated, swirling around him in stupefying passion; a certain voice—a small child's, the same as a teenager and adult—continued long after the other voices had ceased.

Crazy with confusion, Lusilite covered his head with his pillow only to have the voice continue inside his ears and right into his head. *This is madness!* "I'm insane" he yelled.

Flinging the covers off the bed, he attempted to grab at the sound, but to no avail. Dancing around the room, he punched toward the direction of the voice, *here, no here, now there,* it never quit. Now sounding old and frail, the wavering voice was barely audible as it uttered its last prayer. Insane with rage, Lusilite sat down on the bed, fuming.

Presently a younger voice continued where the older one had left off, praying continually. He knew this voice; it was the voice of Emma. W*hat is she saying? 'Protect her? Tell me what to do to protect her from Milton?'* Lusilite's attention was captivated; he hadn't known about this. He calmed himself in order to pay attention to this voice and prayer.

Listening quietly to the words, he saw the scene; Emma, kneeling by her bed while Lucy's body was in a hospice, dying. Milton had ordered massive amounts of morphine before entering the room. *Oh . . .* Lucy remembered the moment: powerless to move or appeal to him, she witnessed the demonic thrill, the "Shareeka" he'd accomplished. Greed was the motivation . . . Lucy had taught him well.

But the prayers of Emma continued. Loving prayers were prayed; though she knew her family had been cheated out of their rightful inheritance. This was an unknown aspect . . . *I thought she'd hate me—I wanted to beat her to it.*

Finally her prayer was finished. Lusilite sat unmoving on the edge of the bed. The prayers had been powerful.

As the morning light crept into the room, he once again noticed the vial: it had not moved and was exactly where he'd left it. Gingerly picking the object up, it felt as heavy as before. Turning it over he found not a thing had changed. Still not locating the opening, he carefully placed it on the shelf.

Something odd had transpired: he wanted to hear the prayers again. This time he would listen to all of them, not just to the last one said on his behalf.

Emma's prayer had affected him greatly. Lucidity . . . that's what it brought to his mind. That someone could love and care for one who'd been conniving and despicable . . . *could she . . .* the thought would not develop further.

Lusilite shook himself. Was he changing? Had the prayers affected him permanently? It was illuminating, listening to the private thoughts of others.

The next morning as he waited impatiently for Jeric's arrival, Lusilite could not purge his mind of the prayers. The little vial in the corner, meanwhile, seemed to dare him to pick it up again. *How do the prayers escape? Are they still in the bottle?*

Jeric arrived, jovial as usual. "Anything special happen?" he asked.

"As if you didn't know," came back the sullen answer. Jeric only smiled.

"No outside therapy today," he informed him causally. "Today you'll stay in your room."

With that statement Jeric abruptly left; but before he did so, Lusilite noticed a small smile playing at the corners of his mouth.

What does he know? He could only guess.

Curious, but still somewhat afraid of the vial, Lusilite finally picked it up once more. As he did, he noticed a tiny pinhole, no bigger in circumference than a microscopic hair. The pinhole was filled with a soft, waxy material. When a finger was placed over the hole, it gave just enough heat for the substance to melt, clearing the opening.

As he watched, a thin, threadlike cloud exited the bottle. Immediately it expanded, filling the whole room with a sparkling radiance. He quickly covered the hole, lest any more prayers escape. *One at a time . . .*

Listening to the first, intense prayer he realized it was the pure voice of his mother, giving thanks for her pregnancy and dedicating her baby to the Lord. *No wonder my secret life of lies was never fulfilling.*

Remembering the archives and what his life could have been, he began to weep softly. Something within him had broken. He had all this time believed kindness was weak, but now he knew: kindness was a killer.

CHAPTER 23

THE YEARNING

You are of God, little children, and have overcome them: because greater is he that's in you, than he that is in the world.

I John 4:4

The next few days were enlightening to Lusilite. Carefully, he listened to each and every prayer said on his behalf. The highest percentage, by far, were the prayers from Karli. Daily, even hourly, her prayers were spoken. *Is this why I couldn't conquer her? What is this power, this power of love?*

On and on Karli prayed: "Lord, bless Lucy today. Give her victory over her addictions. Keep her safe; bring her into a place where she turns to you. Help her to love the truth, to desire truth, let that desire be above all the addictions that keep her from the truth." He was struck by the sheer absurdity of the prayers, said so passionately for the one who loved to lie.

Truth . . . he hadn't considered it to be important at all. *Only what you could make people believe was important. After all, weren't most of the deals and contracts on earth racked with fraud, deceit and dishonesty?*

As Lusilite listened he realized his conclusions were not the case for all. Some humans actually did live their lives in truth, an unseen army of earth dwellers who refused to become part of the deceptive practices of their generation. *Karli was a warrior in her own right, praying for truth to prevail.*

Suddenly, a yearning grew in him like a forest fire. *Truth* . . . he longed for it; the prayers were working. . . . *Is it possible to embrace its boundaries of transparency and honesty? Can it really be a stronger force than deception?*

Listening day after day, Lusilite finally began to understand. Truth was what would endure forever; lies could all be exposed. *What kind of record keeping was this, to keep records of even the prayers that were spoken?* In Hell the records were false. Which was a better world? *I must not falter; I must not give in to the prayers . . .*

At last the final prayer from Emma was heard. From the first to the last the prayers were said with kindness, passion, and openness. *What silent world have I missed out on? Did I ever pray for her or anyone else?* He couldn't remember even one prayer, though he claimed many times on earth to pray and often recited perfunctory prayers at special occasions. He hadn't believed in prayer . . . his method of lying got him what he wanted.

Prayer, trust, forgiveness, honesty . . . these things took faith and strength. Why some on earth lived this way and others didn't was easy to deduct: some chose to do things the right way, others chose to take shortcuts. They actually didn't end up with the same result, as he had previously thought.

Sealing the bottle again was not necessary. The thin wax-like substance once again covered the tiny hole. *It must have an unending supply of wax built into the bottle*, he mused. *Who created such a unique object?*

Humbled, his therapy session continued; for yes, this was the therapeutic plan for now: letting him ponder those things he hadn't considered, awakening in him a longing for righteousness, and preparing him for restoration to the side of Light.

"I am the Light of the world. He who follows me shall not walk in darkness, but shall have the light of life."[128]

---

[128] John 8:12

CHAPTER 24

DRY BONES

Thus says the Lord God to these bones; Look, I will
cause breath to enter into you, and you shall live:
Ezekiel 37: 5

L usilite needed to make a decision. He was currently
being drawn toward the side of goodness and light.
But he was fearful; believing evil would eventually win, he
didn't want to be caught on the losing side.

Lukewarm in his attempts toward the side of good, his
decision was ultimately made for him. Sitting in therapy
one day, he heard the thunderous call of the battle cry. As
the noise resounded over the earth, a wave of demonic
energy flooded every unchanged heart. Rejuvenated in
power, he easily exited the facilities and joined the legions
of wickedness. His heart had once again hardened toward
good, and was focused toward evil.

Lucifer, recently released from his thousand—year
sentence in the bottomless pit, now gathered together all
the faint-hearted, evil, malicious and liars for his army.[129]

---

[129] Revelation 21:8

After strengthening his forces with supernatural power, he gloated, "Evil will win; evil has always triumphed over good."

Satan had seen this phenomenon first hand throughout his years on earth. As "antichrist" he was able to stop the energy productions—coal, nuclear power, gas and oil drilling—through his lies and manipulation of a gullible press. *Easy to fool, this world of man!* The only ones who wouldn't cave to his deceptions were certain conservative Christians . . . but he'd made sure their lives were miserable and their warnings and votes were nullified by the lies of the press.

Winning an election of power from the strongest nation on earth, the whole world called him "messiah." It was a heady title; he milked it for all the adulation he could get, even deluding some of the Christians of earth into worshipping him.[130]

Satan eagerly looked forward to this final battle; winning it would once again put him in power over all earthly nations.

Speaking persuasively and convincingly was definitely his strength. With silver oratory he encouraged his massive army to believe in his cause. "Change will be unprecedented. It is inevitable. We'll win."

But he didn't reckon with the powers of truth, honesty, and love. These so-called mild and weak attributes packed a power he didn't anticipate.

The battle of Armageddon[131] was quick and powerfully fought. Satan's evil empire was no match for the strength

---

[130]   Matthew 24:24

[131]   Rev. 16:16

of the righteous. His force of evil was firmly brought to its knees, his warriors defeated, and reduced to a valley of dry bones.

Suddenly all was quiet as earth's occupants realized anew that goodness and truth had won the final battle. The evil forces were nothing but a pile of brittle bones. Rejoicing for the great victory won, the armies of good began the arduous task of cleaning up the valley.

Korel meanwhile, sat at his desk in the Judgment Hall pondering the events that had just taken place. Because the warrior angels had done their jobs, his duties here were finished. He was looking forward to making the commemorative trip back to the highest Heaven, once more to be in the presence of I AM.

As he emptied his desk he noticed a small plastic bag lodged between the desk drawer and a corner. *What is this?* Peering through the plastic at the contents he discoverd a yellowed swab with a speck of black on its tip. Searching his memory he unmistakably recalled the case. *The unrepentant little imp who thought he could lie his way to power . . . this is his DNA.* After all this time, was it still usable?

Slightly intrigued—and wanting a change of pace from cleaning the room—he placed the swab under the DNA analyzer and waited. Watching the screen, he saw that the material was indeed usable as the earthly life of this creature began to play out before him.

Settling back with one of his favorite hybrid apples he prepared himself for the viewing. There was a fast speed button, which was the normal mode for this type of review, but the machine had the ability to slow down when needed. Racing through the pre-Heaven and pit eras, he slowed the machine down upon entering earth's time zone.

Watching, faint memories surfaced as Korel observed the events before him. The fact that all sorrow had been erased from Korel's memory didn't hinder him from re-acquainting himself with the details of his life. The "bad memory deletion" was a mechanism given to those who had suffered on earth to help them become strong again. Korel was strong . . . he'd been existing in a wonderful state for the last thousand years, making the few years as a human barely worth noting. Yet here he was, reviewing the life of the one who'd once caused him so much grief and sorrow.

Korel felt no animosity nor shame, but only compassion toward his foe. That one could live such a selfish life was definitely sad. Yet, putting it in perspective, Korel realized Lucy's choices were indeed her own, and she'd been as free to make them as anyone else who lived life as mankind. Yet, he wondered if the prayers spoken on her behalf could still be answered.

Korel's tender heart wanted happiness for Lucy even as he'd found joy in his own eternity. Was it still possible change could occur for her? *How?* She'd been given more therapy than most of mankind, yet had refused the offered help.

Pondering the life flashing before him, Korel instantly knew what he must do: find Lucy, and in finding her, find Lusilite/Pinnac. There was unfinished business that needed to be taken care of.

But where was he? Korel knew that all liars had been sentenced after the battle of Armageddon and were being sent to the Lake of Fire. Their bodies had totally been destroyed by fire from Heaven . . . only their bones were left in the valley of Sidron.

Clean up would be a massive task, one that wouldn't be finished for some time. Each bone had to be taken to the analyzer, categorized, and DNA had to be extracted and labeled. This process would be time consuming—but time is ultimately of no consequence in an eternal setting.

Preparing for the possible return of the degenerates was faith and love in action. Impossible? Not with the I AM. As a God who loves, heals and forgives, His desire of restoration would not be limited by time constraints. The price had been paid for all, therefore HE saw a potential to all being restored.[132]

These bones would walk and talk again; for this had been spoken by I AM through his prophets many earth years ago.[133] *The spirits: would they again re-enter their bodies, fully repaired and ready for use?* The answer to this question remained a mystery. Only the I AM knew the future.

Yet at this moment Korel held a gift—a solid sample of DNA. Knowing full well as to whom it belonged, Korel's mind began to work.

Would the DNA analyzer show where Lusilite's body now lay? Moving the screen forward in slow motion, he saw that indeed, the screen gave the coordinates to the bones in question.

What if . . . his thoughts began to rush by in faster and faster succession . . . what if he could take the bones to the plant this very day to have the body restored? Was it premature to even imagine such a thought? Was he judging beyond the boundaries of his authority? *Didn't the most*

---

[132] Jeremiah 51:7 reveals God's desire even for wicked Babylon. See also Philippians 2:10-11.

[133] Ezekiel 37 references the valley of dry bones coming back to life. This was a prophetic allegory referring to the restoration of Israel and not necessarily meant to be taken literally.

powerful Being in Heaven and Earth teach me to love and forgive?

His thoughts were not his own, for he knew the Saviors' love and longing for restoration of the lost was also his.

Looking once more through the record he searched for any act of goodness on Lucy's part that would justify a request of this magnitude. Looking carefully, he found it: Lucy had once compassionately given Karli a drink of water; this act of kindness would not be unrewarded.[134]

Finding the bones and taking them to the DNA plant, he watched in wonder as the cells divided and rapidly formed the body he'd previously known in another eternity. *Pinnac . . . Pinnac!* His body was diametrically beautiful, restored perfectly to how THE CREATOR had originally designed it.[135]

Korel again searched the analyzer for the whereabouts of Lusilite. He was in the spirit world.

"It's too late for me," Lusilite thought to himself. Realizing the foolhardy way he had determined to support the evil creation, he could hardly believe the turn of events during the battle of Armageddon. Memories of eternity in Heaven flooded his senses; homesickness overtook him, but he could do nothing about it. He was lost for this eternity, and didn't know how to come home.

But a loving I AM had not forgotten him. The price had been paid for all, and that payment would never expire. Searching throughout the darkness Pinnac's spirit was snatched from the torment and returned to his newly re-formed body.

---

[134]   Mark 9:41

[135]   Gen 1:27; 9:6

CHAPTER 25

FINAL DECISION

Whoever gives to one of these little ones a cup of cold water to drink, he shall in no wise lose his reward.

Matthew 10:42

Lusilite knelt before Korel. "Can you ever forgive me?"

"I forgave you long ago. Our loving Heavenly Father wants all his creation to return to Him; that will never change. Jesus taught 'What good is it if only ninety-nine of the one hundred sheep come home? The shepherd will go out and look for the lost one, and not return again until it is found.'"[136]

Put so plainly, it was easy to understand. *Of course the I AM still loves me. He is love itself.* Lusilite imagined what it would be like to once again be part of Heaven's domain. Pangs of remembrances stirred up within him. Could he really be restored—body, soul and spirit? For one brief timeless moment, he floated in that heady possibility.

---

[136] Luke 15:4,7

Looking up into the loving face of Korel, he believed his life could change. "I want it," he whispered softly.

Korel smiled happily, finally finding closure with the one for whom he'd prayed so earnestly.

Rising from his knees, Lusilite glanced at the other unrepentants who'd also been restored to their heavenly bodies—their reward for a single act of kindness done on earth.

Beautiful in their original state, he marveled at the DNA restoration. *What fun we could have . . .* his thoughts trailed off, for the addictions of evil were once again begging his attention. Tearing apart the magnificent bodies piece by microscopic piece would be a thrill, but even more would be the killing of the revitalized souls: with *new, fresh souls the moment of Shareeka would be powerful.*

The temptation was too much. Lusilite could not shake off the addictions of evil. As he walked toward the group of liars surrounding the false prophet and Lucifer himself, he glanced back only once. Saying a silent good-bye to Korel, his love-hate opponent, he turned toward the creation that had too long held him in its grasp. *Perhaps later. Didn't Korel say the price had been paid once for all time and eternity? I want to experience one last fling of evil.*

Bringing his attention back to the group he began to strategize. Which one could he catch in his grasp of evil? Which one would first give him the pleasure of Shareeka?

He noticed a rather delicate looking angel of darkness, timid and shy in appearance. Touching him on the shoulder, he purposed to make him his next target. Maybe it would take eons of feigned friendship, but that was part of the thrill of betrayal. *Shareeka would happen again*! He could barely keep his anticipation hidden, so excited was he with the new flesh before him.

"Evil, evil, evil—how I missed it!" he thought to himself. He would never get enough of the creation he had chosen.

Looking greedily at each other, the lust for betrayal completely occupied each of their thoughts. The orgy of treachery had begun.

As this pathetic group clustered together—each with ulterior motives for ultimate betrayal—the ground began to shake and move. A fissure in the earth cracked through the crust, dividing off such a massive hunk of earth that it broke completely through the sphere, sending the newly created comet out to space through centrifugal force.

As the bulbous mass broke free of the earth, it slowly began to ascend toward the sun. On its surface the inhabitants were unaware of the movement, focused instead upon each other and the secret plans they had for destruction.

The gulf between the righteous and the unrepentants grew wider and deeper until it was so great it couldn't be crossed. Though redemption had been paid for all, some chose to not use it. The gulf would continue to expand throughout eternity.[137]

Memories fade, the lost are gone; the redeemed are restored to their estates in Heaven. Only in space, light-years away could be heard weeping and gnashing of teeth.[138] Bodies broken, souls were being destroyed . . . but the spirits lived on.

---

[137] Luke 16:26

[138] Matt. 13:41-43. See also Matt. 25:30.

I, Jesus . . . am the Bright and
Morning Star.
Revelation 22:16

In the world you'll have trouble; but be
happy; I've overcome the world.
John 16:33

BOOK THREE

ƒOREWORD

How well can we know the mind of Christ? As part of his body, can we understand his thoughts, his desires, or his motivations? Jesus' spoken words give us not only a clue as to his character, but as to the questions we all have about life on earth: Why are we here? How did we get here? Why is it we can't remember anything before this span of time on earth? What will we remember when the dark glass is taken away so that we can at last see TRUTH face to face?

Who are the "Sons of God?" Why does the Bible call us "Sons of God?" Who was Jesus before he was "begotten" of the Father?

Hidden within the pages of Scripture is a fascinating story. I have attempted to bring it to you through TWICE SHARPENED, The Two-Edged Sword.

This account is intended to inspire thought and research into the character of Jesus through the scriptures. Though the story is Biblically based, the connecting story line is fictional.

For an in-depth study, keep a Bible nearby to check references as you enjoy the book.

TWICE SHARPENED

THE TWO-EDGED SWORD

By
Marilyn Olson

Book Three

For the word of God is quick, and powerful, and sharper than any two-edged sword.

Hebrew 4:12

CONTENTS

CHAPTER 1

THE END OF AN ERA

That search may be made in the book of the records . . .

Ezra 4:15

Korel[139] and Jano[140] exchanged glances. Best friends and closer than brothers, they needed no words to express what both of them at that moment now realized: the assignment was finished, the era of "mankind" was over, and from this instant their lives would change.

Joyful with the long awaited repentance and restoration of Pinnac,[141] Korel reverted to his childhood boyishness and playfully yelled to his friend, "Race you!"

Jano quickly accepted the challenge. They both took off running as fast as they could toward the housing complex where they'd lived for the last millennium.

---

[139] The story of Korel (Kor-EL') is told in the book <u>The Twinkling</u> © 2008 by Marilyn Olson.

[140] Pronounced JAH'noh

[141] Pinnac's (Pin-NAK') story can be found in <u>Dark Stars of the Twilight</u>, © 2009 by Marilyn Olson.

Shouting and jumping as they raced across the field, they were giddy with the knowledge that their assignment for the past thousand years had been completed. All their efforts had paid off; Earth was once more a heavenly paradise where HIS will was done as in Heaven. Millions of prayers had been answered, the lost were found, all things had been restored to the CREATOR OF ALL and Heaven was whole again. Only a very few in the outer edges of the universe were missing with names blotted out of the heavenly records of the Book of Life.

Reaching the complex together, Korel took the lead as he bounded up the steps two at a time.

"What's your hurry?" asked Jano, catching his breath.

"As if you didn't know," responded Korel. "Ziphotan, here I come!"

Jano knew about Korel's passion for his orchards located on Ziphotan. There he enjoyed experimenting with various fruits, developing new strains of apples and other exotic hybrids. It was a fervor created by the I AM Himself, and Korel was more than ready to return to his former life. "Ziphotan, here we come!" repeated Jano, with emphasis on the "we."

Korel paused a moment, pondering his friend. Jano had been there for him all through his difficult childhood on earth and they'd been inseparable ever since. Being assigned to the same judicial seat for the great Day of Judgment had been a bonus. Together with Christ their team had determined the placement of countless individuals who'd not accepted the available gift of salvation while on earth.[142] It had been a long and tedious job, with many procedures

---

[142]   We shall judge angels. 1 Cor 6:3

transpiring, but they'd completed their assigned tasks together.

Noticing a new message in their communication box, Jano stopped to open it.

"What is it?"

"The code to our next assignment." Punching the numbers into the tiny coding device on his wrist he soon discovered their immediate destination. "Looks like we're headed to Nexor."

Korel broke into a wide grin. "Okay!" he responded, for Nexor was a vacation spot highly regarded for its many enjoyable and unique experiences.

"As former millennial judges, it's essential to take a time for rest and debriefing," Jano continued reading instructions from the decoding device. "After all your residual questions from the past era have been completely and satisfactorily answered, you may then continue the journey to the Third Heaven."

"So, we're headed to Nexor not only to revitalize our strength but to solve unanswered questions?" surmised Korel.

"Do you have questions?" responded Jano.

Silent for a moment in sudden serious contemplation, Korel shook his head. "No, I don't. Do you?"

"Yes, I have to say that I do," Jano quietly admitted.

"Then, Nexor, here we come!" Korel would accompany his friend; understanding the truth about puzzling situations was a vital and attainable element in Kingdom living.

Because the two friends had been busy up to the final days of the era, they were amongst the last to leave for this debriefing necessity. The stop at Nexor was apparently a prerequisite to attending the grand celebrations in the Third Heaven, a seasonal event all angels eagerly anticipated.

Quickly packing, the two friends soon headed toward a small intergalactic skyper to embark for the trip.

As they entered the vehicle, they noticed a diminutive angel named Jeric running toward them. Usually happy and jovial, he appeared now to be in a somewhat somber mood. Nevertheless he stuck out his thumb in a jocular fashion, knowing full well his meaning would be instantly understood.

"You want to join us?" Jano yelled out of the cockpit.

"Beats using my wings. Where're you headed?"

"Nexor, then to the Third Heaven for the celebration."

"That's my destination as well."

"Okay. Hop in." Unknown to Korel, Jeric had just become aware that his earthly charge, Pinnac,[143] had in the end chosen evil over good and was now on the outskirts of the universe with the other enemies of the Kingdom.

Throwing his bag through the door, Jeric jumped into the skyper. Though burdened with his undisclosed information, he nevertheless flashed one of his smiles, for he truly had a remarkably resilient personality.

Nexor was located three galaxies away from the agricultural planet Ziphotan. Well known for its fun, parties, and delightful activities, this little planet was a popular vacation playground. Good restaurants, a buzzing city life, unusual entertainment and drinks of different flavors and textures were offered in abundance; it was an ideal choice of place to rest and be refreshed.

Arriving at the small planet they observed the milling crowds as they landed at the port.

---

[143] Jeric had been Pinnac's guardian angel.

"Didn't know there'd be so many here," noted Korel as they exited the vehicle.

Walking down the corridor to the terminal, they noticed a list of activities prominently placed by the walkway. "Hey, there's a three mile water slide nearby," noted the adventurous Jano. "Want to try it out?"

"I'm game—if you ride the zip lines with me," responded Korel, knowing the little child in him would be satiated by juvenile thrills within the hour.

Jeric, seeing some of his friends in the terminal, made plans for a later rendezvous with his traveling hosts and quickly bid them goodbye. Jano and Korel, after establishing the whereabouts of their rooms, grabbed their suits and headed to the water park.

The next hours were carefree as they hiked, boated, swam, and enjoyed playing the many sports offered at the compound. Rafting down the white water rapids, Jano and Korel rekindled their love for the simple pleasures of life.

It had been tough, evaluating their peers. Yet as judges they'd finished the task assigned to them while accepting the results as just. Some had not, in the end, accepted the free gift of salvation as was hoped. Though every opportunity had been given to those in question, their own personal choice of evil over good had made the final sad decision for them. The proverbial sheep had been separated from the goats;[144] the wheat had been gathered and the tares had been destroyed.[145] It was finished, and the division was accomplished.

So be it.

---

[144] Matt 25: 32

[145] See Matt 13: 25-40

After the hours of fun and frolic the two friends sat down at a well-known eatery famous for its unusual drinks. Observing their surroundings, they noticed the crowd: a boisterously happy group. There were many warrior angels, triumphant in battle, relating to each other the stories of war and victories of the last few millenniums. As expected, their unpredictable stories of temporary defeats all ultimately turned into triumphs for the Kingdom.

Standing quietly by the door was a tall seraph. Seraphim are identifiable due to their six wings and seemingly benign personalities. Created with numerous ways of seeing, they can take in their surroundings in an unassuming way without having much to say. Always content, these angels appear to blend into the background and are not much noticed.[146]

This particular seraph was vaguely familiar to Korel; he determined to know why before the evening was over. Mulling through his memory as to where he'd seen him, he was interrupted in his thoughts by a beautiful angel named Dawn.[147]

"Remember me?" Dawn squatted down beside the table, looking mischievously up into his face.

"How could I forget?" Korel brightened at the sight of her. Smiling, Korel acknowledged his acquaintance, having spent much of their earthly lives together in a deceptive situation. Happily, Dawn had discovered the truth about the lies she'd been told on earth and had found closure regarding the chaos they'd caused.

---

[146] Seraphim angels are defined with having six wings. Isa.6:2. For multiple internal eyes, see Rev 4:8

[147] Karli's oldest sister of her two sisters on earth. Though an eternal being, the feminine usage of pronouns is used to avoid confusion.

"Would you care to join us?" asked Jano. "Sure." Dawn sat in the chair offered and looked contentedly at Korel for a moment before speaking.

"You weren't the person I thought you were," she remarked casually. "We were Kingdom sisters as well as earthly ones. I didn't realize it then, but now I do."

Taken aback, Korel only nodded, for he knew what Dawn was attempting to say. That Dawn had not understood the truth about Karli[148] during her lifetime on earth didn't

---

[148] Karli was Korel's earthly name.

diminish the fact that now the truth was recognized. In the attempt to "correct" her, Dawn had abused Karli; she'd consistently believed their sister Lucy's lies against her. No apology was needed, but Korel was curious.

"Why now?"

"You were my unanswered question, the mystery I couldn't figure out. Why were you so successful when apparently you were so sinful? Now I know that I, not you, had been deceived."

"Lies permeated our existence on earth," Jano interjected. "We were all misled in one area or another. No one had perfect clarity on everything."

"When I understood the facts in light of truth, it brought tremendous healing," responded Korel.

"The heavenly record is accurate," Dawn continued. " . . . Just took me awhile to believe it."

"Thanks for letting me know." Korel smiled, as no more words were needed at the moment. As Dawn got up to rejoin her party, Korel softly sang "—one of the most beautiful people in the whole wide world," knowing Dawn was still within earshot. Turning back, Dawn bowed a curtsy along with an exaggerated swag of the hips in response.

Enjoying the banter, Jano hoped his unresolved issues would be clarified as thoroughly.

"Her issue was me," Korel turned to Jano. "What's yours?"

"Timmy Benito."[149]

"—one of the well-known tele-evangelists of the twenty-first century. I recall his programs."

---

[149] Fictional name

"Timmy Benito spent his life preaching the gospel. His ministry seemed valid: he spoke to thousands, casting out devils in Jesus name, wrote books, and was interviewed many times by Christian media. Yet, the words he heard at Judgment were 'Depart from me; I never knew you.' On the other hand Mac Slater,[150] the sex offender, was welcomed into Heaven as a mighty man of God."

"I remember." As Korel relived the scene, he admitted there seemed to be a juxtaposition of the two cases. "I've pondered this myself, how what was seemingly accurate on earth was so backwards at Judgment."

"So, that's my unanswered question."

"I see."

As they finished their drinks, Korel again noticed the seraph at the door. He once more tried to recall the circumstances but couldn't place him at all.

"Where have I seen him?" he muttered to himself, not really expecting Jano to know. As he again searched his memory, the tall seraph extracted himself from his surroundings and casually walked over to the table.

Too late. Jano was unable to remind Korel that seraphim were able to hear as well as see all that happened in the room.

"Jucola's[151] my name." The seraph spoke clearly—confidently—as if he was at their table by appointment. "You're right. You've seen me once before; it was during your pit existence. Do you remember now?"

"Not really."

---

[150] Fictional name

[151] Pronounced Joo-COE-la

Though Korel had forgotten, seraphim forget nothing. For this reason, being good storytellers came naturally to them.

"It was in the deepest part . . . Do you want me to continue?"

Immediately captivated, Jano and Korel answered simultaneously, "Please do!"

Listening intently, the two friends were singularly attentive as Jucola told the most fascinating of stories.

CHAPTER 2

JUCOLA'S STORY

Above it stood the seraphim: each had six wings;
the posts of the door moved . . .

Isa 6:2-4

Long ago within the massive hierarchy of Heaven the tiniest of details was nondescriptly put into place. A quiet seraph was commissioned as doorkeeper to the inner chambers of a well-beloved angel of Light. With not much to say and seemingly no opinions about anything, this tall seraph was perfect for the assignment, for truth be told, he really did not like to audibly chat.

One of the characteristics of this tranquil angel was that he had a memory that forgot nothing. He could remember days, events, times and places as well as every spoken word and gesture.

His name was Jucola, and he thoroughly enjoyed watching the brilliant angel named Light[152] conduct his many assignments.

---

[152] "Light" is Lucifer's nickname.

Often Light created new instruments of worship within his inner chamber. These would be used to accompany choirs and other musical events as an integral part of Heaven's joyful rallies. Dancing and singing praise to the ALMIGHTY of the Heaven of heavens was an occurrence that never became routine.

Though Jucola said little, his inner life was rich with his work. He enjoyed seeing the implementations of new instruments as well as observing the interesting activity that took place in Light's presence.

As beings of great status were ushered into the inner chamber of this powerful angel, Jucola inwardly chronicled the events. His memory was always busy as he organized his thoughts. Joyful in his placement, he had no desire to change his position to anything other than what he was doing.

Jucola, however, kept a secret only he knew about. Though he obeyed every directional given to him, he was not technically under Light's authority. He'd never been, nor would he ever be under his control, for he was under the order of seraphim that answered only to the I AM.

Light eventually found much favor with the FATHER for his creative works of music. As the ages swept by, he was given more and more of Heaven's masses to oversee. Meeting these new challenges with capable wisdom, he flourished in his new status. Eventually joining the ranks of archangels Michael and Gabriel, he, along with other sons of God, could regularly be in the presence of the I AM.[153]

---

[153] See Job 1:6 for Satan's access to the Lord and the sons of God. This access was apparently still allowed even after his rebellion and subsequent fall.

The fact he was found worthy by the Highest was an immeasurable achievement. Beautifully developing his gift of music, he repeatedly brought the masses of choirs to roaring praise of adulation to the epitome of Love, God Himself.

Returning home, jubilant after his first extended visit in the Highest Heaven with the sons of God, Light happily embraced all who came his way. Joyfully he sang and shouted as he danced down the street to his bright residence, for he'd sought long and hard to perfectly impress his Creator, and had succeeded.

"Congratulations!" he heard the pleasant voice. Greeting him was Jucola, the little noticed seraph who rarely caught his attention. Without a word, Light grabbed his hands and spun him around in a dance.

Amused, Jucola was more than a bit surprised with the spur-of-the-moment merriment; he laughed good-naturedly as he righted his six wings. Folding each one carefully, he meticulously tucked them back into place.

"It's not every day I get a 'congratulations' from a seraph," Light exclaimed. Jucola nodded a happy acknowledgment of his pleasantries.

Because seraphim angels have the ability to stand motionless at their post for an indefinite length of time, they easily blend into their surroundings. Consequently, Light didn't usually notice his doorkeeper.

The irony of his position was not lost on him, however, for though seraphim seem above rank to the general angel population none had ever attained the rank of archangel. Light was understandably ecstatic with the fact that he himself had attained it.

For numerous millenniums to follow the archangel Light served with rigor the I AM. With singleness of purpose he taught all those under his authority to do the same.

As he increased in ability and power, more and more angels were given into his care. His numbers of angels grew until fully one-third of Heaven was under his management.

Life was good. The unpredictable became the predictable, for Light was constantly able to put his creative gifts to use in structuring and delivering new forms of worship, music and praise. For millions and millions of eternities life existed in this pleasant and active state.

During this pre-world existence many subtle changes took place. Now, even as unfamiliar routines began to unfold before him, Jucola still kept an accurate account of every guest that came through Light's door. His position made him privy to details no one else knew; he could not only remember each visitor by name, but could also repeat word for word every conversation uttered in his presence. Jucola had been placed there by the Great I AM, but for reasons no one else remembered nor could have foreseen.

As the ages passed into immeasurable lengths, the mood of the placement continued to gradually change. Intermittently, Jucola would catch a glimpse of Light's distant look—one that both haunted and unnerved him.

These occasional looks, he surmised, were not ones of contentment, but rather longings for something else. Though he'd achieved the highest rank possible to an angel, Light appeared to want more status.

Jucola, quiet as a mouse and just as much noticed was inadvertently privy to the start of Light's deteriorating thoughts: *Who is higher in rank than I? No one! I must be regarded by my subordinates to be equal to the I AM. I must learn the power of THE WORD and use it to my advantage.*

The Word. This was where all power originated. Light longed to be able to speak so that the spoken became fact. He often daydreamed: *to have the kind of eternal, creative power that the I AM has . . . . to speak the Word and the Word creates existence.*[154] This thought grew until it consumed his every thought.

Soon the discontent in his thoughts seeped into his being. He dreamed of creating a new order, one where he'd reign supreme. Desiring to equate himself with God, he came up with a startling idea. Developing it, he schemed a plan to replace the supremacy of the I AM.

Opposites! A new creation with everything the opposite of good. The night of this discovery was for him a tremendous breakthrough. Much like a black hole is a negative to the movement in the universe, his creation would be a negative to the creation of good.

The Father is "love" so I'll be defined as "hate." The Father is truth, I'll be lies. He created life, therefore I'll create death. As he formulated his sinister plan, he chose a name for his new creation: "Evil." *Evil will replace the Father's creation of "good."* Excited about his unique conception, Lucifer[155] carefully schemed how to implement it into law.

Heaven is an orderly place where authority and chain of command is highly structured. Lucifer knew the Father would never break his own laws, so he worked within the premise of that organization; he used his authority to teach his subordinates his new way. Evil, he surmised, was

---

[154] John 1:1-3

[155] "Light" will now be identified by his real name, "Lucifer."

stronger than good, and with that presupposition, Lucifer determined to make himself the sole ruler of his new world.

He began the process by placing restrictive orders within the top echelons of the ranks under him, then letting those restrictions filter down to the rest. Next he sent out special invitations to some of the top leaders, as well as to those not so well known in his domain. Most were clueless as to what was happening.

Jucola's position was such that only through his door could the invited guests enter into the inner rooms of Lucifer's quarters. He could see that those summoned were not only loyal, but also naive as to Lucifer's true motivations. He also realized that his status made him unique among the personages of the conference that was taking place just under his nose. That he was basically overlooked was a design of his position implemented ages ago, long before any thought of insurrection had entered the realms of heavenly perfection. Now he realized that in the Father's wisdom he had set the boundaries in place if ever such a situation should arise.

He had seen much.

CHAPTER 3

THE TRUTH LEAKS OUT

—Bring them that sit in darkness out of prison.
Isa 42:7

The time had come once again for Jucola's seasonal visit to the highest Heaven. With no fanfare and not a shrug of a change from the routine, he entered his personal skyper and left for the journey. Within his memory were the names of all those involved in the treachery.

He mentally prepared what he would say: "Lucifer, entrusted with the well-being of masses of angels, has grown increasingly envious of the I AM'S power and dominion. He's created an evil force and has enacted laws restricting true worship of the Father for all under his authority."

Entering the highest Heaven he quickly transported to the throne room where Michael, Gabriel, and twenty-four elders were gathered. Bowing deeply before the I AM, he realized no words were needed, for HE was instantly aware of the subversion. The loving eyes of the Father were filled with grief for those locked under this evil scheme.

Michael spoke up. "The question now is how to restore the ones affected." The fact that so much authority had been given to Lucifer made this an extremely complex situation.

Obviously, the I AM was not short on ultimate wisdom and power. His creation of good would defeat evil once and for all. However the victory would not come without a price.

Michael quickly put the battle strategy into place. Jucola must return to his post in order to convey all pertinent information to Michael. The news of the insurrection would be kept quiet for now.

"Here, take this." Michael handed Jucola a small round instrument. "You can download your information to this device simply through the flicker of your eye." Jucola looked at the small device. Round, magnetic, and not much bigger than a small coin, he surmised correctly that he could keep it hidden in his skyper: it perfectly matched the other dials located on the dash. Even if found it would be useless without the code. Additionally, it was designed to function only with the unique twinkle of his own eye. It's true use would never be discovered.

"Be alert, Jucola" Michael warned as Jucola headed back to his skyper. "Lucifer's power should not be underestimated."[156]

Knowing his placement was important in obtaining accurate information for the battle ahead, Jucola once more headed back to Nexor.

Nearing the port of entry he was unexpectedly surrounded by Lucifer's elite. *This is unusual. Do they already know my true mission?* As he exited the skyper, he was escorted back to his post by two of them.

---

[156] Jude 1:9 The archangel Michael, during a dispute with Lucifer (Satan), didn't dare accuse him, but said "The Lord rebuke you."

"What's happening?" he asked.

"New regulation. Everyone who enters here must now be cleared."

After a thorough search of his person, Jucola was allowed to return to his position by the door—his true assignment hadn't been discovered. Though outwardly appearing benign, inwardly he'd become increasingly wary. *I must gather information while I can.*

One day a little-known angel named Pinnac excitedly walked through the door. As was customary, Jucola silently led him to the inner chamber; he dared not speak a word of warning. Motionless, he documented all that transpired between them.

Soon after Pinnac's visit, the top echelons of Lucifer's new power elite met to finalize the plans for the takeover rally. The time was set to coincide with the seasonal worship in the Third Heaven; no one would be allowed to leave the planet. For the first time in history one-third of the angels would be absent. All under Lucifer's dominion would be required to stay here and worship only him.

This is it! I must leave while I still can. Finding an opportune time when no visitors were coming or leaving, Jucola quietly exited the structure and cautiously returned to his skyper. The information he had was vital; he needed to get it to Michael as soon as possible.

Entering the cockpit, he quickly downloaded the information into the small storage device located by the dials. This was not hard—all he had to do was stare at the device for a moment in concentration. With just a twinkle of his eye all stored information in his memory became imprinted on the core of the tiny unit. As he punched in the needed code, he knew this vital information was safe and could now only be accessed by the warrior angel Michael.

No sooner had he done this than his skyper was surrounded by Lucifer's newly commissioned thugs.

"Treason," they snarled as they commandeered his ship.

Unwittingly, Jucola had become Lucifer's first prisoner of war—not because his true loyalties had been discovered, however. It was because of another reason altogether: his was the only working skyper on the planet.

Because skypers were programmed, maintained and controlled with the technology from the "good" side, the dark forces hadn't foreseen that their vehicles could so easily be rendered useless. All skypers used by Lucifer's subordinates had been de-programmed.

It was unknown to Lucifer's cohorts why Jucola's skyper hadn't been affected, but it was quickly commandeered for Lucifer's personal use.

Soon war of gigantic proportions broke out in the heavenlies. Lucifer and those under him were quickly banished from Heaven and fell to Earth; a huge barrier swept across the heavenlies to block any attempted re-entry. Eventually the core of the earth became their prison.[157]

Meanwhile, Jucola as a prisoner of war was bound and taken to the deepest parts of the pit. Shackled to the walls for an eternity, he soon lapsed into a state of suspended animation; he wouldn't be released until rescued by the Liberator from Heaven.

Jucola sat down. The room was packed with listeners, all intently focused on the story.

"What happened?"

---

[157] See Job 33: 24-30; also the story is told in detail in <u>Dark Stars of The Twilight,</u> copyright 2009 by Marilyn Olson.

"Simple. I didn't move until I heard the words 'It is finished.' The spoken WORD released me, along with all other prisoner's of war."

THE WORD.

The seraph quietly stood up, signaling the story was over. As the guests clapped in appreciation, he returned to his post beside the door.

So, Jucola had been a prisoner in the recesses of the pit. Korel correctly deduced that this is where he had seen the angel: he'd been shackled to the wall as a prisoner of war.[158]

Fascinated with the story, the two friends bid goodnight to the dwindling crowd and made their way to their quarters for some much needed sleep.

---

[158] For more of this story, read <u>THE TWINKLING</u> by Marilyn Olson, © 2008.

CHAPTER 4

AN ARCHIVE VISIT

There is joy in the presence of the angels of God over one sinner that repents.

Luke 15:10

Though the present was so magnificent in comparison, the Father knew that truth was the best antidote to the residual lies that were still causing unanswered questions. Some of the redeemed needed nurturing as they readjusted to a world where only truth was told. Others were still babies, indeed, having been "born again" into the Kingdom, but having grown very little because of one reason or another.[159]

Archive stations were accessible for the redeemed on numerous planets throughout the universe. These had been set up for purposes of clarifying puzzling issues regarding experiences on earth. Those of mankind who'd grieved missing loved ones and had come to Heaven with some

---

[159] A comparison would be a loving mother who cares for a small baby, teaching it only the things he can handle at each maturity level. See 1 Cor 3:2; Heb 5:12-13; 1 Peter 2:2

misunderstandings as to their real nature could find closure in these stations. Truth not only brought understanding of confusing events, but healing of them as well.

Most of the redeemed had by now taken advantage of this service. Because Jano had been busy up until the last days of Judgment, however, he'd not yet had the opportunity. Jano's unanswered questions about the judging process needed to be resolved.

Why was Timmy Benito rejected and Mac Slater honored?

The next morning before they met up with Jeric, Korel and Jano visited a branch of the archives located nearby. Entering the large building, Korel punched in the code for the twenty-first century. Sitting in the comfortable chairs as the screen came to life, they watched the lives of the ones in question play out.

In looking at the archive analyzer it soon became apparent that the "facts" on earth did not meet the standard of truth in Heaven. The "sex offender" had been falsely accused by an underage and very immoral foster sister. She accused him in order to hide her promiscuous past.

Eighteen-year-old Mac had been taken in for questioning, lied to and threatened. He was questioned hours upon hours without sleep; the interrogators were convinced of his guilt because of the details provided by the foster child.

Having been home-schooled and protected, Mac was no match for the manipulations of this experienced force. He believed them when they told him he'd failed a lie detector test and would absolutely be convicted as a sexual predator. They continued the interrogation with threats that once he was in prison, he'd be repeatedly raped unless he became a "wife" and therefore protected by his convict "husband."

Mac had been so scared that his first sexual experience would be a prison initiated homosexual rape that he accepted the untrue plea bargain rather than take a chance on losing in court. Innocent, he was scared into falsely admitting guilt and accepted the lifelong label of a sex offender.[160]

His life changed forever. Now he couldn't associate with anyone under the age of eighteen, including his own siblings. His probation requirements stipulated he pay for monthly lie detector tests. No longer could he pursue a career in teaching, but had to look for work wherever he could with the restrictions he had. His earthly jobs consisted of pumping gas and doing yard work.

As Mac got older, he attempted to recant his signed statement, but it was no use. His accuser, even as an adult, never found the courage to admit the truth to the authorities. Ultimately, Mac lived with the sex offender label and its restrictions for the rest of his life.

The evangelist, on the other hand, had been a deceiver of many. Greed had been his motivation for preaching.[161] He'd stolen intellectual material sent to him by the trusting and published it as if he had written it himself. His motivations for everything he did were self-exaltation, pride, money, and a quest for power and fame. He was, in reality, a wolf in sheep's clothing[162] that preyed upon the innocent, trusting and gullible. He masked his true goal with a fake humility while perpetuating a fraud upon God's people.

At Judgment he thought he could also fool God. "I've preached in your name, I've cast out devils."

---

[160] Based on an actual case
[161] 2 Cor. 11:13-14
[162] Matthew 7:15

"You've devoured widow's houses. You've stolen from my true servants. Depart from me. I never knew you."[163]

By contrast, Mac Slater had grown spiritually strong as the years went by. He was able to forgive those who'd lied and manipulated him into this situation. He prayed often for those who had treated him unjustly. As a result, he was able to genuinely minister to others who found themselves in similar circumstances. His advice and comfort, birthed from walking through the proverbial fire was accepted and received by the hurting. His ministry was strong as he helped many to find the answers they needed to thrive in the Kingdom.

Faithful to God in life, he was rewarded upon death with the words "Well done, good and faithful servant. Enter into the joy of the Lord."[164]

Upon this revelation, Jano's questions were answered to his complete satisfaction.

Anxious to get started to the Third Heaven, the two friends reconnected with Jeric, who by this time was looking much more rested and refreshed.

"All set to go?" Korel beamed to his friend.

"Absolutely." Jeric flashed his infectious grin. The three headed to the sky port, entered the skyper, and punched in the code for the journey.

---

[163] Mark 12:39-40. See also Matthew 7:22-23

[164] See Matt 25.21-46

CHAPTER 5

ON TO THE THIRD HEAVEN

[One was} caught up to the Third Heaven
2 Cor. 12:2

The Third Heaven was the place where, before the rapture, the redeemed of Earth found themselves after death. A beautiful, welcoming city, each of the redeemed had arrived with personal guardian angels to help them re-adjust to life.

"The beautiful streets of gold . . . I want to walk on them again," declared Jano enthusiastically.

"Righto," Korel responded with a happy twinkle in his eye, also re-living the experience. The unusual pavement, luminous in its golden hue, had caressed his feet as he walked on its sparkling surface. The buildings were also unique, giving musical sounds which blended together into a pleasant symphony as he walked with his own guardian angel, Nagee.[165]

---

[165] Pronounced Na-GEE" with a hard G.

These memories sparked in Korel an interest as well to return to that beautiful place. *My trip to Ziphotan can wait.*

"How was your visit to Nexor?" Jeric, ever the bright optimist, casually asked after takeoff.

"Illuminating," Jano answered in a word.

"Questions answered?"

"Absolutely. I'm glad we took the detour."

"I've also a question."

Surprised, Jano turned to face Jeric.

"You? I thought guardian angels have no need for clarification of earthly events."

"Usually, no. However, one thing has me puzzled." Getting the attention of both Jano and Korel, Jeric continued. "I'd like to visit the archives to see if I can discover the answer."

It didn't occur to Korel that any of the guardian angels would want to see the archives. *Hadn't they already had access to the events on earth? Didn't they automatically understand the facts surrounding each mortal? What information could he possibly lack? He didn't experience a sin nature or exist in a clouded state of reality like we did."* As he mulled over these thoughts, Jeric came out with a startling statement.

"I want to understand the mind of Christ. How is it he alone volunteered to defeat Lucifer on his own turf while none of the rest of us dared?"

It was an astonishing question. To know the mind of Christ . . . this particular thought had never crossed Jano's mind.

"Do we have the right to know?" questioned Korel. "Would his life even be in the archives at any rate? The archives were set up for all who'd been on earth during the long war, but does that include giving us access to the inner thoughts of Jesus?"

"The fact that he lived on earth as 'mankind' might qualify his life as accessible," interjected Jano.[166]

"I guess there's one way to find out."

Intrigued, even Korel, who'd earlier felt he had no need for an archive visit, was interested. Though longing to return to his precious orchards on Ziphotan, his curiosity was again piqued with something of much more interest.

"I'm game," he stated enthusiastically. "How about you?"

"Sure!" Jano was just as eager to explore the possibilities.

Jeric's desire to understand the inner thoughts of Jesus brought about another change of plans for the trio. The fact that Korel and Jano would accompany him would be his delight; for though his assigned Pinnac hadn't accepted salvation, he'd been able to rejoice in Korel and Jano's changed lives.[167] Their recent experiences together had deepened their friendship more than throughout the whole of eternity before the "fall."[168]

"The archives are available numerous places, but since we're headed to the Third Heaven we should watch them there. You ought to see the building!" The memories of the place suddenly overwhelmed Korel's emotions. "Do you remember the city, Jano?"

"Remember? Of course! It was right before the Rapture! How could I ever forget?" Indeed, it had preceded one of the greatest highlights of his existence.

---

[166] See Ps 90:8 and Jeremiah 23:24

[167] Luke 15:10. The angels rejoice when sinners repent.

[168] "Fall" refers to Lucifer's fall, not Adam's. See Isa 14:12

The Rapture!

Abruptly the conversation turned to this event. Also known as the "great catching up of believers" the experience had been so astonishing that it clearly left a deep imprint. The antithesis of "the fall," the catching up had been as joyful as the casting out had been sorrowful. It continued to be a popular topic of discussion among the redeemed.

"Caught up together with Christ our Lord!" Jano sing-songed as they traveled through the galaxies. Jesus was an incredible hero to the rest of the "sons of God," as the redeemed were now also known. Korel and Jeric joined in the song as they entered the heavenly city's atmosphere and prepared to disembark.

Not knowing how long the archives would be available, the travelers decided to make visiting them a priority.

Korel, however, first wanted to look up his old friend Nagee. Perhaps he'd join them. Opening a small directory he found the needed code and quickly informed Nagee of his location. Of course, Jano notified Rutsch[169] that they'd arrived. It had been over a thousand years since either of them had seen their earthly guardian angels and they looked forward to the reunion with great anticipation.

Exiting the skyper the friends soon arrived at the massive archive building.

The structure was unusual, with siding the consistency of sky and the color of a sunset. Surrounding it was an aura of light, fantastic in its color, deep in its hues, and intricately beautiful.

Approaching the building was like walking into a rainbow. Upon entering the sphere of the structure, the

---

[169] Jano's guardian angel on earth. Pronounced Roo-CHAY'

lights would warm them, then cool dramatically, teasing them with their sensations and smells. There was nothing on earth that could compare with the experience.

Jeric was most eager for this event. Though he'd not experienced life as mankind he was, none-the-less, very eager to learn the answer to his question. To be privy to the private thoughts, motivations and workings of such a great mind as Christ's . . . what an adventure this would be!

"Got your message;" a voice halted the procession. It was Nagee and with him was Rutsch.

"Hey!" No sooner had the greeting been given but the friends were slapping each other on the shoulder in jubilant welcome.

"Long time no see," chuckled Nagee. "Where have you been hiding yourself?"

"Earth. Just finished an assignment in the Day of Judgment for the Thousand Year Reign. How about you?"

"Working in Ziphotan."

Korel felt a momentary pang of homesickness. In this breadbasket region of the heavenlies, he liked nothing better than to experiment with new varieties of fruit. It had been a long time since he'd been home; however, the excitement of this present adventure more than made up for the delay of his return.

The small band of friends soon arrived at the door of the archives. Entering, they stopped in the lobby to look at the directory. There were many possible destinations. Jeric read from the list: "Creation, Adam, lineage of Abraham, David . . ."

Contemplating the numerous routes, Jano spoke, "Shall we start at zero BC?"

"No, back it up more."

"To where?"

"How about the beginning? 'In the beginning was the Word; the Word was with God and the Word was God.'"[170] Korel, quoting scripture, had a point, for they all knew the "beginning" for this eternity would include the fall of Lucifer.

"Okay." Jano typed WORD and turned the coordinates to the "beginning." Immediately the directory filled with endless possibilities covering an infinite amount of history. They'd be in the archives forever if the spectrum wasn't narrowed down. "We need to provide a specific point in time. Any suggestions?"

Korel immediately recalled Jucola's story. "How about starting at the point where Jucola sent the information to Michael?"

"Good idea." Punching in a few pertinent facts provided by the seraph's recent narrative, the friends soon found the exact place to start.

As Jano pressed the slight protrusion in the directory the floor began to gently move under them. Chairs appeared, forming a comfortable seating arrangement. Sitting down they watched as the presentation begin. Shown in 360-degree surround mode, the room was soon filled with the most beautiful story of all time.

---

[170] John 1:1

CHAPTER 6

A POINT IN TIME

The worlds were framed by the Word of God.
Heb 11:3

He stretches out the north over the empty place
and hangs the earth upon nothing.
Job 26:7

After receiving the vital information from Jucola, Michael called his warrior angels to the battle and filled them in on the recent events. "One-third are lost, clueless as to the truth of what's going on. By the time they realize they've been deceived, they'll be addicted to the power of evil.[171] Our strategy must be implemented carefully. Anything less than victory on all fronts is not an option."

Watching from the archives, the small group of friends once again witnessed the defeat and casting out of Lucifer and all those under him. It was a war of monumental

---

[171] For deceived, see 2 Tim 3:13, Job 12:16, Deut 11:16, Titus 3:3, Rev 19:20, Rev 20:10. For yoke of bondage, see Gal. 5:1

proportions. Soon the barrier to Heaven stretched across the Universe; the quarantine of the cancer was thorough.

Observing the details of their harrowing deception and banishment brought a sense of sadness to the group. Lucifer, along with all those under his authority, now existed in the pit of the earth.[172] Sitting in darkness, there were those who wouldn't have fallen had it not been for his calculated lies and manipulations.

We were slaves without hope.[173]

The scene moved to the private throne room where THE FATHER and THE WORD were formulating their plans. "We must bring them into the light—let them know the Kingdom of God is once again within reach. Seven days[174] will be the test. 'Mankind' will be the name of the newly created being that can house an eternal spirit."

"As humans they must each be given a chance—outside of Lucifer's total dictatorship—to choose whether to serve good or evil. In order for the choice to be accurate, all memories of former existence will be isolated into the subconscious recess of each memory."

"As long as they live as mortals they'll remember nothing. Faint traces of former memories could possibly make an appearance through dreams and occasional flashbacks, but there should be an atmosphere of safety within the families of man."

"Mothers will be created with a maternal impulse that is sacrificial in nature. Fathers will feel protective toward their

---

[172]   See Psalms 88:6, Isa 14:15

[173]   Psa 107:10, 1 Thes 4:13

[174]   A day is as a thousand years in Heaven. 2 Peter 3:8

wives and children. These natural instincts will balance out the evil that's dominated them for so long."

"Those with abusive parents?"

"They won't be deserted. I'll bring others who care into their lives—even affectionate pets—to teach them about goodness and love. All must be given a chance to choose their destiny. The TWO-EDGED SWORD can divide the intents from the thoughts; quick and powerful, the Word will know who longs to be with us, and who yearns for the kingdom of evil. At the end of the test we'll welcome our citizens home with immense joy."

"The pull of evil is devious as well as strong. Deception is a very real possibility, even for humans created without sin."

"I have a back-up plan, but I hope I don't have to use it."

"Let's begin." These simple words, spoken so quietly, were a gentle contrast to the dramatic events that would soon take place. The WORD was all that was needed to start the redemption process.

The sons gathered to begin the work. Earth, now without form and empty, was to be renovated.[175] A sun, moon, and stars would be created to light up the planet. The mission of bringing home the lost had begun.

LET THERE BE LIGHT![176]

---

[175] Isa 14:17 Indicates that Lucifer not only made the world a wilderness and destroyed cities, but also kept prisoners.

[176] Gen 1:3

CHAPTER 7

THE BEGINNING

In the beginning was the Word and the Word was with God and the Word was God.

John 1:1

It was a joyful bunch, these sons of God. Getting together to decide which planets and galaxies would light up the nighttime of Earth, they shouted for joy when the morning stars sang together.[177] This glorious creation was pronounced "good"—a fine contrast to the evil that had once invaded the heavenlies.

The visible heavens were lighted. *Now to renovate the earth.*

THE WORD planned together with I AM the designs for the project. Together, they placed the sun for upper daytime lighting; they added vegetation, fish, birds, and animals to adorn and beautify the surface of Earth. Not only were the orbits engineered for the galaxies, but also the trajectories of the protons and neutrons were set in motion. Setting up the precise DNA links to be utilized in

---

[177] Job 38:7

repopulating the earth, they put into motion the unique data needed for all living cells to divide and multiply.

All things were formed; nothing created itself. Every element was generated fully through careful planning by the Father and the Word; without the Word, nothing was made.[178]

Soon their planning included concepts for the training of mankind.

"We must teach them to do what's good."

"We'll start with the basics, for they've been so long ingrained in the practices of darkness that they no longer remember how to live in the light."

"They're coming into the world free from all earlier influences and previous addictions. They'll now have freedom of choice to find the path leading to the Kingdom of God."

"We'll make it simple for them. For starters, the first human could get by with just one rule."

"Which is—"

"—don't eat from the Togae tree."

"Togae . . . the flowered tree in the center of the garden with the appealing, pleasant-smelling fruit—"

"—the Tree of Good and Evil. Obedience to this mandate will be the one and only law."

"Perfect. Now, who should be the first to experience being a human?"

"Let's start with Adam."

"Agreed. So be it."

Adam was a good choice. He'd once been a powerfully righteous being; yet caught under the authority of Lucifer

---

[178] John 1:3

he had no choice but to submit to the regime placed over him.[179] He was a suitable pick to father the races of earth.

Once born into the world as mankind, Adam would be free from the domination of the evil one. By obeying the rules he could choose, rather, to serve the God of goodness. Those subsequently born from his seed would have his perfect adherence to the rules implanted in their inherited DNA, making it easier as time went by for those generations to make good decisions. He was the right selection to become the first human being.

Soon I AM created a body from the elemental dust of the ground. He formed it using his own image as the model.[180]

It's perfect.

Admiring his work, HE breathed into the mouth. As the lungs expanded with air, the heart began pumping and all the cells filled with oxygen. God's breath gave the body a living soul. Adam's spirit, snatched from the tunnel, completed the process.

Welcome, son Adam![181]

Adam had a swarthy physical appearance along with a gently strong face. Created with a conscience, he possessed a healthy sense of right versus wrong.

During the daytime Adam worked hard to name all the animals, a job his Creator had given him. It was fun to watch each species for characteristics that would spark a

---

[179] See 2 Tim. 1:9, 1 Cor 2:7, Titus 1:2, John 17:16, Eph 1:4,10

[180] Mankind was made in the image of God. Gen 1:27; 9:6

[181] Adam was a son of God. Luke 3:38

name. He learned which animals made good companions, which ones he could ride and which ones he could train.

Adam also enjoyed exploring the many caves and secret hideouts in the garden, often playing a game of hide and seek with his animal companions. But his favorite activity was to smell and taste all the interesting food from the fruit trees and numerous plants. Crushing some types of produce to make oils and juices, grinding others for flours and experimenting with different combinations of ingredients was a delight of which he never got tired. Life was not dull in the garden!

Interacting with the animals was certainly interesting. He continually worked to discover what each was capable of doing—teaching new tricks to some while harnessing and utilizing the strength of others. Given the job of caring for the garden as well as naming the animals, his life on earth was busy and rich with wonder.

Each evening the I AM would meet with Adam to discuss his day. These times of debriefing and fellowship were great enjoyment for both of them.

It wasn't long, however, until Adam noticed something amiss: each of the creatures in the garden had a special mate. He had none. Howbeit, in earth years he was still very young. God in His wisdom let him finish out his youth before moving to a more mature level.

One evening after their walk together through the garden, Adam heard the pleasant words, "I have a surprise for you."

"What is it?"

"You'll find out tomorrow."

That night Adam was awake a bit longer than normal, pondering the mystery of the secret surprise. *What can it be?* He'd been given many surprises since the beginning, the last being a little puppy that was the delight of his life. *Maybe a new species of animal to discover and name?*

Still excited, Adam suddenly fell into a deep, God-induced sleep.

Upon waking the next morning, still groggy and experiencing a slight twinge from a recent surgical removal of one of his ribs, he saw sleeping quietly beside him a beautiful human, not unlike himself, but yes, quite different.

Being logical in his thinking as well as intelligent, he soon put the pieces together as to whom she belonged and why she was there. Staring at the sleeping beauty beside him he thought long and hard about what name to call her. He finally settled upon the name "Eve." She would be the mother of all their descendants.

Eve, child-like and a bit naïve, had a personality opposite from the insuppressible Adam. She liked flowers and shiny, pretty things. She cared about how her hair looked each day. She also liked to decorate, and had a nesting instinct.

Adam watched in admiration as she organized an area under the trees into a comfortable and secluded home for their use. He had, up to this time, been satisfied with sleeping wherever he happened to lie down at night.

As he learned to please and care for his wife, he also learned how to value her differences from his own. He realized she relied on his strength, his wisdom and his leadership.

Now each evening both would enjoy the fellowship of their Heavenly Father. Shortly before the meetings, Eve would occasionally pick a flower to put into her long golden hair "for the occasion." Adam marveled at her feminine difference; he loved her with all his heart. Together, they learned to subdue the fast-growing foliage, making beautiful and intricate gardens out of the abundant plant life.

Though enjoying each other's company in the garden, there was still inborn within their spirits a dormant memory of their pre-earth state. Occasionally a nightmare would awaken one of them out of sleep. Yet, how wonderful to wake up after a bad dream to find themselves in this beautiful tropical garden, with temperature just right and nothing to cause pain.

As the young couple's days unfolded in joyful contentment, the unseen hosts of Heaven watched. The question remained unanswered: could they live without sin? The Togae tree was prominently placed. The one rule regarding it had been given: DO NOT EAT FROM ITS FRUIT. So far, Adam and Eve had easily obeyed this directive.

Though the tempter was aware of the test, he'd not yet made himself known to either Adam or Eve. His immediate goal was to encourage just one sin. This would get him a foothold in the world and with that foothold he could eventually regain total control.

The wily Satan wanted to thoroughly understand Eve's personality before he made his move. The hope in the heavenlies, of course, was that mankind's choices would always be made correctly, preventing sin and its addictions from entering the world.

As time progressed, the Togae tree, right in the center of the garden, was continually enticing the feminine Eve with its smell and tasty-looking fruit. It wasn't that she was hungry or bored with the other edible delights of the garden; simple curiosity drew her to it. Nevertheless, she obeyed the mandate, suppressing her desire to taste its fruit.

Besides, there are so many other types of fruits to taste and enjoy. I can even eat the delicious fruit from the Tree of Life, so I don't need to taste this one. She often stood by the tree observing its flowers and unique shapes. *There is, after all, no rule about just looking at it.*

Walking by the Togae tree one day she heard a voice she'd not heard before. The tone was silky smooth and surprisingly exciting.

"Did God absolutely say not to eat the fruit?" Hearing another entity was not really startling to Eve. She'd experienced continuous surprises since the day she woke up beside Adam.

Curious, she searched to find the source of the sound. Peering as close as she dared into the tree—for to even touch the tree was forbidden—she saw a beautiful, shiny serpent.

"Yes," she replied honestly. "We're not to eat it, or we'll die." *Interesting. Adam will be surprised to know there's a strikingly beautiful creature in the garden that can communicate verbally with us.* Conversing with the creature did seem a bit weird to Eve . . . she'd never seen a talking snake before. Her conversations up to this point had been limited to Adam and THE FATHER, so it was fascinating to get another view on things. In addition, the serpent's attractiveness increased the believability of his words.

"You won't die," the snake spoke confidently. "This is what you don't know. Once you eat this fruit, you'll become as gods, knowing good and evil. You want that, don't you? Eating the fruit will give you a shortcut to getting back to where you were before this current limited existence."

Shortcut? Eve's curiosity was piqued. *My mind will be open, able to understand our past as well as the details of why we're here.*

"Yes. As gods," he repeated. "This fruit is designed for eating; don't you see? Otherwise, why would it look so appetizing? Besides, *HE* knows its effect will give you insight into the spirit world you don't presently have. Taste it. You'll see I'm right."

The serpent, artfully expressive, spoke with exceptional eloquence. Lustrous and shiny, he was easily the most stunning creature in the garden. Eve, in awe of its charms, became convinced that his assertions were true.

So there is actually no danger at all? We can access superhuman capabilities?

She reached up to grab a ripe piece of fruit. It picked easily. Turning it around in her hands for a few minutes, she bent down to smell its aroma.

This smells wonderful!

At last she took a bite. Nothing much happened, although she did feel a small rush of excitement. *This feeling is pleasant.* Unknown to her, the dormant addiction of doing a prohibited act instantly grabbed hold and attached itself to her spirit; into her memory triggered the latent addictions of evil. It felt pleasurable for only a moment, but that was enough.

Not wanting to be alone in her discovery, she picked some more fruit and took it to Adam. *At this moment, according to the serpent, I'm more knowledgeable than he is. He's got to see that there's nothing wrong with eating this.* She picked a flower for her hair and put on her most pleasing smile.

"Here," she said sweetly. "Eat this. I did and see? Nothing bad happened. It's got an interesting taste I think you'll like."

Adam was adamantly opposed to eating the fruit; every fiber of his being cried out against this disobedient act. But Eve was holding it right in front of him and nothing appeared changed. She obviously had not died, as was the warning. *Yes, even to touch the tree is forbidden, yet here she is holding the fruit with a smile on her face.*

However, Adam was not fooled.[182] He had other thoughts. To leave Eve as a reprobate by herself was unthinkable to him. She was naïve, not understanding the unending ramifications of her act. He knew she had a tendency to be more vulnerable than he.

How can I abandon the love of my life? What will happen to her? He couldn't bare the thought of separation from her. Though his conscience forbade him, his instincts told him to stay with her in order to protect her. If Eve was to die, then he was determined to die with her.

In his thoughts, though, Adam was truly deceived, for he instinctively felt the need to protect Eve from herself. Yet, in this line of thought he placed himself above the mandates of God, not trusting the outcome for her without him. Adam's protective feel towards Eve was God-given, yet now it was displaced. *Do I value her life above obeying my Heavenly Father?*

Adam knew exactly what he was doing. Thinking within himself that God would somehow make everything right again, he succumbed to the treacherous temptation to disobey.

He took the fruit from her hand, bit into it, chewed, and swallowed.

Immediately, both he and Eve became aware of evil. Previously protected, now they were fully exposed to the lure of sin.

Looking at each other they instantly became conscious of the fact that they were naked. *Who else can see us?* There

---

[182]   I Tim. 2:14

had to be unseen witnesses in the sprit world all around. [183] Surely all could see their nudity.

Embarrassment with their exposed situation overshadowed the shame they felt. Gathering fig leaves, Eve put her creative skills to work and helped Adam stitch together some body coverings. Using a quill from the porcupine as a needle and plant fibers as thread she fashioned some suitable clothing. *Yes, this will work.*

They felt better after donning the clothes, yet before the day was over the garments began to dry and shrivel. Fear crept into their psyches and completely took over, dominating their thoughts.

Will THE FATHER find out? We can't let him know what we did. Where can we hide?[184]

In the throne room the angels watched sadly as Adam and Eve failed the test. *Adam is no match for the wily Lucifer.* He'd succumbed to the temptation to sin in an attempt to protect his wife. Oh, the deceitfulness of Satan in misusing God-given instincts for his reprobate purposes!

In Adam's fall the hope for mankind to make consistently right decisions ceased. They didn't have the strength or wisdom necessary to defeat the evil one. But there's always hope in the Creator of Love. A plan had already been formulated to offer forgiveness as well as restoration for all.

A quick meeting was called and all pertinent information was revealed to the sons about Adam's sin. "Now it's not possible for them to live forever in human form. The

---

[183] We are surrounded with a cloud of witnesses. Hebrews 12:1

[184] Story of Adam and Eve taken from Genesis, chapters 1-2.

mandate is clear. As warned, before this day[185] is over both Adam and Eve must die."

It took only one sin for the door of death to open. Adam's DNA was now tainted and would affect everyone born after him. Super-human, uncontaminated blood was needed to absolve the world of sin.

"The tendency of mankind to sin will increase from this point onward."

"How can this trend be reversed?"

"Through his love HE'll win them back."

"But legally, the price for their disobedience must be paid."

"How?"

The Father relayed to them the restoration plan. "Mankind needs a Savior, one who'll be willing to live as a human among them, be tempted in all points like them, yet live his life totally without sin.[186] His perfect life will prevent him from being under the law of sin and death. Therefore, by dying a sinner's death, his innocence will pay for the freedom of all those under bondage to evil and its god."

This was the Father's plan? To take the blame and pay the price? The room was quiet. *Who would be able to make this happen?*

Lucifer was powerful; the Father had given him authority with massive amounts of control. This could not be automatically reversed. Liberation had to be done legally, without an open loophole, and with nothing to cause questioning about the tactics involved. Only ONE

---

[185] One day in Heaven is 1,000 years. As promised, neither reached their 1,000-year birthday on earth.

[186] Hebrews 4:15

with divine intelligence and tremendous strength would be able to accomplish this.

As the discussion continued amongst the sons, THE WORD mulled over the possibilities in his mind. He knew it was not a light thing to volunteer for the task. There'd be temptations—devious, strong temptations. There'd also be pain and abandonment, aspects not allowed in Heaven. The volunteer would experience temptation in the same way as the rest of mankind, yet he must remain undeceived and without sin.

He'd never experienced sin or any of Lucifer's evil inventions. Everything about it was the antithesis of the good he knew and went against every fiber of goodness in his being. This undertaking would require some thought. *There is already a blood ransom owed for Adam's liberation. Who will pay it for him?*

Jeric, Jano and the others watching in the archive room were silent as they witnessed the dilemma. The tragedy of wrong choice was no less dramatic in the present than it was in Adam's day.

Watching from the archives the subsequent gathering of the two-thirds of Heaven's inhabitants, they witnessed the eagerness of Michael's and Gabriel's angels to help with the restoration process. Lining up, they were given jobs: some were assigned to work as warriors, some as messengers, and others as personal guardian angels.

But still a special volunteer was needed. "Who will go to Earth as a human baby, grow up in a sinful world, resist all temptations of Lucifer and die to give his life as a ransom for the rest?"

"Anyone?"

There was silence as they all pondered the question. *Would I be able to live undeceived in a world where deception dominates? Can I defeat the power of evil by one-hundred percent adherence to the law? What about the deceivability factor? As a limited human will I be able to detect Lucifer's cunning tricks? Adam and Eve failed . . .*

Their peers had already shown they were no match for the cunning Lucifer. The only one qualified for such a task would be the all-knowing Father Himself.

"Who will defeat the powerful god of evil on his own turf?" All of Heaven remained silent as the question hung in space. [187]

As the great assembly watched, One came forward. He was magnificent, with eyes like fire; a form of God Himself.

THE WORD.

Made in the image of his Father, his countenance was brighter than the stars. It was HE who graciously volunteered, willing to pay the painful price. It would be the highest act of love ever performed.

The decision was made. He'd been there from the beginning with the Father when the foundations of the earth were put together.[188] He knew the plan and understood the strength it would take. The embodiment of the WORD OF GOD, he was not only willing, but was not deceivable. He would become the Savior of mankind

The purpose was set; the motion of activity went forward. Redemption was the goal as the coordinated preparations were made. Before the evening get-together with Adam, the Father had put his plan into motion.

---

[187] Silence for one-half hour in Heaven would be equivalent to twenty years, six months and twelve days of earth time.

[188] Eph 3:9

Chapter 8

Increase of Disobedience

Be sure your sin will find you out.

Numbers 32:23

Adam had been given the first opportunity but he, along with Eve, failed. Though the world had been cleansed and carefully prepared before the great test, sin entered it through Adam's disobedience. Now sin, like mold, would grow and double in strength with each passing generation. Its grip would have to be broken.

Adam and Eve's eyes were opened, but not in the way they'd expected. Deceived into believing they could achieve a shortcut back to Heaven as godlike beings, they'd failed miserably in fulfilling their goal. Afraid, they hid among the trees.

But God had already put his plan into motion. Innocent blood was shed as HE made clothing out of animal skins—the first leather britches.

Soon the couple felt a cool breeze rustling through the trees, a sign that indicated the Father's presence.

"Adam, where are you?"

"I heard your voice and was afraid. We hid because we're naked."

"Did you eat the forbidden fruit?"

"The woman you gave handed me the fruit, so I ate it."

"The snake deceived me."

No longer talking, the snake just watched, its tongue moving slowly in and out of its mouth. His silvery voice was forever gone.

"Adam, no longer will your garden grow easily by itself; you'll have to battle deep-rooted brambles, weeds and thorns throughout the heat of the day."

"Eve, when you give birth it will always be with excruciating pain. Even then, your desire will be for your husband."

"Serpent, your beauty will be repulsive to every female on earth. No longer will you walk the earth but will slither on the ground."

Lucifer, gloating on his gain, realized he'd not only caused Adam to sin, but also devastation to the poor animal that had the misfortune of being chosen for his scheme. Evil was the most fulfilling to him when it caused destruction to any of God's creation. "Yes! I've changed the world forever," he thought smugly.

The I AM continued talking to Adam and Eve. "As a result of your sin, you may no longer live in this beautiful garden."

Why?

"It's dangerous. If you eat of the Tree of Life now, you'll forever remain in your present sinful condition."

As Adam and Eve pondered these words, the FATHER presented them with the gift of beautifully crafted leather clothing.

"Here, you can put these on."

Adam examined the garments, the source of the material uppermost in his mind. The VOICE, so full of love and compassion again softly spoke. "They died so that you could be covered."

Yielding to sin caused much more devastation than the pair of them initially thought. The heavenly laws could not be broken; therefore the restoration of fellowship with the Father had to be paid for through the shedding of innocent blood.

Adam and Eve left the garden together, knowing their lives had forever changed. There was forgiveness available, yet how was it to be accessed? Through an animal sacrifice? They were, by necessity, eager to learn what they must do to receive a pardon for their sin.

Regardless of their new determination toward right choices, their initial disobedience came with dire consequences. Life became difficult, with weeds growing faster than the produce in the garden. Cattle now often died of disease, weather elements constantly worked against Adam's sweat equity, and arguments between them occurred far too often. It was hard to be pleasant when exhausted, sick, irritated, or in pain. Mosquitoes now caused itching, bees stung, and poisonous weeds made life miserable.

As life got harder, Eve became consumed with regrets. Adam often tried to console her, but usually gave up when he saw that nothing worked. Eventually he simply left her alone during her bouts of crying.

It was during this time that Adam noticed Eve's midsection growing. This was a much-needed diversion from their now difficult and demanding life schedule. Not missing the significance of her expanding girth, he mentally noted the progress of this first human pregnancy on earth.

Notwithstanding, Adam also fell into a deep depression as the full weight of reality hit him. His disobedience had opened the door for sin to affect his children as well as all future generations. The very moment he took the first forbidden bite he knew he'd failed.

"It would have happened anyway," Eve tried to console him.

"You were my responsibility. I needed to protect you. I should have stayed strong. I didn't comprehend at the time that I could have died in your place."

"Adam, don't be so hard on yourself. Our Heavenly Father knows our limitations. I am deceivable . . . no two ways around it."

Adam gently put his arm around her. "I love you so much! I would have gladly given my life for you, yet I went about it wrong. The enemy is strong, and much cleverer than either one of us."

"God knows and understands. He'll make a way for us to be redeemed."

When overwhelmed with guilt, Adam usually handled this by working himself into exhaustion. He became obsessed with thoughts of everything being restored back to normal again. *Will it ever happen? Is it even possible? Is there anything we can do to make it right?*

It was a long time before either Adam or Eve could sleep through the night without waking up in a cold sweat.

CHAPTER 9

THE DECEPTION OF JEALOUSY

Don't be deceived; God is not mocked: for whatever a man sows, that shall he also reap.

Gal. 6:7

Soon baby Cain was born, joined not too long afterward by brother Abel. Though parenting them was a new experience, it was also a natural one. Instincts of protection for Adam were strong; maternal instincts were even stronger for Eve. The family bond was solid, causing contentment even though their home was now outside of Eden.[189]

As the boys grew they tussled and played together, accepting their world as they'd found it. Cain was a gentle boy who loved to grow things in the field. He would often help Adam with the hoeing and weeding and was always excited to discover a new edible plant. He especially enjoyed experimenting with different methods to see how big he could grow his vegetables.

---

[189] Eden was the name of the original garden from which they'd been banned. Genesis 2:15

Abel took over the caring of the animals. He soon discovered which species were easiest to raise, which ones were the tastiest for meat, and which ones could be grown for clothing purposes. It wasn't long before he had a healthy flock of sheep and a strong herd of cows.

Cows gave milk, which could be made into butter and cheese. Sheep gave wool for clothing and meat for eating. As he worked daily with them, he particularly enjoyed playing with the cute little lambs.

Having learned about the need for a blood sacrifice from their parents, the boys prepared to fulfill their sacrificial requirements. Abel chose the most perfect lamb from the flock for his altar. It was tough, killing the baby before laying it upon the stones, but he did so in obedience to the plan.

Cain thought within himself: *I won't take one of Abel's lambs because that represents his labor, not mine. I'll give my largest and best produce as an offering.*

The day came when both boys built altars. Excitedly, Cain placed his fruit and vegetables on the stones while Abel arranged his bloodied little lamb. Cain thought smugly: *My way is better; no animal has to die.*

As smoke poured out from the altars, Abel's smoke ascended straight to Heaven. Cain's smoke, however, just smoldered on the stones before falling to the ground.

Hmm. Maybe I didn't lay the fruit right. Why isn't it burning properly? He adjusted the mess. Soon a burned odor permeated the area, with the smoke still rolling down off the altar. Abel's smoke, on the other hand, continued to shoot skyward from the meat.

Disappointing.

Abel looked his way. "Go get a lamb from my flock. You need blood for the sacrifice."

What does he know? The showoff! "My sacrifice is just as good as yours, even better because no animal has to suffer."

God isn't fair! He honors Abel but not me. Why? I work harder. I give more to the family, and am definitely smarter than he is. Yet now he's accepted while I'm rejected

Cain wouldn't look at his brother. He was more than embarrassed; he was outraged that God would not honor all his hard work!

Unknown to him, a standard for salvation had to be firmly established. Only through the shedding of innocent blood could the sins of mankind be atoned for. The lamb's death was a type and shadow of the ONE who was to come. Those who sacrificed a lamb were, in faith, putting their sins on the tab of the future SACRIFICIAL LAMB of God.

The I AM didn't want Cain to miss out on salvation through his ignorance of not doing what was needed. Yet Cain, instead of correcting his actions to meet the requirements of redemption, chose to be jealous of his brother. He didn't see the big picture of eventual salvation for all of mankind. He only saw his temporal disappointment and opted to feel rejected as a person.

As Abel's love and commitment to God's ways grew strong, Cain's jealousy escalated into hatred. Eventually Cain's anger was so immense that he couldn't even be polite, let alone say a civil word to his brother. Exasperated with the situation, Abel finally approached him.

"What's your problem? I'm ready to talk about it."

"You are, are you?"

"Sure, if it helps."

"Meet me in the field. Then I'll let you know what's on my mind." *I hate him!*

Abel was eager to restore fellowship with his brother; he missed the fun they used to have together. All he ever saw now was Cain's dark, malicious face. Anxious to get things settled he waited for Cain in the field.

"What's the matter, Cain?"

"You think you're better than me, don't you."

"No I don't!"

"Liar!" Without another word Cain brought out the tool he used to hoe his garden. Beating it over Abel's head, his anger reached a passion that surprised even him.

"Stop, Cain. You're hurting me!"

Cain couldn't stop, for something evil had unleashed within him an overwhelming rage. It was a devil-inspired moment, one where he lost complete control, for he allowed the evil from the dark side to thoroughly control his thoughts and actions. In complete overkill, he didn't stop beating Abel until his body was nothing but a bloody mass.

Breathless from exertion, his anger finally appeased, he now looked at what he'd done. Abel, like the lamb on the altar, was dead.

Suddenly frightened, Cain looked around. *Did anyone see me?* No one was in sight. Using his hoe to dig into the dirt, he buried Abel's body in a shallow grave. Covering him up, the ground looked just as before. He determined to keep his actions secret.

Now that Abel was gone, Cain had no one to blame for the desolation he felt. *Does God know what I've done? It's his fault, after all, for He was the one who rejected me. I did my best, yet God overlooked me and honored my stupid little brother.*

Walking away from the field, he felt some of the vengeful anger leave. What had he done? *Nothing that wasn't deserved.* He would tell no one.

That night he heard a voice "Cain, Cain."

"What?"

"Where is your brother?"

"How should I know? Am I supposed to take care of him?"

"Abel's blood cries to me from the ground." Startled, Cain knew he'd been found out.

"Your act of murder has opened up an ugly potential for even worse sin than before."

"If anyone finds out, they'll kill me."

"I'll put a mark on you; no one will touch you, but you may not live with your family anymore."

Cain was marked and banished from his childhood home. All Cain's descendants would now be born with an ever-increasing propensity for hatred and rage, thanks to his murder-tainted DNA.

CHAPTER 10

THE GENERATIONS OF MAN

All the days that Adam lived were nine hundred and thirty years: and he died.

Genesis 5:5

The first human death had occurred. Righteous Abel was welcomed into paradise, having won the battle over evil by obedience and faith in the required sacrificial lamb. His entrance to Heaven was put on the tab of IOU's as a ransom to be paid. Someone would need to make good the debt.

Meanwhile, Cain's behavior changed so much that Eve was beside herself with worry. He'd become deceitful, angry and disrespectful. Helpless, she could only watch in disbelief as he rebelled against everything she and Adam had taught him.

Heartbroken over his conduct, she at the same time felt responsible for it. Their perfect world had changed for the worse and Eve didn't know how to reverse the downward spiral.

That Cain withheld knowledge regarding Abel's whereabouts was apparent, yet he refused to discuss the matter. Abel's absence became a daily topic of heated discussion until the day Cain announced he was moving with his wife to a place at the east of Eden named Nod; it was a bittersweet relief to see him go.[190]

Observing the subsequent intensity of corruption and murder that gained a stronghold with Cain's descendants, Eve was overwhelmed at her lack of power to eradicate it from their lives. After many more years, however, she found peace with the conclusion that she had no choice but to hope in the mercy of a loving God.

I will trust in Him and in HIS plan for redemption.

Saddened with the now-known knowledge of Abel's murder and the subsequent banishment of Cain, Adam and Eve were nevertheless comforted when another son was born.

"He resembles you, Adam."

"Well, what do you know!"

They named him Seth, which means "appointed one." A younger image of his father, Seth was a great joy to his parents. Obedient and conscientious, he was one with which THE FATHER took great delight.

The generations of man will descend from this son.[191]

The first "day" of 1,000 years was almost over and Adam's season as mankind had ended. At age 930 Adam took his last breath and died.

As Adam's spirit entered into the transport tunnel, he knew distinctly he'd failed the test. God had given him a chance to have a part in mankind's redemption, yet he'd not been able to withstand the temptations of the enemy. But he

---

[190] The Bible does not say from where he got his wife. It is assumed that his wife was a sister. See Gen 4:17.

[191] All Cain's descendants died in the flood.

was not without hope. Not only had he, by faith, taken part in the required sacrifices of atonement, he'd also observed his godly son Seth teaching his children and grandchildren the ways of righteousness.

Maybe one of his descendants will be able to pay the price for our redemption.

CHAPTER 11

THE REDEMPTION PLAN

*I will help you, says the Lord your Redeemer, the
Holy One of Israel.*

Isa 41:14

When sin entered the world, sickness and death also
entered. As one by one the banished were born into the
world of mankind, each generation found it harder and harder
to live a healthy, sinless life. None were completely successful,
though a few came close. Only two righteous men went straight
to Heaven without having to go through the dying process.[192]

Meanwhile the sons of God met together to watch the
progress of the test transpiring on earth. Observing the
families as mankind began to multiply upon the face[193]
of the earth, they saw that their daughters were attractive;
some chose human wives for themselves.[194] This resulted in
giants being born within the human population.[195]

---

[192]   Enoch and Elijah. See Gen 5:24; Heb 11:5; 2 Kings 2:11

[193]   Note the usage of "face" vs. "pit."

[194]   Gen. 6:2

[195]   Is it possible that some of the "sons" lived on earth incognito?
See Hebrews 13:2

These giants became men of renown, strong, doing exploits; but this was not the plan of the Father, for mankind needed to solve the tests of life without giants to distract them. They needed one giant, a heavenly GIANT, who wouldn't succumb to the temptations of evil, but would be a willing and perfect sacrifice as the Lamb of God. The sin and sickness of the world had to be taken away through one method only. God's redemptive plan had to be carried out in full and would not work with any shortcut.

One day the Sons of God met together with the Lord, and Lucifer came with them. He'd tried everything he could think of to cause a righteous man named Job to sin, but had failed miserably. The reason? Job adamantly trusted in God's plan for redemption. Job not only refused to give in to Lucifer's manipulations but prayed for the ones who'd troubled him.[196]

During the worst of his misery, God asked Job: "Where were you when the earth was formed?"

There was only one answer, and righteous Job knew what it was: he'd been sitting in darkness in the shadow of death, deep in the depths of the pit.[197] His reply was the battle cry for everyone who trusted in the redemption that was to come. By faith he shouted, "I KNOW THAT MY REDEEMER LIVES!"[198] All Heaven rejoiced at his answer, for it confirmed that at least one human understood the plan.

On the second heavenly day the I AM spoke to THE WORD: "I've put together ten basic precepts of behavior

---

[196] For more on this story, read <u>Dark Stars of The Twilight</u> © 2009 by Marilyn Olson

[197] Job 33:29-30

[198] Job 19:25

that will instruct mankind to live righteously with their limited knowledge on earth."

"The first—"

"—is the most important, to worship only the I AM. In addition, they must not use my name in a non-reverent way. They must not make images of gods for the purposes of worship. They must keep the Sabbath day holy. They must not kill, must not commit adultery, and must not steal or lie. They must honor their parents, and not covet what others have."

"You're right. These ten should do it. Keeping these commandments will convey the basic concept of 'good'."

In the days to follow these Ten Commandments became the guide of mankind to separate right from wrong. The godly judges of Earth wisely utilized these ten mandates in order to make correct decisions. Though justice ruled for a time in the lives of the chosen,[199] there was still something missing: the spirit of loving the truth.

"Search throughout the earth, find me a man who understands my heart."[200]

The Word walked the earth, and found what he was looking for. He was a boy watching his father's sheep, singing "The Lord is My Shepherd . . ."

"This young man has it right. My ancestral line will continue through him; the Kingdom will be firmly established with his descendants."[201]

THE WORD watched in interest as David the shepherd become the most beloved king of Israel. Not only

---

[199] "Chosen" refers to the lineage of Christ, which came through Abraham, Isaac, and Jacob. See Acts 3: 24-25

[200] 1 Sam 13:14

[201] 1 Chronicles 17:11-14

was his worship rich with music, singing and dancing to the Lord, but his decisions toward others were fair as well as merciful.

His example of true worship will strengthen my people.

Yet as the humans of earth continually fought against righteousness on every front, evil reigned in many of the tribes of earth. Deceived and manipulated, humans—even with the written Ten Commandments—were no match for the craftiness of Lucifer and his cohorts. Though the standard of the Ten Commandments had been set, there had to be a better way to implement it.

It wasn't an easy fix. The failure of mankind to perfectly keep the commandments became for them a prison, evoking shame and despair. No one was powerful enough to keep them perfectly, as Adam himself so miserably proved. Therefore the Savior as the unblemished lamb could not be of the seed of Adam, for sin had polluted his DNA. A new, sinless strain had to be introduced to the world.

As the generations came and went, the godliest with the least amount of sin in their bloodline were chosen to father the descendants to continue the line.[202] Abraham, Isaac, Jacob, David—these were men who could be trusted to continue the requirements needed for God's plan.

With this lineage in place the ancestral line for the birth of the Savior was established.

The fourth day was about over. It was time to separate the light from the darkness.

The Day of Redemption had come.

---

[202] See Galatians 3:18-19 The inheritance was given to Abraham"—till the seed should come to whom the promise was made."

CHAPTER 12

THE SON ON EARTH

He sent redemption to his people.

Psalms 111:9

In the I AM and his Word was life. This life was LIGHT to mankind. Jesus, the SON of God, was the Volunteer who chose to undertake the sacrifice of redemption. He would pay the price for all humanity, Jew and Gentile alike.[203]

When the earth was black with darkness on the face of the deep, this LIGHT shined in: the darkness didn't understand it. This Light is the true light, which lights every man that comes into the world. He came into the world that was made by him, but the world didn't recognize him.[204]

Why?

The story of Jesus, from a first hand account, was about to begin. Breathless in anticipation, Korel and his group of

---

[203] The Jews are the descendants of Abraham, Isaac, and Jacob. Everyone else is a "Gentile." See Romans 2:9-10

[204] Text from John 1:1-13

friends could only watch in wonder as they experienced the life of Jesus, the Savior of the world.

Mankind had been on earth for 4,000 years, well over half the time allotted for the great test. The Word, willing as well as worthy for the mission, was notified to return to the Highest Heaven. He bid goodbye to his companions and quickly made the journey.[205]

As his personage appeared on the screen of the archives the room erupted: "There he is!" All in the room were entranced, for the moment had finally come to view HIS personal earth story.

Jano looked at Korel. "Virtual?" he asked.

"Yes." It was settled.[206] They would witness the life of Jesus as seen through his eyes.

What an amazing adventure lay ahead! They settled back, took a breath, and pressed the green button. Soon they found themselves witnessing the greatest story ever told.

The Word

Called into the Father's inner chamber, The Word noticed the others standing respectfully along the hallway. *Are they aware of what's about to transpire?*

The fact that he'd been summoned with a distinct urgency did not concern him. He had enjoyed creating

---

[205] Jesus came down from Heaven rather than up from the pit. In John 8:23 He said "You are from below, I am from above."

[206] In the archives it's possible to experience the life as if you are that person. For more details, read <u>The Twinkling</u>, © 2008.

the sun, moon and stars with the Father. He'd walked the earth, observing the unfolding of God's plan there.[207] Still, he knew he had yet to fulfill a very important piece to the puzzle that had been reserved until this moment.

Entering in the place of pure Love was always a delight. He thoroughly enjoyed being in the presence of his Father.

"How are you, Apple of My Eye?" HIS loving voice resounded through the marble halls.

Smiling, The Word approached the throne. "Delighted, as always. It's time, isn't it—"

"—to enter the world as mankind. You'll be born as a baby with no prior knowledge of pre-earth events. I've chosen loving parents for you. Growing up under their watchful care your physical maturity will be just like any other young Israeli boy. But there'll be a difference. Your DNA will contain no ancestral sins."

"Though your mother will be human, having descended from Adam's line, the DNA strain needed from the father's side will come directly from me. As a result, your blood will be as pure and sinless as Adam's was originally. You'll be both Son of Man and Son of God."[208]

"—A legality required to fulfill the redemption of mankind."

"Your earthly parents are also descendants of King David—"

"—fulfilling certain promises to Israel and his descendants."

"Yes." The Father was quiet for a moment, before continuing. "Though many in this chosen race of people

---

[207] Dan 3:25 mentions the Son of God. See also Dan 10:16.

[208] Mark 1:1, Luke 1:35, Luke 19:10

have followed my commandments, the seeds of evil have sprouted and spread throughout all the earth. There is none righteous anywhere; all have sinned and are in need of a Savior."[209]

"From what I've observed, I have no doubt the rest of the generations of man will follow the same path to destruction."

"They have the Ten Commandments—"

"—but so many rules have been added to them that the original intent is almost unrecognizable."

"What do you suggest?"

"Simplify them. Narrow them down to 'Love the Father with all your heart, and love each other as yourself.'"

"That's good. Simplicity is what's needed here. Use the same approach in telling stories to teach truths of the kingdom. As they believe and grasp onto the Word of Truth, enemy strongholds will be broken."

"There are so many people to reach in one lifetime . . ."

"Start with twelve men; teach them in-depth about the Kingdom. The Word will spread out from there. Those who are truly my people will want to do right. If not, they'll continue to do the deeds of their lying 'father' who is a murderer from the beginning."[210]

Pausing a poignant moment before continuing, the Father spoke softly: "As a human you'll experience pain, sorrow, rejection—"

"—I can endure anything you allow to happen to me."

---

[209] Romans 3:23; 5:12
[210] John 8:44

"There are other things that sin brought: disease, crime, death—"

"—I'm ready to deal with them!" The Word was adamant in his purpose. "I'm more than ready. I'm anxious to bring healing as well as to restore life!"

The FATHER could see his SON'S determination to not be limited by pending humanness. HIS resolve to break the power gripping the fallen was strong.

The appointed time came; the sons whispered "good-bye" to the Lamb of God. Soon a baby named "Jesus" was born on earth to a virgin named Mary.[211]

---

[211] For complete story, see the book of Matthew from the Holy Bible.

Chapter 13

Jesus' Childhood

*Signs and wonders may be done by the name of
your holy child Jesus.*

Acts 4: 30

Life was busy and happy at the home of Joseph and
Mary. Jesus woke up each day with the smell of fresh
bread permeating the house. His mom had to be the best
cook in the village! Every morning as the sun would peak
over the horizon Mary could be seen walking to the village
to buy grain and fresh food for the day. What she didn't
buy, she grew in her well-kept garden. She made bread
every morning during the week, and enough on Friday to
last for the Sabbath.

His hard-working dad was also a strong presence in
the home. Gentle and kind, his responsibilities toward
his family predicated every decision he made. His love for
Mary was obvious in his tender smile toward her and loving
words to others about her.

Oldest of the children, Jesus felt secure in his home. The
many younger siblings that came along in time were a tribute
to the health of his parents. Fighting? Certainly, but he was a
good referee; his siblings could depend upon him to settle an

argument between them fairly. He always perceived exactly what happened, totally understood the situation, and knew how to repair the tension between them.

There was some expected jealousy, especially from his younger brother James. Next in age to Jesus, James couldn't compete with either his intelligence or his sense of fairness in dealing with others. Sibling rivalry—a normal state of affairs for most families—was also in theirs.

Jesus loved his brothers and sisters just as he loved his parents. As the oldest he naturally took on the role of the dominant firstborn, having an instinct to protect them from harm.

Even as a child Jesus knew he was different from others. He preferred to do what was right and did so at all times; never did he entertain even a thought of violating the healthy conscience with which he'd been born. This got him into occasional trouble with his friends and siblings.

Think about it . . . to always be right, to never be wrong, to never give in to the temptations and youthful mischievousness that plagues the rest of youth . . . . this was his manner.

There were times when the thought of a prank gave him enjoyment; however, he never participated in one if it was tinged even slightly with drawing anxiety from the victim. Yet he had a great sense of humor, often delighting his friends and family with his playfulness towards them.

As a child he didn't fully understand all that was ahead of him, but even during those years he experienced a sense of oneness with his Heavenly Father. Jesus subconsciously knew who he was and this knowledge grew with him as he matured.[212]

He didn't question his calling, but only sought to continually learn more about it. Even if initially not fully understanding everything, obedience to his Heavenly Father's guidance was the way he overcame the evil influence of the world's way of thinking. He continually sought to more fully concentrate on hearing and obeying this gentle voice. Daily as he communicated with HIM, HE became his closest companion.

One day Mary took him aside. "Jesus, I want to show you something." From under the bed she brought out an ornate, sweet-smelling box and a decorative cloth pouch. Reaching into the bag, she pulled out three golden coins—all that remained. "When you were a baby, kings came from other countries to worship you. They'd followed a star placed in the heavens, knowing it would take them to where you were. These are some of the gifts they brought." She related to him the details of his unique birth.

As he examined the empty box left by the visitors, he marveled at the loving heavenly provision. Not only had THE FATHER confirmed who he was through a star in the sky, but his parents had been able to buy their house and shop because of the gifts.

---

[212] John 8:23

The next day as he helped his father in the shop, Joseph remarked: "Son, soon you'll reach your twelfth birthday. One year from that day you will be recognized as a man. As you know, there are certain responsibilities as well as privileges that come with that recognition."

Jesus smiled, for he already knew what his father was about to say.

Joseph continued, "At this time you'll be allowed to accompany us to the temple in Jerusalem." His parents had gone there every year since he could remember; at last he'd be able to join them. He eagerly counted the days until the journey.

As the day of departure approached, his excitement grew. He recognized he would be in the temple built to his FATHER'S specifications; a heavenly structural design that housed the Holy of Holies within its gates.

Soon the day arrived and he, along with his parents, joined others from the village to travel together. Jesus and his young companions laughed and played as they walked, enjoying the freedom of the adventure. As evening fell the first day they unloaded the tents from the donkey and quickly set them up. *Sleeping under the stars together is a treat. Let the adults use the tents!*

Camping each night and walking during the day was a slow process, but one of intense pleasure. Before long they climbed the last hill that led to Jerusalem.

Jesus

The temple before me was majestic! Entering through the gates, something welled up within me. This was my Father's House . . . .

Looking around, I saw the activity—some of it godly and pleasing to God, and some of it worldly with thieves and con artists using the temple as a means of defrauding its worshippers. *I didn't expect this.*

We entered the courtyard and continued on through the entrance. In the room to my right the Pharisees and doctors of the law were deep in study. Noticing the scrolls with the Word of God open on the table I knew: *This is where I want to be!*

Taking my place on the floor, I quietly listened as the discussion grew animated and even heated at times. At one point I raised my hand, making a comment about the scripture passage in question.

Suddenly the room was silent, for I'd asked a question not only pertinent to the discussion, but its answer provided keen insight to the group. Eyebrows raised, the bearded teachers turned around to see who had voiced the query. Noticing me, they were more than a little perplexed.

Who is this young man?

They were aware of the strong prophetic word Simeon had spoken over a baby twelve years ago. Every day until his death, he insisted he'd held the Messiah in his arms. The mystery child had not been seen since.[213]

Is this him? He's the right age.

Gathering around me while focusing on my person, the questions began in earnest.

So excited was I to be conversing with these great men of the law that I didn't notice the passage of time. We talked late into the night and into the next day.

---

[213] Luke 2:25

Meanwhile my parents had moved from this room to another, assuming I was with their party. Even while traveling home the following day they didn't notice I was missing; I'd always been, in their eyes, where I was supposed to be.

Eventually realizing I wasn't in the group, Mom began to cry. *What's happened? It can't be time already!* Though she knew I was special, she'd also been told that "a sword would pierce" her soul. *Not yet!* At my present tender age she still wanted to protect me from the world.

Though deeply concerned, Dad attempted to reassure Mom that all would be well as the two of them left the group and hurried back to Jerusalem.

Where is Jesus?

Anxiously they returned to the temple, retracing their every step. Finding a large crowd of teachers in the main hall, they quickly walked past them. But then they heard my young, strong voice amongst the gathering.

"Jesus?" Mom turned around, her worried face lined with grief and perplexity.

"This young boy is extremely intelligent, understanding way above his age level. His interest in and understanding of spiritual things has amazed us," spoke a highly regarded teacher.

Dad, however, was in no mood to be complimentary. Giving me a sharp look, he asked, "Didn't you know your mother would be worried? Why have you done this?" Mom with tears streaming down her face grabbed me, hugging me with all her strength.

"Why did you look for me? Don't you know I must focus on my Father's business?"[214] I truly was perplexed.

---

[214] Luke 2:49

Mom had told me numerous times who my biological Father was. Dad had also relayed to me that I was soon to be considered a man. *Didn't they think I'd been listening?*

Sorry for inadvertently causing them emotional pain, I hugged them both while inwardly deciding to communicate better in the future. The last thing I wanted to do was to cause grief to my dear parents.

CHAPTER 14

GROWING TALL, GAINING WISDOM

And Jesus increased in wisdom and stature, and in favor with God and man.

Luke 2:52

Frustrated, and a bit fearful in letting him out of their sight—for he'd been the target of death by a powerful king in the past—his parents forgot who he was for a moment, ready to reproach. His surprising words, however, brought them quickly back to reality. Yes, he was preparing for a mission, but the time for it was premature.

He needs to be home and protected until he fully reaches adulthood.

Teenage years brought about a different type of newness. Maturing in body as well as mind, Jesus experienced all the growth surprises that his brothers did. Yet, nothing fazed him; he continued to be kind, patient, and honorable to his parents. With an inborn sense of purpose that felt right, he determined to never break the bond of goodness that had hold of him.

Joseph, a skilled carpenter, had an excellent reputation that extended far beyond their village. Jesus loved to work in the shop with him, creating beautiful pieces of furniture. Beds, chairs, tables, desks, and many other items were perfectly crafted with his young hands. Mary often watched him as he worked, marveling at the gift in the Son she was given.

The family never lacked for new work orders as Jesus and his dad completed each project with precision and good craftsmanship. All of their customers were astonished at Jesus' skill and the perfection in his work. People came from all over Galilee to buy furniture from Joseph's little shop.

Jesus' younger brothers would often accompany him in search of suitable wood for the carpentry work. Taking the donkey and cart to the nearby forests was an arduous, all-day event. On occasion they'd find a fallen tree in the village and would offer their services to remove it, saving themselves a day's labor. Regardless of how they acquired the wood, cutting and transporting it was an enjoyable activity for all of them.

James and Joses didn't mind the hard work—it had a good side effect of increasing their strength as well as their physical muscle mass. This was noticed not only by their friends but also the potential employers in the village.

Those in the archive room watched as the boy Jesus grew strong and handsome over the years, increasing in wisdom as well as in height.[215] Everyone in his life was impressed with him; he was trustworthy, fair in his dealings, and by far the favorite babysitter of his younger siblings. Physically strong, he'd become somewhat of a legend when it came to races and other games played in the streets.

---

[215]   Luke 2:52

These years were filled with numerous weddings, funerals, births, and mitzvahs. Along with these events, the work in the shop kept them all busy.

Jesus dearly loved the Father with all his heart. As the knowledge of his purpose grew within him, however, his heart was often grieved with the sin of the world. Faith was so natural for him that he became increasingly perplexed at the lack of faith found in God's people. He struggled to understand the limitations of others—he himself had no doubt he could remove mountains if he so desired. But with his parent's gentle teaching and example, he learned to function within the limited world of mankind.

Jesus

It astounded me, but I said very little about it. Growing up with brothers James and Joses, I understood too well how feelings could get hurt so I usually kept my mouth shut. Still, at times I was totally amazed at the lack of conviction exhibited by my peers.

Sure, I was tempted in every area, same as anyone else my age. Yet, unlike the other boys, I didn't give in to the temptations. It simply wasn't in my nature to sin.

It was in my brother's nature, however, and as a result of not being able to compete with me, I was made the butt of some jokes and snide remarks. Regardless, nothing could stop me from loving my siblings and eventually my attitude toward them superseded any jealous thoughts they had toward me.

We had fun as we grew up together. Laughing, playing and enjoying each other's company, my childhood years were full of enjoyable activity and good memories.

My parents often talked late into the night, discussing different options available to them. Sometimes I could overhear their muffled conversations: "He's noticed in the neighborhood: 'The carpenter's son, so handsome, so kind, so good at his trade!'" Many times they were approached with possible marriage contracts from well-meaning parents of available daughters.

Joseph had been chosen by God for the responsibility of guiding as well as protecting me in my formative years. He'd been an excellent father to me. Hesitantly, one day, he brought up a sensitive subject: "Son, you've reached the age where most parents would arrange a marriage." Here he stopped, looking at me quizzically.

I knew what he was thinking. A marriage would be nice . . . to want to hold a beautiful girl in a gentle embrace was an instinctive desire planted within every healthy human male. I was no different in that regard, desiring to love and cherish a special someone. But I quickly put those thoughts out of my mind, for I realized marriage was not for me. A wife would be distracting as well as present difficult situations of temptation, as Adam and other "sons of God" had previously demonstrated.[216] Besides, I had work to do and marriage would hinder me from that effort.

"Father, you know the answer.—"

"—Hear me out. Your mother has been a delight to me; how could I have functioned without her? It's not good for man to live alone.[217] He needs a helpmate. And you, Son . . ." he choked up, not able to continue.

My father was a good man, a hard worker, gentle in spirit, and righteous in his dealings. He loved me, and the fact that I'd became more skilled than he at carpentry only

---

[216]   Gen. 5:4
[217]   Gen. 2:18

made him prouder of me. He had my best interests at heart; yet, we both knew the answer:

"I cannot now, nor can I ever marry."

Joseph looked at me for a long time, nodded his head, and patted me on the shoulder.

"I understand." I held him for a moment, our earthly roles reversed. My earthly father was a saint. My Heavenly Father had chosen for me the best of mankind to oversee my upbringing.

As I watched some of my siblings marry and start families, I grew impatient to begin the ministry for which God had prepared me. I continued, however, to submit to my parent's authority as I waited until the time was right. Though there were some occasional pangs of loneliness, I stayed resolute to my calling.

Mom was a gracious hostess, many times inviting neighbors and friends over for dinner. One of these friends had a daughter who was engaged to be married. Our family was invited to the wedding. The engaged couple had grown up in our village. I knew them very well; we'd played together as children. The girl was also a friend of my younger sister Salome.

"Judith's wedding is coming this spring," Mother reminded me. "Make sure the boys are ready." I knew what she meant: "Make sure your brothers know the dances."

I not only loved to dance but was also quick to learn every dance step. With each movement having a meaning, putting the steps together was a great way to dance in praise and worship to God. Some of the dances could be traced clear back to our forefather King David. I was the one who usually taught these dances to my brothers.

My family enjoyed these celebrations; the food and dancing, connecting with good friends and joyful music not only gave us time together as a family but also provided a change of pace from our work in the shop.

These were memorable years.

CHAPTER 15

JESUS BAPTISM
AND TEMPTATION

*I have baptized you with water: but he shall
baptize you with the Holy Ghost.*

Mark 1:8

I had a cousin named John. He was known as somewhat of an oddball, yet I knew him as an effective "voice" of the Word. Called of God to prepare people for the coming Messiah, he understood my calling whereas my brothers did not.[218] His message was that the redemption of mankind was near. I knew it was <u>very</u> near. I decided to travel to where he was in the desert for a visit.

Kissing Mom good-bye, I headed out the door. "Make sure you're home in time for the wedding," she added.

Approaching the Jordan River, I could see in the distance the huge crowds gathered there. John was baptizing scores of people while preaching the message of repentance. A mixture of excitement and anticipation welled up within me.

---

[218]   Neither did his brothers believe in him. John 7:5

I was eager to begin teaching about the Kingdom of God, that it was once again obtainable to all. The joy of providing redemption to mankind was before me, and it was within my power to give. My goal: to provide a way for the lost to return to the Father.[219]

As I approached the crowd, suddenly all eyes turned in my direction. "Behold, the Lamb of God which takes away the sin of the world," John shouted as he pointed straight toward me.[220] As I came to the edge of the water he bowed his head in deference to my presence.

"John, I want to be baptized."

Surprised, he looked up. "Oh, no! I need to be baptized by you!"

"Allow it to happen. This is the Father's plan." Humbly, John gave in to my request and lowered me into the water—down, down, and up again.

As my head came up through the watery surface, I felt the Holy Spirit, like a dove, lightly land upon it. A powerful charge immediately ran through my body as a voice thundered from the heavens: "THIS IS MY BELOVED SON, IN WHOM I AM WELL PLEASED. LISTEN TO HIM."[221] Instantly I became aware of a potent sense of complete knowledge. Housed within my body of flesh resided the Spirit of God, which now directed me to go into the desert without delay.

I left without speaking a word to anyone.

---

[219] I am the way, the truth and the Life. No man comes to the Father except by me. John 14:6

[220] John 1:29

[221] Matthew 17:5

Who am I? This question played over again in my mind as I pondered the evidence before me. I had an inner sense that I was not of this world, yet over the last thirty years I'd increasingly wondered about my place in humanity. That I was not only Son of God, but The Lamb of God was a thought that had been confirmed by John's recent proclamation.

All mankind were sons, in a sense;[222] sin caused them to be separated or "fallen," to be sure, but nevertheless still "sons" from a distinct past. In tracing my genealogy back to Adam it was written that Adam was "son of God." I was "the last Adam."[223] Adam had failed the test; I would not fail.

I required unhindered, uninterrupted time with my Heavenly Father to sort all this out. I had to get away from the cares and events of the world in order to hear his voice, to know it, and to not confuse it with any other spirit attempting to dilute the message.

Not one to casually make decisions, I measured each thought against the WORD. That I lived in a restricted human state meant I must weigh every decision for accuracy and signs of deception. I knew I must break through to unobstructed communication with my Heavenly Father.

Determined that nothing would deter me from accomplishing this task, I focused on what needed to be done. Fasting while praying was essential. I absolutely had to be of one mind with my Heavenly Father and eating would be a distraction from that goal.

I will not make a mistake. I will not fail.

---

[222] Philippians 2:15; 1 John 3:2

[223] See Luke 3:38 and 1 Cor 15:22

As the days without food added up, my mission became crystal clear. I was to be the perfect, unspotted sacrificial lamb. I was to lay down my life for the salvation of the world.

After forty days without food my body was on the verge of keto acidosis, a condition that would cause it to utilize the muscles in order to sustain life. But I'd achieved perfect unity with HIM, a truly remarkable experience while in the carnal body of mankind. Now physically hungry beyond belief, the stones began to look like the delicious barley loves Mom would bake. The natural instinct of survival created a roaring desire to eat.

Sure enough, here came Lucifer disguised as an Angel of Light, tempting me to change the stones into bread. Finding me weak and emaciated, this fallen archangel thought it would be an easy task to convince me. He'd defeated Adam rather easily, I reminded myself, using the God-given basic instinct for food as a temptation.

But my spirit was strong, and I defeated the enemy with the power of THE WORD. More temptations followed, but I withstood each one. Finally, he gave up, leaving me alone.[224]

Lying down in a physically weakened state, a sense of joy washed over me. I had experienced using the sharp sword of the WORD to defeat evil. With this victory, everything was possible; I had no doubts that I would be able to redeem all of mankind through my death.

---

[224] For more details read Luke 4:1-13. Also the story is told in <u>Dark Stars of The Twilight</u>, copyright 2009 by Marilyn Olson.

"Bravo!" I opened my eyes to see two angels kneeling beside me. "The Father sent this for you." In one outstretched hand was a tray containing a pitcher of ice water and two warm barley loaves. The other angel had a plate of fresh fruit peeled and ready to eat.

Sitting up, I ate slowly as the two angels smiled and watched. It felt wonderful to be in the company of the holy—plus it was a most satisfying meal!

"Can we do anything for you? Wash your feet? Give a backrub?" I was worn out and happy to accept the generous offer. Finding a shaded area, I enjoyed the pampering.

Soon the heavenly messengers were gone and I was left with a heightened sense of well-being. I had successfully accessed the strength of the spoken WORD to defeat the enemy on his own turf.

I came away from the desert with clear direction, ready to take on the next level of my ministry. I would begin teaching in the Houses of Worship. Here the faithful gathered each week in obedience to God's law. It was the logical place to start.

Returning to Nazareth I entered the synagogue on the Sabbath day. When the appropriate time came, I stood up to read. The book of Isaiah was handed to me. I opened it and found the following passage:

"The Spirit of the Lord is upon me, because

1. he has anointed me to preach the gospel to the poor;
2. he has sent me to heal the brokenhearted,
3. to preach deliverance to the captives,
4. and recovering of sight to the blind,
5. to set at liberty them that are bruised,
6. to preach the acceptable year of the Lord."[225]

Closing the book, I sat down. Every eye was fastened on me. "Today this scripture is fulfilled."

Everyone there wondered at my words: *Isn't this Joseph's son?* Some were not too happy about my statement and threatened bodily harm, but I passed unseen through the middle of the crowd and headed to Capernaum. There, I did the same thing: I taught them on the Sabbath day.

I'm astonished at his teaching!
His word is with power!
From where did he get the authority to teach this way?
No one has ever spoken like he does.

---

[225] Isa 61:2

It was time to organize my crew. Taking the humble from the earth, I gathered together the ones the Father had pointed out to me. Twelve men, each with different backgrounds and personalities, joined me in my mission. From the day I first requested their allegiance, I prayed for each one fervently. I knew I'd soon give my life for their salvation, and if for them, then also for the whole world.

CHAPTER 16

THE WEDDING

Both Jesus and his disciples were called to the marriage.

John 2:2

The week before Judith's wedding Mom sent word for me to come home. I was fully aware of her desire that I not miss it. *Doesn't she understand the importance of my mission?* I had much teaching yet to convey.

"Son, all our friends will be there; everyone wants to see you."

"I've got some guys with me now, Mom."

"How many?"

"Twelve."

"Twelve? Why so many?" Mom was all-aflutter. My sisters required new garments; my brothers had yet to get out their best clothes and their worn-out sandals needed to be replaced with new ones.

I helped to get everything done to Mom's specifications. When all was ready, she sighed contentedly. "I have one more detail." With a twinkle in her eye, she presented to me a special gift: a new robe.

"This is for you, Jesus," she said softly. "It's quality, ideal for you." I looked at it, noticing the fine craftsmanship. It was unique, all right—no seam anywhere. The cloth had been woven into the garment with not a stitch added.

"Thank you, Mom." Lightly kissing her on the cheek, I put the robe on. "It's perfect."

"Just like you," she said softly. I would wear this robe for the next three years.

Dressed for the occasion, our family arrived at the wedding. The music put us all in a mood for dancing and we enjoyed the fun as we moved to the old Davidic melodies.

Not long into the festivities Mom approached me with a worried look as only a mother can give. "They're out of wine," she fretted. "Please do something!"

Mom, is this really what you want? My first miracle? To make wine for a wedding?

I didn't expect this, as there seemed to be much greater need around than providing wine. But I would honor my mother, for I realized some things were very important to women.

Giving her a reassuring look, I planned what to do. Fixing the problem wouldn't be hard: it was easy to divide and multiply molecules. Mom, her faith in me intact, told the servants to do whatever I said.

Instructing the help to fill up the water pots with water, I formulated the procedure in my mind and applied it to the water in the pots. Knowing the resulting wine was excellent, I enjoyed watching my mother's reaction as well as those of the guests. I winked at Mom as some asked the host: "Why did you save the best wine for last?"

The wedding crisis over, Mom looked at me with different eyes. She surmised, rightly so, that this first miracle of the wine was only the beginning. She and Dad at last both accepted the fact that my ministry had begun.

Changing the water to wine was an easy task. Not only did I understand the chemical compositions of all elements, I also understood the power of true faith. With these tools I'd be able to access the formulas needed to correct the problems I found upon the earth.

But I was an oddity to my brothers. They didn't understand me at all, nor could they reason with any logic how I'd accomplished the miracle.

After the wedding, my disciples and I accompanied my family to Capernaum for a few days. Since the Passover was near, I wanted to continue on to the temple in Jerusalem to celebrate it.

The long, steep climb to the city was invigorating. Each step brought me closer to my Father's House. The time for which I had spent a lifetime of preparation, had finally come.

With the advent of the feast day of Passover, I was where I wanted to be: in Jerusalem teaching truths to God's people. *There are many who'll believe my words once they witness the miracles.*

Arriving at the noisy courtyard was a shock back to reality. It had deteriorated into a marketplace! Hawkers were yelling, frightened sheep and oxen were making terrible noises. Doves and other birds were messing up the grounds. Observing this, a determination stirred within me. These merchants had made my Father's house into a den of thieves! Quickly fashioning a whip of small cords, I drove them all out of the area: the sheep, birds and oxen scattered as I turned over the tables and dumped the money onto the ground.

"Take these things away. Don't make my Father's house a place of merchandise."

Skulking before me, the moneychangers crept away. As I watched them, I realized where they were headed: to the area of the temple where the Pharisees gathered for their debates.

Good. As men known for their devout attention to the law they should feel the same way I do about it!

Expecting the Pharisees to support the cleansing of the temple grounds was more of a wishful thought. As they approached me, I perceived they'd not only given permission to sell livestock in the courtyard, but would also receive a cut from the profits.

With one glance I instantly knew the inner characters of the seven men who approached me:[226] *Three complete hypocrites, two scholars who are full of pride and arrogance, a wolf in sheep's clothing, and . . . there's one who actually wants to serve God. All are hiding secret sins.*

"What sign do you give to prove you have the authority to do this?" asked one revered teacher of the law.

"Destroy this temple, and in three days I'll raise it up."

"Forty-six years it took to build this, and you can rebuild it in three days?"

I was more amazed at their lack of knowledge than of their lack of faith. These renowned scholars hadn't a clue that I was speaking about my own body. Many of them at this time, however, were interested in me because of the miracles I performed. Yet I didn't commit to them because I could see the bias in their hearts.[227]

---

[226] John 2:24

[227] John 2:25

CHAPTER 17

THE PHARISEES

Beware of the leaven of the Pharisees.
Matt 16:6

Dogmatic at times, the Pharisees had replaced the joy of attainable salvation with a list of do's and don'ts, making life hard and tedious for those who wanted to serve God. I had to break the yoke the teachers of the law had not only put on God's people, but onto themselves as well.

Nicodemus was one of these. Though misguided, he had a genuine thirst for knowing the truth of the scriptures. He was one of the Pharisees who took notice of the miracles I did in the temple. As a result he wanted to secretly meet with me.

"The counselor Joseph owns a garden nearby," he whispered after most of the group of Pharisees had left. "Meet me tonight."

"I'll see you there," I whispered back with a smile, knowing he was breaking out of the mold the rest were entrenched in.

As soon as I entered Joseph's garden, I knew the place would have a special significance for me. There were olive trees with an oil press at one end. Nearby was a new tomb where two gravesites were being carved out of the rock. A peaceful place, the sounds of chirping birds and the sweet smell of flowers permeated the air. Located a short distance from the Sheep Gate and just out of hearing range from the noise that resonated from the city, it was a perfect place to pray.

Arriving late in the night, I perceived that Nicodemus was honest and sincere in his questions. He'd studied the law for the right reasons: he wanted to be right with Jehovah.[228]

"I know you're from God, for no man can do the miracles you do unless God is with him," he began.

"You must be born again to enter the Kingdom of God." With that startling statement, I'd gotten his attention.

"How can a man be born when he's old?" Though a doctor of the law, he didn't understand what I meant. I was happy to explain it to him.

"Mankind on earth gives birth to human bodies; but it's the Spirit that births our spirits into the Kingdom."[229]

"How can this be?"

"I came down from Heaven to be lifted up from the earth in death. Anyone who believes in me will have eternal life. God loved the world so much that he gave me, his Son, to the world. He that believes on me is not condemned, but he that doesn't believe is already condemned.[230]

God's Light has come into the world, but men love darkness rather than light because of their evil deeds. He that

---

[228] Jehovah is a Hebrew name for God. Ps 83:18

[229] That which is born of the flesh is flesh, but that which is born of the sprit is spirit. John 3:6

[230] He stays in his present lost state due to Lucifer's current authority over him.

lives by truth is happy to come to the light, unashamed of what he does. Those that do evil try to stay in the dark."[231]

I could tell Nicodemus was listening. Intelligent, he understood the concepts I imparted to him. *He's the one who'll speak truth to his peers.*[232]

The next morning as my disciples and I traveled back to Judea we came to a place where there was a lot of water. We stopped to baptize the new believers who followed us there. At the same time my cousin John was baptizing new believers near the town of Salim.

As soon as we entered the water, the Pharisees arrived with their jealousies, manipulations and misguided judgments. Their motivation was obvious: they wanted to cause trouble. After the last baptism was over, they hurried to Salim where John was working, hoping to cause jealousy with the news that my disciples had baptized more believers than he had. But John surprised them with his answer: "He must increase while I must decrease." [233]

True workers in the Kingdom aren't in competition with each other. They work together, encouraging, complementing, and appreciating each one's effort.

I didn't receive any encouragement from the Pharisees.

As we commenced walking to Judea we passed through a little village in Samaria named Sychar. It was about noon when we reached Jacob's well at the city's outskirts.

Sitting down in a shady spot, I instructed my men to go into the city to buy some lunch. Having been up late the night before with Nicodemus, I was tired and wanted to rest.

---

[231] Text taken from John 3

[232] John 7:50-51. See also John 19:39.

[233] John 3:30

Soon a young woman came to draw water from the well. Glancing at me sideways with a somewhat flirtatious look, I knew instantly not only what she was thinking, but her total past history. This woman was miserable, lonely, and had poor self-esteem.

I asked her: "Will you give me a drink?"

"How is it that you, being a Jew asks a drink of me, a Samaritan woman?"

"If you knew the gift of God and who it is that's asking you, you'd ask me instead for living water."

"Mister, you don't have anything with which to draw water and the well is deep. From where would you get this 'living water'? Are you greater than our ancestor Jacob who gave us this well in the first place?"

"Whoever drinks this water will get thirsty again, but whoever drinks the water I give will never get thirsty. It will be like a well of water bubbling within him, springing up into everlasting life."

"All right then. Give me this water so I won't ever have to come here again."

"Go get your husband and come back."

"I have no husband."

"That's right, for you've had five husbands, and the man you now have is not your husband."

She froze, shocked I'd so perfectly nailed her situation. She decided to change tactics; "I perceive you're a prophet . . . . okay, where do we worship? Our fathers worshipped here, but your people say it's got to be in Jerusalem."

"God is a Spirit. He searches for those anywhere who will worship him in spirit and in truth."

"When the Messiah comes he'll tell us everything."

"I am He."

A flush of recognition suddenly came over her delicate features. She recognized the truth, and its revelation wiped out her hidden resistance to it.

Embracing the news, she went through the village exclaiming about her encounter with me. "He told me everything I've ever done," she excitedly proclaimed.[234]

Imparting truth to the spiritually hungry gave me such tremendous satisfaction that it was just like eating a big meal! My disciples, who'd returned by now with food, didn't understand why I was no longer hungry.

There were many new believers from Sychar because of this incident. We stayed two more days to teach them about Kingdom living. Many others also believed during our stay there. It was heartening to see how God's truths satisfied those who were hungry for His Word. "We've heard him ourselves and know that this is indeed the Christ, the Savior of the world."

Experiencing much joy at their newfound hope, we left the new believers in Samaria to continue our journey to Judea. Just before arriving at our destination, I was approached by a nobleman whose son was sick. Having no doubt in his mind as to what I'd do, he asked me to heal his son.

"If you don't come, he'll die," was his humble appeal. In this father's heart was genuine love. I felt his concern; I would not leave him without helping the situation.

"Your son now lives," I stated simply.[235] His faith was strong, so it was an easy task for me to speak the WORD and thereby remove the virus from the child's body.

---

[234] Story from John 4
[235] John 4:50

As the nobleman went home, his servants came rushing up to him with the happy news that his son had suddenly become well.

"When?" he asked. The answer revealed it was the exact moment I told him his son was healed. This was my second miracle in Cana. Word about it spread quickly.

CHAPTER 18

WORK FOR THE KINGDOM

Unless your righteousness exceeds that of the scribes and Pharisees, you shall not enter the Kingdom of Heaven.

Matt 5:20

A fter our visit in Judea, we returned to Jerusalem for the second feast.[236] Arriving at the city we found a good place to rest near the Sheep Gate. Close by was the pool of Siloam; people were camped everywhere, hoping the water would heal them.

There was among them a man who'd been sick many years. Watching him, I knew he had strong faith.

"Do you want to be healed?"

"I move too slowly. Once the waters move others always beat me to it. I've no one to help me."

"Pick up your bed and walk." As the meaning of my words dawned on him, I saw belief arise in his heart. He picked up his bed and was instantly healed.

---

[236] The chronological order is taken from the book of John. John indicated that there were many more events that took place than he reported. See John 21:25

Grinning from ear to ear, he soon headed to the temple. His desire was to worship God within its doors, something he'd not been able to do for the last thirty-eight years.

The Pharisees were perplexed. They knew the man had been sick a long time—they'd seen him daily sitting outside the gates of Jerusalem. Instead of being happy that God had healed him, however, they immediately began a harassment campaign. Their jealousy inspired a search for something for which they could accuse me to my audience. "He can't be of God. He forced this man to work on the Sabbath day by ordering him to carry his bed. We know this man is a sinner!"

Disappointed but not surprised, I made mental notes:

Pharisees:
1. criticized rather than encouraged
2. were angry that believers followed me
3. never smiled at or complimented me on anything
4. were unhappy with my wise answers to them
5. were enraged that God confirmed my WORD with healings and miracles

Conclusion: They were jealous of me in the same way that Cain was jealous of Abel. Unless their hearts changed, murder would be their next step.

The fact that they knew I saw their motivations escalated the troubling aspect of animosity the Pharisees had towards me. One would have expected these wise teachers from the temple to confirm the WORD as they recognized its truths. Their accusing attitude, however, wouldn't deter me from my mission. I determined to move forward no matter what they said.

Looking one of them squarely in the face I stated, "My Father works here, and so do I." [237]

Angered that I'd not only "broken the Sabbath" but now said that God was my Father, they looked for ways to cause my death.

I knew what was in their hearts. Boldly I looked at another of the pompous crowd. "Why do you want to kill me?"

How does he know this? "You're crazy! Who wants to kill you?"

"The Father raises up the dead, and gives them life. So I'll raise up who I will. I'm telling you these things so that you can be saved. Search the scriptures—you say you believe in them. When you do you'll see that Moses himself testified of me.

The Son can do nothing of himself, but only what he sees the Father doing. The time is almost here when the dead of the earth will hear the voice of the Son of God and in so doing, shall live." [238]

I'm offering life to those who want to kill me.

Kingdom Truths

After my discussion with the Pharisees we left for Judea; I planned to celebrate the Feast of Passover there with my family. Leaving Jerusalem, we came to the Sea of Galilee. By now word had spread, and a huge crowd followed me everywhere, giving me no privacy at all. The people were

---

[237] John 5:17
[238] John 5:25.

like sheep needing a shepherd. Teaching them Kingdom concepts was my passion.

A flower-strewn hill was nearby—a perfect place to teach and be heard. I walked up the grassy hill and sat down with my disciples.

As the huge crowd gathered on the hill below me, I began the teaching.

1. Happy are the humble, for theirs is the Kingdom of Heaven.
2. Happy are they that mourn, for they'll be comforted.
3. Happy are the meek for they'll inherit the earth.
4. Happy are those who hunger and thirst after righteousness, for they'll be filled.
5. Happy are the merciful, for they'll receive mercy.
6. Happy are the pure in heart, for they'll see God.
7. Happy are the peacemakers, for they'll be known as the children of God.
8. Happy are those who are persecuted because of their commitment to righteousness, for theirs is the Kingdom of Heaven.

"When people insult and bully you, and say all kinds of false things about you for my sake, be ecstatically happy, for you'll have a great reward in Heaven. You're on the same level with the prophets who were mistreated before you."

"You're the salt of the earth. You are the light of the world. Let your light shine before others that they may see your good deeds and glorify your Father in Heaven."

"Give to others in need. Love your enemies. Bless them that curse you, be kind to the ones who hate you, and pray for those who treat you wrongly."

"Perfection is the goal. Be as perfect as is your Father in Heaven."[239]

The crowd listened, astonished at my teaching. They'd not understood that giving would make them happier than taking[240]—that God himself supplies the needs as well as blesses those who are generous to others.[241]

After the teaching was over I realized many of the people hadn't eaten all day. Turning to Phillip I asked "Where can we buy enough food for them?" Though already knowing what I was going to do, I wanted to see if Phillip had been listening to what I'd been saying.

"We don't have enough money to feed this crowd!" he exclaimed.

"There's a boy here who has five barley loaves and two small fish," Peter remarked, "but they're a drop in the bucket compared to what we need."

"Tell everyone to sit down."

I took the loaves, using the same principle of multiplication I'd used before with the wine. After giving thanks, I broke off pieces of bread into the baskets and handed them to the disciples to pass around. After everyone was fully satisfied, there were twelve basketsful of bread left.

Seeing this miracle, the crowd wanted to make me their king right then and there. Talk about shortcuts! I firmly declined the offer, knowing that this wasn't the right time.

Now both physically and spiritually full, the crowd gradually thinned as the people returned home. Feeling an

---

[239] Text taken from Matthew 5
[240] Acts 20:35
[241] See Mal.3:10 Luke 6:38

immediate need for undistracted communication with my FATHER, I quietly hiked to the top of the mountain while the rest of the disciples took the boat across the lake.

Praying was energizing as I reconnected to my SOURCE of strength; hearing my Father's guiding voice brought a refreshing to my spirit. Soon the night stars were the only light on the mountaintop.

Down below I could hear the wind whipping the waves on the water. I sensed that my disciples were frightened as they battled the tempest in the black of the night. *I must go to them.*

Moving at lightening speed I ran down the mountain and stepped onto the surface of the water. Buoyed up by the rising and falling waves, I jumped across the gullies as I hurried along.

Approaching the ship I heard some yell, "It's a ghost!"

"Don't be afraid," I shouted back. "It's me, Jesus." Entering the boat, I immediately transported it to shore.

The next day the crowds were perplexed as to how I'd crossed the sea; I didn't see a need to explain it to them. Instead, I told them something they didn't expect: "I'm the Bread of life, the living bread that came down from Heaven. If anyone eats my flesh and drinks my blood he'll live forever. I'll give my body to give life to the world."

They had questions. "This is a difficult concept. Who can believe it?"

"Does this bother you? The words I speak are spiritual and give life to the spirit. But some of you don't believe."[242]

---

[242] John 6:48-64

Not understanding, most of the new disciples left, unwilling to follow me anymore. "Will you also leave?" I asked the twelve.

Peter answered for the group: "To whom shall we go? You alone have the words of eternal life. You're the Christ, the Son of the living God."

I've chosen you twelve, yet one is a devil.

This had been a tough day.

CHAPTER 19

DANGER IN JERUSALEM

—Neither did his brothers believe in him.

John 7:5

After this event, I avoided the areas where the most dangerous Jewish fanatics gathered. They were like a pack of wolves, eager to tear me to pieces. I decided to keep a low profile, for I knew it wasn't yet time for me to die.

Not understanding the risk, my brother Joses urged me, "Come to the feast in Judea, as planned."

"It's too dangerous for me to be seen right now."

"Nobody sneaks around secretly if they want to be openly noticed," added brother James. "If you're going to do these miracles, then proudly show yourself to the world."

My brothers don't believe in me either.

"The world doesn't hate you—only me, because I expose its evil conduct. Go up to this feast by yourselves. The timing may be right for you, but it's not for me."[243]

At this celebration I was the subject of most conversations. Some said I was a good teacher, others alleged that I "deceive

---

[243] John 7:7

the people." But the ones who were for me spoke guardedly for fear of reprisals from the Jewish leaders.

"How is this man so highly knowledgeable, having never been educated?" This was a question repeated so often that when I finally did show up at the feast, I answered it.

"My doctrine isn't mine, but HIS that sent me. Anyone who lives in harmony with HIS will knows if this doctrine is from God or birthed from my own skill and knowledge."

"Is anyone thirsty? Come to me and drink; if you believe, living water will flow out of your bellies."[244]

The people were curious: "Do the rulers know this is the Christ? He's speaking openly in the temple, yet they don't stop him. What do they know that we don't?"

The Pharisees had their own opinions: *Jesus hasn't earned the right to do what he does. God, is this fair? I've dedicated my life to studying the scriptures, yet I can't heal anyone.*

Why him? Why not me?

Quickly calling a meeting, the leaders got together to look for ways to discredit me. "Does God break his own rules and heal on the Sabbath?"

"Aha!"

"We've got him!"

"He quotes scripture . . . let's use the Law against him!"

Turning to the officer present, one leader spoke sharply: "Why haven't you taken him in already?"

"No one has ever before spoken like this."

"Are you also deceived?"

Another chimed in, "We know from where the real Christ will come. The scriptures plainly tell us he'll come

---

[244] Healing properties would be in any of Jesus' bodily fluids.

from Bethlehem. But listen . . . ." the teacher gloated proudly with the information he was about to impart; "We know for a fact that this man comes from Galilee, not Bethlehem."

"There's your proof, right there in black and white. This man is definitely not the Christ."

Finally Nicodemus spoke up "Does our law judge anyone before it hears the other side?"

"Are you from Galilee as well? Search the prophecies. No prophet comes from this town." The teachers were at odds.

"We'll test him."[245]

---

[245] Text from John 7.

CHAPTER 20

WISE ANSWERS

—The spirit of the Lord shall rest upon him, the spirit of wisdom—

Isaiah 11:2

After a night of prayer on the Mount of Olives, I returned to the temple early the next morning. As soon as I was noticed, the people ran toward me, wanting me to teach them again. The scribes and Pharisees arrived also, smugly bringing with them a disheveled-appearing young woman.

"Master, this woman was caught in the very act of committing adultery. According to the law Moses gave us, she's to be stoned . . . but what do you say?"

I glanced at the woman and instantly knew her heart. In looking for affection, she'd given herself to someone who didn't love her. When their adultery was exposed, he quickly turned against her.

I felt her sorrow, her absolute grief and suicidal thoughts. Betrayed and humiliated, she was brokenhearted. Glancing up momentarily I looked at each of the leaders. As I focused on their hearts they began to fidget uncomfortably.

He's looking right through me. Does he know about my secret addiction?

"He who is sinless among you, let him throw the first stone." Stooping down, I wrote words in the dust with my finger, paying no attention to the guilty, self-righteous crowd. One by one they left until only the woman remained.

"Where'd they go? Didn't anyone stay here to condemn you?"

"No one."

"I don't condemn you either. Go home, and don't sin any more."

Through a face wet with tears, she smiled her thanks. Scampering off she stopped just once to glance back at me. As she did, I perceived what was in her mind. Her thoughts were these: *Never in my life have I felt so valued and loved.*

Returning the smile, I proceeded to the treasury room of the temple to begin my teaching session. Though now once again amongst the most dangerous of the religious Jews, FATHER assured me I'd be safe; it wasn't yet time to lay down my life.

I looked over the small band of scholars and began to speak: "I'm the light of the world. He who follows me will no longer walk in darkness, but will have the light of life."

"Aha! Because you bear record of yourself, your record isn't true."

"Your law states that the testimony of two witnesses confirms a fact as true. I'm one witness and the Father that sent me is the other witness."

"Where is your Father?"

"If you really knew me, you would also know my Father. I'm not from this world; but I know from where I came and where I'm going."

"Where are you going?"

"You're from beneath the earth, I'm from above. If you don't believe in me, you'll die in your sins and not be able to join me."

"Who are you?"

"When you've lifted me up, you'll know that I AM HE; I do nothing by myself, but only the things which please my Father."

After hearing this, many of the Jews believed in me. Speaking softly, I explained: "If you continue absorbing my WORD into your lives, you will truly become my disciples. Knowing the truth will make you free."

"We, as Abraham's descendants, were never in bondage. What do you mean 'you'll be free'?"

"Whoever commits sin is its servant."

Does he know about my addictions and secret sins?

"If the SON makes you free, than you're truly free from sin's addictions."

Other leaders took offense, trying to trip me up, calling me a "Samaritan" and accusing me of hosting a devil.

"If anyone keeps my sayings, he'll never see death. Believe me, your father Abraham was glad when he saw my day." *He understood what it took for God to sacrifice his Son to save others.*

"You're not even fifty years old, yet you claim to have seen Abraham?"

"Before Abraham was, I AM."

Enraged at my words, some again attempted to stone me. But I hid as I left the treasury room by passing right through the center of the group.

Exiting the temple, I noticed a blind man sitting nearby, who'd been blind from birth. My disciples had a question about him: "Who sinned, himself or his parents?"

"Neither. The works of God will be noticeable through this man." *My saliva has the same healing DNA as my blood.* Spitting on the ground I picked up the resulting mud, placing some on each eye.

"Go wash in the pool of Siloam." The man did as I asked.

"I can see!" he shouted as he skipped around the courtyard. Happy for him, the crowd clapped and cheered as he continued his exuberant dance.

Healing the man born blind, however, caused certain of the Pharisees to become very unhappy. These jealous ones determined that God was making a mistake by validating my message with miracles! There was a division among the leaders.

"He is the Christ"

"He is a prophet."

"He has a devil and is mad. Why listen to him?"

"These are not the words of him that has a devil. Can a devil open the eyes of the blind?"

Return to Jerusalem

It was winter when I returned to Jerusalem to celebrate the Feast of Dedication. Arriving early, I entered the temple through Solomon's porch.

"Isn't this the man they're trying to kill? Yet he again preaches openly in the temple. Do the rulers indeed know that this is the Christ?"

Soon the teachers of the law surrounded me. "How long will you keep us in the dark? If you're Christ, tell us plainly."

"I told you, and you didn't believe me. The works I do in my Father's name, they speak for me."

They still don't believe who I am. I'll refer to one of their favorite topics of discussion: David's shepherd analogy.

"I'm the Good Shepherd who's willing to give his life for the sheep. A hired hand runs away when he sees danger approaching because he doesn't care for the sheep. But my sheep know me, and I know them just as the Father knows me and I know him. Because I willingly give my life for the sheep, the Father loves me. He's given me the power to lay down my life, as well as to take it up again."

"Those who are mine will believe I came from the Father. I'm able to give them eternal life so that they never die. Those who don't believe me are not mine. My Father and I are one."[246]

---

[246] Text taken from John 10, whole chapter.

We've got him. He put himself equal with God. "This is blasphemy!" Eagerly they took up stones to stone me.

"For which of my good works do you kill me?" I calmly asked.

"You, a man, make yourself equal with God."

"Isn't it written in your law 'You are gods'? Do you say that I blaspheme because I told you I am the Son of God? If I don't do my Father's job, then don't believe me. But if I do, then know and believe that the Father's in me and I'm in HIM."

Angered at my logic, they responded by again trying to grab and kill me, but I escaped, traveling quickly to the place where John first baptized beyond Jordan. Though saddened at the state of the Pharisees, I was encouraged by the believers who came to see me.

While there, many others came to understand and accept the truth. Being able to perceive what was in their hearts affected the way I dealt with each one. As usual, I had perfect clarity.

CHAPTER 21

HEALINGS

To you that fear my name shall the Sun of
righteousness arise with healing in his wings;
Malachi 4:2

The group in the archive room watched in fascination as three years of ministry flew by. Every day Jesus taught about Kingdom living; every day his words gave purpose to those with no hope. Explaining how God's law was more than a set of rules, he encapsulated it in one sentence: "Love God and love each other."

Defining love as giving, sharing, praying, encouraging, forgiving, being patient and believing in each other, his premise that "God is Love" went against the attitude of legalism into which Jewish law had evolved.[247] The stories Jesus told to illustrate his teachings were simple, yet profound in their message. People could relate to them on a grass roots level.

The more Jesus preached, however, the more the Pharisees became outraged. "Who does he think he is?" they fumed privately. Yet they were afraid of the people who believed in Him, for they couldn't deny his many marvelous

---

[247] 1 John 4:8; 16

miracles. He cured those who were sick, restored to health the blind and lame, cast out devils and raised the dead.

Still, the spirit of Cain persisted amongst the religious leaders. They continually questioned God: *Why Him? Why not us?* They refused to believe the answer, that Jesus was the Messiah for whom they'd been waiting. God had already confirmed his WORD with miracles. Why would they not humble themselves to simply believe it?

Jealousy has neither reason nor logic to it. Instead of seeking to learn God's true ways, the religious leaders were determined to make God bless them within the context of their misguided understanding. *After all, we've given our lives for service to the temple. We've spent hours studying; we know all the right answers to every question.* Their delusional determination caused them to miss the point in the same way Cain missed the point: they harbored a proud refusal to learn from the one who got it right.

It isn't that God loves one more than another. There's a process that has to be followed in order to fulfill the requirements for salvation. For Cain, a sacrificial lamb had to be used rather than vegetables and fruit. For the Pharisees, their manipulative lies as well as their demanding set of rules had to be exposed to the light of truth in order for their hearts to change. Without repentance their jealousy would be deadly.

Jesus, who'd first started his ministry in the synagogues, now taught in fields, by lakes and on mountain slopes. These open places were better suited to accommodate his huge following, for even the largest synagogues were not big enough to hold the burgeoning crowds.

The friends in the archive room watched as Jesus healed the sick while the Pharisees, envious of his success, seethed with anger. The vehement outrage and manipulative behavior of the leaders did little to stop Jesus from continuing his mission. His Word, sharp as a Two-Edged Sword, would accurately divide the proverbial sheep from the goats. Starting in Jerusalem, the powerful truth would gradually spread throughout the entire world.

Though busy with the crowds that followed him, Jesus still made it a priority to mentor his twelve disciples. Calling them "friends," he showed by example what it meant to be one.

But even with his loving attention the heart of one of them remained unchanged. Judas loved money more than God; in exchange for riches he schemed with the Pharisees to betray Jesus. Aware of his plot, Jesus knew this disciple would not only condemn himself, but also be forever lost.[248]

Sensing that the time of betrayal was near, Jesus went to pray in the garden owned by counselor Joseph. Here, carved right into the rocky knoll was a new tomb in the final stages of construction. Only one of the two gravesites had been completed. Jesus perceived that this sepulcher would soon be his own burial chamber.

---

[248] Jesus knew this from the beginning. See John 6:64

CHAPTER 22

RIDING INTO JERUSALEM

Rejoice greatly, O daughter of Zion; shout, O
daughter of Jerusalem: your King comes to you:
he is just, and having salvation; lowly, and riding
upon the foal of a donkey.

Zechariah 9:9

It was Passover time. Jesus recognized that this seasonal feast was a shadow of his impending death. *In the same way the innocent lamb's blood dripped from the doorposts in Egypt, my blood will drip to the ground. Only then will the ransom for every human be paid for in full.* The pending event was very close; he was restless to complete the task.

His instructions were clearly laid out by his ever-present Heavenly Father as he guided his every move. He was to enter into Jerusalem for the last time, but not as a baby or young boy of twelve—not even to cleanse the temple or to teach in it. It was to be a triumphal entry, a foreshadowing of the future when he would return as a victorious king to rule the whole earth.

Jesus climbed the hill overlooking Jerusalem, his heart breaking with grief. As he looked over the city, he saw not only the present beautiful temple, but also its future as it lay in ruins. A symbol of hatred would be prominently placed where the beautiful courtyard had once been.[249]

Anguished, he watched future generations make the journey to the remaining temple wall to pray only to be accosted by another jealous brother who refused to do things God's way: Ishmael.[250]

Ishmael's apostate descendants would boldly build on the temple's very grounds in an attempt to prevent God's true followers from worshiping him. Their noisy "call to prayer" would be a counterfeit to the genuine methods the Father had put forth. Not only in Jerusalem, but in synagogues and churches all over the world, this dangerous religion would erect their towers in an earsplitting attempt to dominate and control. Whereas Jesus taught love, this counterfeit religion would teach hate. While God's true followers build and restore, the counterfeit religion would teach their followers to kill and destroy.

The motivation was simple: Cain's jealousy of Abel was repeated in a nation that felt rejected by God. Rather than learning from the brother who got it right, they would demand recognition for their misguided religious acts.

Look how holy we are! See, we pray five times a day—do you notice? Never do we allow 'sin' in any form; we control our people through rules and terror. We kill anyone, even daughters and sons if they don't follow our religion. You've got to take notice! See how dedicated we are?

Jesus saw it all, and it made him weep.

---

[249]   Mark 13:14. See also Daniel 12:11 (One definition of the word "abomination" is "hatred.")

[250]   See Gal 4:22-30, specifically verse 29.

"Oh Jerusalem, Jerusalem, you who kill the prophets. How I would have gathered you under my wing and protected you, but you refused!"

Later as he rode into Jerusalem on a young donkey's colt, the people shouted, "Hosanna, blessed is the King of Israel that comes in the name of the Lord!"[251] It was a moment that would be noted and remembered, for Jesus would come again when the last day of testing was over and the Thousand-Year Reign had begun.

Eating supper that evening for the last time with his disciples, Jesus told them again how his body and blood must be consumed for salvation. By breaking the bread with his hands, and drinking from the communal cup, Jesus left microscopic amounts of his own DNA in the food and drink. Still not really understanding how this would pay their ransom, the disciples ate the bread and wine as a token of their faith in His redemptive plan.

Jesus understood. "I am come a light into the world. Whoever believes on me will not live in darkness."[252]

Jesus had one more task to do that night: wash his disciples' feet. "If I, being your Lord wash your feet, you also ought to wash each other's feet." As he lovingly completed this lowly task, his actions imprinted the scene into their souls.

The Messiah is taking a servant's role. This concept is very different from the world's way of thinking.

Jesus spoke again. "I'm going away, but my Father will send the Comforter to continue to teach you all things."

"Where are you going?" asked Peter.

---

[251] John 12:13
[252] John 12:46

"Speak plainly to us," they all begged. "What's going to happen?"

"Don't be troubled; in my Father's house are many mansions. I'm going to prepare your eternal home for your arrival."

With that statement, Jesus gave his final words of wisdom to his disciples. Revealing many details about future events, he ended his conversation with the following words: "I'm leaving my peace with you. Though the prince of this world is coming, he has nothing on me; he wasn't able to cause me to sin in any way."

"The incidents about to take place will occur so the world will know I love the Father. I'll do everything HE requires me to do."

"Pray with me. My time has come."[253]

---

[253] John 14:26-31

Chapter 23

It is Finished!

Behold the Lamb of God, which takes away the sin of the world.

John 1:29

Jesus and his twelve disciples left for the garden. Soon Jesus was praying so intensely that his sweat turned bloody as it ran down his face.

"Father, if possible, let this cup pass from me. Yet not my will, but yours be done." *If the mission can't be completed unless I go through this, then I'll do it. It's why I came here—to give myself as a sacrifice.* Knowing he would soon be reunited with his Father, he determined to see the mission accomplished to the tiniest detail.

The plan was this: Death would come after suffering at the hands of those who should have welcomed him. He would then enter the pit to release the long held captives and bring them to the light where they would be free from the cursed power of darkness.

Soon Judas arrived. With him were the misguided religious leaders who were intent on murder. Approaching Jesus, Judas wondered at the sweaty, bloody face. Kissing him on the cheek, Judas tasted saltiness as Jesus' sweat and blood with its pure DNA entered his mouth; inevitably he swallowed a miniscule amount of the mixture. Unaware, he'd just tasted from the forbidden Tree of Life. His spirit would now live forever in its present sinful state.

Jesus was taken to Pilate's palace where he was mocked, tried, whipped, convicted, and sentenced to death. Not saying a word during the torture, he was as a lamb being led to the slaughterhouse.

Jesus

Unknown to the rest of the world, I went willingly, for I knew this was the process needed in order to redeem mankind. Unlike Cain who wanted the method changed and was bitter that he had no power to change it, I knew that this course of action was not mine to change. I had to fit into the pre-determined plan in order to accomplish its purpose.

The whipping, the abuse—it was painful, but the presence of MY FATHER made it bearable. Surely God would not ask anything that wasn't do-able, and I firmly resolved to endure to the end.

After my conviction I was forced to carry a heavy wooden cross through the streets of Jerusalem. The weight was heavy, and rubbed against my open wounds. More than that, I knew I would soon bear unspeakable agony upon it.

At length we arrived at the crucifixion site. Nearby was a rocky hill that resembled the face of a skull. Also close by was the unfinished tomb.

Here is where I'll give up my life.

My comfort was this: My Father was with me; HE would be with me with every phase of this horrendous death.

The nails were pounded in without mercy. *So much pain!* Pain was created by the evil side and used extensively in its hierarchy. In the flesh, mankind was designed to avoid pain at all costs. Yet the Spirit is stronger than the flesh, and I determined to succeed in finishing my task. Unimaginable joy would soon be mine once salvation for all was achieved through my death.

The soldiers hammered the nails into my wrists and feet, while attempting to keep clean from the blood that splattered and dripped. Picking up my clothing, they divided the pieces between them. Finding that my robe was seamless and not wanting to tear it up, they played a game of lots to see who would win the prize. Mom, eyes streaming with tears, watched the gambling activity.

My head ached with the pounding; the pain was incredible as they placed the cross in an upright position, but my Father constantly comforted me. He had been there with me at the mock of a trial with every answer I gave to the chief priests; HE was also there when I remained silent. Every word out of my mouth was only a repeat of what the Father whispered into my ear. When there was no whisper, I didn't speak.[254]

The agony of trying to breathe while lifting up my battered body on the cross took superhuman strength. With a steady stream of blood oozing out, my body became weaker. Still my compassion was for the thieves on each side of me who were moaning and cursing in agony. It was obvious that neither of them had prepared their souls for this moment. One spoke: "If you're truly the Messiah, save yourself and us."

The other one had a different attitude: "Aren't you afraid? We're all in the same boat. We got what we deserved,

---

[254] John 8:26. One of many references where Jesus says he speaks only what he hears from his Father.

but he's done nothing wrong." Turning his head toward me he spoke haltingly between agonized breaths: "Lord, remember me when you come into your Kingdom."

I answered with words of truth, comforting the dying man: "Today you'll be with me in Paradise." *I offered them both eternal life. One received it, the other rejected it.*

Through my pain I watched the crowd that gathered. If only they knew to believe in me! *They don't understand how short their lives are; they'll return to the pit unless they put their trust in me. Oh, that they'd turn from deception and embrace the truth before it's too late!*

I uttered one last prayer for the world: "Father, forgive them for they don't know what they're doing!" I cried out to save even the ones causing my agony.

Hours passed. Suddenly the earth grew dark. I found myself alone. The Father's presence was gone. *What's happening? Is this part of the plan?* "FATHER, WHY HAVE YOU ABANDONED ME?" My cry thundered out over the crowd. I knew I could call ten thousand angels—oh, the thought did cross my mind. Yet my determination was so strong, pure and focused that the fleeting thought had nowhere to take root.

I will persevere no matter what!

Though I didn't understand why I was on my own, it didn't change my commitment. *I'll die, then, alone.* Such was my drive to complete with my death the redemption of mankind. *I'll not fail, not even in the last moments of my human life.*

"IT IS FINISHED!"

One more agonizing moment, and I felt my spirit leave my body. Though the separation from my Father was more than the worst feeling of loneliness imaginable, my obedience conquered my thoughts. The atonement was complete. The dying was over and the price of redemption had been paid.

I felt a rush of victorious joy, for I had finished everything the Father had required of me.

Elated in knowing I'd broken Lucifer's grip of evil, I watched momentarily as John took my mother's arm and tenderly helped her walk to his house. Yes, she would be lovingly taken care of by him for the rest of her days. I'd handpicked him for that purpose as his gentle personality and strong faith would be an encouragement to her in these days of sorrow.

Warm feelings swept over me as I silently said good-bye to the woman who'd given me birth. She would be honored and loved by millions in ages to come.

As my spirit began to soar in the air, I noticed my body, still on the cross, bloodied and bruised. Yes, I had taken a beating . . . my blood was now gushing to the ground due to a post-mortem pierce of a sword. But because I'd kept my blood pure from sin, it would never deteriorate. Its healing powers would be forever planted in the world of man, spreading through the air and soil as its molecules separated into billions of cells. These particles in turn would eventually permeate every part of the earth and water.

My blood also soaked well into the rocky soil, running down the cracked basalt like a funnel—down, down, until it dripped onto the very mercy seat of the Ark of the Covenant hidden long ago in a cavern beneath the rock.[255]

---

[255] The entrance to Jeremiahs cave is located just a few feet from the place of the skull. The Ark of the Covenant was hidden many years before during Israel's captivity. There is some indication that deep within this cave is the place where it was recently found. The cave entrance, as of today, has been blocked off and is now inaccessible to the general public. See also www.CovenantKeepers.co.uk for fascinating information.

CHAPTER 24

RELEASE THE PRISONERS!

To bring out the prisoners from the prison, and
them that sit in darkness out of the prison house.
Isa 42:7

I had work to do. Gathering my wits about me, I mentally prepared for the task at hand. I knew where the gates were . . . FATHER had prepared me well. Entering into the tunnel, I achieved lightening speeds available only to Deity. As I made my entrance into the pit, an earthquake rocked the chambers. I brought light into this world of darkness, light that could never again be quenched.

"Release the Prisoners!" I shouted. The inhabitants could only gape in wonder, blinking in the blinding light that surrounded me. Those in charge had no choice. They immediately unlocked the chains that had for so long bound the prisoners.

As I turned once again to exit, the released prisoners, in a burst of energy and joy, swarmed out with me. Such jubilation had never been witnessed within these boundaries! I was eager to bring them back into the Kingdom.[256]

Reaching the surface didn't take long. The newly released beings eagerly flitted here and there, enjoying their new found freedom as I entered the tomb where my body had been laid.[257]

---

[256] See Psalms 16:10 and Rev. 1:18
[257] Matt 27:60 See also Isa. 14:13-17

The sweet smell of myrrh and aloes permeated not only the tomb but the surrounding garden as well. These spices had soaked into the linen covering my body. Cold and lifeless, my corpse had been hastily wrapped in a long linen cloth along with the burial spices.

At the moment my spirit entered my body, the light radiating from the reunion slightly scorched the linen, creating a perfect photographic negative. This clue would be preserved; the Father had alerted certain believers to keep the relic safe for future generations.

The twelve-foot linen shroud showed my image, top to bottom, front to back. The cloth around my face also showed my facial features, front and back. Though photography hadn't yet been discovered by earth's inhabitants, in time it would be. Many future generations would find faith because of my image on the cloth.

As I removed the shroud from my resurrected body, I carefully folded and placed it at one end of the tomb's burial bed.

"Good work." Michael greeted me. He and Gabriel were sitting on the other side, watching me as I folded the linen. They were smiling with joy as I readjusted my earthly body to my eternal self.

"Smells sweet," I noted as I laid the face cloth down.

"A bit overwhelming . . . You keeping the body?" Gabriel asked.

"Why not?" I beamed, still savoring the victory. "Sinless . . . It'll never deteriorate."

"The scars remain."

"Battle wounds. Will always remind me of Kingdom victory," I answered, still amazed and elated at knowing the job was completed. "I'm ready to return to my Father."

"Won't be long now." Gabriel said with a smile as he gave Michael a joyous high-five.

Leaving the tomb, I noticed the damage from the earthquake to the stone wall of the opening. Stooping to exit, I saw that the angels had already removed the stone by rolling it back up the slight incline. Smiling a "thank you" to them, they nodded, shrugging their shoulders. They were fully aware that my power now was far greater than theirs.

Two Roman soldiers, felled by my resurrection power, dazedly got up and ran out of the garden as fast as they could. Left on the ground was the broken Roman seal.

Exiting behind me, the angels tussled playfully in the garden before re-entering. I could tell they were excited, and I was too! Though I'd been through an ordeal, the thrill of victory for the Kingdom was extremely energizing.

Standing unnoticed just outside the tomb, I watched in interest as Mary Magdalene came with a basket of spices to finish the job Joseph had started. As she approached, she noticed the stone had already been removed from the door. She quickly left and soon afterward Peter and John ran into the garden.[258]

John, being younger, reached the entrance first, but it was bold Peter who actually bent down to enter the tomb.

Noticing the linen with the photographic negative, Peter's eyes popped open in amazement. The image was enough to confirm the fact that I'd not only been wrapped in the grave clothes, but now was not in them.[259]

They left, too amazed to talk; but Mary, who had once again returned to the tomb, timorously stooped down to look inside. It was then she saw the two angels in white

---

[258] The counselor Joseph of Arimathea begged Pilate for the body of Jesus and laid him in his own tomb. See John 19:38.

[259] John 20:4-8 When John saw the cloths, he believed.

sitting, one at the head and the other at the foot where my body had lain. She began to sob.

"Why are you crying?" I asked gently

"Because they have taken away my Lord and I don't know where they've laid him." She turned around and saw me standing. She assumed I was the gardener.

"Sir, if you've moved him from here, show me and I'll take him away."

Even though she'd seen her brother Lazarus brought back from the dead, I realized she had not expected me to come back from such a death. My blood loss alone would have made my body incompatible with life.

"Mary." Her big brown eyes opened wide. "Master!"

"Don't touch me, for I've not yet ascended to my Father. But go to my brothers and tell them that I'm going to my Father and your Father and to my God and your God."

This message would be repeated until the whole earth would be aware of the meaning: Lucifer's previous authority over them was now legally and officially terminated. THE WORD offered life; those who believed in me could enter the Kingdom of God as adopted sons. It wasn't a list of rules and rituals that made Heaven possible for mankind, but the love a Father had for those who were lost and sitting in darkness.

The next forty days the news of my resurrection spread like wildfire all through Jerusalem and into the outlying provinces. The truth would never be quenched; the sacrifice would never be outdated.

My job on earth was finished.

Returning to the Father was a joyful experience. Running into the inner chamber, I embraced him as he embraced me.

"It's finished; we've won the victory."

"Now we must win the war."

With a couple thousand years of earth time left, our job was to empower each of earth's believers with our Spirit in order to strengthen them to withstand Lucifer's many attacks. Lies were still rampant, and the unwary believed them. But the words of truth had been spoken, the light had been shone, and never again would the world wait in darkness.

From Heaven I saw the Father send His Spirit to earth in a magnificent way. A shimmering cloud descended upon the earth. Rising high into the atmosphere it took on a form consisting of every soul on earth who believed in me. Toes, feet, hands—every cell of this body contained a vital part. The redeemed were all part of its body; the Holy Spirit was in them, and they were in Him.[260]

Every believer down through the ages became a part of this magnificent cloud. From the head, each cell received orders and each cell obeyed. A mighty force to be reckoned with, the forces of evil would never be strong enough to defeat it.

Complete restoration of all things would happen; it was only a matter of time.

---

[260] John 14:20

CHAPTER 25

EXITING THE ARCHIVES

I will ransom them from the power of the grave; I will redeem them from death:

Hosea 13:14

Jeric glanced up, enlightenment in his eyes; "It was the Two-Edged Sword! THE WORD was so sharp it could discern the thoughts and intents of the heart. Unlike Adam, Jesus was not deceivable."

"So you found the answer to your question?" asked Korel.

"Yes. The Word of God was what defeated evil. Jesus, with the anointing of the Father, was the embodiment of THE WORD.[261] Neither Satan with his tricks nor the Pharisees with their evil intents could defeat him."

"We're clean because of the words he spoke to us."[262] Korel added.

"Why go any further?" Jano interjected. "The greatest event in human history is HIS victory over sin and death."

"Fun event to watch!"

---

[261] John 10:36

[262] John 15:3

"Want to see it again?"

The friends looked at each other, grinning at the prospect of viewing it a second time.

"Let's do it."

"I'm game."

"Rewind."

The instant Jesus arose from the dead was the most electrifying moment. Backing the archives to the spot, the group settled back to experience it again.

Only seconds into the replay, Korle caught sight of a figure they hadn't noticed before.

"Wait! See the seraph? Isn't that Jucola?" All their attention had earlier been focused on the massive exodus from the pit. Now they saw that among the crowd was the tall doorkeeper.

Yes! As a released prisoner of war he now was exiting with the others.

The archive room erupted into cheers. Jucola's earlier story had not included this ending, leaving them somewhat curious.

Following Jucola to the surface, they observed him glancing here and there as he refocused his eyes to the beauty of trees, grass, and living, healthy beings. To say he was elated was a complete understatement.

The normally motionless angel, newly reborn into life was dancing and shouting for joy. He ran through the fields and splashed in the water, totally unseen by the humans on earth. Eventually he happily boarded a waiting skyper and returned to his heavenly home.

The story of Jesus had impacted the friends with unrestricted merriment. They danced happily as they witnessed once more the resurrection of the Savior of the world. Jesus had conquered death; they would never forget his gift.

CHAPTER 26

ADVENTURES IN
HEAVEN AWAIT US

In the resurrection they . . . are as the angels of God.
Mat 22:30

The celebrations in the Highest Heaven were thrilling! Jesus, seated at the right hand of the Father welcomed them all back with words of love, appreciation and affection.

In Heaven there's no sickness, disease, cheaters, nor liars. All previous sins were forgiven, and as the eras sped by in rapid succession, the trials and experiences of earth were forgotten by its former inhabitants.

Together again on the eighth heavenly day after creation, the sons settled into a glorious pattern where all worked together and flourished. The adventures of LIFE were many, and inexhaustible.

Jano and Korel met on a regular basis for horseback riding, skydiving, baseball games and other fun sports. Korel's passion of creating new strains of apples retained its fascination for him; he invited Jano to join him in his experimentation and discoveries. Jano readily accepted the invitation.

The Sons of God, many more by this time as all of the redeemed had become joint heirs with their Savior, enjoyed creating new stars and planets. Shouting for joy at the completion of each new realm, the heavens continually rang out with delighted laughter.[263]

Guardian angels were re-assigned back to their original jobs, though this past temporary diversion of work had left a long-lasting impression on them. Forever friends, these angels would still never understand redemption in the same way as would those who'd escaped from the addictions of evil.

Meanwhile Korel, gone from his orchards and gardens for over a thousand years, was eager to return to them; the joy of gardening still held a strong interest for him.

"Ziphotan, here we come!" he exclaimed to Jano and anyone else within earshot. Jano, who now also resided on Ziphotan was just as eager to return. The angelic friends once more boarded a skyper and headed to their homes.

Korel and Jano along with their friends were satisfied, knowing those intended for salvation had all been redeemed. They would not need to worry about the sons of perdition who preferred evil over good. These lost ones had chosen their fate, and the choice had been their own.[264]

Peace had been restored; all was well for eternity.

As they made the journey toward their homes the two friends planned to visit the archives again, but at this point that visit has not happened. Too many exciting adventures in Heaven have prevented their return. Maybe later . . . .

---

263 See Gal 4:4-7 and Eph 1:4-5
264 John 17:12

CHAPTER 27

EPILOGUE

I have waited for your salvation, O Lord.

Gen. 49:18

Millions of light years away deep in a black hole existed the antichrist Lucifer, the false prophet and all liars. Who's to say? Millions of years, millions and millions of eternities, some time way out in the future when eons of eras have passed and no one remembers anything about the days of "mankind," somewhere, perhaps, a repentant Pinnac and others like him will find the miracle of THE REDEMPTION, paid by Jesus for all time and eternity.

In an eternal world with a LOVING HEAVENLY FATHER, all things are possible.[265]—Even the conversion and restoration of the most evil one who caused the banishment of one-third of the angels?[266] That question

---

[265] Nothing is impossible with God. Luke 1:37

[266] See Matt 18:11-13. Even just one lost sheep causes the Shepherd to leave the rest to look for it. Also note Heb 6:4-6 for the likelihood of repentance from those in question.

can only be answered by THE WORD and ETERNAL FATHER OF LIGHT.[267]

The story of sin and its forgiveness should never be forgotten. Jesus, willing to pay the ultimate price made a way for all to return to the loving Father; all can find themselves once again reunited with HIM.

Though the story of Jesus can never be completely told, in reading this trilogy one can experience the truths of the Gospel while imagining wonderful adventures in an eternal world. May all who read the words written in these books find the Savior, and in knowing HIM, discover true joy and happiness.

The way has been made for all to return to the Father. Why not do it today?

---

[267] James 1:17

If you open the door, I'll come in.   Rev. 3:20

About the Two-Edged Sword Series . . .

When I was a young mother up on the farm, I would listen to the Christian radio station as I went about my work. My favorite program was from 8-8:30 every night with Kathryn Kuhlman. She was an early charismatic preacher known primarily for the spontaneous healings that took place during her services.

One night she spoke about the formation of the earth, fallen angels and the creation of man. I was fascinated, as I'd never before heard such in-depth explanations. The desire to write a story on the subject was birthed in my heart and grew year by year. Reading the scriptures throughout the following 35 years with her teaching in mind continually verified the truth of her words.

One Sunday in 2007 our church music minister announced she had a word from the Lord for someone—highly unusual in our denomination. After church she approached me.

"Marilyn, I saw this vision so plainly. I saw a feather pen, paper, and ink. I believe you are to write." Her eyes were misty as she imparted these words.

"Perhaps this is an encouragement to finish the musical I'm working on," I replied.

"It's something different, but you'll have to confirm this yourself. Has God been speaking to you about anything else?"

Yes, he had.

Thus was born the trilogy: THE TWINKLING © 2008, Dark Stars of THE TWILIGHT © 2009 and TWICE SHARPENED, The Two-Edged Sword © 2010.

Marilyn Olson